TOM GALLAGHER

Flight of Evil:

A North British Intrigue

First published in the United Kingdom in 2018
by Scotview Publications, Edinburgh

Printed by Buchanan McPherson

ISBN: 978-0-9934654-2-0

Dedication

To Effie Deans, an astute political mind in Scotland who, with flair and insight, has defended many of the values upheld by the nobler characters in this novel. @effiedeans

Acknowledgements

I am grateful to all those who who encouraged me to press ahead with this novel and who offered practical advice and help at different stages. David Ross provided a distinctive cover which is an excellent showcase for the book. Particular thanks are also due to Ian Wilson of Edinburgh who patiently copy-edited the text.

Recommendations

Tom Gallagher has fun and a glorious multiplicity of targets in this dystopian novel about the uncomfortably near future which explores many of our worst nightmares. England is in a civil war precipitated by far-left zealots who torture and dispossess the old, a sane Scottish government struggles to defeat fanatical nationalist resistance and cope with vast numbers of refugees driven north by foreign fighters, Ireland is a narco-state, and the US bends with the wind. Along the way we meet sociopathic Anglophobes, deluded peaceniks, seditious academics, corrupt corporations, philistine liberals, a sexually voracious female rabble-rouser and many more enemies of decency and reason.

Ruth Dudley Edwards, biographer, crime-writer and columnist on Irish affairs.

Flight of Evil is an original and timely warning of the dangers of political extremism, It shows how it might be possible for the UK to descend into a state of violent dystopia, with outright civil war in England and perilous instability and near-collapse into insurrection in an independent Scotland. Such a state of affairs may seem fantastic but I found the scenario credible enough to keep me reading to see how far it could be developed.

The narrative is fast-paced, eventful and filled with near-recognisable characters. For political insiders, part of the entertainment will be in identifying which real-life public figures match those characters with bizarre and sometimes unhinged personality traits!

Prof. Gallagher demonstrates how political fanatics with unhinged egos (not as rare as you might think in today's Britain) could drive a nation to disaster. A dark, but in many ways believable, vision.

Tom Brown, veteran columnist, editor and reporter in the Scottish media.

There have been a number of futuristic fantasies in recent years which build imagined, terrifying and theoretical scenarios out of the kernels and embers of present realities - PD James' The Children of Men, Michael Symmons Roberts' Breath and Michel Houllebecq's Submission. Similarly, Tom Gallagher's Flight of Evil grows out of the seeds of contemporary extremisms and tribalisms which can seem frightening today, but hopefully short-lived.

All four have unrealisable plots, but just enough truth and recognisability to cause the most sceptical reader a shiver of dread. Scottish readers of Gallagher's book will be the most gripped, discomfited and entertained.

Sir James MacMillan, composer and writer

CONTENTS

Introduction

Chapter 1

The Edinburgh Challenge

Anatoly opened his eyes and took in the bare white walls. Why was he in this strange room, stretched out on a bed? Who was this woman in a blue and white uniform standing over him? At least she had a warm smile. But she was also looking down at him with a concerned expression.

'Mr Yashin how do you feel?' she asked.

Anatoly reflected on this for a moment. He felt shivery and had a headache but the main sensation was one of great tiredness.

'I feel rotten but I hope I'll live,' he said.

'Did I have a heart attack?,' he then asked. He was unsure why he had blurted out this question but it was the first thought that had occurred to him.

The nurse smiled and said 'No you've not had a heart attack. You were found lying slumped on the Meadows yesterday afternoon. Apparently you had collapsed and an ambulance brought you here to the Royal Infirmary. For nearly 24 hours you've been under sedation which means that you will have had a good sleep.'

Checking his temperature, she went on: 'The doctors think there is nothing fundamentally wrong with you but they will take more tests before discharging you. It looks as if you may have been overdoing it and your body decided to cry out "Enough."

'Luckily this happened in south Edinburgh's green lung, the Meadows where there are usually lots of passers-by, so here you are.'

'Thank you nurse for the explanation.'

'Not at all,' she replied 'and, by the way, my name is Moira Torrance. If you like just call me Moira.'

Anatoly smiled at her and said 'I will and please do the same. I'm Anatoly. The name means "sunrise" in my language. I'm Russian.'

'What a lovely name' she replied.

'Thank you for putting my mind at ease,' he then said.

'That's what I'm here for' the trim, middle-aged woman said.

'I have a few more patients to attend to but if you need anything, just press the buzzer at the side of the bed and I, or a colleague, will be along quickly.'

Anatoly tried to piece together what had happened. It was a sultry August day. He had spent the morning trying to make his new flat presentable. This was in the

Stockbridge area north-west of the city centre. Because of the fine weather, he had decided to walk the nearly two miles first up to Princes Street, then up through the old town before reaching his office in the Marchmont district just on the other side of the Meadows.

If he had got there it would only have been his second day in the office. It belonged to the British Elderly Assisted Survival Trust (BEAST). It had been set up by him and associates who had banded together as the crisis in England had quickly escalated over the past year. The elderly had been the focus of their concern as the True Vanguard government in London sought to strip millions of elderly folk of their civil rights and their property. But the situation had spiralled out of control. People of all ages had become casualties of the conflict which had rapidly ensued.

It had taken a horrendous turn in this summer of 2022 when Clive Sutton had pulled off a daring feat. Many thousands of foreign fighters had been brought in under the noses of the Americans and their allies, the British Democratic Authority (BDA). The brutal conduct of many of these men, veterans of conflicts in the Middle East and elsewhere, had caused mass panic. This was above all true of the cities and towns in west Yorkshire and east Lancashire. They had been scenes of intense fighting. Hundreds of thousands of people had fled in panic. Huge tent cities had grown up in the foothills of the Pennines from Harrogate up to Hexham not far from the Scottish Border.

It had been the worst emergency faced so far by the ministry for displaced people. He had agreed to coordinate its work for six months in January. But it was impossible to walk away in the stark conditions of northern England in the summer of 2022. He and his friends Zach Mbarra, Javier Roldas, Livia Morariu and Nadia Misri had worked tirelessly to ensure these tent cities had some of the facilities needed to ensure a modicum of civilized life. But the scale of the numbers needing to be absorbed was simply overwhelming.

Clearly such rudimentary shelters were only an interim solution. Winters in the upland regions of northern England were usually harsh. Not just rain and high winds but sometimes a succession of wild Atlantic storms sweeping over the exposed terrain.

Sam Stockwood, his boss as Minister for the Displaced, had asked him to set up an office in Edinburgh to coordinate relief work. It had gone ahead with the agreement of the newly-independent Scottish government. Prime Minister Gavin Ogilvy had reluctantly declared independence on 19 July in order to reduce the chances of Scotland being pulled into the vortex of violence elsewhere on the island. Vanguard's success in turning the tables on the BDA and the Americans had been terrifying. As Clive Sutton and his foreign helpers won back lots of recently lost territory, there were military analysts who compared his exploit to that of the Israelis in the 6 day war of 1967.

Many of Vanguard's foreign legion were Muslims and would have regarded such a comparison as contemptible. Their propagandists exulted that they had pursued the British imperialist demon right to its own hearth. They were now the masters in cities like Bradford, Huddersfield and Halifax with large parts of the metropoli of Leeds and Manchester still being fought over.

It was expected there would be two million refugees from the northern English battlefields by the onset of winter. Newcastle was bursting at the seams. Medical experts had warned it would be difficult to prevent outbreaks of tuberculosis and typhoid, if the tent cities continued beyond one winter. It was clear that several years of intense fighting lay ahead before the outcome of the struggle between Vanguard and its moderate opponents would be decided.

It made sense to have a base in Scotland. Ogilvy had been quick to declare his newly independent state's non-belligerency. But his United Citizen Party was unionist in outlook. Its name had still not been changed. A defeat had been inflicted on the separatist Scottish National Action Party (SNAP) a few years earlier. So consumed was the SNAP by the goal of independence that it had neglected the elementary business of government and supporters had drifted away.

But now the situation was different. The Scottish economy was reeling from the collapse of trade with the rest of the island, the destination of most of its goods in normal times. Unemployment was rising as revenues started to dry up. The Americans had extended a loan to get the Scottish government through the winter without massive cuts. US negotiators had indicated that if Ogilvy's non-belligerency was interpreted in a way that benefited the BDA, America would remain a good friend of the fledgling state.

But SNAP was enjoying a revival. It had a new rising star, Clova Bruce, a velvet-tongued orator. She had worked in the entertainment industry as performer, impresario, and club owner. Some described her as the Madonna of Scottish politics – a headstrong individual who had a talent for campaigning along with strong lines of communication to the young, tens of thousands of whom were now jobless. Ranged against her was the more cerebral Ogilvy. He had been an actor who had made some epic new westerns. He had made the transition from sitting on the saddle to sitting behind a desk remarkably easily. For now, his appeal was more extensive than Bruce's, spanning the generations but it was strongest among women which surprised some as he had made little secret of being gay.

Anatoly was awoken from an improbable dream -in which Ogilvy was chasing Clova Bruce around a bull ring with a lasso rope - by a familiar voice.

'Anatoly so you finally managed to get some well-earned rest I see.'

That Irish lilt could only mean it was Arthur Gorman.

He opened his eyes and said: 'Hello Arthur. Sorry for the surprise. That's right. But it's a pity that it's involuntary and I'm not resting in my own bed at Cyprus Row.'

'Well at least you seem to have received some excellent care. Nurse Torrance seems a dedicated soul.'

Anatoly simply said: 'Moira is great. Her care means I'm getting out of here earlier than I had expected. This evening in fact.'

'Moira is it?' Gorman looked at him waggishly. 'That's promising to hear. Take her out for a meal to show your appreciation. Who knows where it might lead to'?

'I was hoping we might see each other again and that idea is perfect.'

As the afternoon sun receded, Anatoly was driven home by Arthur. Beforehand he had diffidently asked Moira Torrance if she would like to go out for a meal and she had consented.

He and Arthur sat in the private garden used for residents of the small street, as twilight approached. Gorman was still mostly relaxed and jovial. But there was a new sadness that was ready to break to the surface.

'There is no lack of university folk here in Edinburgh well disposed towards BEAST and our work. That's important as the universities carry a lot of influence in the city.'

'But every time I wander across George Square looking up at its university buildings ancient and modern, I think of Wilford university. I will never get over the terrible fate of Euan Garland, my co-founder murdered in his own laboratory.

'Euan got an honorary degree here for his breakthrough in the treatment of arthritis just before the crisis blew up. There's talk of naming a new building in the medical school after him. So his memory lives on.

'I am trying to write a Margo Forbes novel set in these war-like conditions but, so far, it is just not coming together.

'I need a modicum of hope for the creative juices to flow and there is very little. Vanguard has got a second wind and millions of people will struggle to stay alive during the next winter.

'No doubt as a Russian, Anatoly you will tell me that your countrymen have been through far more hopeless situations.'

'Well yes that happens to be true,' he said. 'Vanguard has enjoyed success with its lightning attack but I think it will be hard to build on and we must do our utmost to ensure Sutton doesn't and that he gets the fate he so richly deserves.'

'Edinburgh will play a bigger role in that struggle than anyone might have expected a short time ago,' Arthur said. 'If you had made it to the office yesterday, I would have told you that Sam Stockwood is due up here for talks with Gavin Ogilvy next week. It's fairly hush hush and he'll be staying at Bella Munday's castle in East Lothian while he's here.

'I am sure there will be an opportunity for those of us who enjoyed the best of times in Wilford to have a reunion with Sam,' Arthur said.

Anatoly quickly interjected to say 'and let's make it an opportunity to resolve to put Wilford back together again, both the town and the university that you helped to found. I am sure it can be done.'

Anatoly had been advised to take moderate exercise and he used the next few days to familiarise himself with Edinburgh. He could see foreign embassies installing themselves in Stockbridge. The neighbourhood that he had moved into was dominated by people from the professions which had given Edinburgh a strongly middle-class profile - financial services, academia, commerce and the law.

They dwelled in mews, flats or imposing stone-clad town houses depending on their status. Foreign flags were starting to flutter from houses that had recently been put up for sale.

Stockbridge had restaurants and a range of amenities able to service this burgeoning diplomatic community. Nearby were the Botanic gardens which had been planned on a large scale in the 19th century. They were a perfect venue for discreet assignations if Edinburgh was to be a centre for espionage and intrigue like Lisbon in the Second World War or Beirut through the endless era of Middle East instability.

Thoughts such as these crossed Anatoly's mind as he explored Edinburgh's New Town, in fact streets dating from the Georgian era of the 18th century. But he had one priority which was to identify property which could be used to house refugees if Scotland agreed to take in large numbers of those camped out on the inclement Pennine moors and hills

The more he saw of the city the more he realised it was capable of absorbing many thousands of refugees, that is if the will existed. Central Edinburgh had experienced a building boom in the decade before war broke out in England. Large numbers of new hotels had been built to accommodate a tourist influx.

Edinburgh had been one of the main beneficiaries as other major tourist venues such as Egypt and Turkey became too dangerous in the eyes of the long-haul travel industry.

The political drama which had convulsed Scotland as separatists made a push for independence around 2014 had increased the country's profile. The new era of Hollywood Western films in which the characters were encouraged to keep their European accents and characteristics had also helped as their main star was the ruggedly handsome young Scot Gavin Ogilvy.

But now many of these hotels enjoyed reduced occupancy and several had closed. Although Scotland was still at peace it had joined the list of potential world trouble-spots. Most tourists had come via London's airports and that gateway no longer existed. Scotland was just too close for comfort to the inferno raging just two hours drive to the south

It was still possible to see plenty of foreign faces in Edinburgh. But they could just as easily belong to the spies, smugglers and arms dealers who were starting to congregate. Their preferred haunt was Princes Street Gardens at least when the weather was dry. At other times, they could be found in the bars, seedy cafes and night clubs in the side streets of the Old Town. The maze of alleys and dark narrow stairways linking a complex set of streets arranged at different levels made the old medieval quarter a natural zone for illicit encounters of various sorts. The massage parlours and saunas which had catered for the carnal passions of a segment of Edinburgh's professional elite, still plied their trade. Perhaps a new era awaited them as Scotland's capital found itself on a new and dangerous frontline and the city started to fill up with all sorts of *louche* characters.

In the optimistic times before the crisis the city planners had thought revenue could be made by studding the Old Town with student halls of residence. Edinburgh University had done well in global student rankings so a massive rebuilding programme had got going. The city's administrators were even prepared to risk the Old Town's status as a UNESCO World Heritage Centre by allowing buildings of architectural distinction to be discreetly knocked down. But the characterless student flats with their banal and uniform facades were now mostly lying empty. East Asian students much preferred Vancouver or Auckland to studying on an island that seemed to be in the grip of madness. Images of cities ablaze in Britain and thousands of refugees tramping along rain-sodden roads repelled them. Most, finding it hard to distinguish between Scotland and England preferred to look elsewhere.

Anatoly took Moira for a meal at a discreet Italian restaurant in the Newington area not far from the university. They both delved into their pasts. Anatoly described how he had found the salary of a physics teacher in Russia impossible to live on during the chaotic post-communist era. He had set up Moscow's first properly-run recycling business. There had been some good years before he had been targeted by a crooked rival and packed off to jail in 2010 after a stash of heroin had been planted in his car. A Scottish couple Ronnie and Jean Laidlaw had written to him, sent him food parcels and campaigned tirelessly for his release. Eventually he was freed in 2020. They offered him a home in their small Scottish town. When he found his feet, he decided he would try and engage in philanthropic pursuits. Back in Russia he had ploughed part of his profits into philanthropic endeavours and indeed was a pioneer in the field there. With the British charity sector heavily involved in politics, or else run like a corporate business, he thought there was scope to offer a fresh approach. But when the crisis in England erupted less than eighteen months after his arrival, he knew that the priority would be saving perhaps millions of people from harm and finding them food and shelter.

Moira had been recently widowed. Her husband Bill a teacher was a keen canoeist. He had suffered a fatal heart attack shortly after he had rescued a pair of young German tourists who had got into difficulties while exploring Fingal's cave on the island of Staffa. He was only 48. She was three years younger. They had been together for a quarter-of-a-century during which time they had raised two children, both of whom had gone into medicine. Clare was a nurse in Inverness but Don was a doctor in York which was now very near the fighting on the northern England military front.

Through Don, Moira had been kept informed about the terrible human dimension of the conflict which only rarely got into the Scottish media. Torture victims who had survived their ordeal sometimes needed to be treated for horrible injuries and this kind of surgery had gradually taken its toll on her son. Moira was not very political. She had voted to retain the Union in 2014 but had not become passionately involved in constitutional politics. However, she was someone with a strong ethical sense. Thanks to what she had learnt from Don, reinforced by Anatoly's own story of the past year, she was persuaded that it would be wrong for Scotland to stay aloof from the conflict down south. Many shared her view but a lot wished to insulate themselves from that conflict.

Scotland was divided, Anatoly learned from Morag, though not nearly as badly as it was in 2014. But how to react to the war in England had the potential to cause a major schism in a very short time.

When Moira visited Anatoly in his Cyprus Row flat, as a house-warming present she brought along a painting of Bamburgh castle in Northumberland. It had been a family heirloom but it had been kept in a store room since she had sold the family's 3-room house and moved into a smaller apartment. As Anatoly gazed at the imposing fortification looking over a rough North Sea, Moira mentioned that before the children had been teenagers, this had been a favourite spot for family holidays. Bamburgh was further north than Scottish towns like Dumfries and almost on the same latitude as Ayr and she had never really considered it to be in a separate land.

Anatoly smiled as she said that. He gave her a gentle kiss as they left the flat to set off on a walk along the Water of Leith towards the once bustling port of Leith. It was early autumn, another fine largely windless day, of the kind that Edinburgh sometimes went for many weeks without. They nonchalantly picked some of the wild blackberries that had grown fat on the bramble bushes. Dippers and finches darted across the water. They noticed how the urban landscape changed from middle-class dwellings to flats and then to warehouses and lock-ups as they entered Leith. But mainly it was themselves they were absorbed with. They held hands, kissed when they rested on a waterfront bench and by the end of that afternoon's stroll it was hardly necessary for either of them to put into words the feelings they had for one another.

Chapter 2

Castle Talks

By mid-September Anatoly had drawn up a report showing the amount of vacant property available to house refugees in reasonable conditions. He reckoned that up to 40,000 could be housed in currently empty student halls of residences as well as hotels.

Sam Stockwood, the minister for the displaced, wished to have the report, as he was due to make a two-day visit to Scotland, during which he would be holding talks with Gavin Ogilvy.

The Royal family had offered the Scottish Prime Minister the loan of Holyrood Palace, the Queen's residence in the Scottish capital. The gesture had been made after what appeared to be a botched attempted on the Scottish politician's life. Earlier in the year, he had been travelling from his official residence, Bute House in the New Town, to the Scottish parliament. It was located at the foot of the long Royal Mile which threads its way through the Old Town. The palace lay just across the road and both were overshadowed by the extinct volcano known as Arthur's Seat. Rather unusually the rugged undulating slopes of this geological feature gave the impression that a touch of highland wilderness had been imposed on this urban landscape.

At Ogilvy's request the media had played down the incident. But it had all the hallmarks of an assassination attempt. As his car halted at traffic lights before heading down to the Grassmarket, it was suddenly rammed from behind by a Subaru. Two men immediately jumped out with Uzi sub machine guns and let loose a hail of bullets. The few tourists sitting in the pavement cafes in the Grassmarket scattered in terror as they heard the gunfire. Luckily Ogilvy's car was armour-plated and the windows bullet-proof. When one of the machine guns jammed, both men ran down an alley way towards the Cowgate.

They were later identified as two dissident Irish Republicans based in Glasgow who had been recruited by True Vanguard. Even with visitor numbers down, Edinburgh streets were notoriously slow-moving, so the royal offer of their Edinburgh home for the duration of the crisis made sense. It would reduce the likelihood of a second assassination attempt that might be successful.

The elimination of Ogilvy would be disastrous for the prospect of a return to all-island stability. He had loyal moderate colleagues, some of whom were able, others merely dependable. But Ogilvy had shown ingenuity and cool nerves as this crisis deepened. He remained a Unionist at heart and had a vision of a reformed United Kingdom, perhaps with an entirely different structure and name. Moreover, thanks to his acting experience he had a flair for communications.

It was not one that was in plentiful supply in the Scottish political world. In regular informal broadcasts, he conveyed the importance of ensuring the safety of Scottish citizens without overlooking the plight of their English neighbours. He was careful not to provoke True Vanguard while at the same time firmly keeping his distance from the regime. Polls showed that the majority of Scots were prepared to trust him to guide them through the crisis.

Due to the exploratory and informal nature of the talks between Ogilvy and Stockwood, it was decided to hold them away from the Edinburgh media spotlight. The location was to be Peebles, a pretty, unruffled town on the banks of the river Tweed an hour south of Edinburgh.

In his will, Chris Baxter, a close ally of Ogilvy's until his untimely death in a Liverpool air attack, had bequeathed his second home to the Scottish government and for the Prime Minister to use at his leisure. It had become an occasional weekend retreat for Ogilvy and his partner Greer McIver.

Stockwood was due to have talks about the extent of cooperation between the Scottish government and the British Democratic Authority based in Liverpool. He would spent two nights at Traquane castle near the East Lothian town of North Berwick. It was the current residence of Bella Munday, the Scottish tourism entrepreneur and co-founder of the university which had until recently stood in Wilford whose mayor Stockwood still was.

He had accepted her invitation to stay while he was in Scotland. They were close friends. She had renovated the old Roman baths which had been a big tourist draw in Wilford that, luckily, had survived the assault on the town. Stockwood was delighted by the additional suggestion that they use his visit as an opportunity for a reunion with his old friends, Arthur, Zach (and his girl friend Nadia) as well as Anatoly.

Arthur and Anatoly set out for Traquane as the first of the autumn storms seemed poised to sweep in from the Atlantic. They drove on a mainly straight road through prime agricultural land. Only a few bales of hay were left exposed in the fields and there were tractors and trailers busy trying to recoup the harvest in the hours before the weather turned.

Eventually Traquane grew visible on the horizon. Its imposing ramparts were crowned by four conical towers. As the visitors drew closer, they could see its dramatic location. It was situated on a promontory that jutted into the North Sea. This meant that it could only be attacked on its landward side from one direction. The entrance was not under the imposing portcullis but instead through an inconspicuous recess, requiring a short descent underground.

Bella Munday was on hand to greet them along with a small team which was normally on call when there were Scottish-themed evenings staged for tourists. They followed her up a set of narrow twisting stairs until they finally emerged into a large room with a long wooden table flanked by two long settees.

The room had the accoutrements which expectant tourists would have delighted to see. The heads of stags and boars were mounted on each of the walls alongside tapestries showing stirring battle scenes. There were several suits of armour and a stuffed brown bear even though bears had long been extinct in Scotland. A thick carpet with a striking red, black and green tartan design lay across the length of the room. Perhaps the most imposing feature was a set of friezes dating from the 16th century depicting some of the dramatic personalities from the Lothian region, such as John Knox, who had put their stamp on this turbulent period of Scottish history.

Central heating ensured that the castle's main banqueting room was warmer than it would have been in medieval times The chatelaine gave her guests a quick tour, taking them to one of the towers which had been erected in medieval times to prevent not just marauding English armies but highwaymen and local factions from easily storming the whole castle.

After seating the pair and offering them a drink, Bella said:

'I'm here less often now and the castle has been largely unused since the crisis erupted. But I thought it would be a good place for Sam to relax away from the Edinburgh hurly-burly.

'He's due at 7pm and he's told me he's much looking forward to a reunion with friends now scattered in different directions.'

At this point footsteps could be heard on the stairs. It was Zach and his partner Nadia.

For some weeks the Cameroonian had been devastated by the death of his mentor, professor Euan Garland. He had helped him discover the plant in his country's rainforest which after analysis proved to have properties that could halt and reverse arthritis. But Zach had recovered some of his cheerfulness and poise thanks to Nadia. Both of them had spent the last few weeks deep in the Scottish Borders at the old spa town of Moffat. Five thousand refugees were already congregated there. Both of them had been leading a team to ensure that such large numbers were being properly looked after. They were the lucky ones compared to the half-million camping out in the Pennines, now in another state thanks to the sudden imposition of a new frontier.

'It will be interesting to see what clues Sam can offer us about the progress of his talks in Peebles,' Bella remarked. 'It's already 7.20pm, so let's hope it's a good sign that he's running late.'

A CD with relaxing Scottish ballads had been put on in the background. So they were slightly surprised when the large iron door handle turned and Sam Stockwood stepped into the room.

It was impossible to miss him. With a reddish complexion, big boned, with a broad face, strength emanating from his hands and shoulders, he would have been conspicuous in any Edinburgh gathering.

After warmly greeting the others and being led off by Bella to freshen up after his journey, he was settled by Bella in a large leather upholstered armchair. She made sure that he had the chance to sample the local craft beer, now enjoying a fast growing reputation.

She turned and said to him: 'Sam doubtless you've had a long day. You may have done enough talking and may prefer to move through to dinner which won't be long now. It's just marvellous that we've been able to get together.'

Sam replied: 'Don't worry it's not been such an arduous day. Some hard talking has taken place. But at the end of it, I was glad to have accepted this assignment. My boss Howard Lorimer had said that it was time for talks to take place between members of both governments. He had asked me to go as the refugee situation was bound to be at the centre of them.

'I suppose the main question I had at the outset was whether there would be enough personal chemistry between myself and Gavin Ogilvy in order for any progress to be made. I'm the son of a Methodist lay preacher and have not got rid of all my strait-laced ways as I try to adjust to modern times. Much of my town is now in ruins after the July assault by the foreign fighters. Mr Ogilvy is a Hollywood actor, sophisticated, not afraid to cover up his homosexuality, and with his partner by his side on a lot of public occasions.

'As I say, my trying to keep up with the times has been a losing battle. I told Lorimer that I might blurt something out that would only set back our relations at such a crucial juncture. But after two sessions of talks punctuated by lunch, I was glad to have gone ahead.

'I must confess I didn't know much about Gavin. All my time has been taken up with the crisis. So I decided to try and allow him to do as much of the talking as possible during the morning session. I asked him how he had got to be Prime

Minister of Scotland before he was even forty. Did he have any formative experiences? Was there a guiding philosophy that shaped his outlook in political and perhaps other matters'?

'How forthcoming was he then?' Arthur asked.'

'At times, he was disarmingly frank,' Sam replied.

'He said that the reason why he felt able to steer Scotland through such difficult times was due to encounters that he had in the formative stages of his life.

'Aged sixteen, he was flying off the rails. His parents had just divorced and this had hit him hard. He was experimenting with soft drugs and showed no interest in education

'He was just drifting aimlessly in Perth where he had grown up. Then one day he had heard that a film was being shot near Aberfoyle in the Trossachs. He had thought of sloping off to Spain for the summer so he decided to check it out to see if he could land a job that would finance his trip.

'He ran into an American in the street who turned out to be the film's director Chuck Redfern.'

'The Chuck Redfern who made "Saddle Me Up"?' interjected Nadia.

'That's right' Stockwood continued.

'He offered him a job as a tea-boy and scene shifter.

'He told Gavin to pay attention to the rules which were pinned up on the set, one of which said "No Smoking."

'Gavin was told that he'd seen one set too many burst into flames due to a cigarette butt carelessly discarded. He enjoyed the job. It took him out of himself. He even kicked the smoking habit for a while.

'But then one day when bad weather halted shooting, he lit up where he thought he wouldn't be noticed. Suddenly, Redfern came into view, snatched the cigarette and angrily put it out.

'He gave Gavin a tongue-lashing and said he wanted people working for him who had standards and kept to any undertaking that they entered into.

'The young man wept. He realised how badly he wanted to hold onto the job that might be the way out of a dead-end life.

'Chuck Redfern looked at him long and hard and said he'd give him a second chance but he would lose a week's wages.'

'"The need to have standards which determine your conduct is a lesson that has never left me since that day",' Ogilvy told me. 'He said: "It was a philosophy that was bound to steer me in a conventional political direction sooner or later.

But I was swayed by the radical left atmosphere prevalent among young people then. So I voted for the SNP in 2007.'"

'Chuck Redfern remained a benign if distant influence over the young Ogilvy,' Sam continued. 'He decided to try and be an actor. He saved up to get into film school. A reference from Redfern secured him a scholarship. He learned to ride a horse, trained in martial arts (including wrestling and fencing). He graduated from being an extra to getting bit parts in films.

'I had to chuckle when he told me how his breakthrough occurred. He was in an historical drama being directed by the veteran Hollywood left-winger Oliver Usher. It was an epic about the revolutionary hero Simon Bolivar that was being filmed in Venezuela. Funding from the crisis-hit government dried up. The lead actor walked off the set. Usher took a bet on Ogilvy. He played the Liberator and became a box office hit across South America and beyond. He conveyed passion and commitment and was spectacularly good in the action roles, doing all his own stunts. So most people simply forgot that for someone playing the swarthy Bolivar his complexion was quite fair.

'Offers of work came flooding in but, on the advice of Chuck Redfern, he chose his roles with care.' Soon he was avidly courted by the SNAP. The nationalists were keen to corral any Scot who had made a wholesome reputation overseas. In no time he was making party-political broadcasts for the leader Fergus Peacock which he shudders at whenever they are recalled. He was saved from accepting the offer of a safe parliamentary seat and becoming voting fodder for the party by an unexpected approach from Redfern.

'His mentor had decided to do a Western movie with a difference. It would be a "British Western" in which the British accents which a lot of the original cowboys had would replace American ones. It was a gamble but it paid off. Cinema goers on both sides of the Atlantic liked the new twist and the lead, Rory Kincaid was played by Gavin. His character was known for his brevity of speech and directness. He earned an Oscar for best actor with the second one and by the fourth he was co-directing along with Chuck. He was only 32 and the series had eclipsed "Game of Thrones" as a top-ranking historical fantasy.'

Stockwood looked up and said to the others: 'I am sure I'm boring you by now.' 'Not at all' they responded in unison.

Bella said: 'I knew a little about Gavin Ogilvy's back-story. We are, as it happens from the same area of the country, Perthshire but a lot of this was completely new.'

'Yes it's quite fascinating' Zach said. 'You must have won his trust for Mr Ogilvy to open up in this way.'

At which point, Bella interrupted to say, 'I'm sure Sam has not finished his story but let's go through and eat.'

Over Venison, salmon pie and vegetarian curry they continued.

Sam asked whether they were settling in up in Scotland and they told him of their experiences. He remembered to say to Bella that the curative waters of the Roman baths which she had restored in Wilford were now being used to treat some of the victims of the conflict suffering from muscle disorders.

He then laughed when he said: 'Perhaps the most amusing part of Gavin Ogilvy's story was his explanation for how he got into politics.

'One day he was visited on the Hollywood set by the bosomy and bossy lady who was Scotland's minister of culture and external relations. She told him that as a patriotic Scot he ought to consider dropping the name "British Westerns" for his films. As substitutes she suggested "Celtic Westerns" or else "Tartan Westerns" which she thought followed on nicely from "Spaghetti Westerns."

'Ogilvy tried to fob her off with his Scottish charm but she was having none of it. The party was running into trouble because of a chain of policy failures and it needed a trademark brand to take the minds of voters off their everyday complaints. He needed to show that he was fully committed to the patriotic cause and here was his chance.

'Gavin told me that this was a turning-point for him. He realised that he had got entangled with a party obsessed with presentation and spin rather than substance.

'He then lost touch with Scotland for a while due to taking up a role as a United Nations goodwill ambassador. Observing at close hand the misery that still stalked huge areas of the world due to exploitation and war brought home to him just how lucky he was and how fortunate people in Scotland were by comparison with all of the places he had seen on his UN assignment.

'It was in a Sudanese aid settlement on the edge of the desert that he met Greer McIver, a doctor from Kirkintilloch about his own age who was looking after victims of malaria which had flared up with a vengeance after previous hopes that it had been eradicated, were dashed.

'He spent a few days first observing and then working alongside him as he did his best, in primitive conditions, to treat hundreds of sufferers of the illness. When it was time to leave, he knew that it was not just admiration that he had for the intrepid medic but a deeper emotion. He invited him to stay at the holiday home he had recently built on the Azores.

'Six months later the world's media were encamped outside Kirkintilloch parish church for their civil partnership ceremony. In the intervening period friendship had blossomed into love and the desire for a lasting union.

'It had been an even more incredible turnaround for Ogilvy than breaking into film. He told me that he had long known that he was gay but that he had preferred to plough his passion and emotions into his film work. He had been careful to steer clear of the tacky and soulless Hollywood gay scene. But he had also known there was a good chance he would not be in the movie game forever. Between films, he had pursued a degree in urban regeneration at one of the better research-orientated universities in California. He even told me that one of his essays had been on Wilford as a model for sustainable development.'

'You must have been proud to hear that,' Arthur broke in. 'Naturally, I was' Sam replied 'but I was even prouder that this young man was talking to me in such a transparent way.

He probably guessed that I wasn't one of life's natural liberals but he decided to break the ice by being straightforward and open. I could only respect that and this morning has certainly broadened my mind. A bit overdue, some of you might be thinking but there we are.

'Ironically it was Greer who persuaded Gavin to spend more time in Scotland. It was the base for his medical work so Gavin decided to film his next British Western on location there. This was a time when the wheels were finally starting to come off the SNAP bandwagon. It was clear the people running things had got in way above their heads and were simply not up to the task of running government departments for a country of five million people. Fergus Peacock's party had grown arrogant and incompetent. It had neglected governing for a succession of propaganda stunts.

'Three years ago he got overtures from the United Citizens party (UCP) to stand. Of course he talked it over with Greer and he turned out to be the decisive influence prompting him to accept. He observed that Scotland had gone through a lost decade of missed opportunities thanks to the constitutional issue driving out more serious matters as objects of government concern. There was now a real danger that it would be a lost generation unless SNAP was pushed out of office and the shambles that was Scotland's public services modernised.

'Both men had been on opposite sides in the 2014 independence referendum. Greer had campaigned to preserve the Union. The fact that he had for a few years been a well-known sporting figure – capped 17 times for the Scottish national rugby side – made him an asset for what ultimately proved the winning side. Gavin's partner observed that one of the things holding Scotland back was the dearth of politicians who had work and life experiences beyond Scotland. Too many people who had done a few years being Special Assistants to members of the Scottish Parliament (MSPs), or had been local councillors, were slotted into ministerial jobs only to quickly flounder.

'Gavin took the plunge and he stood for election in his home town of Perth. The UCP emerged as the largest party and was able to form an administration in coalition with the much smaller Scottish Progressives. He went straight into government as minister of urban regeneration. Until the crisis had erupted he had been making progress in turning around economic blackspots like West Lothian and East Ayrshire. The fact that the government was paying attention to the needs of areas that had backed the SNAP, now in opposition, made a favourable impression. This work was, however, overshadowed by the sudden death of the UCP leader Archie McCrindle. There was no obvious successor and polls showed Ogilvy to be the most popular minister right across the generations.

'Consulting once more with Greer, he decided to see if he was capable of providing leadership at the top of government and he easily won a leadership contest.

'Regrettably,' Sam went on, 'Gavin only had a year in office before the crisis in England erupted. Long neglected tasks were being tackled. Officials in top posts were being appointed on the basis of competence not political allegiances. Investment was flowing in. Previous divisions at last seemed to be fading into the background.

'I knew Scottish independence had been declared with great reluctance' Sam underlined. 'While he was still alive, Chris Baxter had pointed out that the two parties in the coalition were solidly behind the continuation of the Union.

'Gavin Ogilvy confirmed this was the case and that Union sentiment remained strong in Scotland. But he and his government felt they had no option but to pull Scotland clear of the firestorm that was raging through much of England. There were two primary concerns. A relatively small contingent of two or three thousand foreign fighters was capable of wreaking devastation in Scotland where the population was even more concentrated in a few urban centres than it was in England. He had also received intelligence that the militant wing of the SNAP was planning to mount a break-away move. It had already acquired its own paramilitary wing, still small in size, but growing and the fear was that if key buildings were seized True Vanguard might use this as a pretext to intervene in order to "restore order."

'So' Sam said' tucking in to the ice cream and profiteroles which had been served for dessert, 'this was the much needed refresher course I received on Scottish politics from its central figure.

'I don't think Gavin Ogilvy revealed anything to me that would compromise him but I would not have provided a verbatim account of this part of the conversation unless I knew all five of you were souls of discretion on these matters.

'England has a great friend in this Scottish leader and it is not my intention to do anything that will undermine him.'

'That's fully understood Sam and, speaking as a patriotic Scotswoman, I'm glad you are taking a long-term approach,' Bella interjected.

'But is there anything you want to happen in the short term?'

'I hope those in charge of Scotland will be vigilant in ensuring it isn't used by Vanguard forces to harass the British Army across the Border in northern England. Gavin has already shown that he is willing to alleviate the plight of the growing body of refugees in camps just across the Scottish border. A field hospital is being set up near Kelso to treat badly injured civilians and those suffering from life threatening diseases. It will be under the auspices of the United Nations but it is an all-Scottish initiative in reality.'

'Did you know,' Zach spoke up, 'that the Spirit of Freedom football team has been inducted in the Scottish Premier League just a few months after it was founded'? It is composed of young men who fled north to Scotland quite early in the crisis. The team has been reinforced by four top players from London clubs who were made unemployed after Vanguard suspended English league football in case it proved an opportunity for unrest.'

'The team plays out of Peebles and has acquired a large following among Scottish folk in the Borders area who never previously had a strong team of their own to back. It has had a string of wins, sensationally knocking out Aberdeen in one of the early stages of the Scottish League Cup just a fortnight ago.'

'Hopefully sport will prove a bridge rather than a barrier between our two British nations flung apart by this terrible conflict,' Sam remarked.

'Ultimately I hope a lot of the refugees will be able to move to Scotland on a temporary basis. If that was not our goal, I wouldn't have requested that you come here when there is so much work to do in the parts of England under our control. But we will just have to wait and see how the mid-term elections go in the United States. They are five weeks away and if President Wallace's party retains its Congressional majority, then America is likely to revive its intent to force Vanguard from power.'

Stormy winds were now battering against the ramparts of the castle but inside the atmosphere was jovial. It was decided that the guests from Edinburgh would stay the night. There was plenty of room and Bella felt there was no point in traversing along an unfamiliar road where there was the risk of crashing into trees that might have been blown down by the gale.

As everyone got up to make their way to their night quarters, Sam had a final remark: 'I almost forgot to mention that as I was about to enter the car, an athletic figure in shorts and a vest came bounding towards me. He was out of breath having been jogging and he introduced himself as Greer McIver. Gavin was not there as he had been called away to take a phone call from Edinburgh.

'He said that Gavin was a good man who would not do anything dishonourable and that I should not be too impatient with the pace of events up here. There were constraints and dangers. But the most upright and intelligent folk in Scotland knew it was their own kith-and-kin who were going through hell in England and that it was impossible to ignore their plight.

'The athletic doctor quickly said goodbye and disappeared into the house, leaving me with the sense that my visit to Scotland had far from been in vain.'

Chapter 3.

Grassmarket Information Wars

Arthur Gorman was sitting amidst packing cases and shelving that were waiting to be assembled. He was amused that he was in a three-story town house in Edinburgh's historic Grassmarket purveying propaganda for British Liberty and its government in Liverpool. It was an outcome of the recent round of talks between Sam Stockwood and Gavin Ogilvy. There would be an information office putting across the views of the British democrats battling it out with True Vanguard for control of much of the island.

He had received an official letter from Liverpool asking if he would agree to be the director. He would have full control over the British Information Council's programme of activities. Nobody had needed to spell it out to him but his task would be to lessen the possibility of Scotland reaching some kind of accommodation with Vanguard. He would need to try and remind a ruling elite – still in its infancy after twenty years of internal self rule - of the price to be paid for making such a Faustian pact.

An attempt would be made to put across the British resistance perspective to a rather cynical media corps whose members worked out their position on major world issues based on highly selective and flimsy information. Many journalists were on short-term contracts which pre-disposed some of them to ape the line of Vanguard because it had the deepest pockets. He would reach out to the wider public, appealing to humanitarian instincts and a sense of solidarity by showing the heavy price everyday folk were paying not so far away because of the rise to power of a fanatic.

Film events would be put on to show the cruel depravity unfolding on the streets of English cities. There would be talks by well-known figures. Debates might occur provided they didn't spark a riot. There would be photo exhibitions and book launches. He himself would travel across Scotland to give talks.

Arthur knew that he possessed some advantages. He himself had been a best-selling novelist, with one of the detective novels that had been filmed by Hollywood even winning an Oscar. He was Irish which presumably gave him a certain detachment, at least in some eyes. He had the ability to put people at their ease as well as the fluency which were thought to be trademarks of his race. But above all, he believed in the cause of British Liberty.

He had warned in his novels about where a popular culture, increasingly based around febrile emotions and a desire to escape from reality, could lead. He had helped found a university to ensure that at least some young people learned how to be freethinkers and, as adults, show a commitment to improvement and reform rather than bulldozing the social and political order.

He had two of them now beside him, trying to prepare for the opening of the BIC. Kyle Ritchie and Rory Savidge were both Scots whose commitment to opposing Vanguard had impressed him. Kyle would be helping him to build up ties with the media and connect with middle-class Scots. As his name suggested Rory was from an Irish heritage background. The Glaswegian perhaps had a stiffer assignment. A lot of his people had been influenced by the propaganda of Vanguard because the movement was thought to be anti-imperialist. Pro-Vanguard banners sometimes even appeared at Celtic football ground in the east end of the city. There were plenty of sensible young people even among Celtic's fan-base and hopefully they would be capable of exposing Vanguard for what it was - a movement intent on carrying out repression that would dwarf in scale anything the British had done in Ireland in centuries past. If this didn't happen, Vanguard could acquire a 5th column in Scotland's largest and most volatile city.

The first event would hopefully put the information centre on the map. It would be a talk given by Rodney Tripp who, for thirty years, had presented culture documentaries on British television and hosted discussion programmes on Western thought down the ages. Tripp had not pushed any agenda and had won a loyal audience (spanning the generations) because of his knack of transferring his enthusiasm for ideas and their application to his audience. This bluff Lancastrian from Clitheroe, now in his seventies, was never going to fall for the negativity of Vanguard. He had quickly emerged as one of Clive Sutton's most energetic critics. But if he had assumed that he could continue to function as a sceptical public intellectual in the Sutton era, he got a rude awakening.

He had been one of the hundreds of public figures detained after the Remembrance day massacre of 2021. Along with other detainees, he was kept in squalid conditions in the tunnels lying under the Emirates stadium in north London. With football now banned in Vanguard-controlled England, the Arsenal stadium (along with several others) had become a vast makeshift prison in which people who were seen as potential or actual enemies of the regime were kept.

Tripp had managed to escape from his grim captivity thanks to an amazing act of self-sacrifice. It involved his twin brother Julian who was allowed to visit him every six weeks. By April he saw that Rodney's health was fast deteriorating in the fetid and overcrowded conditions. He told his brother that he had a plan that might get him out. As it was usually impossible to tell them apart, he would replace him in captivity. Initially, Rodney was aghast. He told Julian that he just had to endure his lot and hope for eventual salvation. Realising that the visit would soon be over, Julian asked him to stop and think. Out of prison, he would be able to draw the world's attention to the inhuman system of political detention Sutton was operating. He Julian would likely be roughed up but he thought the regime had enough sense not to kill him.

Sutton was even disallowing the United Nations from gaining access to Vanguard's vast prison system. As the guard's footsteps approached, Julian pleaded with his brother to agree. With tears in his eyes he said, 'Alright Julian. I hate the prospect of you being flung into this pit but this is bigger than either of us. So you've persuaded me. If I get out, I won't rest until the world realises what is going on.'

'Good man,' Julian replied and, at that, he quickly left.

At the next visit Julian wore a deliberately tight-fitting suit. Rodney had lost so much weight that it was necessary not to alert the guards to the ruse by having a thin man swallowed up in a bulky suit. Julian, an actor, had also brought some stage make-up in order to disguise his brother's greyish complexion. There were around seven minutes in the 45 minute visit when the guard's attention was drawn to other nearby prisoners. They quickly swapped clothes, embraced, and with as much com-posure as he could muster, Rodney made his way through the dense warren of makeshift dormitories in which hundreds of prisoners had been crammed.

Outside a car was waiting that took him on a two-hour journey to the East Anglian port of Lowestoft. It was under Vanguard control but fiercely pro-resistance. Fishing boats were allowed to go to sea after a search. Vanguard's vigilance had gradually relaxed as no contraband or smuggled escapees had been found for some time. Disguised as an elderly fisherman, Rodney Tripp passed undetected. Out at sea he was transferred onto another trawler from Grimsby. This Lincolnshire port had remained free of Vanguard and 24 hours after walking out of the Emirates stadium, Rodney was recuperating in Grimsby's hospital.

Over the summer of 2022 Tripp had gradually recovered from his eight months of harsh detention. He had met with Ray Lattimore, the most outspoken critic of Vanguard among the by now scattered British press corps. He told Ray that his brother had made a great sacrifice in order that he would be a voice of the resistance. He asked him what was the most effective way that he could speak out?

Ray asked him if he would describe what he had endured at the launch of the British Information Council in Edinburgh? It was likely that such an event would get far more publicity if staged there rather than in another part of the island free of Vanguard's grip. Edinburgh was now filling up with foreign diplomatic missions. Television crews reporting the English fighting often rested up there. Above all, a battle to win the hearts and minds of Scots was underway. Prime Minister Ogilvy had privately indicated that he wished Vanguard to be toppled. But there were many obstacles to be overcome before he could declare his hand. Unmasking some of the real horrors of Sutton's repressive order could make a real difference. It was certainly likely to throw the pro-Vanguard faction in Scottish politics onto the defensive.

These arguments made sense to Rodney Tripp. He met Arthur Gorman and his team a fortnight before the Edinburgh initiative. Originally, Arthur had thought of holding the Tripp lecture in one of Edinburgh University's main lecture theatres. But, so great was the demand for tickets that, with one week to go, it was decided to hire a much larger venue, the Usher Hall.

Since its opening in 1914, it had been Edinburgh's largest public meeting place and it was able to seat 2,200 people. Three hours before the talk, a queue of people was snaking along Lothian Road down to St John's Episcopal church at the west end of Princes Street. Not only was the Edinburgh bourgeoisie out in strength but people from across Scotland, as well as from trouble-free parts of England, who were devotees of Tripp's media output, had come along.

With the help of Zach, Nadia and Javier, Arthur had organized fifty stewards to manage the event. Discreet security had been laid on by the Scottish government and there were police right around the building.

Arthur's spirits rose when the audience got up and gave Rodney Tripp a standing ovation when he appeared on stage. He was thinner and a little stooped but his bouffant mop of hair and expressive grin, made him instantly recognisable. He did not dwell unduly on the discomfort and danger which he had endured but gave a detailed account of what captivity was like for thousands of people. Their only crime had been to oppose some of the more inhuman actions of the regime or else be seen as potential threats in the future. He revealed that several well-known people, very distinguished in their fields, were now dead, either from malnutrition, cold, or by being simply denied medicine, essential for the treatment of long-term conditions. There were gasps when he described how a once very fit around-the-world yachtswoman had been allowed to die in a damp cell when a fresh inhaler would have enabled her to survive the asthma she had acquired in captivity.

He put the repression which Sutton had unleashed a year previously in a long-term perspective. He asked his audience to recall that it was completely alien to

British traditions, stretching back at least half a millennium. It was necessary to look to occupied Europe of the Second World War or else the communist purges in Russia and its neighbours, to find a proper parallel. Drawing to a close, he said it was an honour to be present at the launching of the British Information Centre and that it was his hope that the core nations on the island of Britain would find ways to be in active partnership when this emergency was finally over.

At this point the hall was suddenly plunged into darkness. The front area then filled with thick smoke and it was later found that smoke bombs had been thrown into the audience. After thirty seconds of pandemonium the lights came back on. Arthur Gorman who had been chairing the event, was seen trying to pick himself up from the floor, blood flowing from a thankfully small wound at the back of his head. But there was no sign of the speaker.

Police and security staff managed to clear the hall after half-an-hour. Long before Arthur had become convinced that Rodney Tripp had been kidnapped. He asked Anatoly what could be done? Javier spoke up. Mindful of the audacious kidnappings that had occurred in his native Colombia, he had got the speaker to fit a small tracking device to the cufflink on his left sleeve. He said that if a code was punched into an online programme, then Rodney Tripp's whereabouts could be tracked.

Anatoly hurriedly produced his laptop and tapped in the code. Tripp appeared to be in a vehicle moving at speed on the M8 motorway towards Glasgow. If the car managed to get off the motorway undetected, it would soon be swallowed up in the metropolis. So speed was of the essence. Jack Armour, the police minister, appeared on the scene. Squad cars were dispatched to intercept Tripp's kidnappers at Harthill service station, the midway point between the two cities.

For an hour everyone waited anxiously for news. Finally a call came through to Armour who looked across to the others and gave the thumbs up sign. The dark Volvo containing Tripp, had been forced off the road and the two occupants overpowered before they could use their automatic pistols. There was no sign of Tripp until banging from the boot was heard. Tripp had been shoved in after being bundled out of the Usher Hall. His assailants were unidentified due to wearing masks but one had a Scottish accent and the other a foreign, perhaps Middle Eastern, accent.

It was impossible to play down the kidnapping given that it had occurred in the midst of several thousand people. Next day, the world's press had stark headlines warning that the English conflict was spreading northwards and that Clive Sutton had a very long reach.

The conclusion which Anatoly, Arthur and the others reached was that there had been a botched attempt by Vanguard to seize Tripp and restore him to its captivity. His escape had been a great embarrassment. Apprehending him in the full glare of publicity would have been a propaganda coup. By contrast gunning him down in cold blood would have merely confirmed his case about the viciousness of the Sutton regime.

After such a dramatic debut, the BIC (as it came to be known) settled down to some weeks of routine. A daily news bulletin was edited by Arthur. It contained information about the military position as the BDA held its ground against a slackening Vanguard offensive. Profiles appeared of prominent citizens who had been taken into custody by Vanguard in 2021 and not heard from since. There were appeals to find homes for children who had lost their parents in the fighting as well as notification of talks and musical performances from groups which had been formed among the refugees already in Scotland.

Professor Edgar Hale, the palliative care specialist who had made a dramatic escape from London by barge with Anatoly and several other key collaborators, did a short lecture tour for BIC. He described the human costs of the ageist crackdown still being carried out by Sutton and his terrifying minister of social credit, Sharon Burgess. The one given at the Edinburgh Medical School, in the south of the city next to the Royal Infirmary, attracted a capacity audience. The next day the professor was flying out to New York where the intercession of the US government ensured that he would be giving a presentation on the plight of Britain's elderly to the UN human rights commission.

As the tempo of the BIC's work slowly increased, one morning Arthur looked across to the opposite side of the Grassmarket where a disused pub had stood boarded up. A new shop front was being installed. He thought nothing of it until, later that day, Kyle Ritchie, took him aside. He pointed to the Vanguard emblem, a bright flame against a green background, with a tiny Union Jack in the top left corner. It was next to a sign which proclaimed 'True Britain Hub.'

Arthur was momentarily taken aback that Vanguard was opening premises in Edinburgh and right opposite to BIC. But on reflection it made sense. Vanguard was not outlawed in Scotland. The furore which had erupted when the Scottish army drove the foreign fighters out of the Cheshire town of Wilford, had died down. As for the Grassmarket, perhaps the choice of location was practical. This medieval square was accessible to Waverley train station, the airport out in the west, and to the Scottish parliament, half-a-mile to the east.

Arthur carried on as normal until, two days later at 3.30 in the afternoon, the phone rang. There was a slightly familiar voice at the other end, a touch of a mock Cockney accent, overall smooth and even bordering on the familiar.

'Hello, I wonder if I could speak to Arthur Gorman. I'm calling from just across the road actually, from the True Britain Hub.'

Arthur was momentarily startled but quickly managed to compose himself.

This is Arthur Gorman speaking, can I ask who's calling'?

'Yes, it's Tristram Pannell. London has sent me here to launch its information hub. I wonder if you are free to have a coffee either now or perhaps at some other time?'

Arthur thought quickly. There was absolutely no advantage to be gained from seeing someone from this Vanguard 'hub' especially if it was at their suggestion. And if that person was the failed Machiavelli of British politics, Tristram Pannell, then it had even less to recommend it. It was safe to assume he was up to something.

Arthur decided not to stand on ceremony: 'Mr Pannell, I'm not going to offer you the excuse that I'm busy. Right now I'm not. I hope you will understand when I say that I need to inform my superiors in Liverpool that you have phoned.

'You seem to be answerable to True Vanguard,' he went on. 'I am certainly answerable to the British Democratic Authority. If I am told that it is alright for a meeting to go ahead, I may then decide to accept your kind invitation.'

Pannell responded: 'that sounds like a rather legalistic approach but at least we have made telephone contact and perhaps I will hear back from you in the near future.'

Arthur replied, showing a touch of anger: 'Your government, back in the early 2000s, was zealously legalistic, passing hundreds of new laws, some of which have enabled Vanguard to stamp out liberty in the places that it controls.

'May I also say that there was nothing very legalistic about the attempted kidnapping of Rodney Tripp at our founding event which most people assume was carried out by True Vanguard.'

'This had nothing at all to do with me,' Pannell hastily interjected. 'Since we are virtually neighbours, I hope we can get along despite that spot of bother.'

'We shall see,' Arthur replied. 'But right now I don't think there is anything more to be said. Goodbye' he said, quickly putting down the phone.

What did the dispatch of Pannell to Edinburgh mean? Before he contacted Liverpool, he spoke to his two assistants and asked them to keep their distance from the competitors across the road. They were only in their early twenties and would be unable to recall much of Pannell's ten-year premiership. He felt it necessary to point out that he was a very devious politician indeed – outwardly amiable and capable of charm but utterly untrustworthy.

Later that day, the Council of State in Liverpool asked him to await further instructions concerning the news that Tristram Pannell was operating in Edinburgh on behalf of True Vanguard. These came the next day in the form of an E mail from Ray Lattimore who, since the start of the crisis, had been an unofficial press adviser for the BDA.

It read:

'Dear Arthur, You were right to deliver a rebuff to Tristram Pannell. But it would appear that he is poised to mount a propaganda offensive in Edinburgh. Probably, it will be simply impossible not to have dealings with him. But, as far as possible, they should be on our terms. I'll be in Edinburgh later today in fact. Let's meet somewhere quiet for a meal and a drink, a place where we are unlikely to be overheard or observed.'

Arthur was at platform 2 of Waverley station as the second daily train from Liverpool pulled in. It and the Liverpool to Cardiff line were the only two cross-country services that were still operating. He spotted Ray and as dusk was falling they were soon driving through Holyrood Park with the extinct volcano that squatted in the heart of the city glowering down at them. After ten minutes they pulled up at an ancient drovers pub, the Sheep Heid. It was popular with walkers who explored the mini-wilderness that towered above the city. The food was hearty. There was a good wine list for the more discerning as well as a wide selection of real ales. They decided to retire to the courtyard where the only other customer was a local with his collie dog.

Over the food they discussed the new development. Ray said: 'It wouldn't surprise me if Pannell had been sent up here to dissuade the Scottish government from playing a supportive role in any renewed British-American push against Vanguard. The mid-term US elections are just a month away. If they go President Wallace's way, the signs are that America will return to the fray, committing its troops to land and air combat operations.

'Our intelligence people tell us that the True Britain Hub has rented a three story town house on Ann Street. It is in Dean Village, overlooking where you are in Stockbridge. Adjacent streets are beginning to fill up with embassies. Through Pannell, I strongly suspect, Vanguard will be trying to impose its line on the Edinburgh diplomatic community as the warfare in England looks set to intensify.'

'So what do you think I should do?,' Arthur asked.

'My guess is that there is little chance you will run into Pannell in the Grassmarket,' Ray replied. 'He is too grand to be a shop manager of the TBH. He'll be using his sinuous charm in New Town drawing rooms and over lunch with various Edinburgh grandees to try and get the local establishment and foreign opinion to adopt his own cynical approach to the crisis.

'Provided you are comfortable with the idea Arthur, I would send a note saying you are willing to meet him for a brief chat. I don't need to tell a novelist, one alive to the quirks of human character, to be on his guard. But if the encounter goes smoothly enough, you might put a proposal to him.'

'Oh and what would that be?' Arthur asked, his curiosity tinged with alarm.

'You might invite him to participate in a debate that is open to the public on a theme along the lines of "What is the best way forward for Britain after 2022?"'

'It's the kind of topic that would enable the British Liberty vision of the future to be transmitted to a Scottish audience. This vision would stand in sharp contrast to the Vanguard one but Pannell might see opportunities to present a euphemistic portrayal of events. If London gives him the go ahead, I expect he would wish to take part himself.'

'And who would be representing our side?,' Arthur asked.

Ray replied: 'You debated very effectively in America last winter. But perhaps there is a case for the line-up being an all-British one. I will be seeing Brian Crawford who has just arrived back in Scotland. It would be a coup if the pre-war head of Sutton's communications operation agreed to speak publicly on behalf of British Liberty. There is no love lost between Brian and his former chief. He placed him under house arrest and surely would have killed him if he had been apprehended while fleeing north. Brian is a changed man. He has dropped his Scottish Nationalist sympathies and is well into writing a book about what he saw of Vanguard from the very inside.

'As the other speaker, I would propose Professor Edgar Hale. He is one of Britain's most distinguished specialists on the treatment of the elderly. His detailed report on Sutton's plans for the elderly was submitted to the UN a year ago before the worst had happened. So he is a figure of credibility *and* he helped Anatoly and the others escape from London by boat up the Thames. He continues to regard Vanguard as the worst disaster to befall England since the Black Death. So I would expect him to agree to play a major role in such a debate.

'What do you think Arthur? Is it worth a try'?

'Yes I think it is' he replied 'provided we go into it with our eyes open and it is planned with care. My hunch is that Vanguard will jump at the opportunity to have their case presented in a favourable light. As for Pannell he still somehow thinks that he can charm the birds off the trees with his earnestness and mock sincerity.

'I think it might be worth considering holding it outside Edinburgh,' Arthur went on. 'Glasgow is the obvious location. As the centre of the anti-British push to quit the UK, there would be residual sympathy in some quarters for Vanguard even though Sutton would place Scotland under an iron heel if he could.

'Everywhere some people have the tendency to block out a cause's unsavoury aspects in order to derive benefit from it, however obscure. During the thirty years conflict in Ulster, there were always knots of people in the west of Scotland ready to overlook the brutality and terror and back "the Boys" because they were "our people."'

Rory Savidge and Kyle Ritchie had arrived to meet Ray over a drink.

'Such an event held in Glasgow would have to be choreographed with great care,' Rory observed – 'the right venue, a capable chair, proper security so there was no repeat of the Usher Hall incident or worse. Pannell may still remember the rough receptions that he received in the city after he engineered regime change in Socotra. But he reckons that people have short memories and maybe they have forgiven all that has happened in the meantime.'

The following morning Arthur sent Rory across to the True Britain Hub with a message in a sealed envelope that was for the attention of Pannell. He was handed the message that afternoon.

He had spent all day at Ann Street planning the TBH's first reception. He was grateful for the help of a former British ambassador to Sweden who, after retiring to Edinburgh, had become a well-known figure in New Town society. Dame Emily Montrose viewed events in England through rose-tinted spectacles, assuming that the British revolution she had yearned for from her hard left college days was unfolding and positively thrilled that she was still alive to see it.

Gorman's message had simply proposed a meeting, suggesting as a possible venue the car park next to Dunsapie loch. It was a little-known spot located by the most elevated part of the road going through Holyrood Park. The loch was tranquil, a place where courting couples met, joggers rested, and family groups came to picnic during the fleeting months of good weather. It was now well into autumn. The place got dark by 6.30pm. Gorman hoped that his counterpart might see the worth of meeting there.

Gorman provided an E mail address and Pannell agreed to the venue but, rather surprisingly, suggested 8.15 next morning. He was evidently keen to meet and the timing had some merit. The spot would be quiet. Beyond the park, the roads would be clogged with drivers heading for work or else on the school run. Only the super-fit or dog-walkers would be up at this secluded spot so early.

As it was dry Arthur decided to walk up. It was 25 minutes from his flat in Merchiston. He had made sure Liverpool knew about the meeting.

A blue Jaguar was the sole occupant of the small car park when Arthur arrived. The front lights briefly shone and Tristram Pannell climbed out. He had been seventy that May but he had a brisk gait and wasn't stooped. However, the widows peak that was starting to appear in his final years as Prime Minister was far more pronounced.

Pannell flashed his trademark ingratiating smile and they shook hands. At that point a younger man in a dark suit, with a bulge in the breast pocket, got out of the back.

Why don't we have our chat in the back seat,' Pannell suggested.

'If it's alright with you, I'd prefer it if we stayed in the open air,' Gorman responded.

'We're both wearing overcoats and it's at least twelve degrees this morning so we won't freeze to death and it's a nice walk along the side of the loch.'

If necessary, Arthur had been prepared to enter the car but there was practically nobody around so they were unlikely to be overheard.

Pannell agreed. He instructed his minder to stay back. But as they approached the loch, he put on a pair of dark glasses. As the weak sun gave the loch a cobalt blue colouring, the thought suddenly occurred to Arthur that this hilly parkland in the centre of a bustling city would make a great setting for a new *Margo Forbes* novel.

But before he could see if his writer's block was receding, Pannell said to him: 'I devoted a big portion of my Premiership to bringing peace to Northern Ireland and the stakes are even greater in the conflict that is now tearing apart the bigger of our two islands.'

'We are certainly in a bigger mess,' Gorman replied, 'especially given that the principal architects of violence are currently in power.'

'It is a frightful business and I only wish things were somehow different, but we are where we are,' Pannell replied.

'Obviously our two organizations are in direct competition. We have different explanations for how the conflict started and we differ also over the preferred outcome,' Gorman responded.

'True,' Pannell said.

Gorman then interjected with a question.

'Do you think our respective interests could be served if, instead of firing endless propaganda volleys, our two organizations right here in Scotland debated what is the best way ahead for war-torn Britain?

'This is perhaps a way of doing your job that won't attract much public criticism. You would probably have not just a Scottish but an international audience prepared to hear your case' Gorman continued.

'I don't propose to spell out all my reasons for taking on this mission,' Pannell said. 'There are dimensions that should remain undisclosed at least for now. My overriding motive is that I think I can play a role in the search for a settlement even though there are people who will say that I am tarnishing my reputation by aligning with Vanguard in this way.'

Gorman, a man prepared to see the best in some dubious people, had not warmed to Pannell. He was coming over as both unctuous and shifty. He was tempted to ask just what *reputation* he was referring to but didn't. But he wasn't here to start a quarrel and contented himself by asking Pannell to give the idea some serious thought and get back to him about it.

By now they had almost doubled back to the car. Pannell's man had opened the front door.

'I can give you a lift back to the Old Town if you like,' Pannell said.

'Thank you, that's considerate,' Gorman said. 'It didn't take me long to walk up here and it will take me less time to walk down. I like to make the best of a dry day in a city with such capricious weather.'

'Good point,' Pannell replied.

Gorman didn't shake hands but raised his right-hand in a half-wave and headed down a footpath for pedestrians only.

Perhaps he had misjudged Tristram Pannell, Gorman reflected as he threaded his way down and across the park. Instead of grabbing at any opportunity for renewed fame, the sad creature might be stuck in Edinburgh under redress. As a teenager he had been educated at one of its prestigious schools and was said to have greatly disliked the experience. Now he was back as the minion of a dictator who had taken the cult of youth to far crazier lengths than Tristram and his PR machine would ever have dreamt of.

And there was still no sign of his wife. Her disappearance since the English troubles had started, struck him as curious. But it would be unwise to display undue interest in whatever human drama lay behind his sudden arrival in the city. He had shown tact during the short few minutes they had conversed. They were adversaries

- that much was clear - but as a writer he was curious to see what would become of the ex-Prime Minister's mission to Scotland.

Back in the office, Arthur was soon toiling over a talk he had been asked to give to the West Linton Ideas Society on 'the crime novel in war.' It was quite a demanding topic but at least it had drawn his thoughts back to Margo Forbes, the character who had given flight to his literary imagination as well as bringing him fame and fortune. In all likelihood the intrepid South Manchester police widow had been burned out of her bungalow. East Didsbury, the area in which she lived, had fared very badly in the fighting due to its proximity to Manchester Airport. Hopefully, she would have escaped. If lucky, she might even have made it to Edinburgh rather than being stuck in a flimsy tent on a North Yorkshire moor. As his thoughts of resurrecting his queen of crime in wartime conditions grew, his reverie was interrupted by the ringing of the phone.

A polished English female voice asked if that was Mr Gorman. 'Speaking' he replied.

'My name is Belinda Rice and I'm phoning on behalf of Mr Pannell to say that the Hub is interested in going ahead with the debate. Since this is a collaborative event, we would like to invite you to a planning meeting at his official residence in Dean Village. If this is acceptable to you, feel free to bring along whoever you want from the BIC.'

Gorman thought quickly and decided it made sense to accept the invitation and to go to the Vanguard headquarters in Edinburgh. There would be no loss of face as the meeting would be private. Of course, he would inform Liverpool in advance in case his superiors thought differently.

'I accept your proposal,' he replied. 'Do you have a date and a time in mind?'

Rice replied: 'We were thinking about 11 am tomorrow at Ann Street.'

'Yes I can be there and I'll have an assistant with me,' Gorman replied.

Kyle Ritchie was up in Aberdeen that week so he took Rory Savidge with him.

The walk up from Stockbridge to Ann Street brought the two of them through some of Edinburgh's choicest real estate. The flags of Russia, India and Brazil, fluttering in the autumn breeze, showed the area was keeping up appearances despite the crisis. Rory was amused to see that a Middle Eastern country had put its diplomatic plaque outside a house on Danube Street which was still fondly recalled by some as the site of an upmarket Edinburgh bordello presided over by an outwardly demure spinster.

Ann Street was one street further on. It was tucked in front of Dean Village tennis club. The tree-lined street had pretty well-tended gardens and a range of architectural facades. Vanguard's offices were kept in the largest house on the street. It had a set of Roman pillars on the front with a large triangular roof. But little was visible due to a massive hedge which screened off most of the building from external view.

They found themselves in a large high-ceilinged hallway graced by a crystal chandelier. Instead of a portrait of Sutton, there were oil paintings of Victorian explorers on the wall going up the stairway to a large drawing room. The Vanguard makeover may not have reached this northern outpost. Or perhaps the idea was to maintain a facade of continuity with the British past that would chime in with Pannell's emollient diplomacy.

Belinda Rice had shown them up and she directed them towards a sofa and two leather armchairs. 'Sofa government' had been one of the nicknames given for Pannell's informal style of government. Belinda, pad in hand, was ready to take notes. Rory had been given similar instructions by Arthur.

Over coffee they discussed how to proceed. Gorman proposed that the debate should focus on a relatively open-ended question such as 'What is the best way forward for Britain after 2022?'

He said that a non-contentious question that prompted both sides to try and make a positive case could help to take some of the heat out of the occasion.

Pannell said that he had no difficulty with such a goal nor did he have any objection to the question.

They agreed on a two hour debate with a 30 minute interval. Two speakers would perform from both sides. Some questions would be allowed from the floor.

Gorman recommended an audience of no more than 300 people, one that could be vetted in advance to reduce the likelihood of disruption.

'Who would ensure balance?' Pannell asked.

Gorman suggested the Law Society for Scotland.

Pannell countered with the Electoral Reform Society.

'It probably exists in Scotland' Gorman replied 'but given the controversy surrounding electoral reform in pre-war England, I'm not sure how credible an organization with this title would be.'

'The Law Society up here is really a broad church and by no means a mouthpiece for any particular interest or view.'

'Alright, I'll suggest that to London,' Pannell said.

'Do you have any preference for a venue?,' Gorman followed up.

Pannell said: 'It should be somewhere that has good security and is in an accessible location.

Gorman said: 'In that case could I propose Glasgow? It has plenty of conference venues. It would get our respective organizations noticed beyond Scotland's capital and Vanguard is not without its supporters over in the West.'

'I'll come back to you on that if I may,' Pannell replied. 'But let one thing be clear,' he went on. Britain's government is currently in Vanguard's hands and I am answerable to it in the role I have chosen. I'm not a member of Vanguard and never attempted to join in case you are wondering. I've undertaken this role out of a sense of public duty.'

'Thank you for the clarification. It's something I'll remember in future. It means the speakers will be introduced as private citizens not as representatives of particular organizations.'

'I'm glad you'll consider Glasgow,' Gorman went on. 'If it is acceptable, then I'd recommend the City Halls in the up-market Merchant City quarter. It's a manageable size and its location means that it can be protected.'

Pannell asked his assistant to write down these details. He then asked Gorman about speakers. By now the Irishman already knew who would be the speakers for the BIC but protocol did not require the names to be disclosed this far in advance.

'We are working on this and their names will be disclosed one week from now,' Gorman replied.

'Alright, that brings us to the date,' Pannell said.

'What about Tuesday 24 October, exactly two weeks from now,' Gorman replied?

'And finally,' Pannell said 'who will chair it'?

Some thought had been given to the matter and Gorman proposed that both sides nominate one chair each who would divide up the two hours between them.

'If that is acceptable,' Gorman said, 'I would propose Archie Busby who is a veteran sports commentator and writer. He is in his seventies but he is well respected and enjoys robust health.'

'In that case, I would propose Felix Arbuthnot,' Pannell said. He is from a Scottish literary family and has made a name for himself in London and Edinburgh. His writing shows why the patience of so many young people, frozen out of the professional middle-classes, snapped in the last few years.'

Gorman said: 'Well at least we have agreed on who will be chairing the event. Other practical steps are on the table and it would be good to reach a swift decision on them.

The meeting then broke up and the visitors left. Climbing up to Queensferry Road in order to return to the city centre, Rory asked Arthur if it was true that speakers had still to be identified for the BIC team.

'It's not strictly true,' he was told. 'But its better if we keep one name concealed for as long as possible. I doubt if everyone in Vanguard would be happy with our choice and I don't wish to provide a pretext that will cause them to pull out.'

Rory gave Arthur a sideways look but beyond that he wouldn't be drawn.

Accompanying Professor Hale in the debate would be Brian Crawford. He had agreed to take part. It would be a minor coup for the BIC since he had made no public declaration about his views since fleeing London almost a year earlier. But when Pannell was informed about the BIC line-up, the second speaker was listed as Sir Maurice Brogan, Britain's most noted musical conductor. He was a firm foe of all political extremism and had rallied plenty of moderate Scots working in the arts against the 2014 breakaway bid. But he was not widely known and his appeal was mainly among the older generation.

Publicity was distributed but then, with six days to go, Gorman sought another meeting with Pannell. He was informed that Brogan had decided to pull out owing to exhaustion, having just returned from a series of concerts at military bases in un-occupied England.

Pannell said: 'I am sorry to hear that. Who will be replacing him'?

'Brian Crawford,' Gorman replied.

'Now you can't be serious,' Pannell exclaimed. 'He is a renegade from Vanguard, a volatile figure with an acid tongue.'

'Well exactly,' Gorman quickly interrupted. 'These traits mean that he is likely to be an effective debater. An effective foil for Professor Hale who is very cerebral but not as good with the cut and thrust. He too is someone who ran out on Vanguard in the sense that he opposed the regime and had to evade arrest by fleeing London last year.'

'Well there's nothing more to be said for now. I'll relay your news to London and we'll see if there's still a show,' Pannell said.

'I think there will be' Gorman said. 'The BIC intend to be in Glasgow on 24 October but naturally we hope the evening will be in the form of a debate and not a meeting where Brian Crawford is the main draw.'

Two days later they met again. The True Britain Hub *would* participate. But it had been decided to stand down their second speaker. Instead of the ex-diplomat Emily Montrose, the Scottish journalist Theodore McCusker would be taking part.

Gorman's reaction was dead-pan. But it was a turn-up for the books. Teddy McCusker, as he was known across journalism, was a man of many faces. He was a Celtic football enthusiast who famously lived it up while constantly preaching equality. He regarded the political right as lower than vermin but even worse in his eyes were left-wing politicians who borrowed from the Conservative playbook.

Long after he had vacated the Premiership, Pannell had been pursued by McCusker in scornful articles where he was roasted for having turned Britain into 'a Babylon of the most profane capitalism.' He had pursued him over Socotra and his invective had pushed many readers of his columns in the Scottish media towards the SNAP. He had played a starring role in the 2014 referendum, excusing the rough stuff that occasionally emanated from the defeated 'Yes' side.

Despite remaining extravagantly Catholic in a left-wing way, he had kept silent about Vanguard's assumption of power. Indeed, his by-line had not been visible in the media for at least a year. The rumour had gone around that he had been recovering from the corrosive effects of liquid lunches and late night carousing by a lengthy stay in an exclusive Austrian health clinic. But now he was back in circulation, ready once more to play the wild card, this time it seemed on the side of Vanguard.

Gorman replied by simply saying: 'It looks as if we are all set to proceed. We are in no position to object to Teddy McCusker. He will be a good match for Brian Crawford, so let's go ahead on that basis.'

Along with Gorman and Ray Lattimore, the two speakers met up on the eve of the debate at Maurice Brogan's home. He lived in a small mansion overlooking Lochwinnoch in Renfrewshire just 45 minutes from the centre of Glasgow. He and his wife Helen invited the four for dinner and offered to put them up for the night which each had accepted.

This was lush dairy farming country with a slow pace of life which Sir Maurice found perfect for unwinding between concert tours. He and Lady Helen reared several head of cattle purely for hobby purposes. They were amiable and expansive hosts who soon put each of their guests at their ease.

Brogan recalled the tussles that he had had with McCusker during the 2014 referendum. He had known him since their days at Glasgow University. He had been President of the Young Communists while McCusker had been a much higher profile head of the Young Socialists. He ran it very much as his personal fiefdom, even at one stage persuading the members to put up a Basque militant, just out of prison for terrorist offences, for the Rectorship of Glasgow University. He lost but fought a rumbustious campaign, his trademark through an eventful media career.

Brogan knew that Brian Crawford was likely to have McCusker's measure. But he pointed out to Edgar Hale that McCusker could be underhand in debate and was capable of melodrama and fake emotional appeals that could knock opponents off balance. His wife, from the medical field, said to Edgar: 'Just be yourself. Stick up for what you, and lots of us, believe in, and you're bound to sail through.'

Diplomatically, nobody thought to bring up Brian Crawford's stint with Vanguard before it acquired absolute power in London. Inevitably, there was laughter as the Brogans and their guests speculated how Pannell and McCusker would get along as they prepared for the debate.

'Tristram has accumulated so many enemies in the media that he is probably only dimly aware that McCusker was one of the most uninhibited, Lattimore observed.

'If he had done some research, he might have been amazed at the sheer vitriol behind some of his attacks,' he went on.

'I am sure,' Brogan said, 'Teddy will shelve his brawling persona for one night and try to make nice with the ex-Prime Minister. I can imagine him saying to Pannell, "You know I denounced you night and day back then but, believe me, you do not have a greater friend in Scotland than me. Together we will trounce those defenders of the moth-eaten, neo-imperialist Britain which both of us have had quite enough of.'

The others laughed as he said: 'Tristram might not be entirely convinced but as Teddy filled his glass and refilled his own, he'd probably conclude: "I've no option now but to rely on this huckster to get me through this."'

Fortified by the hospitality they had enjoyed at the Brogans, the four felt cheerful as they returned to Glasgow the next day. The heavy rain lashing down that night slightly dampened their spirits. But they soon cheered up upon being introduced to Archie Busby in the private room of a smart pub just across from the debating venue. As the schedule was gone over, he appeared laid back but authoritative with a vigour belying his almost eighty years. He made a joke about being kidnapped by Sutton's minions and being hauled off to the Tower of London if it turned out to be total humiliation for the other side.

Just at that point the second debating chair arrived. Felix Arbuthnot was rather less of a people's person. His patrician Scots accent was a contrast to Busby's pungent west of Scotland tones. His tight-fitting denims, white shirt and maroon waistcoat also made a contrast to Busby's well-cut suit. Both chairmen pointed out that tight security arrangements were in place. Both sides had nominated one hundred people each, with the Law Society selecting another one hundred. Each one was subject to a metal detector check and a physical search.

The same thoroughness extended to the media. Film crews from Scandinavia, North America, Spain and Austria occupied the left side of the balcony. Probably never had a debate taking place in Glasgow on a dark rainy night been the focus of such widespread interest.

The notes Ray Lattimore took in preparation for his regular contribution to Free Britain television endeavoured to capture the spirit of the evening:

'A toss of the coin to determine the running order for the evening had been won by the British Information Council. Its two speakers opted to allow their competitors to start. Tristram Pannell was the opening speaker. His name conjured up memories of a more peaceful era when Britain had been "cool" and experimental in a usually non-threatening way. He had been out of the limelight for nearly a decade. He had clearly aged but still looked in good shape for a man of seventy. Only the deep furrows around the mouth and a left eye that kept slightly blinking, perhaps gave a clue to the amount of pressure he had been under recently. As the crisis escalated he had been spotted in the Middle East and in Washington but it was unclear whether he was visiting in a private capacity or as an emissary of the Vanguard regime.

'But tonight he was speaking as head of the True Britain Hub in Edinburgh. It has taken over an imposing 18th century building in one of the city's most prestigious spots. Many predict it will soon be Vanguard's unofficial mission in Scotland. If Pannell is placed in charge, his social gifts will undoubtedly be useful as Vanguard redoubles its drive to get Gavin Ogilvy's government to dance to its tune.

'Tonight, instead of a careful minuet, Pannell provided a vigorous fandango. He didn't use the phrase "I'm a fairly transparent guy you know" for which he was once derided. But this is the image he tried to convey in his twenty minute speech. He said that he had learned the folly of war through his own terrible miscalculation in Socotra nearly twenty years earlier. Regime change was alluring but it was difficult to pull off. This was a lesson that he had absorbed and it was one which those seemingly bent on driving Vanguard from power needed to heed before it was too late. They might feel they had right on their side but self-righteousness was rarely a sensible spur to action.

'Yes Vanguard had made mistakes, he declared. There had been too much zealotry. Inter-generational conflict may have been allowed to go much further than was proper. He spoke, not as a member of Vanguard but as someone prepared to work alongside it in order to secure peace.

'Much of England could become a wasteland, its cities levelled, if the war entered the deadly phase that the BIC appeared to advocate. Nothing would be solved. New people might eventually take over. But what would there be left for them to inherit?

'As for Scotland, it was unlikely to escape from any inferno which erupted in the rest of Britain. How could it be expected to absorb millions of refugees? How could it avoid proxy wars erupting on its own territory? Its leaders might hope to sit out the conflict as Portugal and Sweden had done in World War II but its fate was more likely to be akin to that of Lebanon or Cambodia which both became spectacular victims of conflicts on their doorsteps.

'Now was the time for cool heads and statesmanship. If Britain was to recover and become an island of peace and stability once more, war must cease.

'This was the kernel of Pannell's address. He was fluent, spoke largely without notes and he seemed to revive some of the magic of his earlier years. His speech produced cheers and sustained applause from his own supporters as well as respectful clapping from the neutral part of the audience.

'He was followed by Professor Edgar Hale of the BIC. He pointed out to the audience that he had never been involved in politics: "I am a medical doctor. In 2005 I abandoned a lifelong habit of voting for the Progressives because of Mr Pannell's ill-conceived intervention in Socotra. Tonight he has regretted this policy. I suspect that he may, in time, have even bigger regrets about his call for an oppressive regime, occupying large swathes of our country, to be allowed to stay in charge."

'"This is not any old dictatorship liked that of the Greek Colonels in the 1970s or the Turkish generals of the 1980s. It is one pursuing an inhuman campaign against the elderly of staggering dimensions. Already, the confiscation of property and the removal of human rights easily dwarfs what occurred in South Africa during the first phase of apartheid. Clive Sutton's regime shows no sign of wishing to modify its policies. Those advocating a minimalist opposition say that time will smooth out its rough edges. This was the clarion call of the establishment folk from law, academia and big business who jumped on the Vanguard bandwagon. Those who tried to jump off and were captured by Vanguard have suffered cruel fates."

'"Mr Pannell is not one of them. He has nothing to say about the fact that many who supported his government now languish in prison. But at least in one thing he is right. Dislodging the regime will undoubtedly result in major loss of life and perhaps even terrible destruction. But cities can be rebuilt, a new generation, freed from tyranny, can start over. It happened in Japan in 1945 and, of course, in Western

Europe at the same time. But leaving a regime with Clive Sutton's agenda of inter-generational warfare in place is disastrous for the whole island. Scotland is likely to find it impossible to stand apart. The poison will contaminate the rest of north-western Europe and perhaps even beyond."

"'Britain will have a second chance if Vanguard departs. But if Vanguard remains, Britain enters a Dark Age, an almost unprecedented fall from civilized standards into an abyss of horror and cruelty. These are words that I don't normally use. But what has happened to a large part of the elderly population of Britain in just one year must speak for itself."

"'Britain is at a crossroads and, if it continues to go down the Vanguard path, its fate will be sealed."

'There were some boos and more applause as Hale sat down. Ten minutes were set aside for questions. When someone asked Pannell why he, as a 70-year-old, was able to travel freely, while millions from the same generation faced penury and detention, Felix Arbuthnot quickly ruled it out of order. He reminded the audience they had been informed at the start that no question about the current personal circumstances of the debaters would be permitted - a condition which had been inserted by Pannell (though that went unmentioned).

'Hale was asked whether Scotland should take in all, or some of the quarter-of-a-million refugees now languishing in tents in exposed parts of northern England. He made it clear that he was reluctant to make overt recommendations in sensitive policy areas. But it was natural for there to be concern about the fate of these people and he thought the issue was unlikely to go away especially if it turned out to be a harsh winter.'

During the interval Rory Savidge mentioned that he wasn't surprised when some folk booed Edgar Hale. In some nationalist quarters, there was still a great deal of resentment towards elderly folk because they had played a decisive role in foiling a breakaway bid by their massive turnout for the Union in the referendum. So his plea to remember the plight of the elderly was unlikely to be appreciated.

'With Archie Busby in the chair ,' Lattimore's text continued, 'the atmosphere briefly relaxed when he introduced the next speakers and paused at the name of Theodore McCusker saying: "We don't see each other much these days so I hope Teddy will do the appropriate thing when I remind him that he owes me £150 from several years back."

'Many speakers would have been wrong-footed by such a dig but McCusker was unfazed. He was patronising or amusing depending on your perspective.

"'My friend Tristram" he said "is proving himself to be the statesman that most of us knew he was deep down. Ten years ago in this city there was relentless criticism of his record. But that was then. Tonight he showed that he has learnt from Socotra. He is now back among us in Scotland on a vital and principled mission – to persuade us to act wisely towards England as we embark on what I hope is permanent statehood."

"'All nations have their fraught times. England is experiencing its own delayed menopause, if I can put it slightly indelicately." (There were titters but also cries of "Shame" and "You're a disgrace" from a few in the audience).

"'Our great and often generous neighbour is searching for a new equilibrium. It is finally discarding the flummery and empty trappings which I have long railed against as a progressive journalist. Sometimes violence is unavoidable in these situations. But let us not forget that some of the most progressive societies have emerged out of revolutionary upheavals. I refer not so much to Russia as to France, Mexico and of course the United States."

"'I hesitate to compare the remarkable Clive Sutton with George Washington. Clive is more athletic but perhaps they are both somewhat challenged in the humour stakes. Their revolutions were written off. Washington the revolutionary and his successors had a lot to live down. They strove to build a stable and evolutionary order despite terrible mistreatment of the North American Indians and of course the blight of slavery. Few revolutionary causes are clean and virtuous. But that doesn't give us the excuse to pontificate about their faults and misdemeanours from the heights of moral virtue. Like the esteemed Tristram Pannell, I wish the elderly question had been handled with less furious impatience. But what has been done has been done. I am sure that lessons have been learned and that the elderly will have less cause to complain in the future. I compare them with our unemployed a century ago in the 1920s. Their situation looked hopeless but eventually, in 1945, Tristram's party came to office and their lot quickly improved."

"'I think we should give the Vanguard government a chance to show if it is capable of having its own 1945 moment. We should not try to abort the process of change occurring in England with an invasion. This is likely only to lead to a terrible bloodbath."

"'We have no interest in seizing control of Leeds or Manchester. It would be unmitigated folly to take part in any ill-conceived move to try and change the London government by force. If Scotland drops its non-belligerent status and goes on a war footing, then I will put aside my pen and enter politics to try and stop this madness.'"

'"Let me tell you firmly that the sane and prudent course is to keep well out of it. If this means not taking in another refugee, then so be it. Scotland has been engaged in an overdue process of national awakening these past years and the arrival of up to one million refugees will cause dangerous disruption as well as being a major drain on our resources."

'Cries of "hypocrite" and "to think you are *Irish*' came from some in the audience."

'He went on: "You gung-ho Unionists out there can call me anything you like. Britain had an obligation to assist those Irish fleeing the famine of the 1840s especially given the way that their land had been ravaged by British colonialists. But we Scots don't owe a debt of any kind to England or the English. Of course I am sorry for the misfortune of those driven from their homes and I will contribute to any relief effort meant to ease their plight this winter. But we are too weak to play a decisive role and we will be dragged down if we meddle in the affairs of a foreign country, for this is what England is to many of us – a beloved place but definitely somewhere else."

'At this point Tristram Pannell shifted in his seat and stole an anxious glance at his watch.'

'"The British epoch is over. England is inclining, hesitatingly for now, towards a new dawn. Scotland is finally going its own way and should cultivate its own garden rather than peeing over the fence into another one."

'"You've said enough, just sit down," someone in the audience shouted.

'"Maybe I have" McCusker beamed. "But I got a reaction and put my views across. It's what counts for me and I'd say it all again if given the chance."

'There was dissension in the hall as cries of "Bravo" mingled with "Bampot" and "Idiot."

'But there was soon hush when the last speaker got up.

'Brian Crawford said: "I've been away from Scotland for over five years but I see that Teddy, my old colleague on the *Glasgow Bugle*, is great at winding folk up. But what he said tonight is mostly sophistry. He offers a clever and, at times entertaining, case for shrugging our shoulders and looking the other way as much of England burns. It seems to me that he has never properly gazed at what is happening in England or reflected on its significance for us here in Scotland. He has acquired random impressions of what has occurred in the last year and slotted them into his cynical worldview. Thus, he assumes the assault on tradition and continuity has its benign features. Pomp and privilege have had their day in England – a great advance in his eyes. Clive Sutton is even compared to Attlee and George Washington."

"'To my shame I once served Vanguard and was a worse hireling in the service of a rotten cause than even Teddy is likely to be. I was tempted by the good money I was offered at a time when I was spending it at a ferocious rate due to my addiction to gambling."

'Oohs and ahs came from the audience but Crawford was keen to press on.

"'In my defence, I genuinely thought that Clive Sutton, angry and profane though he often was in my presence, somehow represented progress. He was the new broom whose arrival in Britain was overdue."

"'I believed too much wealth was being hoarded by the elderly and I thought that some redistribution was urgently required. But never in my wildest dreams did I imagine that Sutton would go through with a policy of such savage inter-generational revenge. He was strong and implacable but I assumed that the underlying moderation of England would force him to jettison the most alarming features of his programme once confronted with the realities of power. I've written a book showing how I fed the Sutton myth of 'the Redeemer' and how the scales finally fell from my eyes last autumn when bloody events unfolded on the streets of London and soon, all over England."

"'My parents Hector and Marion are here tonight for the debate. I feel a sense of shame that tens of thousands of ordinary blameless folk like them have had their lives destroyed by what I helped to set in motion. I obtain some partial consolation when I recall that it was really electoral fraud and coercion which enabled Vanguard to obtain power last autumn. I find it unbelievable that Tristram Pannell would serve such a regime in any capacity because he must also know that from day one Vanguard has lacked national legitimacy."

"' I have tried to ease the burden of my guilt by writing a book called *England's Rage: What I saw and did*. Any profits will go to help the over one million homeless produced by the war. The manuscript is now in several secure places on both sides of the Atlantic."

"'Sutton sees Scotland as a subject territory. He was raging when, thanks to royal intervention, it was exempt from the new rule that no party could enter parliament that obtained less than 10 per cent of the UK vote. None of the Scottish parties would have got in if this trick had been allowed. In conversation with Sutton, it is clear that he has nothing but contempt for its main political forces. Gavin Ogilvy and his allies are clearly enemies. The Scottish National Action party is just a tool to be used and then discarded."

"'I'm not sure what kind of political destiny I want for Scotland – full independence or else a renewed and different association of British communities. But I am certain that for as long as Vanguard wields significant power in England, Scotland faces mortal danger. Just three hours drive away, in Manchester and Leeds, great cities where we Scots felt at home, are being pulverised in a terrible conflict."

"'If Vanguard is challenged by the resistance led by British Liberty and bolstered by American help, then for reasons of self-preservation, I think Scotland needs to stand alongside them and play a role in banishing this evil from our midst. Scotland's government showed courage when it agreed to the American request to send troops to save the inhabitants of Wilford and liberate other Cheshire towns being threatened by foreign fighters. American strength then prevented any retaliatory action up here by Vanguard. Our future will be more secure if we join forces with those who stand for a decent democratic future in which Vanguard is banished from our midst. To stand aside increases the very real chance that Sutton and his mad crusade will endure. If that happens, we in Scotland will only know a fleeting peace. The man is a fiend. No amount of special pleading from my debating colleagues opposite can gloss over the terrible things that he has done. I am convinced that evil times will be in store for all of us unless his influence is eradicated. Scotland cannot afford to turn its back on what is happening."

'The room erupted into cheers and boos. Crawford spoke with passionate frankness and few people seem to have been unaffected by his words. After a few minutes, the two chairmen managed to restore order. The audience appeared to have been stunned by what they had just heard and there were no questions. Busby and Arbuthnot then summed up the two positions and a vote was called.'

'It was a very narrow vote in favour of the British Information Council's pro-intervention position, 146 in favour to 143 against with eleven abstentions. The significance of the vote would likely reverberate far beyond this hall in the coming weeks and months,' Lattimore's notes of the evening concluded.

Tristram Pannell hurriedly left. Brian Crawford waved to his parents and they crossed the road to the private room in a swish pub where he had been earlier. As Edgar Hale, Archie and Ray chatted, Brian found himself pinned against a wall by Teddy McCusker. Perhaps stung by his defeat, his veneer of bonhomie had deserted him. He advised Brian to promote his book but not to get embroiled in Scottish politics.

'You were once the communications wizard of the Independence side but if you go over to the Unionists, there will be a lot of people who won't forgive you.

Best if you disappear to the Mediterranean, somewhere far from dog tracks or race courses.'

Brian was too drained to argue back and he knew that if any scene occurred, McCusker would likely twist it to his advantage.

But he had not reckoned with his mother Marion who had overheard the remarks. She jabbed her right forefinger into McCusker's chest and said: 'I heard that. Typical bullying when your fake charm doesn't work. You think you're the King Rat of the Scottish media, trying to frighten Brian off. Let him decide how he should deploy his pen and his voice.'

Her husband then intervened: 'That's enough dear. He's not worth wasting your time on. Just leave us alone now Teddy McCusker if you don't mind. We don't get the chance to see our son very often and this is a night to celebrate.'

McCusker said: 'I'm not going to hang around where I'm not wanted. I can see you're proud of Brian and I can see the parental influence that made him what he is. All I was advising was that he proceeds with care in these fraught times.'

He was gone before a freshly aroused Marion could react. Brian then went to get some drinks for his parents. They were joined by a rather excited Ray Lattimore.

'I've had a tweet from someone well able to measure the pulse in Washington,' he said.

'You've met her before Brian.' Crawford pondered and assumed he meant Lucy McKenna. They had met at the Toucan club in Liverpool when she had been US consul there, brought together by their mutual love of jazz.

He put his phone up to the their eye level. The message read: 'Mr Crawford's speech is all folk here can talk about. It will be screened in the W House later. L.'

Just before 10.30pm Brian hailed a taxi for the three of them to return to Linlithgow. As he bent down to tell the driver the destination, a shot rang out. There was a slight cry followed by a dull thud as a body slumped at his feet.

It was his father Hector. Blood was pouring from his chest. Marion quickly knelt down beside him to see what could be done. There was no sign of life from him and she sobbed as the police sirens started to wail.

Edgar Hale had still been in the vicinity when the shot rang out. Having run over, he knelt down beside Marion and quickly saw that the bullet had pierced her husband's heart.

As he put his arm around her, he said: 'I am so terribly sorry Mrs Crawford but there's little to be done. I can't find any pulse. I think your husband would have died the moment the bullet struck him. It has pierced his heart. It is scant consolation, but I think he suffered very little.'

Brian was in shock. He comforted his distraught mother and they were both taken to a nearby hotel and placed under close protection.

Lattimore remarked to Hale: 'The war has followed us here. The bullet was surely meant for Brian Crawford and had True Vanguard's address on it.'

Chapter 4.

Arise and Follow Clova

It was 8.30am and Torquil Niven knocked the door of the master bedroom. He was bearing a breakfast tray with the morning newspapers perched on top.

'In you come Torq' was the reply.

'You're a lovely man, do you know that?,' Clova Bruce said as an afterthought.

'What are the papers saying about last night?'

'The attempted murder of Brian Crawford and the possible repercussions are practically all they have room for,' he replied.

He then put the tray on top of a bedside table.

Gazing at the stately four poster bed in which two people now lay, he reflected that for him, it had been an anchor of stability in a disruptive life.

He had been cuddled in it by his parents on Saturday mornings when they enjoyed a few extra hours in bed.

It had been in their bedroom for nearly fifty years back in Drumclyde. The Reverend Gilbert Niven had been parish minister there for nearly all that time. It was a town near the mouth of the Clyde which had gone from being a bustling centre of shipbuilding to almost a post-industrial shell. He'd noticed the change as a teenager in the 1970s. People once had been too proud to ask for support. But now many a person knocked on the manse door, knowing both father and mother were kindly folk who would likely slip them a pound or two.

He had been an only child who had soaked up the books in his father's library. His mother Euphemia had high hopes that he might become an academic. His father had even expected that he would follow him into the Kirk ministry but these hopes were shelved when he realised that Torquil was largely indifferent to religion, like not a few sons of Presbyterian ministers it had to be said.

His own passion was for art, one that would never quite leave him as he embarked upon a stormy passage through life. He had drawn murals for the stage set of the annual school play and his talent was recognised by various commissions after he graduated from the Glasgow School of Art. *The Ballad of Scotland* was one that he designed for the Edinburgh headquarters of a major insurance firm. It featured kaleidoscopic scenes from Scottish life down the ages. The luminosity he captured in what should have been a grey overcast landscape, and the sharply etched human images, made a powerful impression. An outcry ensued when the firm went into liquidation after 2000 and there was a threat to demolish the building and turn it into a car park. His mural featured in countless tourist guides and Unesco warned that Edinburgh's status as a 'World Heritage centre' would be threatened if the mural was destroyed.

By then people scratched their heads when trying to recall the virtuoso artist. Booze, and a destructive encounter with heroin that nearly snuffed out his life, made his artistic flowering short-lived. The commissions dried up after a drunken scene at the London exhibition which was supposed to launch him on the world art circuit. A marriage followed to someone who wanted to be the spouse of a career artist not a Good Samaritan towards a gifted bohemian drunk. His ageing parents managed to rescue him from a London doss house and nursed him back to health in the mid-1990s. His output was seen as *national* in character and he got a few more commissions after the SNAP started to wield patronage in Scotland. But the fire had largely gone out of him.

In order not to be a burden on his parents, he headed north to the Moray Firth. He was drawn by the light and the warmth of this corner of Scotland, often sheltered by weather extremes thanks to the mountain barriers to the west. He settled in the historic town of Dornoch. At first he belonged to a New Age commune. But, now in his fifties, he found the gentle chaos too much to handle. He was earning money from tourists who appreciated how he captured the delectable light of the Moray Firth, its coastal features, pastoral landscapes and historic small towns and villages. Dolphins swam in its waters. The Moray Firth was the most northerly place in Europe that they inhabited and Niven's portraits of these intelligent and playful sea mammals interacting with man, were especially popular. Eventually, his income enabled him to buy a cottage on the outskirts of the small town of Nairn.

It was there that he met Clova Bruce. She too was in flight. Starting out in a Renfrewshire secondary school, she found that her spontaneous approach to sex and relationships did not make for a long or fulfilling career as a drama teacher. She was popular and got excellent results but she was too popular with some of the male pupils hardly into their late teens.

There were clandestine flings and, when she was found out, her colleagues initially vouched for her. But she had to resign and quickly get out of town when the parents of a 17-year-old whom she had been seeing, turned up at her door one weekend. To make matters worse, her parents were visiting at the time.

Both of them were mortified. Clova had been the apple of their eye. She had been a life force, bright, bubbly and exuberant and they hoped she would channel her abundant energies into the various careers in communications that were opening up in the new Scotland.

They had named her after a beautiful glen in Angus well favoured by nature. The heather slopes, carpets of wild flowers and varied wildlife had made it a regular place for holidays. The three of them had explored the Grampian mountains that lay to the north, even hiking one summer all the way up to Lochnagar, in the shadow of the Queen's summer residence at Balmoral.

But something broke in the family compact that weekend. Her father managed to pacify the irate parents who were threatening to call in the police even, though, on this occasion, Clova had broken no law. Soon after, her mother fell ill, the victim of a stroke.

Aged 27 Clova headed north. She explored new talents as a vocalist in a band. She promoted a new Caledonian (or 'Cally') rock sound, a mixture of rock and folk. Musically, it was hardly original but she stood out thanks to a provocative stage act. Often dressed in a flimsy tartan dress, she interacted sensuously on stage with the male singers while belting out the numbers. There were a succession of male co-leads, none of whom found it easy to keep up with Clova's hard-driving pace on stage and her erotic demands in the large trailer in which everyone lived.

Now at 30 she kept herself in shape. Tall and big-boned, she held her weight down by vigorous exercising. She had large hazel eyes and her long straight nose was matched by high cheek bones and a shapely mouth with full lips. She carried herself well and had the acting skills needed to put on a rousing act.

The occasional reviewer talked of the 'Scottish Madonna.' Un-kinder local critics wrote her off as the reincarnation of Lulu, a Glaswegian pop idol from the 1960s whose stage act was positively Victorian compared to Clova's. For some, perhaps aware of her sexual appetites and who had been on the receiving end of her occasionally rumbustious persona, she was described as an insatiable Medusa.

Nevertheless she flourished and became a well-known figure on the performing circuit. Scotland was finally shaking off its puritanical skin and quickly fast forwarding to being an uninhibited place. At least this was true of many in the younger generation who were coming of age by 2010.

She won a fresh following in the years after 2012 when nationalism swept through popular culture in Scotland. She was a fixture at political concerts, providing suggestive and passionate warm-ups for the political stars of those days. She was seen as one of the 'creatives' regenerating the cultural spirit of Scotland in the musical field at least.

Like so many others, she suffered 'burn out' when the Scots failed to take the great leap forward in 2014 and vote themselves out of the United Kingdom. At such a low-point she ran into Torquil Niven during an arts festival taking place in Nairn. They found they had a similar approach to life. They enjoyed talking and ruminating and found they could handle each other's limitations. She broke the loneliness that had been steadily creeping up on him and moved into his cottage.

Niven had always seen himself as a Scottish patriot in an understated way and Bruce gave him more of a political focus. With the nationalist cause enjoying un-precedented electoral appeal despite the referendum defeat, they decided it was time to move back to see what Glasgow had to offer both of them.

Torquil took up serious painting again. Clova decided to enter politics. Her first foray didn't get very far. She put herself forward for nomination in the 2016 elections for the Scottish parliament at Holyrood. At the vetting meeting to approve candidates, she was asked about her views on civil disobedience. The party elders did not like her answer. She believed it was a form of political action whose potential had not been properly tapped by SNAP. She failed to be selected.

But perhaps it was the best thing that could have happened to Bruce as she in-creasingly concentrated on bursting into politics. 2016 wasn't a good electoral year for SNAP. 2017 was even worse. It was clear by now that whatever appeal it had for young people was slipping away. Old strongholds, such as the North-East, were growing rebellious. Even Fergus Peacock, once the great white hope for the cause, lost his seat in the regional rout. His successor a hard working but shrill and tactically inept lawyer Janey Snodgrass proved not to be the woman of the hour and her star soon faded.

Bruce bypassed the rudderless SNAP and was one of the 'young Turks' who formed a youth movement called *Claiomh tSolais* meaning Sword of Light. It was by no means a direct imitation of New Vanguard but was designed to ensure the next generation of young people were not lost to the nationalist cause. The leadership was unhappy. There were rumblings about expulsions. But a vacuum had grown up at the top and the radicals were left alone.

Defeated by Gavin Ogilvy in the 2020 election Janey Snodgrass soon departed for a middle management position in the United Nations climate change bureau.

By now Torquil and Clova were living in Uddingston, a middle-class enclave in post-industrial Lanarkshire just east of Glasgow. It was ideal for reaching most parts of Scotland (outside the remotest parts of the Highlands) in a few hours. She was still in the musical business but had put aside her stage role and was now promoting bands and taking a management role in organizing music festivals.

As Torquil put down the breakfast tray his gaze alighted on Davy Trainor or his body from the waist down. He was stretched upside down but his upper half was still under the duvet, only his dark curly hair protruding at the bottom of the bed.

Clova was caressing his bum and occasionally tweeking one of the dark hairs covering it. But Davy was still fast asleep.

Torquil was used to such a scene. He and Clova had never been a love match in the conventional sense. They had made love early in their association but by the time they were married by his father, then in his 87th year, it was clear that what they really were was congenial companions. Both would be granted autonomy in the domestic partnership. But it was an unspoken assumption that it was Clova who would take the most advantage of this liberal compact. When love-making got particularly uninhibited and noisy, Clova knew that Torq occasionally spied on her. But his own sex life was largely over not that it had really amounted to much.

Some of her conquests were downright uninspiring. Too many of the young men she brought through the door were obviously just interested in sex or sometimes in sponging off her for money. She was able to slap down any who got too uppity but on one occasion the police had to be called when a young swain, probably under the influence of drugs, got violent, and went for both of them with a large kitchen knife.

Davy at least had a calming effect. He brought Clova down from the highs she was often on after a concert. He had a sense of humour and good house manners. He also treated Torquil with a degree of respect unlike some of his predecessors who had hardly concealed their verdict that he was just an old fossil and probably a pervert into the bargain.

He could see a little of what attracted Clova to Davy. He was handsome with a fine head covered by a mop of dark curly hair. His attractive features were only marred by a slight scar just below his lower lip. He did not seem the violent type and more likely had been in the wrong place at the wrong time, all too easy in Glasgow if you enjoyed an active social life in city centre clubs and bars.

It was clear from Clova's satisfied air after a session in bed with her young beau that they had a good sex life. He seemed to get as much out of their sexual congress as she did. They had been together for nearly eight months, a record for Clova. Maybe the relationship would acquire permanence and it would be time for Torq to seek pastures new. If that proved the case, so be it. Clova had filled a void in his life but they were both birds of passage.

The house was jointly owned. But if they did split up he would leave behind the ancient four-poster bed. It was only appropriate as it had seen far more action with Clova than probably for all of its other occupants put together.

'You're a real pal Torq,' Clova said.

'I'm glad you didn't stay up. I didn't get in until after 12.

'I was selected for Strathglen Central. But by the time the vote had been taken, the news from Glasgow was starting to reach us.

'The adrenalin was already flowing after an exhausting evening. So Davy suggested we just come straight back to Uddingston. I hope we didn't wake you up but I think we both fell asleep around 2.30am.

'My young buck is still dead to the world' she remarked as she gave the 19-year-old's rear a playful slap. 'So I better concentrate on the papers.'

There was only a brief mention of her nomination to contest the vacancy that had arisen in the Scottish Parliament following to the death of Chris Baxter in the Liverpool air raid some months earlier.

She did not expect to win. Baxter's widow Catriona was standing. She had been active in the constituency and there was bound to be a large sympathy vote given Chris's tragic end while serving on the Council of State of the British Democratic Authority (BDA).

Still, Strathglen was a seat the party had captured when it had reached its high watermark in 2011. She would give it her best shot. She'd certainly reach out to the young folk among whom unemployment was rising due to the war in England. But it was unlikely to be enough, she concluded.

Then her eye fell on a statement from the Prime Minister that his government would not stand idly by if it was found that a neighbouring state was behind the fatal shooting in Glasgow.

This seemed like sabre-rattling and it gave Bruce an idea.

It was 10am by the time she was showered and dressed. BBC Lowland TV's Ed Cargill should be up and about by now too, she reckoned. The BBC name had been retained, showing how little had altered since the independence declaration that summer. But Ed had always been sympathetically inclined towards the nationalist worldview - though it still hadn't stopped Fergus Peacock from blasting the channel for failing to emphasise the Scottish dimension and challenge misplaced Westminster assumptions about how Scotland thought and acted.

She ran into Cargill at various parties where media and cultural folk congregated. He had invited her onto a few discussion programmes about that perennial topic 'whither nationalism' and she had proven lively and combative.

Now she had an idea that might take her by-election campaign places.

'Ed, hello, it's Clova here.'

'Once the fall-out from the City Halls debate and shooting recedes, I wonder if you'd be interested in a story'?

'I must add that its time sensitive and would be starting to go stale by the weekend.'

'Alright shoot,' Cargill said.

'I intend to issue a press statement this afternoon warning that Ogilvy's "can't stand idly by" statement could have dreadful consequences for Scotland.'

'I see, he replied.

'If you held over the statement until tomorrow, then I could give you a slot on Thursday's Good Evening Scotland.'

'That's agreed,' Clova said. 'It could be just what we need to set Strathglen on fire, politically I mean.'

'Yes that would be fantastic for us here in tellyland,' Cargill said. 'Now I'm off to Holyrood to witness Sheriff Ogilvy firing his revolver at you baddies' he laughed.

SNAP spin doctors had tried to keep Bruce off the airwaves. They had a decade's experience of browbeating a media which rarely fought back with much vigour. Cargill had complied. Even in opposition a party like SNAP still had the capacity to be awkward if you defied them when they meant business. But he wondered if this was now a time of reckoning for the party. As he patted his paunch and contemplated an approaching retirement, he thought the time for playing safe was over. Ivor Chisholm, the third SNAP leader in six years no longer seemed to be what the party needed as the country stared into an alarming crisis.

Cargill decided that Bruce must be allowed to say what was on her mind.

What that would be she wrestled with for the rest of the day. She believed Scotland needed to avoid being dragged into the conflagration, given phoney inducements for its land and soldiers to be used, then abandoned and spat out by its cynical Anglo-American allies. She decided the best way to put these sentiments across was through song. With 30 seconds of her interview with Cargill remaining, she suddenly burst into song:

Oh Shield of Scotland

Protect us in this Hour

Make Us Stand Tall

Good Scots One and All

Rally to your Nation's Call

Normally not lost for words, Cargill dried up, at a complete loss to know how to follow the bizarre turn the interview had taken. He knew Bruce was not religious but she had suddenly sounded like the revivalist preachers he used to hear at street corners when growing up in Dundee.

Bruce quickly filled the silence by saying:

'I wrote those few lines in the back of a taxi on the way here. The words just came to me as I pondered the bad place that the government seems intent on taking the people of Scotland to. Someone needs to call a halt before we tip over the precipice and, as a musical Scot, this is how I see it.'

Beyond Sinatra and later Blondie, Cargill wasn't really a musical person. He'd prefer a slap up meal in a Glasgow West End Indian restaurant than camping out to hear Clova Bruce at an open air pop concert. He was relieved when the producer signalled that it was time for the next item.

Bruce halted in the hospitality room for a coffee. She was just getting up to leave when a slightly breathless Cargill rushed up to her:

'Hang on Clova,' he said. 'I thought you should know the phone lines have been jammed with comments about your song. Twitter is also buzzing. The feedback is really positive.

'You took me aback with your rendition. Frankly, it's not at all the done thing on a current affairs programme. But it seems to have struck a chord with a lot of people.'

Her story of how the patriotic ditty had come to her was not strictly correct. She had got around the table with Torq and Davy to thrash something out. In the taxi she had thought of discarding the idea. The chances of it backfiring among the middle-class folk who dominated the programme's listeners, seemed too high. But she had nothing else really compelling to say. So what the hell.

Approaching SNAP's electoral headquarters in Strathglen an hour later, she was surprised to see a throng of people spilling into the road. When Bruce was recognised, there was clapping and cheering. When someone said: 'You spoke for Scotland tonight Clova,' there were many shouts of 'Yes' Yes!.'

She had been struggling to get volunteers to canvass the constituency. But no less than 140 signed up to do electoral work on the spot. Big names that had held aloof and cruelly remarked that they preferred the plangent music of the *Proclaimers* to her tartan glam rock, sent effusive messages.

Anatoly's oldest friends from Scotland, Ronnie and Jean Laidlaw, lived in the semi-rural part of the constituency. As soon as they heard that the Russian was in a relationship with a nurse whom he had met while convalescing in Edinburgh, they insisted both of them come to stay the weekend. He and Moira arrived with only a few days of campaigning left. Ronnie and Jean were as hospitable as ever and, out of Moira's earshot, they remarked that he had found a good woman and that he must do all he could not to lose her.

The US mid-term elections had taken place a few days earlier. The President's party retained its control of Congress (though with slightly fewer seats). It meant that the United States was likely to step up its support for British Liberty and the BDA.

Bruce's campaign slogan 'Butt Out America, Don't Bring Your War Here' was already the talk of the constituency. Jean maintained that she had gone from underdog to favourite as the 16 November polling day approached. In the market town of Strathaven where they had first hosted Anatoly upon his arrival in Scotland in 2020, Catriona was still easily the most popular choice. But most voters were to be found in the town of Strathbride five miles up the road. It had been built in the 1960s to absorb people from a then badly-overcrowded Glasgow. It had never acquired a strong local identity. The failure to attract the level of industry its population warranted gave it a makeshift character. When the rain was heavy its wide boulevards and high-rise buildings suggested an aura of North Korean melancholy, a friend who had been there remarked to Ronnie.

Strathbride had last made headlines due to the persistent vandalism of its train station by local youths. Train staff were now refusing to work there because they didn't feel safe.

Ronnie told his guests that Clova Bruce had pulled off another stunt by turning up at the station a few days earlier around 9pm when it was normally deemed unsafe. She had a sound system with her and proceeded to entertain the idle and dis-contented youth with a selection of her trademark melodies. At first, they heckled her but then they gathered around and soon she was giving them her campaign spin. They laughed and cheered when she said she would make sure that none of them were sent down south to die for Doncaster or Billericay. Sixteen of them signed up on the spot to join the Claiomh tSolais youth movement.

'It looks as if it will be her coronation next Thursday,' Jean sighed. And so it was. She beat Catriona Baxter by nearly 5,000 votes. Colleagues gave her a standing ovation when she turned up at the Holyrood parliament a few days later to take her seat.

A nervous Presiding Officer felt the need to point out that no singing would be tolerated before she gave her maiden speech. Soon she was the toast of the party, invited to speak at meetings all over Scotland.

By December she was its leader. Ivor Chisholm was not overthrown in a putsch. He rapidly concluded that the new times required a different person to be in charge, someone with the flair for publicity that Bruce possessed and the readiness to be the demagogue which he, as a douce Edinburgh architect, could not really find in him.

One week before the SNAP's annual conference, he announced that he was quitting as leader. Nominations were announced for a successor. But only one name was on the ballot paper, Clova Bruce's. She won the support of 98.6 per cent of party members who voted. She and the conference got plenty of media attention even as it seemed Britain might be on the brink of intensified conflict.

The new leader sensed the media would be out in force and she told the organizers to make room for an impromptu event that would be in time for the Sunday lunch time news bulletins. It was a short concert in which she wore a pinstripe skirt with a tartan top in the Bruce tartan. Accompanying her were former male vocalists and instrument players with whom she had stayed friendly after she ceased regularly performing.

Weeks of electioneering had made her voice husky but she still had a powerful upper register which enabled her songs about Scotland's coming new dawn to sweep through the Exhibition Centre in Glasgow.

Some said it reminded them of the heady days of 2014 and 2015. Once more the eyes of the world were starting to be on Scotland and its national movement. Hardened journalists from across the world were glad to turn away from the unrelentingly grim situation in England and unwind by writing about an uninhibited folkloric nationalism. Diplomats and intelligence officials looked for contacts in the SNAP who could keep them informed about the new power balance in the party and just who was this leader, who had risen virtually from nowhere.

They quickly assumed that she might be more than an extrovert songstress who, rumour had it, had an insatiable appetite for men and fairly young ones at that. Before the conference was over she had changed the name of the party. Too many puns had been made about the acronym SNAP particularly after the cause had stalled. By a narrow majority she persuaded the party to ditch it and replace it with Action Scotland. Some party heavyweights had spoken against. But Bruce insisted that the new times needed a fresh brand. A lean fighting machine was called for rather than a party dominated by ageing retainers who all too often leant on the side of caution.

She went further. By a tiny majority, she won the party's approval for the Claiomh tSolais movement to be officially recognised as the youth movement of the AS. Under her predecessor it had narrowly avoided being proscribed. A discreet investigation had shown that there were more than a few firebrands, eccentrics and professional English haters, trying to influence the young membership in different ways.

Bruce had never been particularly hung up about England. Her visits down south had been rare. She had always usually hit it off with folk from the music world from the south who were up in Scotland for work. In fact, she had never had any bruising experiences at the hands of English people, ones that could be turned into grievances. But she was unwilling to restrain colleagues who were far more adept at fanning Anglophobia than they were at running the affairs of Scotland now or planning to turn it into a better place in the future. If negativity was what would revive the potency of the cause, then so be it.

Everyone under the age of 35 would be encouraged to join Claiomh. It would hopefully play a central role in helping Action Scotland to take power in the near future and steer the country away from disaster.

A week after the conference, Anatoly and Moira had been relaxing in the centre of Stockbridge. It was a Sunday mid-morning. They had toured the farmer's market at Raeburn Place, buying cheese, olives and delicious German bread for the light lunch they would shortly eat. Relaxing over a coffee in one of their neighbourhood's many small bistros, they heard in the distance the sounds of flutes and accordions along with the beating of several drums. Parades did not usually come through this sedate middle-class area. As the marchers came into view, their eyes alighted on about thirty boys and girls dressed in blue uniforms with a yellow fringe, each wearing red berets. But the most eye-catching thing was that nearly all of them were carrying dummy rifles that had been hewn out of wood. As they passed along, heading up into the New Town and eventually Princes Street, they swung their imitation weapons around. Some were quite expert being able to project them into the air, and neatly catching them as they dropped. At the front was a gaudily coloured banner which showed a large glistening sword held into the light by a young warrior with a map of Scotland superimposed on the background.

Moira remarked to Anatoly that the uniforms and the acrobatics reminded her of the Protestant-orientated Orange walk which had been a colourful fixture at some summer weekends in the small West Lothian town where she had grown up. After lunch both wandered up to the centre. It was a pleasant stroll as the city was then virtually free of traffic, something nobody could recall for many years. Walking up Dundas Street they started to hear a speaker using a sound system and occasional bursts of applause. The blue-uniformed Claiomh people were also milling about.

On reaching the middle of Princes Street they could see that the space between the west side of the national art gallery and Princes street gardens was full of people, perhaps two or three thousand. There were tourists and curious locals but it was mainly a youthful, uniformed audience. Political speeches were being given by

AS people. Clova Bruce was on the platform, beaming and reaching down to acknowledge the greetings of numerous people. Occasionally, the speeches would be interrupted by patriotic ballads from 'creatives' on the nationalist folk scene.

Suddenly, there was a tap on Anatoly's shoulder. He turned around to see Arthur Gorman. He kissed Moira and then said: 'it looks as if the nationalists are getting their act together once more and using the crisis to try to leapfrog back into power.'

'It makes sense that they will try to stir up the huge anxiety that undoubtedly exists and turn it to their particular advantage. Clova Bruce was speaking just before your arrival. She is a powerful orator. She didn't say anything particularly fresh or memorable. But she held the attention of the crowd. As soon as she finished a lot of the youngsters started to drift away. They seem to be from the housing schemes ringing the city. I was up on the slopes of Arthur's Seat earlier and it was possible to see a groups from Craigmiller marching down Dalkeith Road towards the centre.

'Action Scotland appears to be reaching out and involving these marginalised young folk in a way that SNAP simply couldn't accomplish. It's a sign that things are stirring politically. Gavin Ogilvy may soon find that it is not just the English crisis that has to absorb his attention but unrest in Scotland.

'Bruce strikes me as an impulsive and volatile person but one who is shrewd and in possession of cool nerves. She lacks the parliamentary apprenticeship which normally cools the ardour of young politicians. I suspect she will be ready to ride the wave of discontent in the hope that it will bring her to power. She may even be ready to use street agitation to bring that day closer and I certainly don't like the look of those imitation wooden rifles.

'It was young people induced to march around in Dublin over a hundred years ago in militaristic fashion that morphed into the Easter Rising. I just hope that Jenners department store or the National Gallery here at the foot of the Mound is not one day occupied by Clova's young army engaged on a similar destructive mission.

At this point they were joined by a young Edinburgh journalist whom Arthur had got to know as the head of BIC. After introducing Graham Fleming to Anatoly and Moira, the journalist said: 'Gavin Ogilvy has not wasted any time in reacting to this event. The Scottish government has just issued a brief statement, saying the following: 'While public assemblies are a normal and welcome part of the democratic process in Scotland, there is no room for gatherings of a militaristic nature in which weapons, even imitation ones, are displayed. Only the armed forces and the police can display weapons. The risk of an incident occurring when imitation weapons are on display is unacceptably high. Accordingly, a law will shortly be tabled for debate in parliament banning replica weapons being displayed at public gatherings.'

Well, Anatoly said, it looks as if Ogilvy is ready to defy Bruce if she tries to use extra-parliamentary action to get into power. In my part of the world, democratic politicians learned too late that you must not flinch from taking on demagogues in this way. We'll just have to see how great is the adverse effect of this fresh turbulence on our work with the growing number of displaced.

Chapter 5

Clash of Opposites

Greer McIver sometimes chided the Prime Minister for viewing politics through cowboy metaphors. But over breakfast, he listened as his partner explained that the explosive rise of Clova Bruce had something of the appearance of a new gunslinger rolling into town intent on imposing an arbitrary set of values on the place.

Gavin Ogilvy had just returned from an infrequent jog in Holyrood Park. He would like to have gone out more often to keep his still rangy figure in good shape. But this would have involved the park being closed to traffic and guards posted – far above – on approaches to Arthur's Seat. So he usually exercised inside, in the Holyrood Palace gym and played a few sets of tennis with Greer in the open air court whenever time allowed.

On his jog he mulled over his decision to ban displays of imitation weapons at public events. Was it an over-reaction to a new opposition leader searching for a headline-grabbing stunt?

No it wasn't, he concluded. With fighting continuing in the south of the island and the Americans poised to intervene next spring, the move was a sound one. There was growing tension in the air. Overlooking provocative public marches was likely to encourage even bolder defiance of customary political norms. So the legislation to outlaw paramilitary displays would go ahead.

As expected his colleagues endorsed his initiative when cabinet met at 10am that morning. Away from the cameras, Ogilvy encouraged a certain informality and nearly everyone had kept their sober suits in the wardrobe.

He was wearing stylish denims and a dark green polo shirt. It was the first cabinet meeting since the mid-term US elections which suggested that President Wallace had mainly restored his authority.

Ogilvy had made it clear to Washington that he would offer discreet assistance within strict limits during the forthcoming offensive but Scotland would stick to its policy of non-belligerence.

Both Wallace and British Liberty in Liverpool were satisfied with this stance. It was likely that most of the fighting would be some distance from Scotland. Besides, the Scottish armed forces were being increasingly used to guard against the threat of a home-grown insurgency.

The British-American alliance recognised these constraints and appreciated Ogilvy's goodwill. It hoped that soon he would feel strong enough to receive perhaps as many as one million refugees. With new fighting, it was likely that many more would join them. One of Clive Sutton's tactics was to drive civilians out of populated areas often straight into the direction of fighting. There were still many people trapped in the Pennine corridor which Vanguard controlled and who could be used as human shields to slow up the enemy advance.

It was now a question of Ogilvy being able to persuade a majority of Scots that taking in the refugees was the right thing to do. At cabinet, Ogilvy was relieved to find that the united front on the issue remained intact. It was agreed that an effort should be made to give these unfortunates shelter but not at the price of risking a backlash that could bring to power nationalists under the most radical leader in their history.

Just as the cabinet was about to finish, an official placed a note in front of Ogilvy. It was from Colin Ewart, his political chief of staff and stated that the London government had been in touch. Gavin Ogilvy was being invited to go south for talks in light of what was described as 'intensifying warmongering' by the Americans. Ewart's counterpart, Ben Jarvis wanted to know just how things stood between the two governments.

Ogilvy called everyone back to relay the information. A decision would have to be reached soon so a second cabinet meeting would be scheduled for a few days time.

Ogilvy did not relish confronting Sutton. He knew a confrontation was what it was likely to be. But fifteen years in the film business had brought him into contact with plenty of unbalanced people, from producers to agents and columnists. Some of them he had to take on for the sake of his career and his own self-respect. Obviously Sutton would be making demands and, no doubt, issuing threats. He had already demanded that Vanguard be allowed to open a large diplomatic mission in Scotland. Its purpose would have been to gather intelligence and perhaps establish a fifth column which could be bribed with money and kept in reserve in case a full-blown crisis occurred.

The Scottish Government had issued a firm No to the proposal for such a lavish mission. Tristram Pannell's information hub was the compromise. He concluded that he would see Sutton. But the meeting would not be in his lair, the palace of Hampton Court from where he intimidated so much of England.

Over lunch he relayed his thoughts to Greer. A refusal to see his antagonist would be viewed as the gesture of a weakling and, of course, would be exploited by Vanguard. It had now taken on the services of Jerome Roxburgh. He had carved out a reputation as an online rule-breaker during the last Indy surge. The moody and profane Scot had quit the French Foreign Legion to launch a career as an online hell-raiser. He had a genuine talent for invective and his denunciations of the pro-union side won him a fanatical following. He was now part of the Vanguard propaganda bureau, broadcasting most evenings for thirty minutes. McIver had been disgusted by his cruelty and malice. But Ogilvy was less fastidious he recognised that digital technology had carved out a new space for adventurers like Roxburgh. If he had been on the West Coast of America, he would be on a Hollywood contract, producing horror schlock.

Greer thought Gavin was wise to decline a meeting at Hampton Palace where Sutton's ideologists presented him as the sometimes cruel but ever just sovereign, invoking the memory of King Henry VIII by his deeds. The Prime Minister was asked by his partner did he have any alternative venues in mind.

Ogilvy thought and said: 'What about Bradford'? In his Hollywood days, he had given a talk at the National Museum of Film and Photography which was then located in the city. He could recall a city centre with East German style civic offices and motorways cutting through the centre even though it had the lowest percentage of car ownership in Britain. Beyond were terraced houses now mainly inhabited by South Asian Muslims and their descendants.

'Why on earth there,' he was asked?

'Well it's almost right on the Northern front line. I would not need to travel far into Vanguard territory. And, as far as I know, Sutton would be even more a fish out of water than I would be.'

'How come,' McIver asked?

'The war has been going on for over a year. But in that time, Sutton has not paid a single visit to the northern cities which are under Vanguard's control, Ogilvy replied.

'Deep down, he's an arrogant southern snob. He's ditched his metropolitan pro-gressiveness for a post-modern fascism but much of the country is completely unknown to him and I think he probably finds the English North an alien place.'

'But it would do you no harm,' his partner observed, 'if you were to visit one of the refugee camps on the way back to Scotland. It's the kind of work you've taken pleasure in doing as a UN World Rescue ambassador. You would be empathising with the victims of Sutton's oppression. The world would be given a clear signal that you were not being dragged into Vanguard's orbit.'

'Greer that's fine advice,' his partner said as he punched him playfully on the shoulder.

'Now I need to talk to Dr Martyna Sobieski. She'll be able to give me some broader perspectives on the encounter with Sutton.'

Sobieski was a Polish historian specialising in the struggles between the forces of liberty and tyranny in modern Europe. She had taught Ogilvy one of his history modules when he had done an innovative degree on urban regeneration at one of the better Californian universities. On the eve of the crisis he had managed to persuade her to base herself in Scotland after she had won a two-year research grant to examine the British conflict in a wider European perspective.

They met the next day at Ogilvy's parliamentary office. She was a tall, elegant woman with an open, enquiring face. Her manner matched her appearance. She was unlike the superficial, cautious but usually self-important academics whom Ogilvy had often encountered locally as he tried to devise a brains trust to advise him on policy matters.

'So you are entering the den of the jackal, Sobieski said on hearing his news.

'Of course you don't need me to tell you that Clive Sutton hopes to diminish you as a result of this meeting.

'He is unlikely to harangue you and it would be very unwise of him to fly into a rage. We know he is fully capable of Hitler-style frenzies but mainly towards underlings or opponents whom he has cornered.'

'I've read up about how Hitler screamed at the Austrian and Czech leaders as part of the softening up process before the German Panzers marched in,' Ogilvy said.

'Yes, that's right,' she replied. 'But they were largely friendless and isolated. They were being sabotaged from within and their potential allies, France and Britain were refusing to risk war on their behalf.

'You must see that you are in a much stronger position' she went on. 'America is ready to prevent any Vanguard aggression against Scotland because of its strategic importance. It is Sutton's country which is divided and locked in violent conflict.

'My hunch is that he won't utter overt threats. He may try instead to offer you blandishments. Perhaps he will argue that "There is simply no alternative to Vanguard. The best of the English are now on my side." He might say. "I will survive and ultimately win. You will profit if you do not stand in my way. There will be room for two political systems on the island."

'If, however, you remain wary and non-committal, he may become sarcastic and openly write you off to your face as an "accidental" leader in a weak but strategically-placed country which has no chance if it goes it alone. If his ministers are present, he may turn around to them and say that you lack the stature and credentials to be treated with seriousness, even respect.

'These are the stratagems men in his position have used from Stalin to Saddam Hussein when trying to subvert neighbours. Provided you are clear-headed and steady in your attitude, then I believe you won't really lose by seeing him.

'But be warned. When you go there try to eat and drink as little as possible. Sutton is a Machiavellian person and there are slow-working poisons he would not hesitate to use if he regards you as a foe who needs to be permanently got rid of.'

McIver had already alerted him about exactly this point. The Prime Minister expressed his warm thanks to Sobieski and said he would certainly take all her advice very much to heart.

At the cabinet it was agreed that the meeting should go ahead. There was worry from a few ministers that Ogilvy might be putting himself in harm's way. The ruling Unionists knew that he was virtually irreplaceable and, that if he fell victim to the violence of the times, it would be very hard to prevent the Nationalists engineering a comeback, whether by fair means or foul.

Afterwards, Colin Ewart was instructed to contact London to say that the meeting could go ahead. But the Scottish side insisted on certain conditions.

Ogilvy and his team would travel no further than West Yorkshire.

There would be no prior publicity for the event. Journalists would not be present and only photographs would be taken at the meeting which would not be filmed. A list of attendees would be provided by both sides. The meeting would be a formal one scheduled to last no more than ninety minutes.

A day elapsed before a reply arrived from London. Vanguard agreed to all the terms and it was Bradford that was offered as a venue.

Ogilvy was not surprised by the choice of venue. Long ago the woollen capital of the industrial world, Bradford had fallen on hard times. It was the only northern city still fully in Vanguard's hands. What fighting there had been had left very little damage. After the arrival of the foreign fighters, it had rapidly fallen to Vanguard. Much of the white population had quickly fled but so had many of the Muslims who had comprised around one-third of the population.

What trouble there had been involved turf wars and score-settling between different Muslim factions. It had mostly been some distance from the venue that Vanguard proposed for the meeting.

This was Salt's Mill, located in Saltaire, a suburb in the greater Bradford area. It was situated by the River Aire and the Leeds-Liverpool canal in what had started out as a Victorian model village.

Colin Ewart, a history buff, had laughed when he had discussed the venue with his boss. The large mill had been erected by Sir Titus Salt, the kind of Victorian patriarch despised by Vanguard and its youthful metropolitan following. By the standards of the times, he had treated his workers well. Modelled on a palazzo of the Italian renaissance, the mill had finally closed in the early 1980s only for it to acquire a completely new identity.

Its large textile halls were turned into an art gallery, much of which had been given over to the works of the Bradford-born artist, Sir David Hockney. His works spanned a broad artistic range, from portraiture, still life, landscapes and stage sets.

Ogilvy's memory was jogged. The artist had lived intermittently in California for much of his life and he had encountered him at a few Los Angeles parties. He was an affable Yorkshireman who wore his distinction lightly. For a brief moment Ogilvy wondered what had become of the collection at Saltaire.

The meeting was scheduled for Tuesday 14 December and was due to start at 10.30am.

Ogilvy decided to take only a small team with him. Besides his chief of staff, there was a stenographer and just one member of his cabinet, the justice secretary Kate McGoldrick. The four of them spent the preceding night in the spa town of Harrogate. So far it had avoided serious damage and hence was crammed with refugees. The commuter town of Otley, a few miles to the south, was not so lucky. Along with wealthy Ilkley nearby, it had taken a battering as the front line had oscillated back and forth.

It was at Otley that the Scottish party left British Liberty territory. Due to light traffic, they were able to reach Saltaire just after 10 am. Outside Salt's Mill, there were groups of stern looking young men clad in green Vanguard uniforms. Being early Ogilvy enquired if it was possible to view any of the Hockney collection. But he was told by a Vanguard functionary that the gallery had been stripped of all paintings and their whereabouts were now unknown.

A few minutes later the same functionary came back to say that it was time for the meeting to begin. The four proceeded up a narrow set of stairs to one of the, by now, empty galleries. As they entered Sutton was visible, standing at a table at the other end of the long room, flanked by officials.

Ogilvy was required to walk about one hundred yards to this point where a number of empty chairs lay. As he did so, the cavernous hall suddenly filled with music.

Ogilvy instantly recognised it was Elmer Bernstein's score from the 1966 film, 'The Magnificent Seven.'

He could see there was a taut smile on Sutton's face as he drew closer. His host reached out his hand and said 'Pleased to meet you. Since you have declined our offer of lunch, I thought that playing the famous sound track from *The Magnificent Seven* was the least we should do to show our hospitality.'

'I suspect Mr Ogilvy,' he went on, 'you will be remembered for your contribution to the genre of the Hollywood Western long after Yul Brynner and Steve McQueen have been forgotten.'

Ogilvy smiled wryly. The implicit message behind this stunt seemed to be that he was just a cowboy when it came right down to it, in other words Scotland's accidental Prime Minister.

He returned Sutton's smile and said it was an apt gesture: 'seven intrepid heroes tried to save a Mexican village from marauders, almost a parable for our own times.'

Sutton's smile receded and he bid Ogilvy to be seated. Despite many verbal hesitations, Sutton strove to put across his position clearly.

Vanguard was digging in. Any British-American assault would be fiercely resisted. It would be inadvisable for the Scottish unionists to intervene on behalf of British Liberty. Their current position was one of non-belligerence. It would be better if it became one of strict neutrality and complete non-intervention.

Ogilvy, for his part, said there were no plans to alter Scotland's non-belligerent status. However, as Prime Minister, he could not be unaffected by what had been happening across much of England for over a year.

Before Sutton could have any chance to respond, he went on to ask:

'What about the Scots-born people living in Vanguard-controlled parts of England, many of whom are elderly? What is their situation?'

As nervous ministers looked on, Sutton showed signs of exasperation: 'Just try to be reasonable,' he said. 'Wars should not be expected to distinguish between Scots and non-Scots and spare the former.' He looked to his entourage who grinned, some shaking their heads vigorously in agreement.

Ogilvy then asked about the several hundred London-based Scots who had been detained in the various mass round-ups that had occurred. He asked Sutton outright whether it would be possible to obtain access to them in order to assess their condition.

Sutton quickly responded that this was absolutely out of the question. They had been taken into custody because they posed a very real threat to the security of the state.

'You mean musicians, journalists, surgeons, retired diplomats and clergy. Surely you are joking Mr Sutton'?

'I don't joke about anything, especially not this,' his voice growing harsher and louder. 'These people reject the legitimacy of our cause, oppose our ideology. They are a challenge to order. It is folly for them to be allowed to walk the streets when there are enemies seeking to undo everything we strive to achieve.'

Ogilvy remained calm, surprised at how defensive and quick to anger Sutton had become. He could close down this conversation which clearly was striking a raw nerve. But, he thought, there's no point in retreating into generalities. Perhaps it is worth seeing what happens next if I goad him a bit more.

He then said: 'surely the Scots whom you have detained, along with all the others, are far less of a threat to your rule than I happen to be and yet you have invited me to meet and talk with you, even playing the type of music which you thought might put me at my ease.'

'The venue, the music, were my sister's idea,' then he stopped, and glaring at Ogilvy, he said: 'The purpose of our meeting was to advise you not to meddle during the decisive period that now stretches ahead. If you dare, then you badly over-estimate your strength. Let me tell you now – very plainly – that our reach is a very long one.'

By now, Sutton was drumming the table with his fingers. But Ogilvy tried to remain composed as he said:

'I don't need to be reminded of that. There was an assassination attempt last spring as I was going to the Scottish Parliament. I think it is unlikely that the Martians were responsible for it.

'And,' he went on, 'just a few weeks ago, there was the attempt on the life of Brian Crawford in which his father was shot and killed instead. As far as I can judge, only Vanguard had an interest in removing somebody who helped you rise to power but now sees things very differently.'

'Stop, stop,' Sutton screamed. 'You've gone on quite enough. If you don't heed my reasonable warning, then you will have to endure the consequences.'

Then his chief ideologue Brough Mason nervously handed a note to Sutton. He looked at it and quickly exclaimed:

'And as for refugees, just be very careful. Don't think of taking any more in, especially when the fighting starts up again. Do that and Vanguard will view it as a hostile act. Better for your sake that you interpret Scottish neutrality very strictly. Otherwise, as I say, you will live to regret it.'

Noticing Sutton's bulging eyeballs, flushed face and tightly clenched fists, Ogilvy thought: Oh hell, this guy is getting really close to the edge.

Nevertheless, he felt this was not a time for holding back: 'If Scotland has the means to help people who are the innocent victims of war, we won't look away. To leave people to be exposed to the elements, people who are our kith-and-kin, would be indefensible. Probably there are a good few Scots among the refugees. But that doesn't really matter. Any government that believes itself to be civilized, would think just as mine does.'

Instead of replying, Sutton started to shout: 'How dare you come here and behave like some arrogant punk from a movie studio. Nobody has talked to me like this for a long time. Just get out of here you...you...Scottish pervert. Or else I will not be responsible for my actions.'

Suddenly Phillipa Sutton appeared from behind a screen which presumably had carried one of Hockney's murals. She rushed over to her brother stroked his chin, whispered into his ear and seemed to have some success in calming him down. The ministers sitting on the platform looked distinctly uncomfortable, fidgeting, staring blankly into space, obviously hoping that this bizarre encounter would quickly end and they could head back south.

As Ogilvy and his colleagues gathered up their papers, Phillipa Sutton left her brother and quickly crossed over to them.

'Just leave here this instant,' she said. 'You have no right to provoke my brother like that. He has got huge responsibilities and cannot be doing with such pressure. It would have gone so much better if you had allowed him to say his piece and not been so disputatious.'

Hearing angry shouts coming from Sutton's direction, she said: 'For God's sake you had better depart. Now! Just don't hang around.'

By now an angry Sutton was being escorted away by several aides. Further shouts and cries could be heard as the Scots hurriedly left.

'I'm sorry, Ogilvy said to the others. 'I just couldn't put up with Sutton's smugness and his threats. I hope I haven't put your lives at risk. Let's just follow his sister's advice and now get the hell out of here.'

They walked briskly to their car but just before they climbed inside, Ogilvy told the others to stand back. He took out a small mirror from his jacket pocket and made a quick but thorough check just to make sure it had not been booby-trapped. Anything was possible after the most powerful man in England had seemingly had a nervous breakdown in front of them.

When nothing was found, they sped off. They did one hundred miles an hour up an A658 nearly devoid of traffic. They needed to pull in at the Otley checkpoint. To their relief they were waved on and were in Harrogate 45 minutes after leaving Salt's Mill.

Ogilvy again apologised as they stretched their legs by going for a walk on the Stray, the large open air green space which was still one of Harrogate's best features.

'Apologies are not necessary,' Colin Ewart replied. 'It just confirms what a megalomaniac we are dealing with. Twenty minutes in Sutton's presence leaves me in no doubt that he is seriously unbalanced. That might not have come over if the conversation had remained at the level of generalities and oblique messages and threats.'

'The abnormal is now the normal,' Ogilvy said. 'No regime, however radical would have permitted Sutton to stay in charge during the last century. But now thanks to the meltdown in cultural rules and habits, outlandish behaviour at the top is the norm. And it looks as if his sister is able to keep his rages in check. Perhaps she even wields rather more power behind the scenes than we've hitherto thought.'

Then Ogilvy said: 'What should we do now'?

'My suggestion,' Ewart said, 'is that we do nothing, refrain from issuing any statement, and wait and see how Vanguard reacts if at all.'

'I guess there will be some kind of reaction,' Ogilvy said. 'Meanwhile, let's have lunch. We have to be at Catterick two hours from now to visit the refugees there.'

Ogilvy's tour of the camp, his encounters with displaced people of different ages and the staff looking after them, convinced him that his defiant stand had been correct. There was just no reasoning with Sutton. Unless his apparent alacrity to see people suffer in large numbers was checked, soon millions risked enduring a similar fate to the people he mixed with at Catterick.

Boarding the helicopter at Catterick for the flight back to Edinburgh, Ogilvy was pensive. Conversing with the others would have been arduous due to the noise of the engine. It was convenient in a way. His meeting in Bradford had given him an opportunity to to see an uninhibited ruler in action. He saw that he was almost certainly deranged in conventional medical terms. But such terms counted for less and less. The huge cultural shift in British society had enabled a misfit like Sutton to assert his own dark and vengeful personality over a fractured political world. The values enshrined in the Ten Commandments and much humanistic writing, had been drained in a swamp of relativism. Too many young minds had been turned by agitators enthroned right across the British university world. Universities had abandoned their role as places where difficult or opposing issues could be explored in an atmosphere of tolerance. Instead, well-placed academics in the absurdly named liberal arts and social sciences had fostered and imposed grievance and propaganda rather than preparing independent minds through educating and conferring knowledge

The views held by at least half the population were driven out, dismissed as oppressive and reactionary. Too many of the staff had surrendered to the fanatical pressures. Several of them had flanked Sutton at Salt's Mill, cynical careerists or else minor versions of the fanatical leader.

As the helicopter hovered high across the Firth of Forth, with the lights of Fife on one side and the twinkling panorama of the Edinburgh shoreline on the other, he resolved on what he would do. Landing at government buildings in Leith, he took Ewart aside and said: 'We must talk.'

He told his chief of staff that he had made several decisions. Security would have to be considerably tightened up at places likely to be the targets of sabotage or terrorism. Individuals whom Vanguard might be ready to strike out at must be given the offer of protection. He suspected that Sutton, stung by how the meeting had gone, would try to take retaliatory action. He had not seen him at his best. He had been bad-tempered and erratic – that stunt of playing *The Magnificent Seven* sound track as he entered the meeting hall, was the action of an angry and probably demented man-child.

He asked Ewart to notify the government members of a special cabinet meeting the next day. Only one issue would be on the agenda – whether or not to hold a referendum, in the very near future, on the question of giving temporary refuge to the million or more victims of his rule who were camped out in the open in the North of England.

At cabinet, Ogilvy told his colleagues that he thought the thorny issue could not be postponed for much longer. He had not gone back on his determination to keep Scotland out of a fresh bout of intense fighting. But he felt it was reasonable for a neighbour to offer a refuge to victims of the conflict. Indeed, it was probably important that they be removed from their present location. It was quite possible that Sutton would use people still trapped in the cities under his control as human shields to slow the British-American push. Standing aside and allowing him to fight a campaign deliberately aimed at sacrificing large numbers of civilians, was callous. It would be a blight on the story of Scotland's early years as an independent state, if that indeed was to be its destiny.

No colleagues frontally opposed Ogilvy's proposal. But there were questions. He was asked if Sutton would view this as a provocation. His response was that the existence of Scotland as a free entity outside his control was already a provocation. Hostility from Vanguard was likely whatever the Unionists did or didn't do.

Another colleague asked whether a referendum on such a sensitive issue was perhaps just the opportunity Clova Bruce needed to establish herself as a leader-in-waiting. Ogilvy agreed this was a risk. But opposing his plan was likely to place Action Scotland in a bad light among people whose goodwill it needed to obtain. It had long prided itself on wanting to accept economic migrants and even asylum seekers from all parts of the world. Now here was the prospect of large numbers of people turning up whom it would be easy to assimilate. Why. Because these English folk (with Welsh and exiled Scots thrown in) had until a short time ago belonged to the same state. They had shared resources with their northern neighbours, worked alongside them, inter-married, and joined together in acts of solidarity in other perilous times. To suddenly wish to exclude these people from Scotland, when probably many had little desire to stay permanently, would seem small-minded not to say chauvinist.

Bruce would have to work out her stance towards Vanguard before she got anywhere near power. So far, she had talked in platitudes. She had deplored the continuing violence as if it was being carried out by extra-terrestrials. She had been largely silent about the vicious state campaign being carried out against millions of elderly people. She had even talked about the need for sporting and cultural ties to be re-established across the conflict-ridden island.

There were certainly risks in staging a referendum. The crisis was affecting people's living standards and the government was running short of money. But he was convinced that a majority of Scots had not been coarsened by the recent upheavals. They were prepared to give a helping hand to fellow islanders in distress. Providing an effective case for admitting refugees was made, it was Bruce and her colleagues who would look mean and shabby.

Ogilvy had no difficulty in winning the case for a referendum. But there was hesitation among a lot of his colleagues and he knew it.

He instructed his colleagues to work closely with the British Elderly Assistance Survival Trust. BEAST had been coordinating relief since the very first refugees had arrived in Scotland. Anatoly Yashin and his team mentioned to Ogilvy's people that they had identified a range of vacant or low occupancy buildings in Edinburgh in which up to 50,000 refugees could be placed. The drop in hotel usage and the collapse in the number of students coming to Scotland actually meant that there was a huge stock of vacant accommodation. It was in generally good condition as much of it had only been recently constructed in the expectation that Edinburgh would become one of the top West European destinations for tourists and students.

The war had shattered that dream at least for now.

One week after his encounter with Sutton, Gavin Ogilvy met Anatoly Yashin. They went on a tour of inspection of places that could potentially house refugees. It was a bright, cold morning, plenty of leaves underfoot, windless thankfully. They visited empty, only recently-built halls of residence in the Old Town on Holyrood Road and in the Cowgate . They discussed BEAST acquiring the lease of vacant hotels for a twelve-month period. After one last visit to a hotel on Waterloo Place, Ogilvy decided to take some exercise. He asked Anatoly if he was willing to accompany him on the short but steep climb up to Calton Hill. They circled the tower, built in the form of an upturned telescope, in honour of Admiral Nelson. Their gaze alighted on 'Scotland's Disgrace,' the national monument meant to commemorate the Scots soldiers killed in the Napoleonic Wars. It was to be an Edinburgh version of the Parthenon. It acquired its reproachful name because it was left half completed due to funds running out.

Ogilvy said to Anatoly that he hoped at least some of his plans for the reconstruction of Scotland after 'the lost years' of SNAP rule would enable some of his own projects to be completed. He looked westwards, the elevation affording a view of Princes Street with lofty spires exposing the numerous churches of the city.

Turning to the Russian he said: 'There are other British cities with imposing views but few as majestic as this one. Already, in the space of just a year, many of them have become broken shells. Probably my main task is to prevent what lies at the foot of Edinburgh Castle being reduced to ruin and rubble.

'It could so easily happen and it is providential that, so far, our capital has got off lightly. But if foreign fighters had been able to land at Turnhouse airport during the July crisis, it could well have been a different story.

'Vanguard and Sutton,' he concluded with a sigh, 'are only the most irrational recent examples of attempts to use the latest technology and forms of social control to try and destroy the cultural legacy of the West. In architectural terms notable examples from the 18th century are laid out in front of us. But look to one side and you see a hideous shopping centre, demolished already, only for a new one just as ugly to be put up in its place. Perhaps defeating Vanguard militarily will be the easier part and the real struggle will involve trying to prevent new destructive bids by humans to wrest society completely away from the natural order of things.'

Anatoly was struck by how Ogilvy's thoughtfulness – his philosophical cast of mind – was so much at variance with his public image, especially in America. On returning to his office, he turned on the news to learn that the referendum bill had been tabled and it was to be debated at Holyrood over the next twelve daily sessions. A special sitting of parliament would be needed in late December and then debate would continue after the long holiday at the start of the New Year. These celebrations were much more subdued than they had been in times past.

Ogilvy said to Anatoly that he expected a reaction from Vanguard upon hearing the news. That evening on BBC London, there was an interview with Jerome ˙ Roxburgh, the ex-Foreign legionary who was making regular incendiary broadcasts about the Ogilvy junta (as he called it) from High Wycombe. In the weeks since the collision between Sutton and Ogilvy his tone had grown more envenomed.

He made allusions to the Prime Minister and his partner, saying that not since Mary Queen of Scots and her favourite David Rizzio, had Scotland been scandalised by such a flagrant *menage* at the top of the state.

He also directed his venom at BEAST and the British Information Council. Roxburgh described them as 'enemy outposts' in Scotland spreading poison and rancour. He gave out their addresses and hours of opening. By that time guards on 24 hour duty had been posted outside both buildings.

The purpose of the interview was to announce that Vanguard had appointed Roxburgh Secretary of State for Scotland. It was a gesture of provocation meant to show, as Roxburgh put it, that the declaration of independence had been illegitimate: Scotland in major aspects of its governance was still controlled by London.

Of course, Vanguard lacked the means to enforce any kind of writ over Scotland. It was ironic that a fanatical advocate of independence in 2014 was now endorsing London control of Scotland's foreign and defence policy. But much of the impetus behind the separatist upsurge had been based on negation, hostility to Britain and what it stood for from people who couldn't – or didn't - want to fit in. Now a terrifying new Britain that wanted to replace liberalism with savage persecution was ascendant. Roxburgh could tolerate Sutton's version of English power. He was now busy trying to build up what he proudly called a Fifth Column within Scotland itself.

Chapter 6

When the Music Suddenly Died.

For Glasgow it was a mild February evening with the temperature hovering around 8 degrees centigrade. Gordon Hoy was standing behind a tree on the other side of which was a gorge under which the White Cart river swiftly flowed.

He was spending this Friday evening in Linn Park, comprising 52 hectares in the southern outskirts of the city. It was more like a hilly and muddy country park than a well-tended city park of which Glasgow had quite a number. Linn Park attracted people who were keen to escape the bustle or drudgery of city life - from dog walkers to courting couples to youngsters from the nearby Castlemilk housing scheme in search of a few hours of oblivion fortified by bottles of cheap Buckfast wine.

It was a particular couple that Hoy was training his long-range photographic lens on. He only knew the name of one of them, Davy Trainor. Luckily, he was wearing a white-coloured padded jacket. As he made love to his companion, a pretty, dark-haired girl, Hoy snapped away. He was only really interested in Davy. He had entered the public eye in the last few months.

When the young man rested with his back to the tree and his trousers wound around his ankles as his partner bent down to induce a second arousal, Hoy knew that the cold and discomfort were worth it.

In twenty minutes of covert photography he had got what he wanted. He had already tipped off the Irishman Peadar McHale, a stringer in Glasgow for various world newspapers, that he might shortly have some hot photos. He said they were of Clova Bruce's young partner. As she threw herself into the referendum, he was increasingly by her side, especially at public events geared for young voters.

Clova was married to an elderly painter but it was a nominal relationship. A woman almost twice his age being escorted by a dashing guy rising up in the musical business would signify that she was a politician very much in tune with the times.

Owlish and inscrutable behind his thick beard and glasses, McHale had thrown aside his caution and said that indeed he was interested in such a haul.

'Who would take them and what would they be prepared to pay,' Hoy asked?

'There are several publications in the USA's North-East which are regularly taking stories from me and others as Scotland hots up politically again,' McHale replied.

Hoy said he would give the Irishman twenty per cent of whatever profits were made from the transaction but he would want to write the accompanying story. It would be one adopting the line of how the personal so often gets in the way of the political in the story of Scottish Nationalism.

McHale agreed and he was very rapidly able to get back to Hoy to tell him that the glossy weekly *Atlantic Carnival* was ready to offer £150,000 for a five thousand word piece but only if the photos were sufficiently revelatory.

It was not a good idea to check the quality of the photos at the perilous spot where he was located with little between him and the rushing torrent near where he stood. So he gingerly crept away to inspect them in his car. He was relieved to see that there were at least eight good photos showing the different stages of the love-making he had observed. A close-up showing the sated Davy with his back to the oak tree around which he and his girl had cavorted, even revealed the small scar extending from his lower lip.

A provisional contract had been signed with the magazine that laid down he would be paid one-third of the fee upon handing over the photos, another one-third on submission of the text, and the remainder soon after publication. The magazine stipulated that it would own the copyright of the photos as soon as the first part of the fee was paid.

He was heading to his third floor tenement flat in the fashionable Hyndland district in the north-west of the city. He and his wife had bought it together upon teaming up after their respective divorces. Marianna Logan was back to earning an income as a reporter dealing with crime stories on the *Daily Bugle*. It was quite a come-down for someone who had started out in this unglamorous field thirty years earlier and had gone on to do weightier things.

By now she and Gordon were keen to leave Scotland. They were veteran Scottish Nationalists but they had worked out that independence would be no bed of roses for them. Indeed, there were already signs that only grinding austerity offered it any real chance of success. They knew the *Bugle's* staff pension scheme was rickety. £160,000 pounds, on top of savings twice that much, could enable them to buy a condominium in the Florida panhandle. Once they had even higher hopes than this, dreaming of settling down in Fort Lauderdale or even Palm Beach.

That was during the years when they were the power couple of the Scottish media - a mere six years earlier when it looked as if Scotland was poised to emerge from the British shackles and soar heavenwards as a newly independent country.

They had mortgaged their flat and, combined with a large loan from the bank, had launched *Scotland's Own* in 2013. It was a magazine designed for everyone who had some kind of passion for a separate Scotland and, back then, there were many such people. The weekly carried profiles of, and interviews with, personalities from the arts, academia, show business, the media and everyday communities who were committed to 'Indy.' It had witty and provocative columns from Teddy McCusker and others. It kept up with contemporary youth culture but also carried nostalgic pieces designed to retain an older readership.

Within a year, *Scotland's Own* was selling 50,000 copies a week. The loan was paid off, the mortgage redeemed thanks to bumper profits rolling in. Hoy was about to resign from his job as health editor of the *Bugle* and turn his hand to writing a biography of Fergus Peacock, the brash politician who had put the Scottish National Action Party (SNAP) on the map. Peacock agreed to several interviews. But the project never caught fire. Close up, he proved to be a disappointment to Hoy, for long an admirer. He was shallow and increasingly obsessed with his own persona. Hoy concluded that he had got this far thanks to being surrounded by good advisers rather than due to any outstanding personal qualities. Peacock actually lost his seat in 2017 around the time the book was due to appear if he had ever managed to complete it. By now the circulation of *Scotland's Own* had tumbled in line with the decline in fortunes of SNAP. Profits were still being made but they would be toiling in the media world for another ten years before they could walk away and permanently enjoy life in the sun.

Five years later *Scotland's Own* was a monthly selling only 6,000 issues. He had been unable to get his old job back and his name only appeared in the *Bugle* as an occasional outside contributor. His wife agreed with him that the magazine was unlikely to revive even if Scottish separatism took off again. Digital media, dominated by comedians and self-publicists who doubled as performance artists, increasingly absorbed the new wave of nationalists and the pair were simply too old to adapt to the new communications formats.

But, as a concession to modernity, Hoy had begun to discreetly follow Clova Bruce around since her unexpected emergence as head of a party which she quickly renamed Action Scotland. If she consented to give him an interview, he concluded, it was unlikely to be very revelatory. So with small video camera to hand he had hours of tape that could make a video diary if her rise was unstoppable. Besides, he had heard the rumours about her strong erotic drive. While his wife wrote up stories of drug wars, embezzlement and family feuds from the back of the Sheriff's court, he trailed the new separatist star in his Ford Escort.

It was the kind of journalism that he had developed a knack for at an early age. He had tracked runaway Hollywood idols to their Highland boltholes or tracked down Glasgow hoods to their Spanish hide-aways. Hopefully filming in the sub-arctic conditions of Linn Park would be his last such assignment. Once the *Atlantic Carnival* splash appeared, he and Marianna would swiftly disappear. Like most journalists, the last thing they wanted was to ever become the story themselves.

Even before he read Hoy's text, Clayton Pell, the magazine's editor, reckoned he had a major scoop on his hands once he saw the explicit photos of youthful congress occurring in some benighted corner of Scotland. He knew the Scotland Question was coming to the boil as the war drums beat in the rest of the island. Opinion polls showed that in the campaign for the referendum, to decide whether Scotland should take in large numbers of English refugees, the 'No' side had a seven per cent lead. If this persisted, it would be a stinging rebuke to the pro-American Gavin Ogilvy, well known Stateside because of his film career.

Before putting out the magazine, Pell decided to show the material to a contact in the CIA with whom he had a mutually convenient arrangement to pool information on breaking stories. Within thirty minutes, he got a call from the director herself, Verona Phelps. She said the story was exceptionally important. Accordingly, she was asking to be given the final decision on whether to print or not. She said the Agency would provide the money to pay off the Scottish journalist provided it could be allowed to have pre-publication use of the photos.

'Clayton, the situation in Scotland grows more serious by the day and if it goes awry across there, then we can probably wave goodbye to our plans for a spring offensive in southern Britain.

'I wouldn't ask to have prior use of the photos if it wasn't that serious,' she went on. 'The likelihood is that you will probably still be able to run the story but a week or two later than planned.'

'Alright Verona, I hear what you are saying,' Pell replied. 'But if the story gets bigger still, perhaps you could tip off *Atlantic Carnival* about the details. After all, I'm playing ball right now.'

'Clayton,' she said, 'the story may well develop fresh impetus and if it does you are likely to get an even more fascinating piece.'

'Let's hope so Verona. Have a good one' Pell said, ending the conversation.

Three days later a package was delivered to Clova Bruce at her office in the Scottish Parliament. It was marked 'Strictly Private and Confidential.' Her secretary, inherited from her predecessor as party leader and unsure how long she would keep her job, played safe. Instead of opening it, she sent a text message to Bruce mentioning the arrival of a package.

Bruce was indeed planning to appoint a music festival planner as her new secretary and she said she would deal with the package upon her return from Inverness the next morning.

She had a delegation from Norway to meet before heading across to Glasgow for an evening rally. By the time she got to the package, her secretary was on a coffee break. She cut open the top with scissors and allowed the contents to slide on to her desk.

There was no covering note, only 8 A4 sized photos which showed Davy having sex with a pretty brown-skinned girl about his own age.

'Oh the f***ing wee scamp,' she exclaimed. 'There'll be hell to pay for this.'

Knowing her secretary was due back any second, she stuffed the contents into the envelope and shoved them in her computer bag.

The CIA's Scottish desk had decided it would be interesting to offer Bruce an opportunity to see the photos before they were published. 'It might just make waves' the New Age poet and part-time lecturer in literature at Napier University, Carter Bellingham opined. She had a stormy side to her nature and a reputation for being impulsive. 'Let the dice roll and see how they fall,' he recommended to Washington.

It is unlikely that a literary spy like Bellingham could have predicted what would ensue within a matter of hours. Upon her return, Ms Jamieson was informed by her boss that she now needed to be in Glasgow earlier than expected. So the meeting with the Norwegians would need to be drastically scaled back.

She managed to get away after twenty minutes. Even the composed Norwegians were surprised at how subdued the Scottish leader appeared to be, so different from her bubbly and forthright image.

In the car she told her driver to head for the Strathbungo district of Glasgow and then to proceed to the venue for the rally which she would find her own way to later.

It was nearly 6pm and raining. She unfurled her umbrella, pulled up the collar of her coat, and entered another park, Queens park. She wished to collect her thoughts before confronting her lover about his betrayal.

Her behaviour that afternoon suggested that Clova Bruce had not really made the transition from private citizen to elected politician and leader of her party.

All of her thoughts revolved around her partner's deception. She did consider from where the photos had originated. But she failed to ask questions which a seasoned politician, even one with a racy private life, might well have asked.

What does the person who sent them want?

How much is this linked to the referendum?

How much harm can they do to me if they are released to the media?

What is the best way to contain any damage from the photos?

She knew the photos were very recent because she was the one who bought Davy the fur-lined bomber jacket he had been wearing. This was after they had gone on 'a walk-about' in the centre of Dundee several months earlier.

There was a good chance he would be back in his flat since he had been at classes that afternoon up at the Art School where he was doing a part-time degree.

Albert Drive was a wide partly tree-lined street with houses which had once belonged to professional people who had serviced the needs of poorer citizens. It had since gone downhill but it was not as bad as Allison Street which paralleled it to the north. Landlords, some linked to her party, had crammed gypsy families from Slovakia and Romania into once spacious flats which had been endlessly sub-divided. Perhaps six thousand gypsies inhabited an area which had once been a magnet for aspirational Glaswegians.

On Albert Drive, it was still more profitable to rent out tenement flats to nurses or consultants in the nearby hospital or to young accountants starting out in their profession.

As she opened the gate and used the combination code to enter Davy's hallway, she was still rehearsing how she would confront him with his treachery. Pressing the doorbell, she heard footsteps. He was in.

'Oh hello Clova. 'This is a nice surprise' he said as he kissed her.

'I thought you were speaking up at the Coupar Institute a little later. Indeed, I was hoping to get along.'

'Never mind about that' she replied. 'We need to talk because I think you've got some explaining to do.'

'You look out of sorts Clova. Shall I open a bottle of something?'

She said nothing as he took a bottle of 2021 Hawkes Bay Merlot out of the fridge and put two glasses on the table in the kitchen which they had entered.

After sitting down, Clova took out the packet she'd received and flung the photos towards Davy.

'What's your explanation for these' she asked in a querulous voice familiar to Davy whenever she was agitated?

Davy looked at the photos and was amazed to see that it was himself and Gabriella.

'What the hell' was all he could say.

'Never mind "what the hell," what have you got to say for yourself?

'Why are you screwing this trollope? Am I not good enough for you all of a sudden'?

Her eyes starting to redden she went on: 'You used to say that it was the phenomenal sex that we had that was the unbreakable bond between us.

'Who is she? Where did this happen?

'How long has it been going on,' questions which she shouted out?

'Not very long,' Davy replied.

'I ran into Gabriella at Art School where she was an artist's model whom the students drew for their assignments.'

'You mean that you got the hots for her there and then'?

'I suppose I did,' Davy replied, avoiding eye contact. 'She happens to live on Magnolia Street, not far from here. It was last Friday evening that we met up in the park.'

'You mean Queens Park just up from here'?

'No,' he replied. 'Linn Park further out.

'She was terrified about being seen with a *gadjo*, the term gypsies have for us European whites. The *bulibasha*, or chief, of the clan is in the process of making an arranged marriage for her. She's supposed to be a virgin. So we played safe and headed out to Linn Park.'

'So, she laughed scornfully, 'you were afraid of some gypsy minder creeping up on you and beating the shit out of the pair of you, but you couldn't give a flying fuck about what Clova here might think about it.'

'Look Clova,' he said. 'It's been politics, politics, politics for you ever since you became leader three months ago. We're no longer seeing that much of each other. Face the facts, it's true.

'I'm a young guy, I've got a healthy sexual appetite. You know that. It's a large part of what you like in me. Perhaps the only thing.

'We're living in the 21st century for Christ sake, not back in the 1950s.' Suddenly angry, he exclaimed, 'Its strait-laced monogamy then is it? And we're not even married.'

'That's not the point,' she said. 'you might at least have said something, told me it's over rather than me finding out like this.

'I was beginning to have plans for us. There have been some great marriages in our party that have defied the age gap. I even tentatively raised with Torquil the idea of a quick divorce and you and me getting hitched.

'The world knows we are partners. You've been on the platform of some of my keynote events right from the start of the referendum.'

It then dawned on her for the first time that the chances were high that the world would shortly get to know about these photos.

'At least you could have kept your dick out of her hole until the referendum was behind us,' she screamed.

'What an awful mess!'

For the first time she noticed the wine and took a sip. Looking over at an impassive Davy, she flung the rest of the contents in his face. Momentarily stunned, he rolled back on his chair. It fell over and there was a loud thud, then silence.

Clova rose up from her chair and went around the table. "get up you..." she began, but the words dried in her throat and she was immediately filled her with remorse and fear, the fear easily predominating.

Davy appeared unconscious and there was a large pool of blood at the back of his head. She picked up his wrist to feel his pulse but there was no life.

When the chair had come crashing down, the back of his head had hit the iron fire place. It was the equivalent of a heavy blow to his skull administered by a sharp instrument.

She had got into such a state that she just stood there motion-less. She thought of phoning the police and saying there had been a terrible accident. But what about the meeting only 45 minutes from now? She was the star event. If she failed to turn up, there would be an avalanche of media speculation.

If she was helping the police with their enquiries, it could ruin the chances of a historic victory for Action Scotland.

Gradually, she calmed down and started to think quickly. 'I must get through to the Glasgow South campaign team' she said to herself.

She managed to reach Jimmy Dobson, a dependable local stalwart who would act on any instructions from her.

'Jimmy' she said. 'It's Clova.

'I'm running about an hour late. Traffic hold up. I suggest you kick off without me. I'll aim to be with you by around 8.45pm and I'll give my speech.'

Despite being known as the bull terrier of the SNAP for his 'take no prisoners attitude,' Dobson was quite a sensitive character. He felt something was not quite right.

'Clova are you okay? Where are you right now?'

She immediately put the phone down and knelt down beside Davy. At least the bleeding had stopped, but there was no sign of life, no pulse.

The young Apollo with his coal black curls looked beautiful as he now lay lifeless in front of her.

Tears started to flow as it dawned on her that she had behaved in an unreasonable manner and there had been some force in what he had said to her before she lost it.

She stroked his left cheek and planted a kiss on his lips.

If, at this point, she had concluded that she must notify the authorities straight away, some hellish weeks would have ensued, but she might have been able to pick up the threads of her life.

Unfortunately this period of rational detachment proved to be a fleeting one as the name Roy Semple floated into her head. He was a cop and a fellow nationalist. She used to know him and now he was an inspector based somewhere in Glasgow.

She had established a warm but platonic relationship with Semple earlier in his police career. That was when he was supervising the largest concerts in Scotland that drew thousands of young people and which she helped to organize. They had worked on security together and, over drinks, she had quickly realised that he was as fervent a nationalist as she was.

As a policeman he was hardly alone in this regard. One of the first things Gavin Ogilvy had felt it necessary to do in 2020 was to install a new national police chief whose instructions were to depoliticise the senior ranks and not to ignore hardball tactics from any political quarter but especially SNAP.

Semple was now a middle-ranking officer, possibly on his way to the top. The last time they had met, he had passed on his mobile phone number and said that she should not hesitate to call him whenever necessary.

'My job is to uphold the law,' she remembered him saying 'but I'm a patriot too and I will always do my best for Scotland whenever I have to.'

Semple answered when she rang.

'Clova, so great to hear from you,' he promptly said. 'It's a rare night off for me and I was thinking of going to your event at the Coupar Institute. So many people I've met have said they intend to go so there is likely to be a huge crush tonight.

'Is that where you are already,' he went on? 'I'm based nearby and it would be a chance to see you in action before the referendum next month.'

'That would be fantastic Roy,' she replied. 'But something has come up which means I probably can't make it.'

Before he had the chance to say anything, she asked: 'Roy could you come to 51c Albert Drive? it's where I am right now. I wouldn't ask if it wasn't important.'

'I'll be there in fifteen minutes,' he replied, putting down the phone.

As Semple got his long legs out of the car, he recalled this was practically the quietest street left in Govanhill. As fog started to descend, there was nobody to observe a tall spare man in a dark Ralph Lauren winter coat ascending the stairs.

When Clova greeted him, he saw that she was drawn and red-eyed. She brought him into the kitchen and showed him the body.

'There was a dreadful accident an hour ago, she said.

'Davy and I were arguing. It got heated and I threw the contents of my wine glass at him. It caused him to lean back on his chair. He lost his balance and hit the back of his head on the fire surround. It was a loud thud and I think he must have died on impact. I could certainly feel no pulse.

'Oh my god Roy, what's to be done? I'm not afraid of facing the music but the referendum is only weeks away. If I'm detained for questioning and charged with a serious offence, then it will be devastating for the cause. The Yoons will probably pull off a victory and a big one at that.

'You see where I am coming from Roy? Do you?'

She looked at the red-haired policeman with his sharp, angular features as he surveyed the scene, the boy on the floor clearly dead, the distraught woman standing over him.

His hawk-like nose twitched as he fixed his stern gaze on Clova.

'This is a big mess right enough,' he said. 'What was your quarrel about if you don't mind me asking?'

It was about these photos. They showed that he was two-timing me. I lost the rag and came over here to confront him.

'I'm no emotional weakling. If he had just been a temporary fling, I would have brushed it off. But Davy and I had grown close. Torquil had retreated into his painting studio. I relied on Davy for emotional support during this critical time.

'Everything has been so frenetic these past weeks that I didn't have the detachment to step back and see things in perspective. He's young just as I was once. He needed other outlets and the girl he was with certainly looks beautiful.'

Semple was already picking up several of the photos.

He thought to himself: so somebody else knows about them and thought it worth spying on their love-making even in some freezing park at nightfall.

He saw that she was on the verge of tears.

'Clova sit down and listen' he said.

'You've been foolish. If you were a friend and this had happened in a private capacity, I would be sympathetic but, in the end, I'd leave you to face the music.

'With a good lawyer you'd probably be acquitted, If unlucky, you'd get a suspended sentence. But it's Scotland that would be on trial if this erupts into a huge scandal just as we have the chance to finally break out of England's grip.

'That's why,' giving her a steely looking, 'I'm prepared to risk my neck and keep the story out of the press for the next twenty days.

'The first thing that occurs to me is that you should get on to your media officer and say that, owing to a personal bereavement, you can't speak at the meeting and that you will be suspending your campaign for 48 hours.'

'I am in your hands Roy on this. I'll go ahead and do that.'

Semple's next task was to try and identify the girl. The pictures suggested that she might be one of the East European Roma whom he had encountered in the overcrowded streets beyond Albert Drive.

For three years, the Govanhill area had been part of his beat. He searched around in a bureau where the dead boy had kept papers. There was a diary. The entry for Friday 11 February said: 'Linn Park, 7.30pm, Gabriella.' An earlier entry said 'G' and next to it was a phone number, 08843 371992.

Clova was sitting in an armchair with her head in her hands, having just told her team that she was out of action for the next 48 hours.

Semple said: 'I'm going to make a phone call to the person I think Davy was seeing. I'll ask her to come round. You must keep out of the way, staying in the bedroom preferably.'

A woman's voice at the end of the phone answered: 'Da, Gabi aici.'

Semple immediately said: 'It's the Scottish police here. I'm at the home of Mr David Trainor. There has been some kind of incident.'

'I think you know Mr Trainor. Is that correct?'

'Da, I'm sorry I mean yes,' she replied.

'What is your full name and address?'

She answered: Gabriella Preda, 27 Magnolia Street.

'That's just a few minutes from here,' he replied. Can you come to his flat? There is no need to come immediately. Come in 30 minutes.'

In the interval, Semple contacted the divisional office in Shawlands and asked what information there was about anyone with the name Preda living at that address.

Within minutes he was informed there was a file on a Ionut Preda. He had been cautioned several times over attempted shoplifting and he had one conviction for house-breaking.

'Is there anything on a Gabriella Preda,' he asked? 'No that's all I've got' was the reply.

Fifteen minutes later, Semple was escorting a young woman into the kitchen.

'Do you recognise this man,' he asked.

As soon as she saw Davy Trainor's lifeless body, Gabriella burst into tears and bent down to kiss the dead man on the forehead.

'What happened'? she asked a few moments later.

'That is what we are trying to find out,' Semple replied.

Passing her a handkerchief, he said: 'I have a few questions to ask you.

'You have been seeing Mr Trainor. Is that correct'?

'Yes,' she replied.

'Did you see him last Friday'?

After a pause, she said 'Yes.'

'Where'?

'In a park far from here.'

'The intention was to have some fun there?'

She hesitated again and finally said 'Yes.'

'Why did you need to go so far away?'

'We didn't want to be observed,' she replied.

'But surely you could have made love here. After all, it's a quiet street with few people usually about.'

'We did meet here a few times' she said.

'But I got nervous about being followed.'

'Who would have done that,' he asked?

'My brother or my cousins.'

'Why is it a problem for them,' he asked?

He knew from having to separate quarrelling Roma factions that a young woman enjoying independent relationships could be incredibly destabilising, especially when one of the elders of the clan was arranging a marriage. Usually money was involved and status and honour would also be big issues.

'I would be seen as a violator of the rules of my community' she said. Especially when it got out that I was seeing a 'foreigner,' a *gadjo.*

'And what would your brother do'?

'He would probably thrash me and attack Davy if he could find him.'

'So if your brother had known about you and Mr Trainor, he could have been responsible for this'?

'Yes...but no of course not,' she quickly corrected herself.

'What are you saying? My brother has been home since lunchtime. He has a bad cold.'

'We need to go,' Semple said. 'I am taking you back to your flat.'

He placed her in the back of his car and locked the door.

Now he had to phone the local police station.

'Inspector Semple here. I'm reporting a death that could be suspicious.

'I was called to a flat in Albert Drive where I discovered a body.'

He then gave further details to the desk sergeant, Paul Mathieson.

'I'll notify the Procurator Fiscal's office and hopefully a pathologist will be available in the next few hours,' Mathieson said.

'But we have a problem Inspector. we're very short staffed due to the flu epidemic which is starting to badly affect the force.

'Somebody from the division covering Govanhill will be required to take the case on' he said.

'Do you think you could handle it at least for the time being,' he asked?

'Alright sergeant I'll do that. It helps that I'm familiar with Govanhill and its social problems due to having served here a few years ago.'

The journey to Magnolia Street took only a couple of minutes. During that time Semple concluded that he should slacken his pace. He would not seek out and detain Ionut but simply take Gabriella back to the flat so that the family would know something was wrong.

As he got out of the car a large rodent scurried past him. If he had looked up, he might have been able to make out a CCTV camera. Upon entering the flat, he was introduced to Gabriella's parents Andrei and Raluca. They looked at the tall policeman with enquiring eyes and a long pointed nose.

'Your daughter has been helping us with an incident that occurred several streets away. At this stage she is not suspected of any offence. But it is likely that we will need to speak to her again and perhaps to her brother. Where is he now?'

'Ionut is in the bedroom asleep. He has a bad cold,' his mother replied.

'I see' Semple said and with that he left.

He knew it was almost certain that his parents would drag the whole story out of Gabriella. Ionut would also get to know. 'What would he do if he assumed the police were now targeting him,' Semple asked himself?

Flight would be the stock response of someone whose community distrusted authority and who himself had had several brushes with his force since arriving from Romania four years ago.

Back in Albert Drive Semple advised Bruce to get some rest and then to work hard to limit the damage caused to Action Scotland at such a crucial moment. They tried to minimise evidence that she had been present at the time of Davy Trainor's death before the arrival of the pathologists.

He had thrown caution to the winds by involving himself in this murky affair, he considered later. But if he could keep the national cause on course for the victory many were predicting, it would surely be worth whatever risk there was to his career.

Later that evening Clova broke the news to Torquil that Davy had been found dead. Even though her lover had effectively supplanted him, Davy had never been malicious or arrogant towards him. He wiped away his tears and held Clova's hand but when he peered into her eyes, they had a glazed look and her thoughts seemed to be far away.

Messages of sympathy came pouring in and, by the following lunchtime, bouquets of flowers were piling up in the front room of their Uddingston home. Some commentators were already talking about a sympathy vote reinforcing the Action Scotland side in the referendum, making the result virtually a foregone conclusion.

On the evening news Bruce heard that someone had been brought into custody in connection with Davy's death. The press reported that an 18-year-old local man had been picked up in a disused warehouse and was helping the police with their enquiries.

In reality, Ionut Preda was supplying few answers. He had indeed acted in the way that Semple's instincts assumed he would. By the time he slipped out of the flat, the inspector had arranged for one of the informers he had used in Govanhill to keep watch. He followed him to a derelict industrial estate and Semple was informed of his whereabouts.

He arranged for a friendly journalist on the *Evening Bugle* to be on hand with a photographer when the swoop occurred. The interrogation drew a blank. Preda denied having anything to do with Trainor's death or knowing about his sister's relationship with the man. But he could not offer a satisfactory reason as to why he had gone into hiding two hours after the policeman's visit.

After getting the pathologist's report, the procurator fiscal noted that forensic evidence was lacking linking the Roma to the incident. But he decided that his suspicious behaviour afterwards warranted him being held in custody.

By Friday 18 February Bruce was back on the campaign trail. Her entourage and others whom she would encounter all noticed a big change in her. She was no longer the bubbly, sardonic and wise-cracking politician who had electrified Scotland in the past three months. Whatever inner life spurred her on appeared to be flickering. She was still fluent and in charge of her brief but she seemed suddenly diminished.

Once back in the office, the first instruction she had issued was to lay off the denigration of Gavin Ogilvy. He had sent her a cordial private message after hearing of her lover's mysterious death. But that was not the reason for her tactical shift. She knew that if anything leaked out linking her to Davy's death, the fact that a lot of times her campaign had been very abusive to the Prime Minister would look bad.

One of her campaign's accusations was that normal democratic government was on the verge of collapse in Scotland. Ogilvy had dispensed with his cabinet and was being steered in disastrous directions by the sinister Dr Greer McIver. 'Queer Greer' was his nickname on a growing number of outspokenly nationalist online sites. She had done nothing to discourage the portrayal of the Prime Minister's partner as a malevolent favourite who was usurping the government of the country.

She knew that the evidence for this portrayal was flimsy but anything that contributed to the isolation of the ruling Unionists was merited in her eyes, given how high the stakes were.

But now she issued a statement saying that, in the last weeks of the campaign, it was important to stay focused on the issues which the electorate would shortly judge and not to dwell on personalities.

Privately, she issued a directive instructing all elected officials of the party to un-follow Jerome Roxburgh and not to quote his vituperative broadcasts from High Wycombe, however strong several of his arguments may have been.

In their regular get togethers, Anatoly Yashin and Arthur Gorman observed that a note of hesitation had crept into the Action Scotland campaign despite its clear poll lead.

Three days after Preda's arrest, Anatoly had received an unexpected phone call. It was from Dacian Ursu, the Pentecostalist minister in Windcambe with whom he had discussed Roma gypsy issues when he had spent time there with his friend

Luke Tanner in 2021. He had remembered him as an energetic pastor who while offering spiritual solace for his flock was also keen to build up good relations with the host community in this Lincolnshire town.

The Romanian said that he was planning to come to Scotland in a few days. It was at the behest of his religious colleague in Glasgow, the Reverend Tudor Cornea. He feared a serious miscarriage of justice was occurring. It concerned the young man arrested on suspicion of being implicated in the murder of the Scottish politician's lover.

The man's mother worshipped at Cornea's Pentecostalist church. She had approached him to say that her son was being framed. He had been in trouble with the law previously but was mending his ways. The evening when the death had occurred, he had been at home, in bed suffering from the flu.

Ursu arrived in Glasgow on Tuesday 22 February after a laborious journey up from Lincolnshire which involved a wide detour from the fighting still raging along the Manchester-Leeds corridor. Preda had been formally charged with involuntary manslaughter the day before.

The main evidence against him was that he had gone into hiding soon after his family was notified about the crime. Forensic tests on Trainor's remains and at the scene of his death were continuing.

After Ursu had met the family, Anatoly asked if a lawyer had been hired to defend Preda. He was told that lack of money meant that they were relying on advice from a local law centre.

Anatoly said that his relief organization, BEAST, would be prepared to hire a competent lawyer who would defend the young Roma. Meanwhile, ever pro-active, Ursu tried to get to know the community a bit better. He saw that Govanhill had some of the classic features of a community where settled, and often quite elderly, people found it difficult to adapt to the noisy and sometimes extremely disruptive ways of the Roma.

Wandering around the streets, he noticed surveillance cameras pointing out of some doorways. If switched on, they would have a record of who entered and left a building. There was one outside the tenement where the Predas lived,

He expected the council had put these cameras up in order to deter muggings and other forms of anti-social behaviour. But it turned out not to be the case. The council was floundering in its handling of the noise, safety and cleanliness issues that had arisen as a clash of cultures ensued with the arrival of the Roma after the year 2,000.

The security cameras had originated with a local campaigner Gillian Aitken. She looked after her aged mother who had lived for much of her life in a tenement in what had long been considered a desirable street. Even as conditions steadily deteriorated, Aitken thought a move would kill her 84-year-old mother. For ten years she had fought a lonely struggle in order to try and draw media attention to the social crisis in her community. But the media mainly kept its distance for fear, it said, of stoking racism but in truth because it did not wish to embarrass city elites who had mishandled so badly the Govanhill situation.

Ironically, many of the people who had faced difficulties as a result of the influx of a culturally very separate community were Pakistanis and Irish as well as indigenous Scots. Indeed, Govanhill had been considered one of the multi-racial success stories in the city before the arrival of a group with its own rules for living and an aggressive sub-culture.

Daçian Ursu had no hesitation in seeking out Gillian Aitken and he brought Anatoly along to meet her. She was a smartly-dressed and still attractive middle-aged woman who had worked as a conference organizer in Australia and England before returning to tend her mother. She made them welcome and said that a charity had supplied the funding for the security cameras. They had been placed out of reach, above the doors of tenements where someone had been mugged or robbed, usually an elderly person. The purpose was to instil a greater sense of security.

The Rev Ursu explained that the cameras in 27 Magnolia Street could hold vital clues that might prove the innocence of the Roma in custody and facing charges relating to the death of Davy Trainor. He asked if she would allow him to have access to the tape in that CCTV machine. She agreed to do what she could, conceding that a lot of the Roma were law-abiding and primarily concerned to make a living without harming others. She would do her best to try to prove that Ionut Preda was not one of the disruptive minority who preyed on others.

That same afternoon, a technician removed the cassette with the film and played it before Preda's lawyer and the two others in Mrs Aitken's living room. They were paying attention to the hours between 4.30 and 6.30pm on 14 February when Trainor met his death. The video footage showed that Preda had returned to his own flat at 2.15pm and there was no further sighting of him until he left hurriedly at 10.30pm. Unless he had climbed out of a window (unlikely since the flat was on the third floor}, the evidence pointed to him not being at the scene of the death. It was what his mother had been vainly insisting.

In his routine report to the government in Liverpool, Gorman mentioned the puzzling information that was starting to emerge about a death with striking political overtones.

The British Democratic Authority (BDA) copied in the US State Department whose sources of information on Scottish developments remained limited.

Within 72 hours, the story which *Atlantic Carnival* had been sitting on for several weeks had appeared. Much of the detail concerned the tempestuous Clova Bruce and how she was the latest high-profile nationalist to try and push the undecided Scots towards independence. But the main thrust of the article concerned the mysterious death of her lover and the fact that photographs had been taken of him engaging in open-air sex in a Glasgow park shortly beforehand.

The magazine at least had the grace to alert Gordon Hoy that the publication of the story was imminent and there was added information that might make Glasgow a rather hot place for him to be in. He and his partner Marianna Logan had already concluded the same thing. The day after Trainor's death was announced, they let out their flat on a long lease. The appearance of the magazine found them high above the Atlantic on an aeroplane heading for Florida.

Curiosity prompted Hoy to keep on his E mail account and he was bombarded with lucrative offers from the *Bugle* and other Scottish publications to provide whatever other salacious details he might still be privy to. But he preferred to lie low in his Florida condominium as the political storm raged back home.

The headline above the 4,000 word piece read, 'Mystery Glasgow Death Could Decide Crucial Scottish Referendum, West Now Holds its Breath.'

The original dispatch of the photos to Bruce had been meant to unnerve her and hopefully impede her campaign to keep Scotland from assisting the Americans in their bid to crush Vanguard. The US intelligence officer responsible had no idea how she would react but the psychological profile that had been assembled suggested that she was unlikely to stay impassive.

Now the pressure was ramped up with an article unveiling her colourful personality and her prodigious sexual appetite but also asking just what she knew about the death of her lover.

A boxed article by 'Another Correspondent' revealed the evidence unearthed by the Rev Ursu and categorically stated that it meant the gypsy languishing in prison was unlikely to have brought about Davy Trainor's death.

The Chief Constable of Police Scotland confronted Semple. He was asked why he had not taken into consideration the vital information that others had so easily obtained from CCTV footage. When he could give no satisfactory explanation, he was taken off the case. A frantic investigation then occurred into his handling of it. The circumstances of how he had come to lead the case even though the death had not occurred in his area, came out. When it was revealed that he had known Clova Bruce for a period of years, he was suspended from the force.

Only eight days remained before the referendum. But these twists in the Trainor case were starting to drive the referendum off the front pages. Bruce cancelled all press conferences and most public events as advisers broke the news to her that she had gone from being the 'No side's chief asset to its main liability. Polls now showed that the 'Yes' side, in favour of admitting English refugees, was on the way up.

On the day that *Atlantic Carnival* appeared, Kevin Ingram, the deputy leader of Action Scotland, had opened a package which contained the 8 A4 photos taken in Linn Park on 11 February. He was old school nationalist ready, like much of the party, to try something new if it meant bringing the cherished goal of Indy nearer. But he was also unwilling to see the party held hostage by a capricious leader whose private life was becoming virtually the only big story for the media. Glancing at the photos and reflecting on the week of lurid headlines there had been in the media, he decided to seek a meeting with Bruce.

She was unusually composed when he told her that he had come to the conclusion that, for the sake of the independence cause, she should consider taking a back seat for the remainder of the campaign. Looking across at her, he could see that her normally flushed cheeks were white, there were bags under her eyes presumably from lack of sleep, and her left hand appeared to be shaking slightly.

'Clova' he asked. 'Are you alright? Can I get you anything? Water perhaps?'

'No Kevin,' she replied, 'Just get on with what you have to say.'

He then told her: 'I'm terribly sorry but you've become the story. The referendum issues are being forgotten about. A lot of people are going to base their vote on an assessment of your judgement and character.

'My hunch is that the headlines are not going to get any better for Action Scotland in the next week. I think you should drop out of sight and I'll take the flak. This is not a coup. You're still leader. You have plenty of support. People want to see you get through this. For the sake of the party I would ask you to pass the baton on to someone else.'

Ingram looked across for her reaction. He had expected that this would be a stormy encounter and he had chosen a room in the opposition wing of parliamentary offices where any shouting was least likely to be heard. But she just looked defeated, all fight gone.

'Alright Kevin I hear what you are saying. You've made your case and I accept it. Someone should draw up a brief statement offering a rationale for my withdrawal from the campaign.'

'Thanks Clova,' he replied. 'As time is of the essence, I've gone ahead and drafted something. Do you wish to check it?'

'No Kevin, you are a lawyer, a good one, I'm sure what you've written covers all the bases.

'If you'll excuse me I'll just go now' she said, hurriedly getting up to leave.

Greatly adding to Bruce's sense of despondency was the message she had received just beforehand that Roy Semple had been found at his home a few hours earlier with his throat cut. She had also been informed that there was a suicide note but, as yet, its contents were unclear.

She drove to Uddingston and closed the door behind her. Amazingly to her, there were only a few media folk present, ones she quickly brushed past. Most of their colleagues were, instead, besieging Roy Semple's bungalow in Newton Mearns, a posh Glasgow suburb.

Inside Torquil said: 'Is that you Clova'?

'Yes dear,' she replied.

'I've got the kettle on. Let's sit down and have a cuppa' he responded.

Clova said: 'I've got myself into a right mess. You see Davy died as a result of a horrible accident. I was there. Not only did I witness it but I was to blame.

'Oh Torq,' she went on, 'If only I'd had the presence of mind to go to the police straight away and not seek out a pal like Roy Semple, the media furore would soon have died down.

'Now I've got some very tough times to face. There's going to be huge fall-out.'

'Inevitably, you'll also get unwelcome attention Torq. If you think it best to abandon me and this place and go back north, I won't blame you in the slightest. It might even be a very sensible decision.'

Torquil's surprised and quizzical expression as he heard her news gradually altered to one of compassion and he went over and put his arm around her.

'Clova we're an unusual pair. But we're man and wife however liberally that has been interpreted, "in joy and in grief, in sickness and in health, till death do us part" and all that.

'I did sense something was not quite right these past days. But I held back, thought it best if you sorted out what was troubling you, or decided in your own good time, to let me know what was on your mind.'

At this point sudden pandemonium erupted outside.

'Clova, Clova, open up. Roy Semple's letter has just been released. We want to know what you have to say.'

Someone then pushed a single sheet of paper through the letter box. Torquil picked it up and handed it to her. It read:

'I wanted justice and freedom for my country. But I interfered with the workings of the law in the process. Nobody was going to be framed. The important thing was to prevent a tragic but accidental death having a disastrous impact on a referendum that could finally help to set Scotland free.

'Ionut Preda would have been released soon after the result. No serious evidence would have been found linking him to the incident that had any chance of standing up in a court of law. I took unacceptable liberties with the law. I now have no future in the police which I tried to serve to the best of my ability. I am disgraced but the disgrace is mine alone. Nobody else influenced the way in which this case was pursued. All the decisions were mine alone. Now it's over for me.'

Torquil hugged Clova again: 'I'm going to try and get you through this,' he said. 'Don't fall to pieces. It will all pass in time, maybe sooner than you think.'

Looking straight at him, Clova said: 'I know what I have to do.'

She immediately opened the door and was almost knocked back on her heels by the glare of the flashes from the many cameras suddenly furiously filming her.

'Ladies and gentlemen,' she said, 'I can understand your interest in these developments. If you'll permit me, I've decided to go to Glasgow police headquarters where I'll make a statement. It's appropriate that's the place where it's made. I think it's likely to be divulged in good time before next morning's papers go to press.

'So if you'll just let me get to my car, I'll be on my way.'

She must have known that this would have been an extremely difficult task. By now there were at least fifty journalists and photographers standing in her way. Their quarry was right here in front of them and few wished to be fobbed off with a press hand-out hours later. Just as she was on the point of losing her balance and being dragged to the ground, a beefy hand reached out. It was Ed Cargill.

'You guys,' he shouted, 'watch your manners now.

'You'll get your story. But Clova Bruce is still a human being and right now she's coming with me. We press people need to behave like adults now and then. So gangway please.'

Momentarily taken aback, the wall of media folk suddenly parted as the burly 'Good Evening Scotland' anchor man took command. He showed surprising nimbleness as he directed Bruce to his Range Rover.

'Clova, let's go in my car. We have a driver. Okay?'

'Sure Ed, let's just get out of here,' she said.

The thirty minute drive to the Scottish Police headquarters in Baird street, just off the M8 motorway, occurred largely in silence.

As they pulled into the station, Cargill said: 'It seems to me that you've got a lot of thinking to do. I hope in the last thirty minutes you've worked out what to say once you're inside.'

Throughout the journey Bruce had been absorbed in her own thoughts. Cargill was curious to learn about how Scotland's most charismatic politician had got herself into such a gigantic mess. But he showed restraint. Something at the back of his mind told him that her own ego had got the better of her and events had spun out of control. Stretching his mind back over the era of devolution he could see that the new Scottish-focussed politics had attracted plenty of driven figures whose personal appetites and impulses too often overwhelmed the pragmatic and responsible sides of their nature. It was difficult to forget the young lady (promoted far too soon) who gave up the leadership of her party to be blasted into orbit in order take part in a well-paid reality television show that involved her defying gravity with other publicity-driven personalities. Reprimanded by her party, there were more headlines when a relative sought to deprive her of part of the eye-watering fee that she had acquired.

Then there was Fergus Peacock, the great 'Kingfish' of separatist politics himself. His perennial hunger to be noticed had taken him beyond the comfort zone of his party to perform in theatres, putting on sketches and blethering with his chums. It was undemanding fare but he hastened the decline of his party when he accepted an offer to perform a weekly show on a television channel that was widely viewed as the propaganda arm of a dictatorship which was threatening small, recently independent countries that were not dissimilar to Scotland.

At least the foibles of the political elite had kept him busy with stories. His work would have been more tedious if the professional loud-mouths, grievance mongers and expenses junkies had been leavened by a corp of achievement-orientated politicians keen to get on with projects that would make a difference long into the future. But builders and visionaries were even thinner on the ground than they had been during the political tundra of London-rule. Only Gavin Ogilvy had shown real interest in the much-needed infrastructural improvements or in schemes to overhaul the country's costly and often wasteful public services.

Cargill contented himself with saying to Bruce: 'I don't know what happens next and now is not the time for me to hold you up. I admire you. We don't have an identical outlook on Scotland's future but I share a lot of your aspirations. Be brave girl. I just hope you get through it.'

Bruce tried to smile, clutched his beefy hand and walked through the doors. Cargill now had to put a programme out but all was not lost. Trainor's mother had agreed to be interviewed about the death of her son. She blamed Bruce for leading him astray and was angry that the politician had not even been in touch to offer her condolences.

Bruce knew that if she hadn't made this journey, in all likelihood the police would have come looking for her.

The convoy of journalists who went in hot pursuit of her and Cargill camped through the night outside the police station. Right up until 4am North American journalists were speaking to camera for their evening news shows about the amazing medley of events in Scotland.

A police spokesperson stepped outside to issue a statement to the media nearly twelve hours after Bruce had entered the building.

It read:

'At 3.30am Ms Clova Bruce was charged with deception and conspiracy to pervert the course of justice. She is being held in custody until a later court appearance.'

The official hurried back inside without answering questions. A few of the journalists were listening to the first news bulletins of the day. 'She's gone' someone shouted. 'Action Scotland has announced that she's no longer leader. Ingram's in charge for now.'

'Well the music's died for Clova that's for sure,' one of the older journalists remarked 'but she's left a right mess behind her and a lot of other people might soon pay dearly for it.'

Chapter 7

A Nationalist at Bay

Scotland entered into the last lap of campaigning before the vote on 14 March 2023 in a subdued mood. The implosion in Clova Bruce's leadership meant few in her party held out much hope of averting defeat. The priority became pulling out the Nationalist vote and preventing internal recriminations spilling into the open.

Any relief which Gavin Ogilvy's Unionists had over the revival of their side in the referendum was tempered by the need to maintain tight security on the day of the vote and later at the different counting centres across Scotland. It was recalled that the civil war in England had originated from a riot in Clacton when the result was disputed in the 2021 election which brought Vanguard to power. Ogilvy was therefore taking no chances. His intelligence people told him that so far they had been unable to establish links between Claiomh tSolais and Vanguard. Nevertheless, armed police stood guard outside most police stations. The army was mobilised to convey ballot boxes to the main counting centres.

By 2am it was clear that Ogilvy's gamble was likely to pay off. As in the 2014 referendum, the compact district of Clackmannanshire was the first to declare. The Yes side had 58 per cent over the No side's 42 per cent. Similar results came in from the north-east and the south-west of the country. These were areas unlikely to be greatly affected by the arrival of refugees since, with the exception of Aberdeen, they lacked major cities. The small town and rural populations were also unlikely to have been impressed by the meltdown in Action Scotland or the extraordinary conduct of its leader.

It was the Edinburgh result which preoccupied the Prime Minister as he and his partner sat up with a few friends in Holyrood Palace. It came in at 3.20am and was much closer. The Yes side got 53 per cent and the No side 47 per cent. At least the turnout had been a respectable 63 per cent. But in Glasgow, a smaller turnout of 56 per cent was registered when the result was declared thirty minutes later. Moreover, the No side won albeit by just half of one per cent. Worryingly, an unusually high percentage of ballots were spoiled and afterwards Ogilvy was informed that nearly two hundred contained personal threats directed at him along with numerous pejorative remarks about his relationship with Greer McArthur.

Claiomh tSolais made its presence felt at the Glasgow count as it tried to drown out the announcement of the returning officer only to find that its side had won.

Overall, the country had voted by 53 to 47 per cent to accept large numbers of English refugees on a temporary basis. A statement was quickly issued by the White House praising the Scottish people for both the 'maturity' and 'generosity of spirit' that had been displayed. Secretary of State Lucy McKenna announced a substantial aid package for Scotland a few days later. There were other messages meant to convince wavering Scots that they had not made a mistaken decision. On holiday flights to Las Vegas and Florida, the visa restrictions which had made it very irksome for most Europeans to enter the USA in the last five years were relaxed in the case of Scotland. Duty on whisky and Scottish craft and knitwear products was also significantly lowered. A few days later it was announced that talks meant to lead to the conclusion of a defence pact between the USA and Scotland, would commence shortly.

Gavin Ogilvy was usually low-key when addressing Scots and he strove to avoid any sign of triumphalism in a broadcast to the nation on the following evening. He said the Scottish people had delivered their verdict – in his view the correct one - in the troubled circumstances which Britain found itself in. Preparations were in train to settle refugees in ways that would cause minimum inconvenience to the communities they were joining. They would only be able to enter the labour market and compete for jobs in sectors where shortages existed. He appealed for the rancour exhibited during the six-week campaign to now be put aside. He said the government would listen to any reasonable concerns which citizens had about the way the induction of the refugees was being handled. His door was also open to Action Scotland. But he was not prepared to tolerate opposition that spilled over into anti-parliamentary agitation. His government had won a clear majority in 2020 and was determined to serve out its four-year term.

Before March 2023 was over large numbers of people were starting to move from the by now overcrowded camps dotted across the north of England. Luckily, the winter had been significantly milder than the one of 2021-22. Anticipated deaths from exposure and even diseases like cholera, had not arisen. But an outbreak of contagious tuberculosis had occurred and tens of thousands of people were in a fragile state both physically and psychologically.

Anatoly Yashin was the head of the Scottish office of the British Ministry for the Displaced. His boss Sam Stockwood had negotiated directly with Gavin Ogilvy with whom he had a growing rapport (one that flowed from their first meeting in the autumn of 2022). Anatoly reassembled the core team with whom he had previously tried to carry out relief and rescue work in England. That is until war conditions made it virtually impossible to operate in many areas.

One of the biggest refugee centres was situated in Moffat in the Scottish Borders. Zach Mbarra and his partner Nadia Misra were based there. They and a team identified the needs of the new arrivals. Who required medical care? Which settlements were best suited for particular refugees? Who was available and willing to work in economic sectors where there were clear shortages? The main one was the food sector owing to the supply of labour from East-Central Europe drying up arising from the difficulty of reaching even North Britain from the continent.

Livia Morariu's task was to oversee the needs of elderly refugees. As a doctoral student in palliative care the exhausting work often gave her invaluable experience. She struck up a rapport with civil servants in the Scottish health ministry. Thankfully, she found no lack of decent people willing to be of help.

It was heartening for Anatoly's team that a movement to smooth the path of the refugees spontaneously sprang up in Scotland. It was called Friends of the War Victims. Funds were raised for specific initiatives such as holidays in the Highlands and islands for refugees. A wide range of social events were arranged from literary festivals to local dances and walks in the hills. These gatherings brought hosts and newcomers together. Friendships were kindled that sometimes led on to romance and marriage.

One unexpected but welcome by-product of the arrival of so many people from England was that it broke down stereotypes. It became less easy to portray the English as sullen, arrogant and self-centred when so many different types were to be spotted. Mistrust had sprung up and become established in some areas during the years of nationalist fervour. Jerome Roxburgh, from his propaganda centre in Berkshire tried to rekindle rancour. However, the impact of his nightly tirades was limited outside a few hardline nationalist areas, increasingly confined to parts of Clydeside.

Scots could now see the refugees close up. Some were problematic and demanding but the great majority were stoical and some were prepared to offer something back whenever the opportunity arose.

Definitely to be included in this category was the Spirit of Liberty football club. It had formed among the first wave of refugees in 2022. Talented footballers from the English Premier League, such as Dilbert Roderick, Gerry St Clair and Brian Pidwell, helped put together a team which was making its mark in the 2022-23 Scottish football season. They had resisted overtures to move across the Atlantic and embark on lucrative careers in American football. They clung to the hope that the conflict would abate before it was too late for them to resume their footballing careers in England. Meanwhile, their team was rising up the Scottish Premier League and progressing in the Scottish Cup.

In the teeth of opposition, Ogilvy had made the case to the Scottish Football Association that the rules should be relaxed to allow the Spirit of Liberty to engage in Scottish football at a senior level. In the acrimonious and sometimes petty-minded world of Scottish football, the Prime Minister's stubbornness paid off. Among the public there was renewed interest in the game. Peebles was the home base for the Spirits as they were soon called. For a time it became a favourite destination for afficionados of football. But the team's drawing power meant that a new stadium was urgently required and one was found in Lanarkshire where a large steelworks had once stood. The area had been renovated and grassed over and, within, a month, a stadium had been constructed able to contain 40,000 fans. Soon, there was also a demand for merchandise associated with the club – strips, scarves, pennants with two shops opened in the centre of Glasgow and Edinburgh selling nothing else.

Jerome Roxburgh soon realised that it was counter-productive to direct his hate speech towards the Spirits and he ignored the club. But there were a few unsettling incidents: random attacks on refugees, graffiti daubed on the walls of the buildings they stayed in or used. Such hostility became far less noticeable after several of the perpetrators were arrested and handed stiff sentences by the courts.

Ensuring acceptable levels of security, so that refugees would not feel at risk, had been one of Anatoly's chief priorities. He had utilised the services of the junior Colombian army officer Javier Roldas who had worked in this field back home. They soon built up cooperative links with the police and most local authorities.

Anatoly even reached out to Action Scotland in the hope that it might be persuaded not to exploit the refugees presence in order to hasten its recovery. The separatist force had tried to throw aside its recent troubles by electing a new leader.

Tony Shand was a 34-year-old urban heritage designer. He would be the sixth leader in nine years. As AS found itself at the mercy of events which it could not control, a feeling had grown in the party that it needed to rebuild its appeal perhaps with a different brand. This was largely the view of political moderates content to see incremental change lead on to independence rather than relying on the kinds of political stunts favoured by predecessors. The Big Bang theory of the rapid dash to freedom, under outsized personalities like Fergus Peacock and the ill-fated Clova Bruce, had not worked. Seizing upon the disorientation of the fundamentalists after recent calamitous times, this moderate minority had managed to install the young articulate but low-key man from Falkirk, a place located right in the geographic centre of Scotland.

Shand's message was that Indy remained as crucial as ever. But the party would throw its energies into trying to fix some of Scotland's intractable social and economic problems before the great day dawned. Previously, the unspoken assumption had been that everything could be safely left to the onset of liberation when a torrent of released human energy would transform the country. Shands's contrasting approach involved trying to make better use of the built environment. He was soon throwing his energies behind campaigns to ensure that people came before roads when major planning decisions were made by councils. He won an early success when councils were persuaded by vocal protests to cancel the construction of large shopping complexes in architecturally sensitive areas of the country.

Anatoly was received courteously by Shand who indicated that he had no intention of offering a sanitised version of Jerome Roxburgh's stance towards refugees. As long as they were not expected to settle permanently in Scotland and they did not prove to be a vastly disruptive force, then his party would try to concentrate on other matters in its quest for power.

Action Scotland remained wholeheartedly opposed to Scotland intervening forcefully on the British-American side of the conflict. A military push against Vanguard had already got underway in southern England. Territory that had been recaptured by Sutton with the arrival of the foreign fighters, was won back. The siege of Portsmouth was lifted, a renewed push into Sussex occurred, and a new front had opened up in East Anglia after troop landings at Kings Lynn and Lowestoft.

The regime got a shock when the Vanguard commander in Norwich, surrendered the main city in East Anglia to British-American forces. Colonel Brian Manning had been one of the small number of regular officers who had decided to obey Vanguard's orders. But he had baulked at the command to destroy the cathedral and other historic buildings as enemy forces bore down on the city.

Manning had ensured that his family had gone to ground before his mutiny. Vanguard then ordered that at least one close relative from officers with an old military background be taken hostage to prevent further acts of treachery. Its response was pitiless when Ralph Toynbee, the Minister of Culture attempted to flee to France on a cross-channel ferry disguised as a crew member. He was detected in a spot-check by the frontier police. A swift trial followed and he was publicly executed at Tyburn in west London three days later. He had been best known for his novels about bohemian hipster society and neither his desire to abandon Vanguard nor its reaction, came as a surprise to those observing how it was rapidly becoming a ruthless militarised force.

Less than three months before he had signed a protocol of cooperation with Clova Bruce on cultural matters. She herself was in dire straits but only facing the possibility of a lengthy prison sentence rather than execution. Her trial for culpable homicide was due to get underway in the Edinburgh High Court in July 2023.

She had been kept in custody due to the seriousness of her alleged offences. She faced charges of culpable homicide, perversion of the course of justice, and corruption of a public servant. It would be very unusual for anyone to secure bail in these circumstances.

But a Friends of Clova group had been set up whose main purpose was to get her out of Cardross woman's prison. It was a recently-opened institution erected in west Dunbartonshire, north-west of Glasgow. Formerly it had been a Roman Catholic seminary which had only lasted for three decades. The dysfunctional nature of the modernist concrete structure which had won it awards for its pioneering architectural design, had made it impractical to maintain. Not only its inability to shut out the relentless west of Scotland wind and downpours but the steep fall in religious vocations had turned it into a white elephant.

Teddy McCusker had been a seminarian during Cardross's brief heyday. But he soon realised that the priestly vocation was too onerous for someone unwilling to subordinate an extrovert personality to a higher religious calling. He mentioned this during a visit to Bruce. Her husband Torquil Niven had moved back to the Moray Firth, unsettled by the scandal and desperate to shake off the pack of journalists who stalked him after her arrest.

Bruce had been in low spirits and McCusker felt it was his job to raise them. He bustled in, displaying a knowing attitude to the guards whose sympathies might be appealed to later on – one just never knew. He could see how subdued she was and he immediately tried to bring her out of her shell. He told her that she had not been forgotten. She had lit a flame for the nationalist cause by her inspired leadership which had not been extinguished. There were plenty of people who were determined that she should spend even less time shut up in Cardross than he had done as a seminarian.

Unfortunately, the current leadership of the nationalists were not among them. Tony Shand and his allies were busy trying to erase memories of the four months that she had been in charge of the party. She had been in Cardross only a few weeks when a special party conference was held to accelerate that process of forgetting.

The nationalists renamed themselves the Independence Party. The noisy and, at times, provocative youth wing was not wound up but instead placed in cold storage. Any initiatives had to be cleared in advance with the party bureaucrats at central office. Three-quarters of the five thousand strong membership, promptly quit.

McCusker was appalled. The party which he had extravagantly championed had fallen victim to a hostile takeover. It was the kind of thing he was all too familiar with in the media world but rarely had it occurred in politics with such suddenness. This safe, sanitised nationalism clearly had no room for a mischievous free spirit like him. Opportunities for writing on politics were starting to dry up. Shand preferred to air his thoughts to more cerebral reporters.

McCusker put Bruce in the picture about the situation on the outside. Dressed in a grey prison uniform, she was despondent, often seeming lost in her own thoughts. McCusker decided that the only way to rekindle the defiant flame that had once burnt brightly within her was to level with her.

'Clova,' he said, 'you are suffering unfairly because of a terrible quirk of fate which led to the death of poor Davy Trainor. A lot of people wish to get you out of here before your trial. It would put you in a better position to fight the charges that you are facing. As it is, your current incarceration is a rallying-point for those who wish to rescue the party from the trimmers – perhaps even traitors – who have seized control.'

'I see,' Bruce smiled wanly. She had always been slightly on her guard towards McCusker. They were on the same side politically but he always seemed to have schemes on the go that were also bound up with promoting his own cause.

'And just how is this going to be done,' she challenged him?

'It can be done, you have my assurance of that,' he said, putting her right hand in his. 'Money is already being raised to get you out on bail. Lots of it will be needed but there are well-wishers with deep pockets who are prepared to contribute to a campaign. Our people in the world of Scottish folk and tartan rock music are planning to hold a special concert. If you give us the signal to go ahead, it will be called "Justice for Clova."

McCusker was relieved to see that the phrase produced the first flicker of interest in her eyes.

'Clova,' he went on, 'we are doing this both for the cause and for you. Your situation parallels the terrible state the country is in, its freedom choked by the jackals who currently control its fate.

'We want to seize the keys of the kingdom from Ogilvy and his gang. I'm sure that as one of the leaders of our generation, you do too.'

'This sounds worthwhile Teddy,' she replied. 'But if I involve myself in a fresh political struggle when I am confined in here, it is likely to mean that I walk away with a far stiffer prison sentence.

'If you and others wish to turn me into a martyr for the cause, then you might indeed be going the right way about it.'

'Clova, it's really not like that,' he interjected. 'Nobody intends you to be a sacrifice. There are twin goals, to secure your release from here and then ensure that you be found not guilty of the charges that you face.'

'Angus Dalglish, my lawyer, has said that there is no precedent for anyone facing such serious charges ever to be granted bail. I fear he is right,' she said.

'Angus is an honourable nationalist and a good lawyer when handling a straight-forward case,' McCusker answered.

'These are extraordinary times we are living through when precedents no longer apply perhaps even in the world of law.'

'I am here to make one recommendation that stands a reasonable possibility of making you a free woman soon.'

Taking both her hands in his he said: 'Discharge Angus Dalglish. Hire a new lawyer who has the ingenuity and daring to enable you to triumph over your current adversity.'

'Oh and just who might that be,' Clova asked, now smiling at McCusker because of his unquenchable optimism?

'His name is James Hinde. He only qualified as a lawyer last year and you would be his first major case.'

'So I'd be a kind of guinea pig who would be experimented on to see how good he was.'

'There is no need to be quite so negative as this,' Teddy said, betraying some irritation that she was slow to grab the lifeline that was being extended to her.

'I know James Hinde well. I wouldn't be recommending him if I didn't think that – young as he is - he has the right combination of talents to help you in your hour of need. He started out as a journalist fresh from taking a politics degree at Glasgow University. His timing seemed to be good. It was the aftermath of the 2014 referendum. Things were still on the boil. New nationalist publications were springing up both online and in print. He took the fight to the Unionists and was tireless in reporting how the Scottish struggle was seen from Dublin to Berlin. But the new nationalist media was not robust enough to sustain the cause. It fell on hard times. After three years James concluded that he was pouring his talent and energy down the drain. At best he might end up an MSP at Holyrood by the time he was forty. He decided to turn his hand to something new.

'I was sceptical when he said he was going to become an Advocate. Not only did he think that he had the temperament and skills for the calling, but he was convinced there would be a lot of work for a dedicated nationalist lawyer in the times we are living through.

'The law is another world to me Clova. I just try and keep on the right side of it but, unfortunately, the number of libel cases I've needed to defend, means I've often been unsuccessful. One thing I'm sure of: the great disruption we are facing in Scotland means a lot of nationalists will need a resourceful lawyer. And this is what James is. I am now convinced of that.'

'Oh I remember the guy now,' Clova said. 'Unlike many journalists very punctual, disciplined and all for the story. Almost monk-like in his dedication even.'

'You got it Clova,' McCusker said, relief clearly visible on his face. 'James is not the complete ascetic. He married Lorna, a young librarian and they have a baby son.

'But if you took him on, he would fight tooth and nail on your behalf.'

'Teddy, you clearly mean well and are doing the best you can for me. So I'm willing to talk to James Hinde and we'll see what can be done. That's all I'm committing myself to at the moment.'

'I don't think you'll regret it,' McCusker said as he rose to leave. 'Just hang on in there Clova. This is merely a temporary setback for you and for the cause we hold so dear.'

A week later she had a visit from Hinde. He was dressed soberly in a slightly ill-fitting black suit with matching tie. He could easily be an undertaker, Clova thought. He was a thin young man of medium height with a long Celtic face and a heavy lock of black hair almost falling over his pale blue eyes. He had a formal manner and extended his hand politely.

Bruce said: 'Teddy has told me a lot about you. He thinks that with you defending me, there is a chance that I could secure my freedom. How would that be possible?'

Hinde said: 'It is ultimately down to the fifteen people making up a Scottish jury. A majority verdict is needed to secure your conviction. I believe that if you defend yourself in the courtroom with the vigour and conviction you displayed in politics, many of these people would simply refuse to convict you.'

'That's very consoling' Bruce said 'and I've heard nothing similar from the lips of Angus Dalglish.'

'If you decide to take me on,' Hinde said, 'my main task would be to try and get one of the three charges dropped. It seems to me that the grounds for convicting you with "corruption of a public servant" are very flimsy ones. The late Roy Semple handled the investigation of Davy Trainor's death entirely on his own. He wasn't influenced by you -as at that time you were, I believe, in a state of shock.

'He was a nationalist policeman pursuing this case in his own unorthodox way. He didn't intend anyone to be permanently framed. And his suicide note makes it clear that nobody else was responsible for the course which the investigation took after he arrived at Albert Drive.

'If the charge can be dropped Ms Bruce,' he went on, 'I think it would introduce a strong element of doubt in the minds of members of the jury about the viability of the entire case that's been mounted against you. You really have nothing to lose.'

'Alright James' she said. 'you've convinced me that I've a chance of getting out of here after all before I reach the age of fifty. So I am going to take you on as my lawyer. Let's now get to work.'

Hinde said: 'I'm glad to hear it as there's everything to fight for. But please let's keep to the formalities at least until the case is over.'

'I see... Mr Hinde,' she replied. 'On reflection, that is perhaps a very good suggestion.'

As Hinde assembled his case and the 'Justice for Clova' campaign unfolded, the news was dominated by the offensive of the British-American coalition. Its architects were not seeking a knock-out blow against Vanguard. They knew how well dug in it was, particularly in densely-populated parts of southern England. The goals of the first stage of the military push was to regain control of East Lancashire and West Yorkshire. A lot of dedicated foreign fighters remained on the ground. There were local militants for them to make common cause with. Often these had been radicalised by involvement in Middle Eastern conflicts. But supply lines were badly stretched. It was difficult for London to send reinforcements or basic supplies to the various garrisons. By early April 2023 a No-Fly zone had been successfully established. It was no longer possible for Vanguard to use Leeds airport. But, unlike in East Anglia, there was no sign of capitulation. Brutal fighting, street by street, was now the rule as coalition forces pushed towards the centre of Leeds from the north.

Desperate civilians fled on their own volition or else were pushed in the direction of the coalition lines by Vanguard fighters. Soon the refugee camps to the north, which had been emptied of people who had been moved on to Scotland, were filled to capacity with fresh occupants.

Thankfully across in east Lancashire the fighting had been less prolonged. The towns of Bolton and Rochdale were recaptured with many of their inhabitants cowering in basements or seeking escape on nearby hills. Nevertheless, the fighting further east had produced another 300,000 refugees whom Anatoly Yashin's ministry was having to rescue and find homes for.

He found he had an invaluable ally in Greer McArthur. The doctor used his experience with the United Nations, and the contacts he had made there, to build up an efficient and well-resourced relief campaign. There was no burden on the hard-pressed Scottish Exchequer and by June an estimated two million refugees had been settled in Scotland without any major disruption. The existing population had increased by nearly 40 per cent since the outbreak of the conflict twenty months earlier. In modern times, no other country in Europe had to cope with such a massive influx of people fleeing conflict.

Many Scots were absorbed by the fighting raging a few hundred miles to the south. But by June there was a new focus of attention – in the sporting world – which even gripped many Scots who normally paid little attention to football.

The start of the Scottish Cup had been delayed by the upheaval in the second half of 2022. A lot of players had been temporarily called up when the government mobilised the defence forces in case Scotland was the object of an attack.

By June 2023 the competition was still taking place and, remarkably, the Spirit of Liberty had reached the cup final.

On 24 June the English team found itself facing Celtic at Scotland's biggest stadium, Hampden Park, just south of Glasgow city centre. Whatever the result, there was likely a thrilling game in prospect. A team reliant on the support of the burgeoning refugee community had stormed its way to the final. Celtic had its own dedicated following, perhaps as many as 30,000 fans that day. Around 25,000 fans were either sympathetic to the English team or were unconcerned about who won as long as there was a feast of thrilling football. In the VIP box Gavin Ogilvy was watching along with young Princess Fiona who would present the cup to the winning team.

Football pundits agreed that both teams were almost evenly matched. Spirit's strikers, Pidwell and St Clair faced a tight Celtic defence which had frustrated most rivals that season. Except for a brief recovery by its rival Rangers at the start of the

2020s, Celtic had been long dominant. It looked as if the story would be repeated when its centre-forward Damon O'Hare broke through the Spirit defences and put the Glasgow side ahead in the 34th minute. The Celtic end was in rapture. But the second half was increasingly dominated by Spirit. There were several near misses against an increasingly defensive Celtic side before Pidwell scored with a precisely aimed free kick that the keeper had little chance in saving.

The indignation of some of the hard-core Celtic fans was shown when flares were set off and several banners were unfurled depicting a masked man carrying an automatic weapon, under the sign 'Foreign fighters,' followed by a capital 'V.' Pandemonium occurred when these banners were spotted. There was booing from the Spirit end where fans of Rangers, Celtic's longstanding rival, could be found. But there was also consternation from a lot of Celtic fans. They shook their fists at the ultras, many shouting 'No' 'No.'

For some years the Celtic following had been divided over the militant tactics of the Shamrock Army. Its several thousand stalwarts saw the club more as an extension of anti-imperialist politics rather than as a football side. Palestine had been a burning issue. And a section of the Shamrock Army, very likely under the influence of Jerome Roxburgh's broadcasts, now embraced the Vanguard cause. It possessed glamour because it wished to cast aside existing conventions and had provoked America and the Scottish Unionists, traditional foes for these embattled fans. But plenty of Celtic fans felt the ultras had gone too far with their political grandstanding. The club's name was being dragged into the mud through identification with a sadistic regime which persecuted the elderly and was now even going after hipsters.

Coins started to be thrown in the direction of the Shamrock Army by disgruntled fans. It responded by letting off more flares. The police then waded into the crowd. The authorities were afraid that the smoke could start a mass stampede, leading to the kind of terrible tragedies that had occurred at Ibrox and Hillsboro. They also feared that scuffles could get rapidly out of control. Order was re-established after fifteen minutes. Soon the ninety minutes of playing time were up. Emotions cooled during the fifteen minute interval before a further thirty minutes of play occurred. Both sides rose to the occasion, throwing themselves at the goal mouth of their adversary. In the 17th minute Celtic snatched back the lead with a goal that seemed to come out of nowhere. But Spirit equalised five minutes later and, in the very last minute of play the game was decided when Dilbert Roderick knocked a header into the back of Celtic's net.

The Scottish Cup was duly presented to the English victors by Princess Fiona. Most of those present were entranced by the artistry that had not been on display in a Scottish Cup final for many years. The thrilling match made world sporting headlines. But the next day the Scottish press would have a major story of its own to contend with.

During the disturbances in the Celtic end of the stadium, after Spirit had equalised, the cameras had focused on the spectators in and around that spot. A woman dressed in a smart dark coat and light blue scarf was noticeable among a sea of mainly male faces. She was standing next to the easily identifiable Teddy McCusker in his pin-striped suit, fedora hat, and outsized Celtic scarf.

One of the camera crew who had covered the Action Scotland conference in 2022, remarked in the press gallery to a senior sports journalist, Douglas Naismith: 'I swear that is Clova Bruce.'

He replied: 'It can't be. She's in Cardross woman's prison, awaiting trial.'

'There is probably one way to find out,' the cameraman replied, 'See if McCusker has his phone switched on and ask him.'

Naismith duly phoned and asked him straight out: 'Who is that elegant female with you in the Shamrock Army section. A colleague said it looked like Clova Bruce. Surely it can't be'?

'It's Clova alright. She was released on bail yesterday. We requested no publicity so the press statement was withheld.

'She's had a hard time and wanted a quiet re-introduction to society. But today she felt up to attending the match and being among her own folk again.

'It looks as if you've got a story there,' McCusker said. 'Well done for being so sharp. I cannot win them all but there will be plenty more front pages for Clova in the weeks and months ahead.'

Chapter 8

Trial and Error

Clova Bruce's trial was taking place in the High Court. As a solicitor who had barely started out on his career, it would have been highly unusual for James Hinde to be her chief defence lawyer. A barrister was required to direct the defence and Teddy McCusker hit on a strategy to give Hinde a role. He got a legal friend, imbued with McCusker's persuasive skills and who was friendly with Angus Dalglish, to take the latter aside. Bruce's barrister was already well aware that the case was a highly unconventional one. It would need qualities which he as a Scottish legal luminary had never really displayed. On those grounds he was persuaded to take on Hinde as his junior counsel. He was fully in tune with political conditions which Dalglish, with his passion for outdoor country pursuits, disregarded as far as possible. He might also be able to flesh out political aspects of the case in ways that could sway the jury.

Dalglish still held out little hope that Bruce would be acquitted so he felt there was little to lose by giving Hinde a role. The two men agreed on a division of labour. The senior pleader would dwell on the personal dimension while his junior would try to convince the jury that the wider political dimension must be taken into account.

It was Hinde who persuaded Dalglish to make an appeal to the Procurator Fiscal that the third charge hanging over Bruce be withdrawn. It was hard to see where exactly lay the evidence that she had explicitly tried to get the late Inspector Semple to behave corruptly. The Procurator Fiscal knew there was no point in trying to make a political martyr out of the accused and it was the importance of that realisation which led him to agree to drop the third charge and also to accede to a request for bail.

The bail terms were onerous. A surety of a quarter of a million pounds was requested. Prohibitive for most defendants, it took only 36 hours for this sum to be raised and lodged with the court. It was a reminder that the nationalist cause enjoyed continuing appeal for people of means (albeit a minority of them). Indeed, during the 2014 referendum a tour of middle-class areas of Glasgow and Edinburgh would have revealed window posters in streets occupied by younger-aged doctors, lawyers and accountants.

Proceedings began with the swearing in of the fifteen-person jury. They were broadly representative of Edinburgh society. A bus driver, a housewife, a park cleaner, a supermarket check-out lady and a brewery worker were matched by a medical consultant, a senior investment analyst, a betting shop manager, the head of a small computer company, and a retired Salvation Army officer. In addition, there was an electrician, an airline steward, a tour guide of historic Edinburgh, a restaurant chef originally from Zimbabwe, and a Spanish waiter in one of Edinburgh's best-known hotels.

It was a representative enough slice of life in what had been a tourist-orientated city which was also a national centre for a wide range of services. Hinde volunteered to find out what he could about the jury. He discovered that the electrician had a pro-Indy 'Yes' sticker in the back window of his van nearly a decade after the 2014 referendum. The Salvation Army volunteer was a supporter of the 'Scotland in Union' group which had been an effective foe of separatism in more recent times.

Until the 1990s it had been possible to challenge jurors for a whole host of reasons, including their political leanings. But this was no longer possible. Nevertheless, it was helpful to obtain information on the outlook of some of the jurors who would decide the fate of Scotland's leading female politician.

Farquhar Mitchell, representing the state was a well-organized and confident lawyer, usually able to make a formidable case from the facts before him. His only defects were a certain pomposity and a slowness in responding when an unexpected turn occasionally occurred in cases that he was involved in. He led the court through the circumstances leading to the death of Davy Trainor and the defendant's role in the matter. Her unwillingness to notify the authorities in the proper way, relying instead on her private friendship with a police officer, had led to a miscarriage of justice. The cross-examination of the apparent fall-guy, Ionut Preda, was meant to confirm the prosecution's argument and it seemed to have worked. Bruce's defence had no questions for him, not wishing to keep the spotlight on his weeks of detention for a death that he had no hand in. Nor did it cross-examine Linda Trainor, the mother of the deceased. She had been encouraged to dwell on the fact that the accused had made no effort to contact her after her son's death. The message she relayed was that Bruce, having used her son in life, had callous disregard for him in death, a death she had been responsible for.

Angus Dalglish naturally tried to portray Bruce in a more sympathetic light which meant supplying a context to the deed which had led to her trial. For weeks she had been at the very centre of a dramatic political campaign into which she had thrown all her energy, leaving her drained as a result. It had knocked her off balance and blunted her critical antennae. Thus she had over-reacted on being presented with graphic evidence of her lover's infidelity. Throwing the contents of her wine glass at him may have been harsh but it did not amount to culpable homicide. Dalglish argued that, in the circumstances, she should really be facing a charge of involuntary manslaughter and that the grounds for her guilt on the lesser charge were flimsy ones.

As for perverting the course of justice, none of the witnesses so far called, had been able to offer evidence that Bruce had influenced the direction of Semple's investigation. Taking the stand, Torquil Niven confirmed that she had been taciturn and withdrawn in the days following the death. This impression was reinforced by the testimony of her campaign team.

Naturally, the trial was making headlines far beyond Scotland. But the journalists assembled in hotel restaurants and bars were intrigued by something else. From the second day of the trial, dozens of small explosions had been occurring not just in Edinburgh but also in Glasgow, Aberdeen and a few other places. No one was killed or even injured. The bombs were placed in out-of-the-way spots such as the flower beds of parks or behind a rock on Arthur's Seat. But to anxious spirits, these mysterious blasts were an unmistakable sign that the war was closing in on Scotland and that the authorities were left helpless.

The high-point of the trial was the arrival of the defendant in the witness box. Bruce had been the guest of the owner of a safari park and health farm in her constituency. Due to the fall-off in tourism, both businesses were closed for most of the year. Doug Baillie had sympathised with her plight though he was not an ardent nationalist and had offered her a suite free of charge. It was an hour's drive to the High Court in Edinburgh's Lawnmarket where she was being tried. Since her release a month earlier, she had benefited from plenty of rest and nourishing food.

In the witness box, she was wearing a fawn trouser suit set off by a dark brown turtle neck sweater. Her costume indicated dignity and defiance. Certainly Mitchell did not set out to break her spirit, perhaps realising that would not be such an easy undertaking. His aim was to show she had behaved in a highly irresponsible manner which contravened the law. She conceded that her behaviour had been ill-advised both immediately before, and especially after, Davy Trainor's death but that she had not meant to kill or even harm him. Afterwards, she had gone to pieces. Her disorientation stemmed from the realisation that the referendum cause would be damaged. Her main purpose was to prevent defeat being snatched from the jaws of victory. Her responses had not been about trying to save her own skin. Once her deputy leader became aware of the pictures which led her to confront her lover, she did not hesitate to remove herself from the campaign. She had also gone to the police rather than the force having to come looking for her after Roy Semple's suicide.

'It was a bizarre happening, an unprecedented situation, a grotesque situation, an almost unbelievable mischance' she insisted on one of the few occasions when she raised her voice. Peadar McHale the Irish journalist covering the story for a string of international media outlets pricked up his ears. These very words had been used by the wily Irish political chieftain Charles Haughey forty years earlier when his minority government had been engulfed in crisis. The man responsible for two vicious murders turned out to be a friend of the then Attorney General and was apprehended after staying at his home as a guest. 'Grotesque, unbelievable, bizarre and unprecedented' entered the language in Ireland as GUBU.

Perhaps Bruce had been reading up on this colourful episode in Irish politics and had been cheered upon discovering that Haughey, a kind of Irish Berlusconi, had later made a resounding comeback. McHale entitled his story on Bruce's testimony 'Does Scottish GUBU Explain Mystery Death'?

Mitchell's summing up for the prosecution emphasised that nobody was above the law. This was an era when lawlessness, emanating from the top had done huge damage to Britain. On the occasions when their transgressions brought them before the courts, politicians had to fully answer for them. Otherwise the rule of the mob became a real possibility. While the defendant had not deliberately set out to kill someone, nevertheless she bore prime responsibility for Trainor's death. Her behaviour afterwards had been indefensible and a lengthy custodial sentence was deserved owing to her callous and irresponsible actions.

These points were made coherently but without passion by Mitchell who seemed to assume that the gravity of Bruce's wrong had imprinted itself on the minds of the jurors after what had emerged in the trial.

There were a few exclamations of surprise from the press bench when it was James Hinde who summed up for the defence. The young solicitor argued that it was neither just nor appropriate to make an example of Bruce. She had suffered a great deal already. She had ended up in prison, had forfeited the leadership of her party, and had seen the cause which she had been championing in the referendum go down to a shattering defeat. It had been a desperate effort on her part to avoid the 'No' side losing which had explained her reaction to Mr Trainor's death. She had been disorientated and distraught and this had led her to place her fate in the hands of a misguided senior police officer. If Semple had advised her to play it by the book and explain her role in the affair to the authorities, she would undoubtedly have done so. Her high-pressurised, almost manic, campaigning role meant that she was deserted by common sense when she needed it most.

Turning to the jurors, he asked them to seriously think how they would have reacted if faced with such competing pressures. Scotland was being stretched to breaking point, he claimed melodramatically and it was Clova Bruce who found herself on the rack. Of course, she carried real responsibility for Trainor's death and this thought was likely to torment her until the end of her days. But it was hard to make a convincing case that she was guilty of culpable homicide. It would be a huge waste if someone like Bruce, who had shown an aptitude for public service, was deprived of her liberty just as Scotland badly needed single-minded politicians ready to shield the country from danger. She had already probably suffered enough and why should Scotland now pay a heavy price for her lapse? Now surely was the time to wipe the slate clean.

The intensity with which Hinde deliberated, combined with his simple and expressive English, had held the attention of the jury. Some old hands on the Edinburgh court scene could not recall rhetoric of such force especially from someone just starting out on his legal journey.

Attention then focussed on the presiding judge. Whatever opinions Hazel Raeburn may have had on Scotland's constitutional future, she had kept to herself. The rather prim and humourless 42-year-old was best known as an advocate of women's rights and had lent her name to a campaign to get more women onto the boards of Scottish companies. She had courted controversy in a rape trial where she had strongly sided with a woman accuser despite a well-marshalled defence indicating the strong probability that the student defendant was innocent.

Angus Dalglish had lost count of the times that male colleagues had complained in the bar about her PC views amounting almost to misandry, undermining the presumption of innocence for some of their male clients. They saw her as someone who found men an inconvenience and who was ruthlessly prepared to use the equality principle to advance elite women like herself irrespective of the cause. He found her officious and blinkered but thought that, on this occasion, her feminist worldview might redound to the benefit of his client. It was only when she began her summing up that it dawned upon Farquhar Mitchell that the judge's outlook, combined with Hinde's oratory, could snatch the case clean away from him.

Judge Raeburn enlarged upon the seriousness of the charges which the accused faced. She pointed out that the number of offences Bruce faced had been reduced but the charge sheet against her was formidable. The jury had to ask what role she had played in the death of her lover? Was the wine incident just the first part of an assault that she intended to wage on him? What role had she played in the way the matter had been investigated by the police? By giving herself up to the authorities had she shown genuine remorse in the wake of Semple's suicide? Or at each stage of this wretched episode had she been guided by her own narrow self-interest?

The judge stated that it was hard to avoid the fact that she had been the agent of her own downfall and had brought about the premature death of a young talented individual who perhaps could have done a lot with his life. But then, shifting gear, she asked how serious a crime did this constitute? When weighing up its verdict, she argued that the jury should not altogether discount the fact that Bruce was one of the few women still active in politics at a time of unprecedented crisis in the nation's affairs. The feminine voice in national affairs was vital in order for the nation to be guided wisely at a time of such contention. For a voice as prominent as Bruce's to be silenced would undoubtedly leave a vacuum. Theirs was a heavy responsibility and as she dismissed them, she wished them clarity of thought in their deliberations.

As she finished another dull thud was heard, indicating that a bomb had gone off, by the sound of it probably a mile or two from the High Court. By now it was 3pm on 5 July. Journalists and film crews from North America mingled with the local press corps to await the jury's decision. Excitement rose on the High Street when news leaked out around 8.15 pm that one was imminent. A few minutes later the 15-person jury was assembled before the judge. When the foreman was asked how did he find the accused, he stated that, on the first charge, culpable homicide, she had been found not guilty by a majority verdict. On the second charge of conspiring to pervert the course of justice, a not proven verdict was returned.

There was silence in court. But one of the jurors, the elderly Salvation Army major, held his head in his hands clearly unhappy with what had been decided. It later transpired that there had only been a one vote majority in favour of the not proven verdict. The undecided Edinburgh housewife was finally swayed by the electrician who repeated Hinde's assertion that the defendant had simply been placed in an impossible situation by the march of events.

The judge thanked the jury and pronounced that the trial was now at an end and the defendant was free to go. The media were stunned by the verdict. It was not what they had expected as headlines next day such as 'Clova the Nationalist Houdini,' 'Shock Verdict brings Firebrand Back from Dead,' 'What Next for Volatile Clova' showed? Only one columnist stuck her neck out and argued that the judge had done women no favours in her summing up. In an article headlined 'A Bad Woman Will Flourish in front of Judge Raeburn,' Maeve Cochrane wrote:

'If a woman has seriously violated the law, then surely her profession or the condition of the country have no bearing on her guilt or innocence.'

Bruce was carried aloft out of the courtroom by young supporters flanked by the leaders of 'the Justice for Clova' campaign, McCusker prominent among them. Traffic noise prevented them from speaking to the media outside the court. Instead, they crossed the road to Parliament Square. It was sheltered from traffic by the bulk of St Giles Cathedral. Bruce stood with her back to the large equestrian statue of King Charles II that dominated the entrance to the Court of Session. She told reporters:

'I am glad to have been vindicated. It shows so many people are still with me. Many deeds that were critical in deciding Scotland's fate were played out in this corner of historic Edinburgh. Too many signified the loss of our freedom. I hope my release will put that trend in reverse and there will be a new freedom surge after this. More than ever, with no end in sight to the English war and the Americans ever more closely involved in our affairs, Scotland needs to be the mistress of her own destiny.'

'Will you not give us a song then Clova,' asked a mischievous local journalist? 'What better moment to exercise your vocal chords than this personal triumph for you'?

McCusker promptly intervened, saying: 'this is a very serious business. Ms Bruce nearly forfeited her liberty and she needs to recharge her batteries and decide what's next. But soon you will be hearing more from her and the wider radical patriotic movement. I can assure you of that.'

With that she was bundled away in a taxi, heading for a townhouse in Musselburgh just east of Edinburgh where a party celebrating her win was already far advanced.

The Prime Minister had been disappointed but hardly surprised by the verdict. Emotions were volatile. Scotland was going through a whirlwind of change that had not been seen since the Lowlands had been transformed by a wave of industrialisation two centuries earlier. He had already been thinking what should be done in the event of that outcome. He had one move to make. That was tabling a new bill in the Scottish Parliament for the introduction of identity cards. A case could be more easily made for them than in the past. With the threat of terrorism growing by the day, the police needed to be able to identify people who were acting suspiciously or had no means of identifying themselves. It was too easy to forge driving licences or even passports. The request had come from the police and after consulting with his party colleagues, Gavin Ogilvy decided to back the proposal.

He had reservations about the uses that could be made of identity cards especially if the nationalists were back in power and had access to a data base with personal details on every citizen. His preference was to try out the scheme for a trial period. But he decided to leave that out of the bill. It could be the basis of a compromise later on if the Independence party showed a readiness to come on board in return for some concessions. If the upshot was that a split occurred in their ranks, then he would cry no tears over that.

There was a brief pause in the festivities when Bruce arrived at the Musselburgh residence of Calum Goodlad, who had risen from being a garage mechanic to running a multi-million pound business that dealt with the decommissioning of equipment in the North Sea that had been associated with the previous oil boom. She was cheered to the rafters as she entered the palatial hall. Looking around she was surprised and gratified by one thing. Her well-wishers consisted not just of staunch nationalists but movers and shakers in Lowland Scottish society. She spotted Fred Rankin, the king of the estate agency business and the radical Church of Scotland minister Denzil McTavish. There was the principal of a major university, even a sheriff and plenty of up and coming lawyers. Finally, it was Trevor Colvin, the owner of a string of care homes, who came forward and delivered an impromptu speech of welcome.

Bruce had reflected that none of these people had sent her even a message of sympathy during her months of incarceration. Probably she would have been dismissed as a sad case with much head-shaking and even tut-tutting if she had been sent down for seven years. The messages of support had come from ordinary folk as well as some in the music business determined not to forget one of their own who had risen so high and now seemed destined to be locked up in a dungeon, her public career in ruins.

Bruce was back in business and she knew that she was an asset for these suave, self-confident but sharp-elbowed folk. They were made anxious by the acute instability undermining their business and professional futures. For some she was a reminder of the boldness and at times unorthodox methods they had used to climb to the top in their own professional callings. They were placing a side-bet on her once again becoming a force in Scottish politics. Anyway, she was glad of their presence though under no illusion about what had caused them to show up. She was also glad that a foxy Teddy McCusker was discreetly photographing the gathering with his smart phone. These photographs could prove useful in the future when a lot of people might have to stand up and be counted.

Back at Holyrood after nearly six months absence, Bruce was soon able to see which of her 44 colleagues genuinely welcomed her return and which inwardly groaned at the presence of a stormy petrel ready to disrupt Tony Shand's agenda of quiet reconstruction for the party. Within days the Identity Card bill was being debated. Strains were revealed at the strategy meeting of the party to decide tactics. A majority backed Shand's proposal that the Independence Party should back the law in return for concessions. Not only should it be temporary but a special parliamentary committee should be set up to monitor its effects.

One quarter of his MSPs were opposed to this approach. Many refused to comply with the chief whip's recommendations for who should speak as they felt his selection was bound to favour the leadership. There were already signs of a formal split when the bill was passed just before parliament adjourned for a delayed and shortened summer break.

Several weeks of behind-the-scenes manoeuvring ensued until on 26 July it was announced that a new party was being set up. The launch took place in Strathaven and Anatoly Yashin's friends, the Laidlaws were able to inform him about how it went when they came over to Edinburgh a few days later.

Symbolism had singled out this tranquil, harmonious South Lanarkshire town. It had once been the starting-point for a rising of radical weavers against the government which had gone down in history as the 1820 Insurrection. The rebels were few in numbers and their march on Glasgow was easily broken up and the ring-leaders executed. During the heyday of modern Scottish nationalism, an annual commemorative march had been one of the regular events in the calendar of separatism. Bruce had often sung a few ballads and now she was back, in what was part of her constituency, to announce a new political departure.

Teddy McCusker was the master of ceremonies. He announced that a steering committee had been formed to launch a new party, the Scottish Freedom Front (SFF). He introduced people who had assembled on a makeshift platform erected in the small town's market square. They included nine of the 45 MPs in the Independence Party. It was one-fifth of the Independence Party group but one-quarter had opposed the introduction of identity cards. In response to questions, McCusker admitted that for some it was a big step to leave the party they had spent a lifetime serving. But he was confident that the new party's presence at Holyrood would grow. Few self-respecting nationalists could endure their party turning into an echo chamber for a still-Unionist government.

As he said this there were vigorous nods from the platform. These came from a group of MSPs already known as 'the awkward squad.' These included the outspoken leftist Martina Norris who, ironically, had first come to fame by trying to storm a detention centre in her constituency where asylum seekers whose claims had been rejected were being held prior to being sent back to Third World countries. Beside her was Donald Abercrombie, the former trade-union official who had moved effortlessly into the private sector after setting up a flourishing pet care business. (Ironically, it mainly employed English refugees as dog walkers and pet sitters). Standing out from the group of defecting MSPs was the flame-haired folk singer and ex-nun, Ariadne McDowell who had promised to write a stirring anthem for the new party.

Journalists also noted various luminaries from Scottish civil society who felt they had nothing to lose by publicly identifying with the new grouping. It would have been strange in the eyes of many of them if Finlay Jardine, Scotland's best known public intellectual, had been absent from the gathering. He had patronised every new radical departure for thirty years often turning against them if they failed to meet his exacting standards of socialist purity. He was keen to see off any competition from rising left-wing talent which might deprive him of the various sinecures he had acquired, including the plum spot of reviewing the Sunday newspapers on Sky television each Saturday night.

There was more interest in the press corps at the appearance of Sir Basil Dempsey. The ageing astronomer was now rather more famous for his pronouncements on various issues of the day than for any scholarly works. He had boosted the Independence cause among young west of Scotland Protestants and Catholics by holding public meetings in church halls during the 2012-14 referendum drama. He was a part of a group of Catholic professionals who had long complained of being marginalised in stuffy unionist Scotland but who had quickly built up their own sources of influence once Fergus Peacock and his ruling nationalists realised their value. However, he had stayed out of the referendum on the refugee issue. Some said it was because the contradiction of championing the Irish Famine immigrants to Scotland while refusing to admit English refugees (in hardly better condition many of them) would have appeared too glaring. Others put it down to less lofty motives. They said that a man with heroic self-belief was still smarting at the refusal of the outgoing Snodgrass government to find several million pounds for a new television series on unidentified flying objects in Scotland which Sir Basil was keen to front.

Journalists covering the launch quickly recognised one of their own on the podium. Suzanne Pittock had been a perennial fixture at Indy events for over a decade. She had re-invented herself as a handmaiden of nationalism after listeners to her Radio Clyde 'hour of contention' found her shrill invective too unsettling on the morning commute. Books, think tanks, study-visits, round-tables, television debates on nationalism, all needed to include Suzanne Pittock to have the right level of evangelical fervour. Journalists wondered how long the honeymoon period would be for the new party if this dedicated but intense champion was one of its public faces.

Completing the platform party was Murray Cairns. The hirsute bespectacled radical was perennially optimistic about the revolutionary potential of the Scottish people. He had even set up his own Starry Plough party, promising a workers and students republic but so far it had failed to retain any of its electoral deposits. The party had recently split over whether it was sustainable for the bulk of funds raised to provide Cairns with a living wage and the rent on a studio flat in the heart of Glasgow's bohemian West End. But his 'can-do' approach to the national cause made him a cheerful Pied Piper and a good draw whenever a re-invention of the cause was felt necessary.

Bruce knew that it would be hard to keep in line folk whose truculence sometimes made them hard to work with. She had asked herself and McCusker, who had become her muse, whether she should plunge into the political maelstrom so soon after all that she had just been through. He understood her reservations but insisted that they must seize the hour. Things were coming to a head in Scotland. Ogilvy's Unionists had gambled heavily on Britain being stabilised thanks to American intervention. There was no guarantee the gamble would succeed. Already, a vacuum had opened up in the ranks of Scottish nationalism due to the perfidy of Shand and his moderates. If solid patriots like themselves didn't fill it, McCusker warned that the wild men would soon do so and the consequences for everyone could be incalculable.

In her keynote address Bruce eschewed dramatics. She set out what were already the clearly agreed aims of those setting up the SFF. Strict neutrality was a must to avoid Scotland being dragged into a conflagration that could result in worse devastation than anything seen in England. As for the defence pact being negotiated with the United States, it made a catastrophe even more likely and must be opposed.

A quick normalisation of ties with England was essential as soon as conditions allowed. There was no point in trying to promote regime change in England. Scots who had done this in previous disturbed epochs, such as the 1640s, had got their fingers badly burned in the process. As long as there was a large refugee population of English people in Scotland, then relations would never settle down.

As for its domestic policy, the SFF advocated a sweeping tax on land values to reverse, as she put it, the cruelty of the 18th century Highland Clearances. Inherited wealth would also be subject to new taxes and the proceeds would be used to launch a new youth fund which would enable Scottish young people to enjoy start-ups in the property and jobs sectors. She thought such an approach to inter-generational imbalances was innovative and humane and perhaps even Clive Sutton's government might take notice and act accordingly.

She was questioned about her approach to refugees. Until just two years previously the English now in Scotland had been fellow citizens. Had it been difficult for the new party's founders to agree on a policy which effectively meant most of the refugees would be sent packing within eighteen months irrespective of conditions in England?

No Bruce replied un-hesitatingly: 'It is unrealistic to imagine that a poor country like Scotland can absorb such a volume of people. There are economic constraints. Also ethnic and cultural ones which would make it difficult for a lot of English newcomers to fit into Scotland compared to ones from Somalia or Jordan who are carrying less cultural baggage.'

'The British English people are likely to be manipulated by the Unionists,' she went on.'

'It means that Scotland will find it difficult to settle down and find its own natural rhythm after years of instability. It is more humane if the English are speedily relocated perhaps to North America or Australia if any are reluctant to head back south.'

What if these people were reluctant to leave Scotland, Bruce was asked. 'Well, she replied the SFF would have no alternative but to withhold social welfare payments.' But, a journalist interrupted, much of this money was coming from the United States. Bruce simply shrugged her shoulders and went on to say that if any refugee committed an offence, whatever its gravity, then instant deportation would occur.

In relating what he had heard Bruce say in Strathaven, Laidlaw expressed his revulsion. It was a neo-Vanguard solution for Scotland. The SFF's putative leader seemed to have learned little or nothing from the English experience. Most of the world had shown its abhorrence towards Clive Sutton's rule and now here was a Scottish politician contemplating something not so very different.

Anatoly and his partner Moira Torrance tried to put their friend at his ease. Most Scots would simply not stand for such an agenda. But Ronnie was afraid that enough could be found to implement it if the right set of circumstances enabled her to make it to the top. There were always unbalanced or unscrupulous people with a mercenary outlook who were ready to implement loathsome instructions from on high. He saw Bruce as a clever Jezebel without too many moral scruples. She would allow all sorts of wickedness to go on underneath as long as she got recognition and was able to parade on the national stage as a political star.

At one level the gaping split in Nationalist ranks made life easier for Ogilvy as his responsibilities grew. Parliament took up less of his time for one thing. But the SFF soon proved a headache. Public protests started to occur outside doctors' medical practices in areas where refugees had been settled. The protesters claimed that the newcomers were straining local services to breaking-point. In fact this was untrue. Medicine was the one area where the arrival of the refugees created the least inconvenience. Greer McIver was heading a team that was busy creating a parallel medical service. He utilised his UN connections to create an international task-force comprising 1200 doctors, nurses and specialist staff. Within six months it was being hailed as one of the few successful humanitarian initiatives of its kind in recent times. McIver worked closely with Anatoly Yashin and the British Elderly Assistance Survival Trust.

He was regularly seen entering and leaving BEAST's Edinburgh office. It was usually well guarded but would-be assassins had used a five minute changeover period to plant an explosive device under his car. It would have gone off as soon as McIver turned the ignition key. But ever since the attempt on the life of his partner in 2022, he had been vigilant and he spotted the device after doing a routine check.

The assailants were also detained trying to escape across the Meadows. Under interrogation, it emerged that they were part of a Vanguard hit squad that had successfully slipped in by pretending to be refugees. The Intelligence service reported that there were probably others on the loose.

The SFF made the introduction of identity cards a big issue. It also continued to insist that English quarrels were being imported into Scotland. An opportunity to test the extent of its appeal occurred when a by-election in North Ayrshire was announced following the death of an Independence Party MSP. It was a socially-mixed constituency with post-industrial towns, prosperous suburbs and villages, and service hubs. There were strongly pro-Union areas where people had close ties to Northern Ireland as well as militantly pro-Indy ones.

Sir Basil Dempsey was talked into standing for the SFF. The intention was to use his reputation as an intellectual heavyweight, well-known on television and public platforms, to inflate the vote of the new party. He was up against Grant Stevenson, the son of a trade-union hero of the 1970s who was wary of the extremism of the SFF. As was the case during the recent trial, dozens of small explosive devices went off in golf courses, refuse dumps and other spots usually distant from built-up areas. Nobody ever claimed responsibility but, by now, it was clear a strategy of tension was being pursued.

Stevenson endured fierce hostility from SFF activists. His campaign rallies were frequently disrupted by organized barracking. Fist fights erupted at several of them. When canvassing, he was followed around by SFF militants with megaphones who urged people to stay indoors. A few days before the election, Ogilvy intervened, warning the country that it was the hardball tactics of the SFF which opened the risk of serious destabilisation. Soon after it was announced that the Unionist candidate was standing down in order to allow the two rival nationalists to fight it out.

Floating voters did not find Dempsey convincing. As he aged, he had grown stiff and imperious. In earlier peaceful years he had been an advocate of immigration. Doubts about the ability of Scotland to absorb newcomers had been dismissed by him as the stupidity of men in pubs. Now he was the standard-bearer for a party which wished to exclude war victims in England who until a year earlier had been fellow citizens.

It was a jarring message and, in the event, Dempsey lost by two thousand votes. Disconsolate, his strength taxed by the campaign and in truth disgusted by the methods of some of his supporters, he announced his retirement from politics. Soon after he cut his ties with the SFF and retreated permanently to his holiday home on the island of Iona.

Increasingly, the initiative now swung to radical figures. Teddy McCusker acted as their mentor. His speeches and articles were now increasingly irascible and uninhibited. It was he who encouraged Bruce to launch a campaign of non compliance with identity cards. They were disappointed with the take-up. Only 16,000 people signed a petition stating that they would refuse to cooperate with the scheme. He decided that a public event with a bold denouement was needed to ensure that the campaign caught fire.

Realising that a major confrontation might be hard to avoid, Ogilvy reshuffled his government. He created a new post of Minister of Public Security and, in a sensational move, Grant Stevenson was offered, and accepted the post.

He had soaked up plenty of punishment in the by-election campaign and by its end had come to the conclusion that defending Scottish democracy against desperate people in the radical wing of his own movement was the chief priority of the times. Ogilvy also decided to change the name of his party to the Scottish Citizens party which meant diluting its unionist character.

The subtle shift away from Unionism, adopting a wait-and-see approach to Scotland's future with the rest of the island, was also enough to persuade Brian Crawford to team up with Ogilvy. Sutton's spin master until the eve of the dictatorship, he had lain low since fleeing north in the autumn of 2021. His book on what he saw of the Vanguard movement from the inside had been a worldwide sensation. He had a flair for publicity comparable to that of Yanis Varoufakis, the controversial Greek academic who had created a huge rumpus in Europe several years earlier with his revelations about the seamy side of EU politics.

But Crawford was a chastened figure. He had seen his father Hector cut down by a Vanguard bullet meant for him after he had debated with ex-Prime Minister Pannell in Glasgow in late 2022. The huge royalties he earned from his book were nearly all donated to the Friends of the War Victims, the Scottish charity doing valuable work to integrate the English refugees. He still remained a Scottish patriot at heart but he shuddered at the recklessness of Bruce in stealing some of Vanguard's political clothes.

Whenever he was in Scotland, Ray Lattimore would try to meet up with Crawford. Over an evening, usually at a jazz club down at the port of Leith, they would discuss the war, conditions in Scotland and delve deeper back into the past to ask themselves, over a bottle or two of Rioja, just why the British story had gone so horribly wrong.

Lattimore said to Crawford that it was ridiculous a journalist of his calibre was allowing himself to go to seed. He asked him what he would like to do. Crawford said there was no entry back into Scottish journalism, especially as local hacks were often jealous of colleagues who had shone in London and then returned to Scotland expecting to be big fish there.

Lattimore asked him if he would be interested in working for the Ogilvy government. Crawford knew he had lived down the shame of helping to launch Sutton into politics and was not seen as a security risk. He was aware that there was even sympathy for him in government ranks, especially because of the murder of his father. But it all just seemed a bridge too far.

However, a week later, with the North Ayrshire by-election campaign in full swing, he agreed to meet the Prime Minister. Ogilvy told him that he was not the kind of man to bear grudges and that he admired the lucidity and courage he had showed in recent years. He told him that there was a pressing need to get an effective information bureau set up, especially one able to rebut the disinformation spewing out from Jerome Roxburgh in High Wycombe. So he wondered if Crawford would consider taking on the role.

Given a few days to think it over, he agreed just as long as he would not be a propaganda mouthpiece for the government and he would be given the resources to set up an efficient operation. On that basis, Crawford joined the government.

It was another remarkable twist in the career of someone who had first come to prominence as the spin doctor of SNAP's Fergus Peacock during the 2014 referendum. Soon the world's media were becoming accustomed to a low-key and professional Scottish perspective on the news and Edinburgh's reputation as a hive of rumour and conspiracy began to diminish.

A large Glasgow protest rally was announced for 23 August. It would start at the Botanic Gardens in the north-west of the city, proceed down Byres Rd, often seen as Glasgow's radical Left Bank, file past the university and Kelvingrove park before going through the city centre and ending up in George Square. The idea was that several hundred people, some of them prominent in the arts and academia, would burn their newly-acquired identity cards in front of the city's imposing City Chambers (or town hall) and be filmed doing so. A gauntlet would be thrown down to the authorities to see what action they would take. Ogilvy had already envisaged that such gestures were likely and had urged his civil servants to try to avoid making martyrs.

Both Anatoly Yashin and his partner Moira were in Glasgow on the day of the march. There was a routine meeting at BEAST's west of Scotland offices. It was only due to take a couple of hours. Afterwards, they planned to have a leisurely late lunch before attending a concert in the evening.

The venue of the meeting was in the Park area of the city. It stood overlooking Kelvingrove Park and was seen by some as a mini-version of Edinburgh New Town. It consisted of two gently curving crescents made up of offices, many of which were gradually being restored to private dwellings. It was chosen as the site of BEAST's office not because of its high-end status but due to its access to the M8 motorway which could be joined after a few minutes drive. It was also thought to be more easily defensible with only a couple of ways of getting in and out. But these expectations were found wanting that day.

The two visitors from Edinburgh were just finishing up from their meeting. Thankfully, most of the other participants had left when a shot was heard and three masked men rushed into the lobby pointing guns at the four people left in the building. Moira had just enough time to look through the window and spot the single armed policeman who had been left to provide protection, prostrate on the pavement with blood flowing from a head wound. Moira, Anatoly, the office manager Kirsty Douglas, and Tommy Keegan, a BEAST worker based in Croy, north-east of the city, were then bundled into the kitchen at gunpoint by three men.

They were asked to stand against the wall as a tall, sturdily-built man with a broad Yorkshire accent, began to speak to them. His head was almost completely covered by a mask but there was enough space for part of a red beard to protrude at the bottom.

When he told his captives that he was a deacon of the V-demption church, each of them separately concluded that if it was a kidnapping, it was a very bizarre one.

Chapter 9

A Hi-Jacking with a difference

What Anatoly remembered about the brutality of hostage-taking back home in Russia did not make him optimistic about where they would end up. The hostages in the Beslan school and Moscow theatre sieges were treated abominably by their captors. In the end, it was the callous incompetence of the authorities which sealed the fate of hundreds of them.

He, Moira and Kirsty Douglas, and Tommy Keegan were pushed into the kitchen by the most physically imposing of the kidnappers. He ordered them to sit on chairs while a smaller accomplice bound each of their wrists together.

As this was happening, the Vanguard headquarters in Bradford released a statement. It said: 'A team of fighters has recently taken control of the Glasgow office of BEAST, the bogus relief agency. The people in the office are under its control. They will be released unharmed provided BEAST is willing to wind up its activities in Scotland and the government there releases the Vanguard members it is holding in Scottish jails. Failure to comply with these demands is likely to lead to unfathomable consequences. Our Vanguard fighters are resilient and ready to sacrifice themselves for a glorious cause.'

The helicopter whirring over Park Circus and the sound of screaming sirens on police cars racing to the scene of the incident, was noticed by those at the end of the march. Twenty minutes later, as the speeches got underway in George Square, news of the statement began to spread. The fashionable radical doctor Sir Hugh McTear had the microphone. Since 2007 he had been producing for order a stream of reports damning the opponents of separatism for the inhumanity of their social and economic policies. He served on numerous well-remunerated government quangos. For all his perceived devotion for the welfare of Scotland's poor, he had very little contact with them, dwelling in a castle which he had renovated after it had been partially burned down during a rave held by the Pictish Fairies, the Indy rock band.

Before an expectant and mainly middle-class audience, he was about to set alight his identity card when Clova Bruce whispered in his ear and he quickly stepped aside for her. Picking up the microphone she said:

'Friends and fellow patriots, this is a great moment of defiance against the Ogilvy government's sinister authoritarian move. Hugh McTear, a fine Scottish doctor and a tireless champion of the under-privileged, was about to light the flame for our movement. But I have just been informed that there is an ongoing incident at Park Circus near Kelvingrove Park. It looks as if it could be quite serious. In light of that, the organisers think that it's best if now is the time to wind up our rally.'

To groans and shouts of 'No,' 'No,' Bruce continued: 'Don't worry. Other days of action will happen. There will be no going back from offering fierce resistance to this attempt by a crumbling government to squash our civil liberties. But today's event is over. The turn-out is amazing. Now is the time to go home.'

People who had walked from the west of the city now found that they were unable to take a short-cut through the park. It was crawling with police whose attention was directed to a hilly bluff where 203 Park Circus was located.

It would be the first major challenge for Grant Stevenson in his job as minister for public security. He decided to play it long. A letter was pushed through the letter-box inviting the hostages to state if they needed any supplies for themselves or their hostages.

Ahmed Hedley read the note and handed it to his colleague Tariq Aslam. They were both in the large office of the 5-room building. They had removed their masks. The four captives remained in the kitchen with two armed teenagers, Rashid Sharif and Osama Khan watching over them.

Aslam had obtained a serious wound in his knee as he had attempted to overpower the guard outside. He was in considerable pain due to the bullet having smashed into his knee bone before re-emerging, ricocheting off the pavement and hitting the guard in the head. Although injured the guard would live.

The authorities decided it was best to appeal to the better nature of the captors rather than to rush the building and overwhelm them before they could kill their hostages. Nobody knew what weapons and explosives they had.

Tariq Aslam was a hardy, stoical figure. He had fought in Yemen against the Saudis and had seen much suffering. He read the note and said to Hedley: 'My situation isn't good but I am reluctant to take any help from these people.

'If they send in a doctor, he could be a crack policeman in disguise.'

Hedley said: 'Brother, we have little choice. You need treatment otherwise the state of your leg means you could soon die.

'I propose we tell them there is a wounded person. They may already have guessed going by the drops of blood that are visible on the steps outside.

'We can say that we will allow a woman inside but it must be a woman over the age of fifty.'

'I will not be treated by any woman,' Aslam snapped.

'All right then,' Hedley quickly said. 'Let's ask for an elderly male doctor,' to which Aslam agreed.

Hedley was a convert to Islam. He had found in his new faith a model for the conservative family living that came naturally to him and which his Methodist church no longer provided. It had been the last straw when the leading Methodist in his area had been exposed as someone who had spent huge amounts of money on cocaine and crystal meths as well as habitually using rent boys. He had financed this dissolute life from his salary as chairman of a well-known financial institution. It in turn plunged into financial crisis as this scandal surfaced and to the then Paul Hedley the revelation was a bitter blow.

Christianity no longer seemed to offer a moral design. Islam he had his suspicions of. But he could not help noticing that there were plenty of well-adjusted Muslim families. After long talks with his wife Samantha, they decided to convert to Islam and bring their four-year-old son Dean up in the faith.

He had had few regrets afterwards although, close up, he saw that, locally, Islam contained plenty of hypocrisy and self-serving conduct. Nevertheless, there was something decisive in its favour. It was waging implacable resistance to a dissolute and hedonistic society. Christianity, by contrast, had made the fatal decision to broadly rub along with the ugly conventions of the times.

The violent upheavals which had swept through West Yorkshire had been a nightmare for him. He had lost friends and relatives to the conflict. Many of his workmates in the textile mill where he had been employed, had become casualties or else had fled.

Islam had been badly smashed up too. Factionalism between Deobandi and Baralwi strands of the faith had become violent in their intensity. In addition, the young radicals who rejected conventional Islam used the chaos to establish their own local fiefdoms.

He could fit into none of these categories until Vanguard had sanctioned a new religious path. 'Vdemption' claimed to be redeeming mankind from its sins. Everyone who pledged themselves to fight for justice and who showed valour in doing so, could enter 'the Realm of the Elect.' The new faith had some quirks. In its pantheon it included figures whose lives were thought to be inspirational. They included Moses, Saladin and Muhammed Ali but also David Bowie, George Best, Mo Mowlam and perhaps most remarkable of all, Professor Euan Garland.

Initially, Hedley had been confused by the attempt to rehabilitate Garland. It was his cure for arthritis that was responsible for making him a hero. According to the new official line, he had been accidentally killed in the Cheshire town of Wilford in July 2022. He had been trying to cross over and join the Vanguard side when the tragic accident occurred. Why else would he have stayed behind during the fighting when everyone else had fled the University of Wilford?

Garland's elevation to the Vanguard cosmology was a sign that 'the Age of Fire' would give way to 'the Age of Amnesty,' Hedley believed. Once true justice had been restored to England, it would no longer be acceptable to wage any kind of war against the old. Honour would be restored to them. They would take their place in the Vdemption church even as preachers as well as carers and those who merited care in return.

Greatly appealing to Hedley was the emphasis on equality for men and women in the new religion. The subordination of women was one of the features of Islam that he had been least impressed by. So he decided to throw himself into the effort to implant this new faith. He was uplifted by a talk which Philippa Sutton gave on how to be an effective Vdemption deacon . She was practically the only Vanguard leader from London who had bothered to come up and talk to people since the election of 2021.Whatever complaints folk might increasingly have about her scowling and withdrawn brother, she seemed a serious but approachable person. She was ready to take risks to bring the message of Vanguard to people who had so often been cast aside by the powerful lot down south.

So he had taken the lead and set up his own church in Wibsey, an ethnically-mixed suburb in the south of Bradford. Initially, guards had been needed at the Vdemption tabernacle church when it took over an empty mill. But soon a church that emphasised attending to the material as well as spiritual needs of people in the vicinity no longer needed them.

Hedley's church was in good standing but what was the point if the effects of war were causing people to flee. It would be impossible to usher in the 'Age of Amnesty' if this part of England became a wasteland denuded of people.

So here he was in Glasgow taking a stand to try and stave off depopulation and ruin. He wished to reverse the Scottish government's decision to allow much of the Yorkshire population to relocate to Scotland. He was convinced that what was described as a temporary measure would acquire permanence.

Occupying the BEAST office in Glasgow was the only obvious way he could get the Scots to stop meddling. He did not believe in murder though the Vdemption team had brought explosives with them. He was certainly prepared to die if necessary.

Fast-running out of options and with its territory shrinking, Vanguard's West Yorkshire leadership had approved the idea. They were increasingly left to their own devices by London and it seemed to be a way to persuade those at the top not to abandon what was left of West Yorkshire.

Along with the other three Hedley had slipped into Scotland by embedding himself with the refugees. It was troubling to discover that so few had regrets about leaving their home communities. They knew life was likely to be hard for them in the future but hoped for a chance to build a new life if not in Scotland then certainly in North America.

With his military experience, Aslam had been sent along as the team's logistical leader. But now Aslam was out of action and he would have to take the decisions. It was imperative that the vulnerability of the operation be kept from the prisoners. He would also have to learn more about them in order to devise a strategy that might still bring success.

Hedley phoned the number on the note that had come from the police. It was answered by a calm-sounding officer who said: 'Thanks for phoning. What would you like to say?'

He replied: 'There is a wounded person inside. It is not one of the hostages. I would like you to supply a doctor. But it must be a man who is over fifty. It would help if he could bring painkillers and bandages and – oh yes – a mattress for my colleague to rest on.

'Please also understand that we have no intention of giving up without a fight. By now the message containing our demands will have been circulated. These haven't altered nor has our determination to accomplish our mission. Is that understood'?

As soon as the policeman said 'Yes,' he put the phone down.

When Hedley moved next door, he decided to reveal his identity to the prisoners.

'My name is Ahmed Hedley and I'm from Bradford. This action has been carried out by Vdemption which is the religious voice of Vanguard. The purpose is to stop the emptying of West Yorkshire of so many of its people.

'Now I'd like to ask who each of you are and what you do.'

Moira Torrance was the last to respond and when she revealed that she was a nurse, Hedley's ears pricked up.

He then asked her: 'If I release your bonds and you promise not to escape will you look at a comrade who is lying wounded next door?'

'Of course' she replied. 'It's my job to offer medical help in all circumstances.'

As she was led out, Moira smiled tenderly at Anatoly and waved discreetly to Kirsty and Tommy.

As soon as she saw the extent of Aslam's injury, she turned quickly to Hedley and said: 'This man needs specialist medical attention urgently.'

He replied: 'A doctor has been promised. Bending down to start washing the wound and apply a bandage, she replied: 'I doubt if that will be sufficient.'

He returned to the other room to look over the prisoners. Anatoly sensed by his manner that Hedley was not a psychotic. In appearance he was a strapping athletic man with a ruddy complexion. His red flowing beard gave him almost the appearance of a sage. He just did not seem to be an edgy and unpredictable terrorist.

Anatoly decided to see how far he could get in conversation.

He said: 'What do you hope to achieve'?

Hedley replied: 'I want some of our prisoners freed and BEAST to stop encouraging people to desert England. At the rate people are leaving, soon there will only be the sick and the very elderly left in West Yorkshire.'

Anatoly replied: 'people wouldn't flee north if they didn't expect to receive better treatment. I haven't heard of any trying to flee south, deeper into Vanguard territory. Have you?.'

He wondered how well his captor would take such sarcasm. But Hedley simply said: 'That's beside the point. We are struggling to create a new and better society. These transformations always involve some pain. But the Vanguard faith church that is springing up promises an Age of Amnesty and a reconciliation between the generations.'

'If you don't mind me saying so,' Anatoly responded, 'that sounds a bit too convenient. The elderly of this present generation have been stripped of their wealth, property and status over much of England. Many have died prematurely or have forfeited their liberty. Nothing can stop the biological clock. Soon your leadership will be approaching the age when they too are old and this amnesty idea would appear to arrive at just the right moment for them.'

Hedley glared at Anatoly and the others fidgeted nervously afraid that their assailant might be pushed over the edge.

Suddenly he turned to Osama and said: 'Go over to them and release their bonds.'

He then asked if they would like a cup of tea.

The mood lightened at that point as everyone said they would.

Osama's gun remained pointed at the captives as they drank tea and munched some biscuits.

Anatoly decided to see if there was any chance of appealing to Hedley's rational side. His manner of speaking suggested that he had received a good education and he was religious but hopefully not in a fanatical way.

'I'm Russian,' he said. 'My country is not free. I lost my liberty because someone powerful wanted to seize my property. There was no state ready to intervene and defend the rule of law.

'I'm afraid I don't see the English under your party being any better off. A lot of people have got rich by seizing the property of others. Many of them were already well off. They succeeded because they were well-connected. Just as in my country.

'I don't think this pillage will end soon. Indeed, it is likely to become the norm. I've known you for less than an hour. But I've reached this conclusion: you don't seem to be the type who would relish that kind of society or indeed flourish in it.

'I've read about the religion which you are clearly proud of and it has some uplifting features. But let me say this.

'Probably it will come as a surprise given what you have heard from Jerome Roxburgh and others. But the government of Gavin Ogilvy is trying to pursue basically just policies and it tries to act with restraint. Probably life would be much easier for him if he simply erected a large fence where Hadrian's Wall used to be in order to keep everyone out.

'I don't know how long you have been here for. But what are your impressions of Scotland right now? Is it the cruel, unjust and corrupt place that Roxburgh describes in his nightly broadcasts?

Hedley remained silent for around thirty seconds. Then he said: 'Since I'm on a mission I find it hard to observe what everyday conditions are like here.'

Anatoly then said: ' I take it that you blended in with the latest refugee flow coming up from Yorkshire?'

'We were treated alright,' Hedley replied.

'You would have been in one of the refugee camps. You must have noticed what the atmosphere was like.'

'Yes conditions were decent, I'll admit that.'

Just at that moment, Hedley's mobile rang. It was the police. A doctor had been found. He was ready to come in.

Hedley said: 'Good. But he must be on his own and unarmed. He will be searched.'

A few seconds later there was a knock at the door. It was swiftly opened by Rashid.

The doctor was a man in his sixties, wearing a light suit. He said: 'I'm Dr Alistair Clunie. By all means search me but you won't find anything.'

Hedley looked at the slightly-built GP who didn't seem to have any bulges in his clothing and said: 'Alright doctor I believe you. Come this way.'

Dr Clunie checked the wound of Aslam who was drifting in and out of consciousness. He administered some painkilling drugs and said: 'the cartilage in this man's right knee has been smashed by a bullet. It narrowly missed an artery so he is lucky. But if the leg is to be saved he will need to be operated on before the day is out.'

Hedley said: 'Do what you can for him while you are here.'

'Can the operation be done in this room?'

'No' the doctor replied. 'It would need special equipment that cannot be transferred from a hospital.'

Hedley went back next door. He briefly explained the medical position to Anatoly and then said:

'I want my comrade to live. I've looked up to Tariq. He's been in tough situations but has tried to live his life honourably. He would disagree with my decision but I want him to go to hospital. That means three of us are left and we are rather less likely to get what we came here for. We can go out in a blaze of glory, blow ourselves up, perhaps you also.

'Then there is the surrender option. Don't imagine I haven't considered it. BEAST and the Ogilvy government will proclaim it as a victory. We will be sent off to jail. But what of our families in Bradford? It is likely they will face reprisals in that event. So we are in a grim position.'

Anatoly said: 'yes I can well see that. You've summed up the situation succinctly. That last remark of yours indicates to me that you have a rather clear understanding of Vanguard rule. It is cruel which means that there is no hesitation about sacrificing innocent people to save face or strike a note of defiance.'

Hedley put his head in his hands. It was only for a few seconds. But it was enough time for Anatoly to rush him and snatch the gun he was carrying while his accomplices were busy elsewhere in the building.

Instead Anatoly put a hand on his left shoulder and said: 'we all get into sticky situations at some point in our lives. If I try to suggest a possible way out will you at least listen'?

'Alright say what you intend, I'm listening.'

Anatoly asked: 'could you let me propose a compromise deal with the Scottish government? This is what I have in mind. Ogilvy will announce that any refugees who want to return to England at any time will be free to do so. The courts will be asked to review the sentences of those convicted of kidnapping Rodney Tripp and the murder of Hector Crawford. In addition Tariq Aslam will be treated in hospital for his serious injury. And you and your two remaining accomplices will be allowed to return to Vanguard territory.'

'The government would presumably say that it was willing to make this exceptional gesture because the siege had ended without any loss of life.'

'Alright,' Hedley replied. 'I'm going to think this over and after that I will need to discuss it with the others.'

At this point there was a knock at the door. It was Dr Clunie. He immediately said: 'I've done everything I can for the injured man. But for his leg to be saved he needs to be operated on. I also feel the shock he is experiencing could kill him. I certainly don't rate his chances of surviving as at all good if he remains here for another 24 hours.'

Hedley listened attentively and asked Osama and Rashid to come through. He then asked the doctor to repeat to them what had just been said.

'Lads,' he said, 'this is a tough call for us. If Tariq remains here, he is likely to die. I think we should allow him to be taken to hospital for the treatment that he needs.'

'But what will we get in return,' Rashid asked?

'That is a good question,' Hedley said, turning to Anatoly.

Anatoly thought and said: 'if the authorities want to appear reasonable people, then they should publicly offer an undertaking that they will make no move for 48 hours. It will allow you – us too – to get some rest.'

Rashid shook his head in agreement. Osama quickly did the same and Hedley said: 'We will allow our comrade to be taken from us if those are the terms.'

He then dialled the number and said to the policeman: 'two people wish to speak to you.'

Dr Clunie then repeated his grim diagnosis of Aslam's condition. Next, Anatoly said he was suggesting terms under which Aslam would be removed to hospital. He promised they had not been made under any kind of duress. The doctor would be able to vouch for that later. Fifteen minutes after the conversation, the police rang back to indicate that the terms were acceptable.

Hedley asked if a public statement would be made, declaring that the authorities were planning to take no action in the next 48 hours? After the pledge was given the front door was opened. By now, there was an ambulance drawn up. Two stretcher bearers came in and gently placed the by now unconscious Aslam on a stretcher.

Hedley asked for, and was given, a promise that he would be kept informed of his condition. Darkness was setting in. Several mattresses had arrived by now and he indicated it was time for everyone to try and get some sleep.

The hostages were placed in one large room and each of the remaining kidnappers took turns at watching over them until 8am the next morning.

Sleep came easily to an exhausted Hedley. When he woke next morning, he decided to give Anatoly Yashin's idea a try. It had taken him a day to conclude that he had no stomach to kill these hostages. Most were ordinary, blameless folk who had done nothing to warrant being blown up. The Russian's idea of bringing the siege to an end by some face-saving concessions seemed to be the best way out. But it would involve negotiations. So he decided that he would release Yashin if he was prepared to broker a compromise that would lead to a peaceful outcome.

But first he would need to explain to the other two what was on his mind. It could only work if each of them was in agreement. As Rashid was in the kitchen preparing omelettes for everyone, he explained the plan to him. He agreed that it meant they would leave in dignity so he was ready to back the idea.

When next he took Osama aside, he was perplexed by his reaction. He told Hedley that he must do what he had to do. But he had decided that he did not want to return to Vanguard territory. He had nobody now in Bradford. His family had either been killed or had fled. As a barber he had no job to return to. Since men had been encouraged to grow beards, half the barbers in Bradford had shut down. He had seen enough of Scotland to conclude that he would likely be happier here than in west Yorkshire given what had become of it.

Hedley thanked him for supporting the plan but said nothing about his desire to stay behind. It made things awkward as it meant that only two of the original team would be coming back, something bound to raise suspicion. He himself understood how Osama felt. But he was not renouncing the idea that the Vdemption church could turn into a spiritual movement that would rid Vanguard of its terrible impurities. Beside, his wife now called Samina, and their young son, remained in Bradford and he would shift heaven and earth not to be parted from them.

After breakfast Hedley took Anatoly aside to tell him that the others backed his proposal. This meant that Anatoly would be allowed to leave the building. There were benefits and risks. He could betray them, disclosing to the authorities where their vulnerabilities were, providing a description of the situation inside the house. He was now prepared to take that risk, saying to Anatoly:

'I trust you. From what you've told me of your life, you've abided by a code of plain-dealing and honour. That's also my code.

'I see it as an advantage if you are able to talk directly to your contacts in government. Doing it over the phone and via online communications, is time-consuming. It may also raise suspicions that you are doing this under duress.

'So you will be free to go any time from now if you wish to try and bring this siege to an end with honourable terms agreed.'

Anatoly grasped that his captor was thinking very coherently. He said: 'I agree with what you've just said. Let me now make a phone call. In fact two of them.

'First, I'll inform the police that I'm coming out. But it will be on clear condition that no rash action is taken after that. I will be a negotiator and during my time outside, you will be left undisturbed. Indeed, I will send a tweet to that effect before I leave, so the world knows it...if you allow me.'

'Of course' was the reply.

'I will also phone a journalist whom I have known and worked with since the British crisis erupted. He is well-connected, has covered many conflicts, and I hope will see the good sense in what we are both trying to do.'

When he spoke to the police, he said that he would like to see someone who had authority and so, would be able to make important decisions concerning the hostage situation.

He didn't say much to Ray Lattimore except that he would be outside, negotiating an end to the crisis, and that they should try to meet later in the day.

He reassured Kirsty and Tommy that he would be doing what he could to secure their release and he asked Moira to continue to show fortitude. Having never been a stranger to death and anxiety during her nursing career, she had kept everyone's spirits raised and had got on well with the kidnappers. He thought there was light at the end of the tunnel and he looked forward to seeing her very soon.

When Anatoly stepped out onto the porch of the BEAST office, he was glad to see there were no journalists. They had been moved far back and he was quickly placed in the back of a police vehicle which drove off towards the city centre.

A police inspector sat next to him who asked how everything was inside. Anatoly said: 'It is much better than anyone had cause to hope at the beginning. I think we might be dealing with rational people. Unless mistakes are made, I think the incident could well end peacefully.'

'I hope you're right' the inspector replied.

He told Anatoly that in a few minutes they would be arriving at Glasgow's City Chambers. It stood on the east side of George Square and it was the first major building visible to anyone who stepped off a fast train from Edinburgh.

Anatoly was certainly familiar with the 145-year-old civic building erected at the height of Glasgow's economic prowess. It was a bold example of renaissance Classicism upon which no expense had been spared. Glasgow in 1888 was widely known as the Second City of the Empire and, when he stepped inside, he was impressed by what awaited him. A Carrara marble staircase led up towards a domed mosaic ceiling decorated in gold leaf. He passed along a corridor leading to a council chamber that was decorated in Spanish mahogany panelling. It was an architectural feast which only ended when he was shown into a plainly furnished office where Grant Stevenson awaited him.

Once the minister established that he was in good condition, he asked for coffee and sandwiches to be brought and they began to talk.

Stevenson asked Anatoly to explain what the hi-jackers were looking for and, when he did so, the younger man looked pensive.

'It would be a huge loss of face for our government if the hi-jackers were allowed to return to Bradford and that after receiving some concessions.

'I just don't see how that can be justified,' he continued. 'We have prided ourselves on adopting a stern approach to serious law-breaking. It's vital to be unflinching in the highly-charged situation we are now in.'

Anatoly suddenly realised that things were more complicated than he had assumed they would be. The man whose job it was to manage the crisis was proving inflexible. The irony is that up until a few weeks ago, he had been a convinced Scottish Nationalist.

Anatoly looked more closely at Stevenson. He took in his well-scrubbed features, conventional suit and tightly-knotted tie and realised that he might be dealing with a rather rigid person.

Until the independence movement had splintered, quite a few such people had coexisted, often uneasily, with the dreamers and the fanatics. People like the legalistic and earnest Grant Stevenson had prevented the SNAP pursuing a violent path when it had been unsuccessful after 2014. Stevenson's kind were vital in countries building institutions from scratch. They believed in the rules but now, his stubborn sense of propriety, could thwart a neat end to the hostage crisis.

How much could he tell him. He decided he had nothing to lose if he levelled with him.

'Mr Stevenson, there are particular aspects to this crisis that you should know about.'

'You better go on then,' he replied.

'The lead figure Ahmed Hedley, a convert to Islam, is losing faith in the Vanguard cause. He is motivated by the quasi-political religious offshoot Vdemption but I don't know how long he will stick with that.

'I doubt if he will harm the remaining captives. There might be a suicide pact but, since he is a man of God, I doubt that too.

'He wants to return to Bradford where his family is. To be with them and share their ordeal in a city at war is what chiefly motivates him now. This is the impression I've acquired after what were candid conversations between us.'

'I'm sorry Mr Yashin,' Stevenson replied, 'Hedley may be on the road to Damascus but what he has done still makes him a terrorist. A guard was injured in the attack but, luckily, the bullet that struck him only caused a superficial head injury.'

'I'm relieved to hear that the officer's injury is a superficial one' Anatoly replied.

'If we play this by the book, there is a spectacular trial and Hedley is condemned, it is likely that his family will be harshly punished as an example to any other fighters who falter in their commitment. The North Korean approach to dissent is now part of Sutton's armoury of control. After he was apprehended in full flight, the public execution of the minister of culture confirms that.'

Stevenson chewed momentarily on a pencil and then flung it aside.

'Alright,' he said. 'I'm beginning to see some of the complexities. But I still find it hard to be seen to publicly exonerate someone who clearly started out as a terrorist. I'm just new in my job. It would be a terrible example to home-grown terrorists.'

'Not if you make it clear that there are exceptional features to this particular emergency,' Anatoly said.

'I think if there is a trial, Hedley and the other pair will be revealed as civilians caught up in a conflict not of their making. They will be swallowed up in jail for decades and their families back home will have been destroyed. This will not look good in the battle for hearts and minds which it is crucial that our side wins.'

There was a long silence before Stevenson asked about the British Democratic Authority in Liverpool. What would its main component British Liberty think if terrorists who tried to disrupt the refugee programme are left off with no trial and returned to Vanguard jurisdiction?

'That's a good question,' Anatoly replied. 'One of the things I was hoping to do before returning to Park Circus was to talk to Sam Stockwood, the minister and someone to whom I'm directly responsible. I can ask him if you like?

'I promise not to go over your head' Anatoly continued. 'You are in charge of this emergency. You have done a brave and responsible thing putting to one side your previous loyalties and taking on this tough job in such a strained atmosphere. I admire you for that.

'Yes,' Anatoly continued, 'rules and above all the rule of law need to be respected, but sometimes there is no alternative but to pursue an unorthodox approach if in the end justice still manages to be served.

'I'd merely ask you to think it over. No doubt we'll have the chance to talk again.'

Stevenson's features had softened. Part of the dilemma which he had been wrestling with had been acknowledged.

'There is another day and a bit of the ceasefire' he said and I'm not inclined to make any unilateral or rushed decisions.'

Anatoly's photo had been plastered all over the media so he had to be careful about where he met Ray Lattimore. They decided it would be easier if he came to his four star hotel to which there was a discreet entrance.

They both retired to Ray's room where Anatoly was offered a large vodka. Ray listened as Anatoly explained how it had been turned into a siege with a difference. Aslam, probably the most intransigent assailant, had hardly counted almost from the start due to being badly wounded. Hedley had revealed himself to be a tortured soul, ultimately ready for compromise. The other two Rashid and Osama took their lead from him.

The main impediment to a deal which Anatoly thought made sense was the new minister of public security. Anatoly could understand his qualms but feared that his caution could prove disastrous. At least, Anatoly said, the meeting had ended amicably once he had reached out to try and understand the minister's point of view.

Lattimore took it all in and said: 'I don't have an answer but it would help a lot if you made contact with Sam Stockwood. If you can persuade him to raise no objections to a face-saving end to the siege, then it will have strengthened your hand.'

Anatoly decided to waste no time and phoned him. After asking him how both he and the other hostages were, he listened to what Anatoly had to say.

He responded by saying: 'I understand both you and Grant Stevenson. You have a solution to the immediate crisis. He is concerned at the optics, how it will look and whether it might encourage copy-cat actions in the future.

'Nevertheless, releasing Ahmed Hedley and the others can be portrayed as a wise and proportionate measure in a time of raging cruelty.

'If the Scottish government continues to take a tough line against trouble-makers who dislike its anti-Vanguard stance, then any fuss is likely to quickly die down. I don't think Vanguard will be able to make huge capital out of a peaceful resolution of the siege. And back in Bradford Hedley might be able to do some good that is if he has renounced his previous views.

'So I'll contact my ministerial colleague Albert Tomkins who deals with security and hopefully he will agree.'

'What do you plan to do now Anatoly,' he asked?

'I think it best if I return to the BEAST office, spend the night there so that I can be in direct contact with everyone prior to the whole affair being over.'

'Good thinking,' Stockwood replied. 'Let's hope there's a soft landing. You've got a good plan and I'll support it as best I can.'

Before returning to Park Circus, Anatoly confided to Lattimore that there was an added difficulty. One of the young assailants Osama, now had no desire to return to Bradford. But he couldn't be allowed to stay in Scotland or go to a free part of England without Vanguard smelling a rat.

It was hard to see what could be done.

'A tricky one indeed,' Lattimore said with a half-smile. 'But perhaps we can cross that bridge when we come to it. It's not a unique situation in my experience covering numerous wars, especially in the Middle East where loyalties often prove to be fluid. I'll certainly give the matter thought.'

Anatoly was relieved that there was no deterioration in the atmosphere when he returned. Takeaway food from one of Glasgow's best Indian restaurants had been delivered and everyone had eaten well.

Anatoly told everyone that the plan for a peaceful end to the crisis was being actively considered by the government. It was likely that others who had an interest in the situation, such as the government in Liverpool, would also be consulted. He couldn't say when there would be a categorical response from the authorities but he hoped it would be tomorrow,

It was not until Noon the following day that Anatoly's phone rang. Ray Lattimore phoned to say that agreement seemed to be in sight. Grant Stevenson's reluctance about allowing terrorists to walk free was endorsed by several other ministers but their unhappiness receded when the BDA government in Liverpool revealed it had no objection to the plan.

An hour later an unarmed policeman stepped up to the door and slipped an envelope through the letter-box. Hedley read the contents and passed the message to Anatoly.

It was a short communiqué which said that the Scottish government was prepared to allow the hostage-takers to go free as long as the people they had seized were un-harmed. It would also not stand in the way of any refugees who, as a result of a change of heart, wished to go back to Vanguard territory. Finally, it mentioned that sentencing for crimes related to the conflict were subject to periodic review and recent sentences would be looked into.

The message had been released to the media and it concluded by reiterating that the government would display absolute firmness in its response to attacks from whatever quarter which put civilians at risk and threatened the security of the Scottish state.

Anatoly was relieved that the moderate line had prevailed. Stevenson would have to defend it even though his heart was not in it. Being a disciplined politician he expected he would do so to the best of his professional ability.

The spirits of Moira and the others soared when they learned of the likelihood of beings set free before the day was over. In fact it wasn't until 4pm that they walked into the pale autumn sunshine. There had been talks to work out how Hedley and his colleagues would be brought back to England. Anatoly had been involved from 2pm. When he told the minister that one of the assailants was now declining to leave Scotland, the minister slapped his forehead with the palm of his hand and ex-claimed: 'Christ. Isn't this all we need. A terrorist who decides he likes us after all.'

That morning Lattimore had mentioned to Anatoly that he might have a plan for solving the problem. Anatoly told the minister that it would be worth at least hearing what the journalist proposed. He had long experience not only reporting troubled conflicts but trying to allow reason and humanity to prevail where possible. He discreetly let it drop that he was also romantically involved with Secretary of State McKenna.

'Oh well, I suppose I don't have any choice Stevenson said wearily. How soon can Lattimore get to the City Chambers'?

'I believe he is probably right outside as we speak,' Anatoly replied.

The Russian had no idea what Lattimore's plan consisted of and when he heard the details even his eyebrows were raised.

Lattimore said: 'I am convinced that the peaceful return of Ahmed Hedley to Bradford will work in our favour in the long run. I think it will also be relatively easy to swat away criticism from Bruce's side and the press, arguing that the government has mishandled the crisis, creating an ominous precedent.

'However, the refusal of Osama Khan to leave creates a problem. If we agree to keep him here Vanguard will assume that the hostage-takers have gone over to the enemy. The chances of Hedley and his family remaining unharmed in the face of an increasingly paranoid Vanguard leadership, would be slim.

'My suggestion is that Khan be persuaded to go south with the others but that *en route* – and still within Scotland – a problem develops on the road which enables him to escape (the details of this can be worked out later).

'Now minister here's the tricky part. This subterfuge stands more chance of succeeding if Vanguard are "involved."'

'What!' The minister exclaimed, half rising from his chair.

'Yes, you heard me correctly.

'By Vanguard I mean the True British Hub, the information agency the regime has been allowed to establish in Edinburgh.'

'This is giving Vanguard the right to operate openly in Scotland,' the minister proclaimed. 'Jerome Roxburgh will have a field day as he boasts how they were allowed to escort back to England people who had been sent to Scotland to wage terror.'

'Indeed I can understand how you might see it that way,' Lattimore replied smoothly.

'But if they are taking several of their own operatives out of Scotland and one of them runs away,' it removes rather a lot of the shine from their PR exercise.

'Moreover, the person who is likely to be escorting them back is Tristram Pannell.'

Stevenson's attention became more focussed as Lattimore said: 'ever since a peaceful end to the hostage crisis became possible, he has been taking great interest.

'I think if he was asked to take charge of the return of the kidnappers, he would jump at the prospect and try to ensure that his allies in London promote the idea.

'Of course we would need to exercise vigilance. The Vanguard people in the vehicles would not be allowed to carry any weapons in case they shot at the fleeing Osama.

'I suspect that once they arrived in Bradford, the welcome awaiting them would be subdued and Pannell would have a lot of explaining to do.'

'Evidently you don't have a lot of time for Pannell,' Stevenson observed.

'No I don't,' Lattimore replied. 'He's played a shabby role in this crisis right from the outset. All he really cares about is reviving his own political career and playing a king-size role in any realignment that occurs in London.

'He still has admirers in America and Europe from his time as Prime Minister. Anything that can be done to clip his wings will only be for the good in the long run.'

After making a few phone calls, Stevenson agreed to Lattimore's proposal. The Bradford 3, as they were now known in the media, would be kept in comfortable government lodgings until the arrangements were finalised for their trip back to England.

Back home in Edinburgh as Anatoly and Moira reviewed the last convulsive forty-eight hours, he suddenly turned to her and said: 'Shouldn't we think of getting married? The kidnapping shows danger can leap out of the shadows at any moment.'

'Taking Moira's hand,' Anatoly went on: 'you are the best thing that has happened to me since I turned up in Britain nearly three years ago.

'You're a kind and loving person who has brought stability into my life. You were vital in helping to calm the spirits of the hostage-takers and your treatment of the wounded Aslam won the respect of the other three.

'I just want the world to know how attached we are to one another whatever awaits us in the future.'

Tears had welled up in Moira's eyes as Anatoly spoke. She simply said: 'I want that too and I think you know that. Let's not waste any time about it' and then they kissed.

On Tuesday morning Anatoly explained to Moira that it was likely he would be accompanying the Bradford 3 as far as the border with England. He told her it made a lot of sense to do so. It was a plan that he had worked out with Hedley that was being put into effect and perhaps it was likelier to proceed smoothly if he was there. What he held back from telling her was that there would be a ruse to enable Osama Khan to escape.

That afternoon news came through that Tristram Pannell would have a role in the handover. After this had been agreed, the plan was worked on.

Two escort vehicles of the Scottish government would escort the Bradford 3 to Berwick-upon-Tweed. They would be in another two vehicles. Pannell would travel with Hedley while Anatoly would be with Khan and Sharif. A member of Pannell's staff would be in each car.

They would be unarmed but the escorting vehicles would contain armed police to guard against an ambush.

The small motorcade left the centre of Edinburgh on Wednesday 27 September and would wind its way through the eastern suburbs and onto the A1. The journey to Bradford was expected to take four hours. The cross-over into Vanguard territory had been expected to be the only tense moment. But as the convoy was slowly driving past the service station at Grantshouse in the Scottish Borders, a motorcycle suddenly turned out onto the carriageway at considerable speed. It hit the last escort car which then ploughed into the back of the vehicle carrying Anatoly, Khan and Sharif. The other two cars drove on and it was only after about a mile that it was noticed that they had become separated from the others.

Back at the scene of the collision all attention was directed at the motorcyclist. He looked to be a biker, possibly as old as 75. The front of his Harley Davidson bike was a tangle of twisted metal. The driver was lying on the side of the road, his helmet having rolled down an embankment. He appeared unconscious, blood flowing from a gaping head wound.

Anatoly joined the two police in the escort vehicle to see what could be done. Medical assistance was called up and, as gently as they could, they carried the biker to the grass verge to avoid him being hit by another vehicle.

Ten minutes elapsed before they returned to their own vehicle. Rashid had joined them but now Osama was nowhere to be seen.

At first it was assumed that he might well have entered the service station to use the toilet. But a search soon proved fruitless. By now the other two vehicles had doubled back. Pannell was indignant when it sank in that he would be showing up in Bradford with one fewer of the hostage-takers.

'How could this have happened? He must be found. This is just not good at all' were his strained remarks.

Hedley stayed silent. He had known about Osama's unwillingness to return. The young man had no family now and the regime could not easily take reprisals if he had absconded.

The head of the escort's security told Pannell that every effort would be made to find Khan and, once that was done, he would be sent south. But it was best to continue as another three hours on the road lay before them.

At Berwick-upon-Tweed the Bradford pair were transferred to another vehicle and a different escort, belonging to the British Democratic Authority, took over. Farewells between Anatoly and Hedley were formal even stiff. It was important not to give the impression that they had ceased to be adversaries and that Hedley had acquired Anatoly's view of what lay behind the conflict and what must be done to move on.

Anatoly did not need to ask about the condition of the injured motorcyclist. He was a stuntman in the acting business who was known to Gavin Ogilvy. He had contacted his old colleague as soon as the plan was laid before him. It appealed to the buccaneering side of his nature. Lyall Burnett, the stuntman, was an expert in his craft. With the help of copious amounts of fake blood, he was able to pretend to be unconscious for half-an-hour. He knew how to mimic a serious crash while jumping clear a split second before impact.

As an admirer of the job his old colleague was performing in politics, he asked for no fee and, of course, agreed to remain silent. Osama would go south but much further than England. Kayley Wright, the New Zealand ambassador, greatly admired the work of BEAST. She had accepted Anatoly's assurance that there was every likelihood Osama would be a productive citizen if granted admission to his country.

The strange and anti-climactic ending to the Siege of Park Circus helped kill the story after only a few days. Of course Jerome Roxburgh fulminated about a humiliating climb-down but increasingly he was seen as an empty vessel, at least among the international press corps.

Vanguard made far less of the drama than might have been expected. Only two of the original four had returned (though Aslam might do so after his injuries healed).

Anatoly and Moira had both been impressed by Ahmed Hedley. He was one of the many essentially decent characters whose life had been disrupted by the war. Anatoly hoped they might meet up again and, towards that end, had shown him a discreet way of establishing contact if the need, or the opportunity, ever arose.

Chapter 10:

Ireland's Singular Downfall

For the duration of the siege Gavin Ogilvy had kept out of the limelight. He had accepted the advice of his communications director Brian Crawford that there was nothing to be gained by dramatising the crisis.

It was in fact his preference to be low-key at such times and he was glad that a key adviser who had helped to launch the Vanguard bandwagon at the start of the 2020s possessed similar instincts.

The hostage drama was a test for Grant Stevenson and he had passed it well. He shelved his own preference for a cautious approach when it became clear that the novel strategy devised by Anatoly Yashin might just work. And it did.

Besides the Prime Minister's attention was diverted by other security concerns. A mysterious spate of bombings had continued ever since Bruce's trial and the North Ayrshire by-election. There may have been few casualties and limited damage but Ogilvy and his advisers were not complacent. They feared that a 'dirty' chemical bomb in a densely populated area could be detonated that could cause huge loss of life. Vanguard might now be back on the defensive but it was fully in character if Clive Sutton launched one spectacular operation in Scotland just to show that he was still a force to be reckoned with. He was slowing down the advance of coalition forces in England by using scorched earth tactics that were causing immense suffering to civilians.

His only real backing was to be found among pockets of sympathisers in west-central Scotland imbued with an ingrained anti-British outlook. There were firstly Irish-origin Scots who clung to an enclave mentality. Then there were others, often middle-class, and from a conventional religious and professional family background for whom Scottish Nationalism had acquired the status of a new religion. Ironically, several of the most avid promoters of this line were Church of Scotland ministers who had turned their parishes into arenas of a 'feel-good' religion stripped of any meaningful spiritual core.

For the first group of ethnic irreconcilables, Scottish Nationalism was merely a tool to express their anti-Britishness. For the second it was a means of shaking off bourgeois conventions and exploring a wild and elemental side to their natures. Both managed to overlook the cruelty of Vanguard towards the equivalent of their own grandparents in England. Even by acting like a latter-day Genghiz Khan, laying waste the land that had long prevented Scotland's 'destiny' being realised, Clive Sutton was objectively on the right side of history. He was a 'bad' guy doing a lot of worthwhile things. It was his 'progressive' dimension which only really counted for these restless Scots.

Such views about Vanguard could only really be expressed *sotto voce* in the SFF where the neo-Vanguard Scots made up a large fringe. Clova Bruce was aware of their presence. As a showbiz celebrity who had gravitated to front-rank politics, she also had a tendency to see what primarily suited her interest of the moment. She was not gripped by anti-English prejudices but she was almost completely numb to the suffering millions had experienced for several years. She was not wilfully cruel like Sutton but, as a supreme egotist, the distress of others beyond her immediate line of vision meant very little to her. She had certainly put Davy Trainor's death behind her and had had two fleeting affairs with men of similar age to his after she had dodged prison.

Vanguard's Scottish fifth column would not have been of such concern to the Prime Minister but for the support it was able to derive from the Republic of Ireland. The smaller neighbouring island had not been sucked into the English conflict. But there had been no lack of turbulence in the early 2020s there as well. The reasons were mainly internal ones. The gulf between a mediocre and self-serving political elite and much of the rest of society had grown to be an unbridgeable one. In the past Ireland's democratic institutions had been preserved by encouraging mass emigration. But this outlet had been closed off by the English crisis and the reduction in transport links between Ireland and much of the rest of the English-speaking world.

The quality of people entering politics, never high in the years since the Irish state had been founded, had fallen to a very low level by the early 21st century. Increasingly, many politicians were little more than rent-seekers. Often they occupied a parliamentary seat in order to derive the maximum financial opportunity for themselves and their families. In turn, they dispensed favours to well-placed individuals and groups in the constituency who could ensure their re-election.

Increasingly, it was also hard to tell the parties apart. Fianna Fail (Soldiers of Destiny) had long ceased to be nationalist and was an ardent exponent of a European Union that was far more centralizing than Britain had ever been when it ruled Ireland. Its great rival, Fine Gael, once a pillar of social conservatism, had become an advocate of experimentation across the social spectrum. As for the Irish Labour Party, it had gone from being a force promoting greater economic equality to one championing the interests of some of the most privileged groups in society.

No party backed open borders with such zeal even though the result was that real wages tumbled in many sectors and inequalities widened along with heavy pressure on badly run social services. But the greatest surprise was perhaps the one provided by Sinn Fein. Long committed to abolishing the border by militant means, many were astonished at how quickly it embraced the spoils system and put aside its territorial preoccupations.

A form of dynastic politics exacerbated the low quality of political representation. A lot of seats were handed down three or four generations as family heirlooms. In government, often grasping but poorly prepared figures made regular blunders. They had backed Ireland's acquisition of the Euro in the 1990s even though it left it with a different currency from its main trading partners in Britain and the USA. After the year 2,000 a policy of easy money produced a credit splurge which led to a sharp economic contraction when the global financial bubble collapsed in 2008. Half-a-decade of crippling austerity ensued with the major financial players at the heart of the gambling frenzy being quietly looked after by the state.

Perhaps most extraordinarily of all, a previously conservative elite sought to shore up its legitimacy among the young by ardently championing a lifestyle revolution. It was not just gay marriage but championing transgender relations and promoting polygamy where Ireland became an outrider in the West.

It enabled the political class to parade on the global political catwalk wearing halos of political correctness. But the run of luck enjoyed by one of the most mediocre ruling elites in Europe was about to come to an abrupt end by 2020.

Irish youth revolted about the same time as Vanguard took off but not for identical or even similar reasons. Far from it. There was a backlash against hedonism from the segment of Irish youth which had never derived much benefit from exploring every point on the compass of the permissive society. The media forgot that a lot of young men and women still had age-old wants. They desired to settle down, acquire a stable job, a roof over their heads, so that they could start to raise a family.

Paschal Rogan was a 27-year-old carpenter from Sligo who had the eloquence to express the disappointment and sense of exclusion of such young people with the Dublin elite. He first came to notice by protesting about the state's inaction in face of the swelling population of homeless on Irish streets. He got flung out of the Irish Parliament, the Dail after TDs had made themselves the highest-paid parliamentarians in Europe. His movement was called Muintir which means 'people' in Irish. It attracted the support of other age-groups and took off following the disruption by secularists of a religious procession in Galway on the feast of Corpus Christi.

Rogan and his supporters drove the secularists off the streets. He stayed in the public eye as clashes occurred outside school gates due to attempts being made to remove the last vestiges of religious influence from state schools. His Muintir party won 16 seats in the 2020 general election, helped by the establishment of an online news agency to promote its conventional outlook.

The established parties watched the challenge to their monopoly with horror. But someone else was paying even closer attention – the Dublin drug lord Emmett Macklin. He had, for some years, been seeking to acquire absolute control over the criminal underworld of the Irish capital. Turf wars over territory between criminal families had made Dublin a more violent city than Belfast. Macklin's sheer ruthlessness meant that he prevailed (although he was left with a permanent limp thanks to a botched assassination). By the end of 2020 everyone involved in the drug trade who refused to owe allegiance to him, had been driven out or killed. As criminals went, Macklin was well-read and even scholarly. While serving a four-year jail sentence early in his criminal career, the 42-year-old had done a degree in law and politics at Dublin City University, earning First Class honours. His immersion in political science literature convinced him that even the present Irish political elite might pose a threat to his criminal empire. There was always the danger that a politician would break away from the pack and make a name for himself by launching a drive against serious crime. He recalled how the crisis over Britain leaving the EU had convinced some Irish leaders that they could be the architects of a united Ireland by playing hardball over the terms of Britain's withdrawl.

Macklin concluded that the only way he could expect to stay on top was to set up a new party and try to build a new political order geared to his interests. Politicians would have to be answerable to the narcotics industry in the same way as they upheld the interests of property developers, lawyers and big farmers. After all, he told his closest allies, no other sector of the economy enjoyed such a large flow of revenue as the Irish drugs trade.

He knew that if he was to get anywhere he would need to confront Sinn Fein. This would mean breaking the hold that the party exercised in many working-class areas of Dublin. A new party, Irish Sunrise, took on the Republicans. Away from politics, Macklin sought to break their hold over large working-class estates from Tallaght in the south of the city to Ballyfermot in the north. Intimidation and terror were the means that came handiest to him. Candidates who stood for Sinn Fein received a rough time. Any voters who displayed Republican posters had windows smashed and their cars burned out. In 2010 provoking Sinn Fein like this would have been suicidal. But by 2021 it had moved too far into conventional politics to be able to defend itself. Dissident republican groups, long cynical about the late 20th century peace settlement which had ended the conflict in Northern Ireland, stood by as the squeeze was put on Sinn Fein. The violent power struggle of 2021, which gave Dublin the nickname of the Beirut of Western Europe, was one master-minded by a very smart criminal brain.

After six months of urban warfare, Sunrise was the new political master of proletarian Dublin. Macklin was shrewd enough to base his domination not just on fear but also respect. He organized a programme of renewal in these neglected neighbourhoods. Medical services, housing and road repairs and social welfare provision improved. It meant elbowing aside, sometimes roughly, the conventional parties and taking over big chunks of the local state.

Macklin's appetite for power was tempered by wisdom. He knew that it was probably futile for him to try and extend his control over the whole of the Irish Republic. He decided to concentrate his energies on Dublin and its environs. It was an area that corresponded to what became known in medieval times as the Pale, stretching from Dundalk in the north to Dalkey in the south. It corresponded to the full extent of Anglo-Norman power in the east of Ireland. In a world full of countries where power did not extend far beyond the capital, 'the Pale' had become much used as a term to describe limited central authority.

Macklin had decided that he would have more staying-power if he established a form of indirect rule. His would be a fiefdom where he operated from the shadows, dispensing both coercion and rewards. Besides, Dublin and its hinterland contained by far the bulk of the population, so keeping it under his heel would always be a full-time job.

He installed a loyal lieutenant in the south-east. Its ports were closest to south Britain and indeed to the continent. A southern ally whom Macklin decided lacked the daring to challenge him, ran the important province of Munster from the city of Cork.

The west of Ireland and the Midlands were a headache. The Muintir movement was dominant in a region where organized crime had always been weak. Paschal Rogan had watched the rise of Macklin and his Dublin Narco party with alarm. He had accurately perceived that it lacked any real political content and was just an audacious front for organised crime. But he ceased to count when his body was washed up on the beach at Enniscrone in the west of County Sligo. He was a fanatical surfer who took full advantage of the ideal conditions for challenging the waves in this part of north-west Ireland. He had been seen going out on his board on an early spring day in 2022. Conditions were fair but when he had not returned by lunchtime, a search was organized only for his body to be found on a remote stretch of beach a few hours later.

There was no apparent sign of violence on his body but an unfamiliar yacht had been seen off the coast at the time of its disappearance and there was no trace of it afterwards. Rogan's wife Dymphna suspected foul play since there had been several angry phone calls between Macklin and her husband just before his death. She and her children fled to Northern Ireland taking her husband's body. A post mortem later found that he had been strangled by a nylon fishing line meant to leave few traces of violence.

Rogan's successor fell into line and accepted Macklin's broad overlordship in return for some autonomy. West-central Ireland became one of the four constituent parts in a semi-federal state. Macklin had enough sense to allow the Muintir people in Galway to pursue the kind of socially conservative policies which most people elsewhere thought had summed up Ireland for centuries.

For Macklin wielding power was more satisfying than enjoying the trappings of office. Being involved in ceremonial protocol was energy sapping and afforded too many opportunities for his enemies to strike back through another assassination attempt. He contented himself with presiding over a directory of four high septs as they were called. It enabled him to keep a beady eye on potential foes and ensured that any regional challenges to his control were contained with pitiless efficiency.

The first man in Macklin's regime was a former librarian Louis Carmody. Under a revision of the 1937 constitution Ireland became a semi-presidential republic. The President had control of foreign affairs and defence and had a large budget to play with.

Carmody had been the respectable face of the Dublin Sunrise party. This portly figure with his shock of white hair, jowly face, rolling gait and trademark red braces became a regular figure on the media whenever bloody happenings had to be explained away. He was genial, disarming and slippery. His sense of humour and coolness under pressure were spotted by Macklin who saw that they could be real assets for him. He could help Dublin Sunrise acquire a respectable image which belied its murderous nature.

Carmody ran the Irish Pale Book Festival. Like similar ventures, the post-2008 economic crisis had hit it hard. Macklin ploughed money into it. Big names in the world of literature were sought out. They included Arthur Gorman. He politely declined an invitation to transfer his role as a university reformer back to his own native land.

Even though he was offered the full cost of establishing a new university in the Irish Midlands where he could shape the curriculum, he was highly resistant. It did not take him long to spot that the finances for the new seat of learning would be from dubious sources. He learned from family and friends that lively discussions occurred at the book events but they were confined to very narrow limits. Any writers who were prompted to move beyond safe and picaresque subjects could very soon place themselves in harm's way. Gorman may have stayed away but the big money persuaded many of the top players of the publishing world in Britain to relocate to Ireland from London. Few were as fastidious as Gorman about the tainted nature of the patronage available.

Gorman had few illusions about some of the titans of London publishing but he was sad to see that Carmody, flush with narcotics proceeds, had won over a large portion of the Irish cultural elite. The roguish populist Charles Haughey had tried to seduce intellectuals with tax breaks and sundry state favours fifty years previously. But he was an amateur compared with Carmody who put a portion of his bottomless coffers at the disposal of the literary world. Book festivals increasingly resembled lavish parties that went on for days. Writers who discussed their work received fees unavailable anywhere else in the world. Publishers and travel firms who transported them to the venues also benefited. Huge adverts promoting the book festival calendar appeared in the censored press. Online there was also energetic promotion of what some irreverently called 'the Island of No Saints, Some Books and Countless Drug Pushers.'

The genial, patient and resourceful Carmody presided over this vast intellectual shadow land. Any writer, agent or publisher who refused to toe the line soon found that there was a harsher and quite unforgiving side to this roly-poly literary impresario. Macklin's coercive apparatus would be directed against any ingrate. Nobody was ever killed but intellectuals who stepped out of line were roughed up, their houses set on fire and their tax affairs investigated by the state.

Macklin admired Carmody's handiwork so much that he thought there was nobody better than him to act as his frontman. He enjoyed being the centre of attention at formal occasions and bestowed a pleasing image on the regime at United Nations gatherings and the annual St Patrick's Day ceremony at the White House.

But invitations to President Carmody dried up once it was pointed out to his US counterpart what some of the downsides of the Irish narco-state were turning out to be. The United States had learned to live with regimes whose severe levels of internal violence were sometimes orchestrated from the very top. President Wallace grew impatient with the Dublin regime when signs grew that Irish citizens were aiding extremists opposed to his key Scottish ally.

Macklin had discouraged cross-border activity meant to destabilise the British-ruled north-east of the island. He was well aware that the USA had invested much in the 25-year peace process. It had limped on despite acute difficulties at times. Indeed, for some years Northern Ireland was the most stable part of the British Isles, a contrast to England as it was descending into violence on a previously unimagined scale.

It was also very late in the day when the Dublin regime discovered that dissident Republicans were shipping guns and explosives to Scotland. Vanguard agents based in Dublin were paying for these shipments. Fishing boats slipped into sleepy ports in south-west Scotland to land their deadly cargo. Intelligence agents had seen the leading SFF politician Teddy McCusker in Dublin on several occasions and it was assumed that he had a role in the arms smuggling.

The Scottish journalist was on good terms with President Carmody. After the British Democratic Authority warned him there could be unfortunate consequences, Macklin took steps to block off the weapons route. The Irish ambassador was simultaneously summoned to the State Department and given a dressing down by no less a person than Secretary McKenna herself. Soon the pressure yielded results. Macklin put his foot down. Surveillance was tightened on all fishing ports from Dublin to the Ulster border. The Muintir authorities in the Irish west were ordered to curtail shipments of weapons from County Donegal to the nearest Scottish island, Islay.

However, a huge cache of arms and explosives had already made it to Scotland. It was enough for an armed putsch to be mounted against Ogilvy if the right conditions presented themselves. And by the late autumn of 2023 it was still a mystery where the munitions and arms were located.

The threat posed by a Scottish fifth column of Vanguard became sickeningly obvious for the Prime Minister with the abduction of Greer McIver in the first weekend of October 2023. It was a Saturday morning and he had been showing fellow physicians, from the UN's World Health Organization, around the gardens of Threave near Castle Douglas in south-west Scotland. A lush micro-climate, aided by the Gulf Stream, enabled some of the sub-tropical plants to be found in Madeira, to flourish there. Dry weather and decent temperatures had made it a splendid autumn. The rhododendrons for which Threave was especially renowned, continued to bloom in abundance.

It was from the middle of a rhododendron bush that three masked men rushed at McIver and his guests as they passed by. They were held at gun-point and tied up while the Scot was dragged away.

An hour later they were discovered by one of the gardeners and the alarm was raised. Gavin Ogilvy was working on a speech that he was due to give at the UN General Assembly when he received the news that his partner had been kidnapped. He knew Greer's work re-settling English refugees in such large numbers had made him a prime target. He occasionally wondered what he would do if he was suddenly taken from him. Now that moment had come. His partner was in mortal danger. That is if he was even still alive.

Ogilvy knew that he must somehow retain control of his emotions. It was something that he had been trained to do as an actor and was a skill that he had further honed as his political responsibilities grew ever heavier. But he knew desperate dangers now confronted him and he fought back tears as he thought that he and Greer might be separated forever.

He quickly composed himself when there was a knock at the door of his study. It was Grant Stevenson, the minister who would have the chief operational role in this new crisis.

Ogilvy had grown to respect the former Nationalist for his flinty approach to his duties. He was cool-headed, albeit ready to err too much on the side of caution.

'Awful news Prime Minister' were his first words.

'I know Grant. But we just have to carry on as best we can. I have no other option but to adopt that attitude.

'Do we know anything concrete at this stage,' he asked?

'A speed boat had been spotted near Port William just before the abduction. There had always been strong suspicions that it had been one of the places into which weapons were being smuggled. It is now nearly three hours since the incident and if Greer McIver had been put on board a fast-moving craft, he could have landed in Ireland by now.

'The County Down coast is near' Stevenson went on. 'There are different ways in which he could be smuggled across the border without the authorities being able to detect anything.'

At this point they were joined by Brian Crawford, the communications chief. He asked Ogilvy whether some kind of statement should be issued.

The Prime Minister threw the question back at him.

'What do you think Brian? This is your field after all.'

'Well Prime Minister I think we need to say something. It will be unfortunate if it is the kidnappers who break the news first with a bold and threatening statement containing their demands.

'I would suggest a short statement to the effect that Greer McIver the co-ordinator for refugee resettlement went missing this morning. He was seized by armed men and his whereabouts are unknown. This is the latest in a series of violent actions meant to disrupt the peace of Scotland which Mr McIver has contributed to with his work in the refugee field. The government remains resolute in the face of this despicable incident. Of course it will do all in its power to secure the release of Mr McIver unharmed while doing nothing to place in danger the security and safety of Scotland and its citizens.'

'I think an important balance has been struck there Brian,' Ogilvy replied. 'Thank you. It shows we are not panicking nor must we in the coming days however grave the situation becomes.'

At that point Ogilvy got up, straightened his back and said: 'We all have work to do. My schedule remains unaltered. I still intend to be in New York next Thursday. We must go on. Terror has struck very close to me. But I will try to remain unflinching. I owe this at least to you my colleagues and advisers and many others who have placed their trust in me.'

Stevenson and Crawford were relieved that the Prime Minister was able to display such fortitude in what was sure to be an ordeal for him. The lack of news added to the sense of foreboding. Then 24 hours later events occurred in quick succession. First, a burnt-out speedboat was found in a remote creek on the Cooley peninsula. It faced onto the Mountains of Mourne in Northern Ireland, separated by Carlingford Lough. The place was a home for small farmers and fishermen and had been a bolt hole for Republicans from Belfast during the Ulster troubles.

A Dublin dentist with a holiday home in the area had found the wreckage of the boat while exercising his dog. He had heard a loud explosion during the night but knew better than to exercise his curiosity at an hour when subversives could well be on the prowl.

Amos Dooley, the Irish Foreign Minister, placed his index finger under the tip of his nose as he assessed the news. He had been talked into taking the job by President Carmody a few months before. He had accepted on the understanding that it would be an essentially decorative role with any political heavy-lifting left to Louis and of course Macklin.

A light protocol role suited him well. He had been one of Ireland's first sommeliers. His wine-tasting skills had made him a well-known figure in the Irish hotel world during the good times. The *nouveaux riches* relied on him to identify the best wines as they stocked their cellars in what was thought to be a never-ending boom. But when the music stopped with the crash of leading banks in 2008, Dooley found that, virtually overnight, the demand for his services had dried up.

His villa in the affluent Dublin suburb of Howth was facing repossession when Carmody threw him a lifeline. He bowled him over with the request to be Foreign Minister in the government he was forming. Dooley was a suave fellow able, from his hotelier's training, to find the right word for most occasions and also to overlook unseemly behaviour. Near the end of the boom, he had become briefly known to Irish television viewers when he hosted a series on the art of wine tasting. Now he was all set to emigrate to Australia to see if he could break into the world of the sommelier Down Under until Carmody came along with his intriguing offer.

Dooley's main asset was that he was unruffled and dignified, some might say unctuous. He would be expected to display a serene countenance while murders and beatings periodically took place.

But when the crisis occurred Carmody was 5,000 miles away in New York, preparing for the UN General Assembly. Dooley was on his own.

He knew it was certain that the Scottish authorities would be shortly breathing down his neck. Within minutes of the burnt-out boat's discovery, a group calling itself Irish Vanguard Solidarity (IVS) issued a statement. It was the second major development and it read:

'Greer McIver is one of the most destructive figures in Britain. He has been trying to alter the social geography of the north of the island by emptying Yorkshire of a large part of its population and moving those people to Scotland. He is therefore responsible for major crimes against the anti-imperialist cause in these islands. At the request of our Vanguard comrades in England, McIver has been taken into our custody. He was seized in a revolutionary action. There is no intention to harm him unless the Scottish government tries to release him and Irish accomplices are reckless enough to help it. In due course McIver will stand in judgement for his crimes. The Vanguard government in London will know how to deal with him. The IVS will do all in its power to ensure that revolutionary justice is not long delayed in the case of the people's enemy Greer McIver.'

Just to show that this was no ruse, the statement was accompanied by a head and shoulders photo of McIver who seemed to be holding up a copy of that morning's *Irish Times* whose headline proclaimed: 'Mystery of Top Scottish Doctor's Seizure

Continues.' If the statement was true, then Clive Sutton's regime was dragging its western neighbour into the conflict. There had been complaints in London that Ireland's neutrality was being interpreted in ways that benefited the British-American coalition. Now Dooley realised that he was in for a hard time from Edinburgh and possibly Liverpool and Washington also.

As he massaged his delicate nostrils with the tips of his fingers, the desk phone buzzed. It was the Scottish Foreign Minister Catriona Douglas, asking to speak to him.

She was one of those terse and abrupt Scots unlikely to be put off by honeyed words from a pillar of the Irish hospitality industry.

True to form she got right to the point: 'I'm phoning because of the kidnapping of Greer McIver. He is a dedicated public servant who has played a key role in relieving suffering on a mass scale and keeping my country safe. Irish citizens have been involved in his seizure. The likelihood is that he is being kept prisoner in your country. The authorities in Dublin must not rest until McIver is set free and his assailants detained. As a sign of your good will, I would be grateful if you would allow Scottish and also American intelligence agents to play a role in this operation.'

Dooley said that he would ensure that this request would receive the earliest consideration but it was not one he was authorised to decide upon. Douglas interjected to say: 'It's no secret that power does not only rest in the hands of President Carmody. Please talk with whoever you have to in order to ensure that our people can be on the ground in Dublin as quickly as possible.'

His heart pounding Dooley phoned the feared Macklin and found him to be less forbidding than he had anticipated. The *eminence grise* of Dublin politics urged him to stay calm and to await orders. Meanwhile sympathisers of the SFF living in Dublin would be taken into custody and questioned.

Those raids on people, some of whom turned out to be little more than vocal supporters of Celtic's Shamrock army, were given blanket attention by the Irish media. They were paralleled in Scotland by a much more systematic crackdown. It did not just stop at Irish-orientated militants who had lauded Vanguard for capsizing British power. Jimmy Dobson a well-known Celtic supporter and one of Bruce's Glasgow stalwarts, was picked up. So was Teddy McCusker. His journalism had grown so bellicose that he could only find outlets in fringe nationalist publications. In one hard-hitting piece he had warned that Ogilvy was bound to directly feel the heat for refusing to see that Vanguard was here to stay.

The SFF organized protests outside Barlinnie prison where McCusker and the others were being detained. The nine SFF parliamentarians brought proceedings at Holyrood to a halt the day after, all of them having to be physically removed from the chamber after shouting down the Presiding Officer. Most citizens, however were appalled at the latest and worst terrorist action on Scottish soil. Greer McIver had become widely respected for his selfless and very professional approach to the refugee issue. Civil liberties activist had criticised the detentions but after 36 hours of questioning, McCusker and the rest were quietly set free.

Five days after McIver's kidnapping, BBC Vanguard urged viewers to get ready for a sensational edition of the Jerome Roxburgh show later that evening. The leading propagandist was dressed in combat fatigues. He announced that there was an extra-special guest on the show. A blurred figure appeared who was behind a set of bars. The camera then panned in to reveal someone in a striped prison uniform. He was in a cage and above his head was a placard which read: 'Vanguard's Convict Number 1.'

It was not immediately possible to tell that it was Greer McIver. The captive's hair had been removed. He sported a black eye and his lower lip was puffed up. By the state of him he had suffered a beating at some point in the recent past.

McIver had kept out of the limelight but people who knew him from the worlds of medicine, Scottish rugby and refugee work soon saw it was him. An impassive man just stared grimly ahead.

Gavin Ogilvy was with some rugby-playing friends when the programme came on. He could not hold back his emotions as he saw his partner alive but in such a reduced state, his thick mop of brown hair shaved off and marks of a beating on his face. For the first time since the news that Greer had been taken came though, his composure deserted him. He felt the tears well up and he began to weep copiously. As his friends tried to console him, he jumped up and ran from the room, saying 'Oh my god, Oh my god.'

Ogilvy left just before the next act in Roxburgh's grisly show. The propagandist opened the door of the cage and stepped in. He rudely picked up the prisoner's right hand and asked the camera to pan in on the ring he was wearing, one with a small garnet stone that had been a gift from Ogilvy when they decided to make their lives together.

'So much for the unbreakable bond this ring is supposed to signify,' Roxburgh cackled. 'Clive Sutton warned Gavin Ogilvy, when they met in Bradford, that Vanguard's reach is long and don't we now have proof of that before us'?

Unless Roxburgh had somehow been spirited across to Ireland, the place where McIver had last been heard of, it was almost certain that the captive had been moved to somewhere in England.

The Scottish authorities remained determined to investigate how the Irish operation had been staged and how high was the level of involvement. But now attention swung to England. The next day Vanguard announced that McIver would shortly be placed on trial. The charge would be treason which had always been subject to the death penalty. Needless, to say Vanguard had expanded the number of offences for which capital punishment applied, including defacing Vanguard symbols in a public place.

The headlines were grim in the Scottish evening press: 'The End Could be Nigh for Greer,' 'Prime Minister's Partner faces the Hangman,' 'Ogilvy's Worst Nightmare.'

The Prime Minister curtailed all official duties for the next few days. He was suffering an emotional crisis, having seen what had happened to Greer. At least he was alive but only agony and further humiliation seemed to lie in store for him. To make matters worse, there was so little he could do for his partner despite the power he exercised.

At least he had found some solace in prayer. He received consolation from the Rev Alan Smithers. He had played rugby for Scotland before going on to pursue a ministry in the Free Presbyterian Church. They briefly prayed together at dawn in St Giles Cathedral on Edinburgh's Royal Mile, reciting Psalm 130, De Profundis:

'Out of the depths have I cried unto thee, O Lord, Lord hear my voice: let thine ears be attentive to the voice of my supplications….

Lord, hear my prayer...'

A few hours later, Ogilvy was airborne, heading for the United Nations General Assembly but knowing that it was the relentless march of events at home which would determine so much that was dear to him and vital for the future of Scotland.

Chapter 11

An Old Bailey Trial Interrupted

A week later, the Vanguard authorities announced that the Irish barrister Phelim Armstrong would be representing McIver at his forthcoming trial. This was seen as a climb-down following a stern warning by both the US State Department and the International Council of Jurists that the defendant must not be subject to a show trial. He should have access to an outside lawyer who would not be inhibited in conducting his defence.

Armstrong was a larger than life character. His height, long mane of what had been dark, and was now silvery, hair, his trademark dark suit and white ruff, enabled him to stand out. His oratory, allied with his forensic skills, had made him a legend in his own lifetime at the Irish Bar. He specialised in taking on the cases of people who had suffered at the hands of the Irish state. So successful was he in getting heavy damages from the authorities for medical errors that he forced the state to launch a long overdue overhaul of its medical services.

He also represented wealthy clients which enabled him to make a good living at the Bar. An iconoclast who defied easy classification on left-right lines, he was one of the first to speak out about the menace which Emmett Macklin posed to Irish freedoms. He successfully defended some of Macklin's still living victims in court when other lawyers were frightened off. But soon the time arrived when he decided it was best to quit Ireland. The kidnapping of his 15-year-old daughter Moya convinced him that his continued defiance was futile. It would only exact a very high price and others were likely to suffer before him.

Moya was only released after he announced that he was moving to the USA. There he quickly made a name for himself at the Philadelphia Bar. In reality, it was hardly a big transition since the common law underpinned the justice systems of both countries. His theatricality also found a natural home. There were far more legal 'performers' in the American system than back home in Dublin where a lot of staid colleagues despised his melodramatic ways.

Armstrong's eldest son Lorcan had studied law at Wilford University. The place had been chosen because it challenged the straitjacket of political correctness which had seeped into nearly every pore of most Irish universities. On visits Armstrong soon struck up a friendship with Arthur Gorman. They shared a similar outlook on how the disastrous retreat from free thought in higher education had caused basic liberties to come under fierce assault in many parts of the West. Both of them were also unprepared to lie down and curse the darkness.

When it was clear that Vanguard was prepared to bend a little in face of the international outcry over McIver's seizure, Gorman had gone to see Ogilvy. He suggested to him that Phelim Armstrong might be a suitable defence lawyer. He was courageous, quick-witted and a master of any brief which he undertook. Since the defendant had initially been taken to Ireland, there was an advantage in hiring a lawyer familiar with the Irish dimension. He had also been too busy building up his practice in the USA to make any public statements about events in Britain though he was appalled that his son was one of those who had to flee for his life when foreign fighters burned down Wilford University in 2022.

On 26 November 2023 Armstrong reached London. Air links had been cut since the summer and he arrived on one of the cross channel ferries that still operated. He based himself in the South African embassy at Trafalgar Square. Its staff had proved to be trustworthy when Anatoly Yashin had led an ill-fated mission to London just before the war had taken its bloodiest turn in mid-2022.

It was the Afrikaner head of security Piet Joubert who drove Armstrong to visit his client. McIver was lodged in Wormwood Scrubs Prison. Armstrong was relieved to find that he was not in too bad a condition. He was receiving adequate food and rest and there had been no fresh beatings. Since the trial would be held in public, it was in Vanguard's interests to ensure that their star prisoner looked outwardly well.

Armstrong left the jail convinced that McIver's spirits were holding up. Probably his medical training helped. He was serene in manner and even his dry sense of humour had not deserted him. He told Armstrong that he had always assumed that he faced the risk of attack but he had never imagined it would occur in a spot as peaceful as Threave gardens.

Armstrong was working on a cryptic form of language which could enable him to pass on sensitive information in ordinary E mails. So Gavin Ogilvy was able to find out how his captive partner was as well as the conditions in which the trial was taking place. Much of Armstrong's information about the wider political scene was gleaned from conversations with embassy staff. From Piet Joubert he learned that the Vanguard army had acquired greater influence at the apex of the regime. This was hardly surprising given the central priority of fending off British Liberty and its American ally. Neither Sutton nor his sister had shown much aptitude for military affairs. Jason Gamble, Vanguard's Oxford leader, had acquired increasing sway over military matters after successfully repulsing a push to capture the city back in the spring. He had shown utter ruthlessness: several prominent dons who had refused to endorse Vanguard but who were too respected abroad to detain, had been seized when it looked as if the city was poised to fall. They included the archaeologist Martin Childs and Dolly Travers, Master of Lady Amelia College, by now a gravely-ill woman. Their execution was threatened unless British Liberty drew back.

Gamble proved to be well-named and the besiegers pulled back, allowing Vanguard reinforcements to be rushed to Oxford from elsewhere. He had originally been a radical, all for levelling Oxford's pristine monuments. But he had grown increasingly pragmatic as he had become a power in Vanguard. He stiffened the army's resistance by ensuring that all ranks were well-paid and received regular rations. He did this by making clever deals with Vanguard's business backers. They sponsored the creation of various new regiments which meant that Vanguard was able to maintain a large standing army despite appreciable losses.

For the first time, according to Joubert, fissures were beginning to emerge in the Vanguard monolith. There was a business section which he suspected now longed for a cessation of the war. He had heard from informants who knew the London club world that many had been unnerved when the US government issued a travel ban on thousands of people who had collaborated with the regime and that Secretary McKenna expected all its allies to follow suit. Those in the hi-tech dot.com sector in particular watched with mounting impatience as their American counterparts consolidated their wealth. In the past murmurings of dissent would have been ruthlessly squashed by Sutton. But it seems Gamble had restrained him. He pointed out just how crucial business backing now was for the military survival of the regime.

Armstrong thought to himself that perhaps these tensions within Vanguard could be exploited so as to avoid the bleakest of outcomes for his client. They both decided that the best line of defence was to argue that the original kidnapping had been an outrage and that the accusation of treason was invalid since Vanguard had no jurisdiction over Scotland. Its separate status had been recognised when Sutton had established an informal embassy in Edinburgh under Tristram Pannell and then gone on to meet Ogilvy in Bradford.

The main thrust of the defence case was that McIver was engaged in humanitarian relief. Several million English refugees had been taken into Scotland to avoid huge loss of life due to exposure and disease. McIver was a medic engaged in humanitarian work who had no ulterior motive for the action that he had taken. Armstrong's clients would be glad if most of the refugees could return safely to the places where they had originally come from. Their safety was his primary concern. This was widely recognised internationally.

This line was strengthened by the announcement, on the eve of the trial, from the Nobel Peace Prize committee in Oslo that many chapters across the world had nominated McIver for that year's award.

Both lawyer and client knew that they were being bugged. Not only did they speak in low voices but they kept their conversation to a minimum. Instead they employed a kind of sign language which Armstrong had picked up from a resourceful County Limerick tinker whom he had defended on cattle-rustling charges.

The trial got underway on 2 December under 28-year-old Justice Martin Emberry. He had been a criminologist at a former Polytechnic in the west Midlands. He had taken part in the fast-track process to enter the judicial system. In his case it had involved three months of night classes. There was an urgent need to cleanse the magistracy and higher judicial ranks of people with stuffy attitudes and besides many were deemed to be too old. Emberry had presided over several major trials thanks to having helped draft laws enabling Vanguard to curtail civil liberties. He was suited to presiding over a show trial and Armstrong knew that his selection was hardly a good omen. But he also knew that the verdict would be decided by the political authorities and conveyed to the judge. There was also a jury composed of citizens who had enough points in the regime's social credit scheme to be regarded as trustworthy in this legal farce.

The trial played out very much as Armstrong assumed it would in the un-free city London had become. He made his case as vigorously as he could. He was up against an oily prosecuting lawyer, Ambrose Dyson, who tried to develop a legal case for the seizure of McIver. He even cited the seizure of Adolf Eichmann by the Israelis as a worthwhile precedent.

The defendant remained composed when he was subjected to a barrage of tendentious accusations from the prosecution. After four days it was time for Armstrong to deliver his closing defence. The evening before, while working on his speech in the embassy, he was interrupted by a knock on his door. It was Piet Joubert who said that someone who was clearly from the authorities had asked that this message be delivered to him. When he opened it, he saw that there was just one type-written sentence. It read: 'you and your client have absolutely nothing to lose if you stretch out your closing defence speech for as long as you possibly can.'

Armstrong passed the cryptic message to Joubert and asked if he could shed light on it. He replied that if someone within the regime wished him to drag proceedings out it might mean that there was disagreement about what the verdict should be.

The lawyer decided that he had nothing to lose by padding out his speech over two days. There was no lack of arguments he could deploy.

He noticed that nobody had instructed Ambrose Dyson to adopt a less accusatory tone in his summing up. For several hours he assailed Greer McIver for his all-round villainy.

Armstrong then got into his stride. To the obvious annoyance of Judge Emberry, he spent a morning and half an afternoon pointing out the various sanctions which would blight the lives of Vanguard's backers for years to come if any kind of judicial execution took place.

Afterwards McIver asked Armstrong why he had slowed down He replied that he had his reasons which it was best not to go into in the no doubt heavily bugged Old Bailey. But it was nothing for him to be concerned about.

The judge also noticed that Armstrong was taking his time and he showed his irritation at several points that day. He said he would give him until the end of the following morning to wrap up his defence and that no further time would be available. There was a rather disconsolate lunch with McIver who continued to display grace under pressure. The judge was only ten minutes into his summing up when an official rose up and handed him a note. Visibly annoyed at being interrupted, he glanced at the note at which point the colour rapidly drained from his cheeks. Then, in a quavering voice, he said:

'Ladies and gentlemen, I have just been given very grave news. There has been an incident in Bradford. It is of such seriousness that I feel I have no other alternative but to suspend trial proceedings. The prisoner will be returned to his place of detention and everyone else will be informed about the date on which the trial will resume.'

Armstrong looked at the judge who was clearly shocked and then at his client who raised his eyebrows in surprise. The lawyer quickly said to him: 'Something momentous has happened for the trial to be brought to a sudden halt. I thought something unexpected might occur when I got a signal to extend my summing up for the defence for as long as I could.'

As McIver was about to reply, he was yanked to his feet by a guard and taken away. As the lawyer left the Old Bailey, he could clearly see that something was amiss. Passers-by no longer had that fixed expression, looking straight ahead or down at the ground, which was a feature of authoritarian regimes. They were talking animatedly to one another at bus shelters and in doorways. Newspaper sellers were being asked if they knew anything more than what was in their drab tabloids. All the while police range rovers and the Vanguard pick-up trucks, often used for seizing people in broad daylight, raced up and down the Strand. Pausing in once bustling Covent Garden, he heard one stall-holder say to another: 'I hear someone up North pumped a lot of bullets into that geezer Sutton.'

Armstrong lost no time in heading back to the embassy where he expected that hard information would supplement the swirling rumours. Once inside he sought out Joubert. He found him, along with other staff, listening to the voice of Ray Lattimore. The Free Britain channel was reporting that Clive Sutton had been shot and seriously wounded. He had been due to address a rally at a stadium in Bradford where American football used to be played. The assailant was a local man who had been cut down in a hail of bullets fired by guards within seconds of the attack. A curfew was being imposed from 8pm right across the country. Anyone who was caught on the streets, without official paperwork or a valid explanation, was likely to be shot on sight.

Lattimore said:

'With so little information at our disposal, it is futile to speculate who was behind this attack. The terrible suffering many in the English North have experienced, means there is no lack of people there who wish Vanguard's leader harm. But he would have been carefully guarded on what, for him, was a rare trip to the frontline. Recent history shows that authoritarian leaders often have more to fear from people in their own entourage when the tide turns against them. Much of England has been at war now for several years and the balance of power within Vanguard's ranks has shifted. To survive militarily, it has been necessary for Sutton to recruit people who are not just adept at spreading fear and terror. He has needed capable lieutenants able to plan military strategy, organize supply lines, and pursue espionage and covert attacks. The kidnapping of Greer McIver shows what a priority irregular warfare has become for the embattled regime. We should not discount the possibility that the attack on Sutton was an inside job. That simply acknowledges there are now growing numbers of regime officials who see Sutton as a threat to their interests and the survival of the regime. It would not have been the first time that regicides have sprung from within the power structure. The lynching of Nicolae and Elena Ceausescu by his second echelon comrades is the textbook example. There are others and if this is what happened, the supposed assailant, conveniently mowed down in a hail of bullets, could turn out to be an innocent dupe.'

Lattimore's provisional analysis made Armstrong ponder again about the strange message he had got two nights ago. He was deep in his thoughts when he heard gasps in the room. Looking across, the television screen now had the bold banner headline: 'It's official, Clive Sutton Dead.'

After a day of non-stop drama even a man of his immense stamina was feeling drained. By 11pm he was in bed. But four hours later he was awakened by the screeching brakes of a car outside the embassy. His room was on the left side of the building above where vehicles entered and left. As he came to life he heard another more powerful car screech to a halt. He heard running footsteps and then several shots rang out before a door loudly slammed shut.

Other vehicles converged on the building and soon search lights were being beamed at it. On going downstairs to the main entrance hall he saw the ambassador Desmond Mapende in his dressing gown. He was kneeling over an injured man. He was a medical doctor and Piet Joubert turned to Armstrong to say that the man had been wounded. Soon a pool of blood gathered from what appeared to be a bullet wound to his left thigh.

When he asked what was happening, Joubert discreetly pointed to a woman standing alone in a corner of the entrance hall. Armstrong looked over and saw that it was Philippa Sutton. She was pale but still retained that composure that made her such a contrast to her brother. She was also clutching a thick leather-bound book and she seemed absorbed in her own thoughts.

With the commotion outside increasing, Armstrong suspected that events might hurtle forward at a furious pace. He decided to go straight over to Sutton and introduce himself.

On doing so, she said: 'I know who you are. Your presence is one of the reasons why I came here. I want the world to know that the explanation which the regime is giving the world about how and why my brother met his death yesterday is a fabrication. He wasn't killed by a disgruntled local citizen unless the gun was placed in his hand by our security people and he was led directly to my brother.

'The protective shield around Clive has always been high and would have been higher still due to him being almost right on the front line. I pleaded with him not to go but he said that security advisers were exhorting him to see that such a visit was essential in order for him to maintain his standing with the troops at such a crucial time for the regime.'

Armstrong interrupted to ask: 'So how is it that after your brother was shot you are now in the South African embassy? Shouldn't you be involved in arranging his funeral?'

She replied: 'I don't know what kind of funeral Clive will get but it is sure to be an absolute travesty and it will be organized by elements who had decided that he had become an impediment to their survival.

'I was at Hampton Palace when news of the shooting came through. When I looked out the window, I could see that our customary guards were being replaced by others whom I didn't recognise.

'I assumed that some kind of internal coup was in progress and that unless I tried to make my escape, I would be detained.'

'Who do you think is behind it,' Armstrong asked?

'There is only one person and that is Jason Gamble,' she replied. 'He was appointed Chancellor of the government in the spring when the coalition offensive was resumed. I had backed the move. I knew it was a risky one as he was clearly ambitious and had a history of violence and intrigue. But I had observed how he had quelled factional strife in Oxford and later organized the city's defences.

'But,' she continued, 'as the military issue came to dominate Vanguard's policy making, it only took a few months before Gamble was acting as an independent power-broker complete with his own bodyguard. The military-industrial complex - some of the commanders in the field and the economic moguls who kept their regiments supplied with armaments, food and clothing – began to bypass my brother. He lacked the attention to detail that was vital for overseeing military matters. He was also suffering terrible migraines and bouts of depression (though claims that he was mad are exaggerated).

'I had advised him to think about announcing a ceasefire and making terms with his opponents. It would be an enormous *volte-face* and he would have much to answer for but he didn't rule it out. He said he would think it over. Perhaps it could occur after a magnanimous gesture had been made such as the pardoning of Greer McIver or the release of political prisoners.

'By the way, the kidnapping of McIver was none of our doing. Clive had been surprised when Gamble told him it had been staged. It was the first major sign that he was starting to be sidelined. Gamble said that speed had been of the essence. The aim behind it was to prompt the coalition to get bogged down in Ireland in the hope that it would give Vanguard a breathing-space here.

'Afterwards, it was far easier for me to persuade my brother that he had created a situation in which some of the underlings he had chosen were now openly defying his authority.

'Anyway, I had no contact with him in the 24 hours before he went to Bradford. I now wonder if he was in fact taken there by force. It neither served his political interests nor that of the wider Vanguard cause for him to be there. He would have seen that. His political antennae were still acute. Perhaps he had been consumed by the monstrous engine he had created. It had destroyed so many lives and finally it became his turn.'

As she sighed, she looked down at the book, she was carrying: 'This is a diary which I have regularly kept since the start of 2021 when the road to power opened up for Vanguard. It contains my observations of those tumultuous but increasingly awful times. I was close to my brother, advised him when I could and watched him being destroyed by the movement that he had created.

'Ours was a regime of frantic propaganda but I tried to be detached and, increasingly, I asked what was the point of our supposedly cleansing revolution. True Vanguard had gone from hedonism and social justice for the young to a grim puritanism enforced by arbitrary violence. The dregs of society were mobilised in order to smash opposition and terrorise the population. Foreign fighters who habitually used terrible methods, were enlisted. My brother has so much to answer for and many will say that I do too.

'We started out convinced that we were utterly right to embark on this inter-generational crusade. We possessed not only strong convictions but complete moral superiority. Our standards were good ones based on transferring power from the elderly to the young. At least in the West it was a new departure and we felt uninhibited in vigorously implementing what we believed in. Our ideas had been rejected in past epochs so those who stood for the old ways needed to be firmly dealt with.

'In the beginning my brother was convinced of his own infallibility. It was then that some of the worst decisions were made, ones that it is impossible to live down. But eventually he realised that it had been an error not to review some of the assumptions behind Vanguard rule. Too late he saw that he did not have coherent enough answers for sending Britain down a fresh historical path. We were improvising but doing it in very crude ways. By the end of Clive's first year in power the arsenal of repression was acquiring a momentum all of its own.

'Recently, he began to ask some searching questions of himself but his epiphany, if that's what it was, came too late. By the time these moments of lucidity occurred, he was a leader in all but name. And these were only moments. At other times, his old ferocity took over and if I was not the sister he had always had regard for, god knows what would have happened to me.

'I wrote this diary surreptitiously. I told nobody that I was keeping such a record of events and I doubt that anyone knew of its existence. But I suspect Gamble might have worked out that a peace overture could be in the offing. Perhaps he bugged our apartments. It would not surprise me as he is devilishly resourceful.

'Anyway, I sensed that my brother's fate was sealed and that if he perished, it would soon be my turn. Then, Gamble could assume power in his own right. It would be fully in character if he were then to proclaim himself to be the apostle of peace. He could justify our violent removal by saying that it was a peace we had stood in the way of with criminal obstinacy.

'I determined to make a break for it and at least get this far.

'You hear the din outside. As my brother's funeral is being prepared, those who have succeeded him in power are determined to lay their hands on me. Of course, I accept that I may not get much further than this embassy.'

'Thank you for baring your soul in this way' Armstrong replied. 'I appreciate it and I am certain others will too. But do you mind explaining just how you got away?'

'It wasn't easy but I had always assumed that, one day, there was a risk that people close to us would turn on us. From the moment Vanguard took charge and Clive switched the seat of government to Hampton Palace in Surrey, I looked for people who could possibly be of help in our hour of need. I persuaded Clive not to purge the Surrey police even though there were suspicions that it included sympathisers with the resistance. I cultivated links with senior officers and discreetly used them as an auxiliary protection force.

'I also saw to it that a secret tunnel was built from Hampton Palace to a small jetty on the banks of the Thames. Two hours after Clive's death was confirmed, I was making my way through that tunnel. When I emerged at the other side, I was met by a Surrey police sergeant, in plain clothes, and an unmarked car. Sergeant Hyland, the driver of the car, is lying across there. He was shot in the thigh as we were running to the entrance here. I had used what I thought was a secret number to alert the embassy that I was requesting diplomatic immunity but the call must have been intercepted.

'I hope Damian will live. Contrary to what most people surely assume, I am not without feelings as anyone can see who reads this diary. I would like to give it to Ambassador Mapende for safe-keeping. But in case Gamble violates diplomatic immunity and storms the place, perhaps an extra copy could be made. You can have it if you want: it increases the chances of my story reaching the outside world.

'Is there anyone here who could be entrusted with photocopying it,' she asked?
'I think there is,' Armstrong replied.

He looked around to try and spot Piet Joubert. When he did he then waved to him.

'Piet,' he said when he came over, 'this is an important document. Is there any chance of making a photocopy in the next few hours?'

Joubert looked quizzically at the picaresque lawyer. Underneath the theatrics he had found him to be a shrewd and humane individual.

'Sure,' he said. 'Let me see to it. I'll try to have a copy ready by daybreak.'

Philippa Sutton stared anxiously as he disappeared upstairs with her testament.

'Don't worry,' Armstrong said. 'Piet is one of the good guys. He can be trusted.'

He then said: 'I assume you are hoping to be offered diplomatic asylum'?

'The ambassador has behaved as impeccably as he could in these years of crisis. But I'm really not sure if Gamble is going to respect the normal diplomatic conventions, ones which are supposed to apply even in times of war.

'The trouble is that I simply know too much. The longer I am here, then the more people will get to learn particularly of recent happenings. So it is likely that Gamble will put huge pressure on the embassy. But I hope Mr Mapende will draw the line at handing over Sergeant Hyland.'

Armstrong thought to himself: this calm and collected woman has been at the centre of terrible happenings. There is much that she will surely find impossible to explain away. But she has exposed a valiant side to her personality and it is clear that she is not trying merely to save her own skin. If her former underlings are hell bent on seizing her and shutting her up permanently, then surely it is worth trying to offer her protection.

As these thoughts occurred to him the ambassador approached and said that the Grand Council of Vanguard had just issued an ultimatum. Ms Sutton was to be handed over no later than 9am or else she would be forcibly removed from the embassy.

Turning to Sutton he said: 'an announcement has been made stating that you have taken leave of your senses since your brother's death and that there are fears that you will leak information vital to the war effort.

'Naturally, I have vigorously asserted that the embassy is a neutral space which cannot be violated but I very much fear that an assault may be mounted on the building in the next few hours.

'We are also getting reports from different cities that fighting has broken out, including here in London. So Mr Gamble's succession is not a smooth one.'

Armstrong then spoke up: 'Mr ambassador. I have an idea. At a briefing in Edinburgh Anatoly Yashin gave me the name of a senior police officer whom I could contact if I encountered any difficulties while here.

'His name is Ian Rampton. He is not a particularly admirable figure. He is very much concerned to save his own skin by making sure to emerge on the side which is likeliest to win.

'Shall I try to make contact with him,' Armstrong asked?

The ambassador said: 'Please go ahead if it means my embassy might be spared and more bloodshed averted.'

The lawyer then rang the number and when it was answered, he quickly stated his name and that he was an associate of Anatoly Yashin.

Rampton was up and about and he said: 'I am following the trial at the Old Bailey, so I know who you are. What do you want?'

Getting right to the point, Armstrong said that if any more prominent people were killed, it would cause an international scandal and blacken the regime's name even further.

He handed the phone over to the ambassador who emphasised the point that bloodshed in or near the embassy was likely to produce immense diplomatic fall-out.

When put back to Rampton, Armstrong said: 'Time is very short. If you and others want to avoid a bloody showdown, then I suggest you come here as soon as possible.'

Rampton simply said: 'I will consider what you say. Goodbye.'

An hour later the policeman arrived at the embassy. He was not alone. Accompanying him was Tristram Pannell. Armstrong wasn't surprised. From what he had heard of both men, their primary objective was to be blown clear in any political explosion and to emerge with reinforced influence.

Rampton left the speaking to the former politician. He came right to the point: 'as time is short permit me to say the following.

'We are in a new phase. The regime's orientation and outlook are much more realistic than before. I am here to convey an undertaking that the trial of Greer McIver will be called off. His seizure was an excessive act carried out in former times. He will be released forthwith. Both he, and naturally you as well, will be free to go.'

He looked expectantly at the lawyer, perhaps expecting a positive response.

Armstrong thought: This man is lying. I believe Philippa Sutton when she says her brother did not authorise the kidnapping. 'Tricky Tristram' was his nickname when he was Prime Minister. He is surely back to his old tricks.

He said: 'Just what credence can be placed on your promise, welcome though it certainly is? The internal Vanguard fighting which is occurring right now, indicates nobody may be in charge and that your offer may be worthless.'

Rampton then handed a mobile telephone to Armstrong, saying: 'If you want to speak to your client, then he is on the other end of the line.'

Armstrong picked up the phone and said: ' Phelim Armstrong here.'

A voice replied: 'It's Greer. I've been taken from the prison. I'm now at a motorway service station near Reading. They say it's likely I'll be formally set free and allowed to cross over into coalition territory in the next few hours.'

'Good,' the lawyer replied. 'Is it calm where you are'?

'Yes,' McIver replied. 'I'm extremely well-guarded. But I'm in civilian clothes and I no longer feel such hostility towards me.'

'I hope the ordeal is now drawing to a close for you,' Armstrong said, at which point Rampton snatched back the phone.

'You see now,' the policeman said. 'This is no hoax. McIver should be home soon.'

'But,' Pannell interjected, 'There is one condition. Philippa Sutton must be handed over to the authorities. Her mental state means that she is a political danger. Mr Gamble, our new leader, will not tolerate her presence here in this embassy for much longer.'

Pannell then looked at his watch and said: 'She must be handed over in one hour but preferably before.

Armstrong asked: 'As one lawyer to another, why should my client's release be contingent on such conditions being met? Surely the fact that the charges have been dropped means that he has no case to answer. Does it not?'

Pannell sighed and said in that wheedling voice he used when trying to sell an audacious proposition:

'Phelim, if I may, the proposed release is a gesture of goodwill. It has no bearing on your client's guilt or innocence. It is a political act. Many people have entered or, in a few cases left, prison purely for political reasons.

'So I urge you to grasp this offer. It may not be on the table for long. Nothing is standing still at the moment.'

He almost winked at Armstrong as he flashed him a knowing look.

The lawyer thought: 'Pannell remains every inch a political spiv. He wishes to trade Greer McIver for Philippa Sutton. On the surface it's an offer to be jumped at. But I wonder: what if the survival of Sutton holds the key to an early cessation to this conflict on decent terms'?

Armstrong decided to chance his arm and said: 'I had the opportunity to talk to your quarry. Philippa Sutton is naturally shaken up after her brother's death. But having met more than enough unbalanced people in my time, I don't consider her mad at all. Her decision to come here seems to me perfectly rational. Her life is in danger. She and her bodyguard were shot at as they entered here. She could easily have been killed. Who is to say that she won't meet with an accident or else perish "while trying to escape" a second time?'

Neither Rampton nor Pannell had expected such a reaction. The policeman was smouldering. The politician had a mixture of amazement and annoyance on his face. Before either had the chance to speak Armstrong put his cards on the table.

'I only think Ms Sutton should walk out of here if the ambassador receives a written undertaking from someone in authority that no harm will come to her when she is transferred into the custody of Vanguard.'

So looking squarely at the pair of them, he said: 'Will one of you get back on the phone to secure that authority'?

Rampton then looked at Pannell who nodded. He then picked up the phone and said: 'Put Helena on the phone. It's urgent.'

He then moved away from the rest of them and talked animatedly for ten minutes.

When he returned he said: 'I've talked to our foreign minister Helena Sagunto. She will see what can be done. But I am very much afraid that your obduracy will ruin what is a very good plan.'

Armstrong replied: 'I understand your concern. But if Britain is to have a second chance, it will do no good eliminating someone like Sutton. She is a danger to the regime at its present stage because she simply knows far too much. Her brother's cruel spree was not carried out unaided. This woman, as a dead person, can tell no tales. But she has to have the chance to answer for whatever her own crimes were in a court of law.'

'Romania was impeded for decades because the Ceausescus were never given that chance. Figures who helped them despoil the country and oppress its people got a clean identity. They shaped the transition and indeed wrote the main rules of the semi-democratic game. As a result the country was held back for a generation.

This Irishman doesn't want that to happen to our closest neighbour. England has already been through far worse than even Romania.'

Pannell shifted uncomfortably but didn't reply. He saw what the lawyer was implying only too clearly. It would not be easy to turn a new page and put the past to one side simply by disposing of both of the Suttons. Rampton merely looked grimly ahead. Outside, a loud sound system was starting to blare warnings that unless Sutton was handed over the building would be stormed. When the speaker said 'unfortunately any loss of life will be down to your stubbornness Mr Ambassador,' Armstrong looked over to Mapende. The ambassador looked at his watch and said: 'There are twenty minutes before the deadline expires. I'm going to do nothing until we hear from the authorities.'

With ten minutes left, the first secretary rushed over to the ambassador carrying a sheet of paper. It was signed by Helena Sagunto and said: 'Once delivered into safe-keeping, it is the intention of the interim government that no harm comes to Philippa Sutton.'

As the ambassador took the contents in, Pannell's phone rang. It was the foreign minister. She spoke to the politician who quickly handed the phone over to Armstrong:

'It's the Foreign Minister here. You will have received the electronic message giving our undertaking that Philippa Sutton will be unharmed after she leaves the embassy. As there is very little time left, I hope you will now encourage the ambassador to allow matters to take their proper course.'

Armstrong said: 'Thank you. I will convey your assurance to both him and Ms Sutton. She must decide in the end.'

An angry sound came from the phone but Armstrong handed it back and said to the ambassador that they should speak to Philippa Sutton as a matter of urgency.

When Mapende conveyed to her what had transpired, she got up, brushed down her jacket, briefly arranged her hair and said: 'Thank you so much. I am ready to go.'

But as she approached the main exit, she turned and said: 'There is just one thing. There is no mention of Sergeant Hyland. He is still in danger.'

The ambassador said: 'don't worry. I will do my utmost to ensure that he is covered by diplomatic immunity. Besides he is simply too ill to be moved right now.'

He accompanied her to the door which was opened by a junior staff member. She was also flanked by Pannell and Rampton but as she stepped out into the drizzle of a London autumn, they both hung back. She walked towards a waiting unmarked hatchback car whose doors were already open. She looked straight ahead of her. It would have been impossible for her to miss the mass of scaffolding in the middle of Trafalgar square. It stood on the spot where Nelson's Column had lain until it was blown up along with thirty other historical monuments in a single night during the previous February. Nobody approached her as she drew nearer to the vehicle. Suddenly a single shot rang out. The sound indicated that it had come from a high-powered rifle, perhaps from the direction of the scaffolding. She uttered a sound that was more a sigh than a cry of pain and slumped to the ground.

She was left lying on the wet concrete as blood oozed from a wound in the position of her lower back. After about ten seconds a man rushed out of the embassy carrying what looked like a doctor's bag and a blanket. It was Ambassador Mapende. He knelt beside her and gave her mouth to mouth resuscitation. Then he looked up and shouted, 'she's alive but badly wounded. She needs to go to a hospital now. I will go with her.'

He looked up perhaps hoping to obtain the backing of Pannell and Rampton. But they were still nowhere to be seen. Phelim Armstrong and Piet Joubert joined the ambassador. The head of security asked his boss if she was fit enough to be driven to St Bartholomew's Hospital. Mapende said that he thought she could make it. Joubert then rushed into the embassy's carport and emerged in the driving seat of the embassy limousine.

The ambassador turned to his remaining staff and said the embassy must be placed on lockdown so that nobody could be allowed in without full authorisation.

Rampton then re-appeared and approached Armstrong. He said: 'If you still want your client to be released, then there is no time to lose. You must come with me and you will be driven to where Greer McIver is waiting. It is not far from the frontline cutting through Berkshire.'

The lawyer asked him to wait. He needed to quickly pack. He would only be ten minutes. In truth, he was only concerned about Philippa Sutton's diary. He carefully placed it in a bulky legal briefcase and covered it with his trial papers. He re-emerged after five minutes.

Rampton looked at his bag and said: 'Is that all you have?'

Armstrong replied: 'I have no time to gather up my clothes. Perhaps I will be reunited with them one day via the embassy. Just let's get on our way.'

They were escorted by two other armour plated vehicles, the front one with sirens blaring. They travelled along the near-deserted streets of west London, heading towards Reading.

Rampton finally spoke, saying: 'It is a pity Ms Sutton was shot. But she and her brother made so many enemies. I hope a different side of the regime will be shown from now on.

'I am already hearing that the new government has announced an amnesty for several hundred prisoners. Jerome Roxburgh's broadcasting station in High Wycombe has also been closed down and a warrant has been issued for his arrest. But I hear that he has gone on the run.'

Armstrong showed interest but decided not to engage in conversation about these political events. He suspected that this outbreak of moderation was designed to distract attention from the tyrannicide at the top of the regime with Sutton major killed and Sutton minor possibly fighting for her life and almost certainly in the hands of people who wished her ill.

His priority was to cross into British Liberty territory with McIver as quickly as possible.

After an hour on the road, he was re-united with his client. To his relief there was no checking of papers or searches. The Vanguard authorities seemed still unaware of the existence of the diary or else he would not have been allowed to proceed with it out of their jurisdiction. He said little to McIver other than ascertaining that he was all right. By 12.45 pm they had left Vanguard territory and were preparing to board a helicopter that would take them north and finally out of danger.

Chapter 12

Hebridean Calm and then the Storm

Greer McIver and Phelim Armstrong reached Edinburgh one day after the abandonment of the Old Bailey trial. They spent the night in Liverpool where the British Liberty government was naturally keen to learn more about the convulsions at the top of Vanguard. Armstrong told officials what he knew without disclosing the fact that he was carrying Philippa Sutton's diary.

It had, after all, been given to him, in a private capacity. The dead leader's sister wished it to be preserved for posterity. That was now likely to happen. In time, the English resistance would be able to unlock the secrets that it contained.

Armstrong accepted an invitation from Gavin Ogilvy to stay at Holyrood Palace while he remained in Scotland. The Prime Minister and his partner were re-united without fanfare. Cameras were kept well away. Brian Crawford had been asked to treat the end of a sensational trial in a low-key manner. It was not framed as a triumph. His statement merely emphasised that more needless death had been averted in this tragic period. After recovering from his ordeal, it was expected that McIver would resume his refugee work in the New Year.

The roller-coaster sequence of events in London had sapped the energies of the barrister. Christmas was approaching and Armstrong decided to stay in Edinburgh and recharge his batteries before rejoining his family in Philadelphia.

He had several meetings with Anatoly Yashin who had briefed him about what he was likely to find in the South African embassy. Yashin was eager to find out more about the sensational denouement to the trial and the role played by people he had got to know at the embassy when he had lodged there just before the English civil war had entered its bloodiest phase with the descent of thousands of foreign fighters primed to bring death and destruction.

He also had some news. Jason Gamble's new regime was requesting Pretoria to withdraw Ambassador Mapende. Presumably, the envoy's quick thinking and bravery in the aftermath of Clive Sutton's shooting, had disrupted plans to finish off his sister as well. Yashin had learned from the South African mission in Edinburgh that Mapende had refused to leave St Bartholomew's hospital until he was certain that Philippa Sutton would receive proper medical treatment. He even remained outside the operating theatre during a three-hour operation that resulted in the removal of the bullet lodged in her lower spine. It was successful but the damage to her spine meant that she would almost certainly be confined to a wheelchair for the rest of her life.

Immediately after the operation, Lucy McKenna had issued a strongly-worded statement. In it she baldly stated that she hoped Philippa Sutton would be able to hang on to life. She believed that she was capable of offering a detailed account of Vanguard's role in the period when her brother ran much of the country. She publicly warned Jason Gamble that he would enter the United States' worst graces if he liquidated a figure whom he had loyally served for over two years.

In some knowing minds, McKenna had no need whatsoever to save Sutton's skin other than for *realpolitik*. At the height of her power, the British woman had outsmarted the American politician when they had met in Mexico in June 2022 on the eve of the arrival of the foreign fighters. She had allowed Vanguard to play for time and the results had been calamitous. But she had acquired a grudging respect for Ms Sutton's capabilities. There was much political information she could divulge if she ever managed to leave her closely-guarded hospital bed. McKenna was not alone in wishing to learn why she remained loyal to her brother as he pursued policies that ravaged their country and ultimately consumed him.

She would have been even more intrigued to learn that during those years of turmoil, Sutton had managed to be one of the most dedicated political diarists in English history. But Armstrong remained tight-lipped about the existence of the diary. Its author had written 140,000 words. It took him a week to read it, the lawyer hardly noticing that Christmas had come and gone. He was struck by her detached and elegant style. Initially, her enthusiasm about Vanguard's march to power had grated on him. She depicted incidents like the assault on the lecture given by Professor Magnus Fontaine at Thurlow University as regrettable staging-posts on the way to a brighter future. She did not exult in violence but seemed desensitised by it. Her mood undeniably darkened, however, on describing the Remembrance Day massacre in London later in 2021.It was shocking and inexcusable. This she not only admitted to herself but spelled out in a confrontation with her brother, only the first of many. She claimed that her intercession prevented the wholesale execution of political prisoners. This had been planned following blanket arrests of opponents in November 2021.

Armstrong found it interesting that she regarded Tristram Pannell with the utmost suspicion ever since the former Prime Minister had offered his services to the regime. Her disdain persisted even after she saved him from a beating after he had mishandled his diplomatic mission in Edinburgh. She grew despondent as her brother opened Vanguard's ranks to what she saw as riff-raff and religious extremists.

Her entreaties failed to dissuade him from adopting a harder line towards the bohemians and hipsters who had done so much in the beginning to launch Vanguard.

Clive's last major coup in which he had displayed the leadership qualities which had helped place a troubled nation at his feet, had been the secret plan to ferry thousands of foreign fighters into England in mid-2022. She wrote with some relish about how she had tricked Lucy McKenna at their meeting in Cuernavaca, leading her to advise against closing airspace over Vanguard territory in the hope that a peace effort might succeed. But she was soon expressing her horror about the carnage in the north of England that resulted in several million refugees.

She revealed that only with difficulty had she talked her brother out of killing Gavin Ogilvy when he was still in Vanguard territory during the immediate aftermath of their stormy meeting in Bradford in the autumn of 2023. From then on she tried to dissuade Clive not only from further excesses but from staying on at the head of a regime which was fast spinning out of even his control. Sometimes he listened when she argued that whatever ideals the regime had possessed were now being washed away in a torrent of blood. The elderly had suffered too much and their misery had spread to nearly all sections of society. She warned him of the danger he faced not from British Liberty and the Americans but from some of those around him. The opportunists and psychopaths who had come to the fore no longer had any loyalty to Vanguard's ideals nor to him as a person. Whenever she was sure they were not being overheard, she raised the possibility of them ordering an aircraft to be made ready so that they could flee across enemy lines and place themselves at the mercy of the coalition. It was only on walks in the woods and gardens of Hampton Palace that she dared to give voice to these thoughts. But towards the end she was convinced that sophisticated bugging devices had relayed their conversations to some of the people now making the operational moves and political decisions.

There was one man she feared the most because of his underlying cleverness and ruthlessness. This was Jason Gamble. In the journal she cursed her naivety for recommending that he be plucked from Oxford and appointed Sutton's right-hand-man. He had displayed military talent in breaking the siege of the city. She offered unflattering portraits of the schemers he brought along with him as his influence rapidly increased. By the autumn of 2023 she was candidly admitting that things had got out-of-hand. It was too late to restrain Gamble never mind remove him. In entries written in October, she described her shock over the kidnapping of Greer McIver. She didn't think it was in Vanguard's interests to seize the Scottish leader's partner and then put him on trial. It would just stoke international antagonism at a time when the regime was already losing the propaganda battle. Gamble haughtily dismissed her when she asked for a cancellation of the trial. In the diary she let her fears spill out that there was more to this trial than met the eye. She wondered if it was part of a wider scenario which would result in formal power passing to Gamble.

A week before her brother's death, she described an emotional meeting while they strolled in the grounds of Hampton palace. He was more lucid than usual. They both looked back on their lives and what had led Clive to become ruler of a country now awash with blood. He admitted to Philippa that he may indeed have gone too far and that he was perhaps just a marionette who had been thrown up to take the uninhibited risk-taking instincts of their generation to a terrible conclusion.

It was their final meeting. As soon as news of his death came through, she hurriedly wrote, in her last entry, that Clive's fate had probably been sealed before he had gone to Bradford. He had, in all likelihood, been stripped of his authority in London, the victim of an internal putsch. She speculated that he had been taken to Bradford against his will, and that he probably knew in advance that he was unlikely to leave the place alive.

The entries stopped at that point.

Armstrong decided there was no time to lose and that he should inform Gavin Ogilvy of the existence of the diary. After all, he had got involved in the British crisis through being hired by him.

Ogilvy was unperturbed. It had been given to Armstrong in a private capacity. Naturally, he wished to read it and he asked if he could make a copy. The reading tasks would need to be shared for such a lengthy work. He would ask Greer and Brian Crawford to help him go through it. As someone still haunted by the pivotal role that he had played in the rise of Vanguard, Brian was bound to be absorbed.

Ogilvy and his partner were making plans to see in the New Year on the island of Vatersay in the Outer Hebrides. As well as Crawford he had invited Anatoly Yashin who would also bring his partner Moira Torrance. He wondered if Armstrong would like to join the party. It was a small fertile island with nice beaches.

Armstrong thanked him and dared to ask: 'Won't it be rather bleak at this time of year. After all, there can't be many hours of daylight.'

'Less than seven it is true,' Ogilvy replied. 'There is also the risk of gales. But these are soft gales. Thanks to the benevolent effect of the Gulf Stream the temperature will be higher than on most places here on the mainland. The winds nearly always blow from the south and the air is clean. If we are lucky, there might be a sunny day and, if so, it will be one of bright beauty.

'If I remained at Holyrood Palace, then there is the work finalising the terms of the defence pact with the USA to occupy my time. I'm going mainly for Greer's sake,' he continued. 'He needs a rest and surely you do too.'

'Yes, being here in the palace has been great but I feel as if I do. So I'd be glad to accept your invitation.'

A small plane had been hired for the six visitors. It took off from Glasgow Airport early on New Year's Eve. Freezing fog made the morning even bleaker. The passengers witnessed the arrival of dawn as they flew over Islay, an island famed for its distillation of malt whisky. An hour after forsaking Glasgow they were touching down on the island of Barra. It laid claim to the world's only regular beach runway. But the landing schedule was never the same due to the variation in the flow of tides. The Piper Cherokee landed smoothly on Traigh Mor, a silvery coastal beach on a wide shallow bay.

As they climbed into a bulky Land Rover to travel down the 12 mile length of the island towards its southern tip, Ogilvy pointed to a house standing facing the beach. He said with a smile: 'in case you are unaware, over there lived one of the founders of the Scottish National movement.'

He went on: 'His name was Compton Mackenzie. He was a World War I spymaster in the Eastern Mediterranean and he was knighted for his efforts. He was not really Scottish, certainly he had no Scottish ancestry. But he fell in love with this island. He converted to its Roman Catholic faith and became committed to Scottish renewal. He felt that could only occur through the main decisions shaping the fate of Scotland being in the hands of the people who lived there. He was one of the founders of the national movement in 1928 and he spent the next few decades living on the island. He was not an Anglophobe. He did not feel that Scottish renewal must come at the expense of long-term ties of British fellowship. He did not urge the men of Barra to spurn service to the Crown in World War II. Indeed, a disproportionate number died while serving in the merchant navy.

'He died in 1962 before Scottish Nationalism became a major force. I doubt he would see much to inspire him in Clova Bruce's movement. He inspired me to some extent. When I need my spirits raised or my imagination challenged, I pick up one of his books.'

Turning to picturesque Barra, Ogilvy observed to the others: 'Unlike many other parts of the Highlands, the people of Barra have proven to be indomitable survivors.

They kept their land and many of their rights. Perhaps holding on to a strong religious faith made that possible.'

'We seem to be in luck,' he said. 'It's going to be a clear, fresh day. There is a causeway joining Barra to Vatersay.' Let's have lunch here in Castlebay. The locally-sourced seafood landed here is superb. After that I propose to go for a walk around the island. I hope Greer will join me. Anyone else who wishes to do so is more than welcome.'

The other five joined Ogilvy on the stroll. They were advised to put on waterproof boots as the terrain was boggy in places. But there was no need to don the waterproof clothing that everyone had packed. 2023 had been another terrible year but its last day was a clement one. The southern part of the island was especially beguiling. They strolled along white beaches, deserted but for them. They stumbled upon Iron Age hill forts and gazed at standing stones as they crossed the machair, the flower-strewn grassland unique to the coastal areas of north-west Britain.

They had rented a comfortable lodge, normally used by fishing parties. It could easily accommodate all of them. Nearby, in a small annexe two well-armed detectives kept a discreet watch. Everyone assembled for supper around 8.30pm after grabbing some rest and sleep.

Moira was the first to notice that the Aurora Borealis, or Northern Lights, were going to be visible that night. When she mentioned this to the others, Greer suggested having a barbecue outside. It was cool but dry and certainly wouldn't be dark with the disco lights dancing animatedly far above.

For several hours all thought of food was cast aside as they gazed upwards at the vivid green and turquoise competing with a fringe of red as the shapes danced across the sky. The lights changed in formation and intensity every few seconds. It was a captivating sight. 'The aurora borealis are not nicknamed the merry dancers for nothing,' Brian Crawford remarked at one point.

A small bonfire had been lit. It helped insulate them from the wind-chill. Photos were taken, toasts were drunk. Nothing was said about recent events. This was a time for casting aside the savagery which had touched each one of them in different ways. They were in a place where it was possible to reconnect with a world of elemental beauty. Man's inhumanity could be lost sight of for these precious hours.

Greer turned out to have a good memory for the folk songs that had been sung in remote taverns after rugby tour matches. Moira knew some of those songs too and she had a fine singing voice. They entertained the company with their ballads into the small hours of the New Year.

Everyone was glad of the respite from the storms that had turned their lives upside down. Nobody wanted to dwell on the future. It was enough to make the most of a few days of contentment snatched from the vicious epoch that they were living through.

As tiredness descended everyone slept it off in their respective quarters. When they all rose late, it was to find that the weather had turned. It was a windy and overcast day with persistent drizzle.

As they relaxed in leather armchairs in the library, the talk gradually swung back to politics. Anatoly mentioned that just as they had been leaving Glasgow, he had heard that the identity of the assassin who had supposedly killed Clive Sutton in Bradford had been divulged. Vanguard were saying that it was Ahmed Hedley. He was being described as a double agent who had been turned by the enemy after the Park Circus operation had fallen apart.

'So your handiwork in persuading poor Mr Hedley to repent has finally been acknowledged by these bastards,' Brian Crawford said.

Smiling grimly Anatoly said: 'This story just reinforces my conviction that the removal of Sutton was an inside job. Ahmed did not believe in violence. Prior to the Glasgow siege he had been disorientated by the loss of family members and by the intensity of the war in Yorkshire. He soon showed that he lacked the callousness to go through with killing his hostages. He had been motivated by a set of complex religious reasons, having grown to believe in the potential of the 'Vdemption' cult which had been cynically thought up to cloak the Vanguard cause in religious garb.

'Nobody tried to turn him, at least as far as I am aware. But the regime probably held him in suspicion because he had come back, his mission a failure. In Stalin's Russia, anyone who returned from a mission, even if successful, ran into immense suspicion. The same level of paranoia has infested Vanguard for much of its existence.'

As Brian nodded his head in agreement, Gavin turned to Phelim and said: 'you were in the heart of the Vanguard labyrinth until a few weeks ago, defending Greer at the Old Bailey. So you are bound to have views on this murky affair.'

'If you mean Sutton's abrupt and terrible end, then I do,' he replied.

'I did my best to defend Greer but, from the very outset, I was aware that whatever chance he had of avoiding the hangman's noose depended on events far beyond my control.

'It was a political trial and, of course, I would do what I could to point out the disadvantages for the regime of carrying out a high-profile political lynching. There was just no point in appealing to anyone's decency or sense of natural justice.

'As the trial was approaching its end, a note was passed to me from an unknown source - but presumably from a regime insider - urging me to pad out my closing speech. This was a day before Sutton was shot. It convinced me that something was afoot but I had absolutely no idea what it was.

'The story of Philippa Sutton's arrival at the South African embassy in the company of a wounded policeman, hours after the death of her brother is, by now, well-known. But what is known to only three other people in this room, the man I was defending, the Prime Minister and Brian, is that I left the embassy with a journal that had been painstakingly written by Philippa Sutton. It sheds a great deal of light on the blood-letting.'

'Well well,' Anatoly said, 'Philippa Sutton actually had the presence of mind to keep a diary with all the terrible things going on around her and she, no doubt, responsible for some of them.'

'She did,' Armstrong replied.

How did it fall into your hands,' he asked?

'She gave it to me.

'She said preventing the journal falling into the hands of her enemies and getting her story out into the wider world were her chief motives for fleeing Hampton palace and seeking refuge in the embassy.

'She had calculated that I would understand why she was so desperate for her account of events to reach a wider audience. She worked out there was a high probability I wouldn't be searched as I left Vanguard territory.'

'Was this really her motivation,' Moira asked? How could the diary wipe away all the terrible deeds she was inevitably bound up with'?

'I am not sure if Sutton's actions sprung from a determination to rescue her reputation or save herself physically. She must realise that it is virtually impossible to justify her brother's conduct. But having read the whole thing – when it comes to diary writing she's an Olympic athlete – I was given food for thought,' Armstrong said.

Drawing breath Armstrong went on: 'the primary motivation for getting her diary into the open was to seek revenge for her brother's murder by his closest advisers and to prevent them consolidating their power.

'She actually told me this. Personal feelings explain much about the past conduct of this intelligent woman, one very much a creature of her times. She's just one of millions of middle-class Britons for whom emotions have trumped rational calculations during these tumultuous years.

'But without sharing her feelings I applaud her move. We are not any nearer to peace with the rise of Jason Gamble. He is as ruthless as Sutton in his prime but he is far more calculating. He has been in the thick of the fighting and attendant political intrigue these past few years. It has made him a dangerously formidable figure with an arsenal of skills. I am convinced that it is his intention to try and persuade the Americans that it is better to reach an accommodation with him. Allow him to rule his part of England and he will dismantle the most objectionable features of Sutton's rule. Indeed, it will be spun as a kind of liberation. Plenty in America are receptive to this kind of argument. The high tech billionaires are one significant grouping and increasingly their campaign funding is vital for victory in US elections. Gamble is betting on American weariness with getting involved in complex global undertakings. After Iraq and failures in the Balkans, many lack the stomach for the urban warfare, followed by years of painstaking reconstruction, that appear necessary before England can ever be back on its feet again.'

At this point Brian Crawford's mobile phone rang. Everyone had kept theirs switched off during the short holiday, including him. But he had turned it back on after hearing that Jason Gamble was going to deliver a New Year's Day message to the long-suffering people of Vanguard England whose fate now appeared to lie in his hands.

Crawford picked up the phone and, turning to the others, said 'It's Ray Lattimore. I really have to take this.'

He stepped out on to the porch that was sheltered from the rain and said 'Happy New Year Ray.'

'And the same to you. I wouldn't dare to disrupt your Hebridean get-away but for the fact that there's been an important development.

'In the last hour Jason Gamble has made what was billed as "a speech to the nation." His main purpose seems to have been to try and demonstrate that a new and better regime is now in charge. It has put the fanaticism of the Sutton era behind it. There is a readiness to seek common ground with past adversaries.'

'I can't say that I'm astonished to hear this. Nevertheless, I'm all ears,' Crawford replied.

'It was a slick performance,' Lattimore continued. 'Gone was Gamble's trademark Mao suit and his tussled unwashed hair. He was suited and booted even wearing a conservative tie. At one point he broke off his speech and the camera panned in on a group of frail and unhealthy looking individuals, most over the age of sixty.

'They were dissident figures who had been held captive under various London football stadiums. Vanguard had released several hundred of them in a New Year amnesty. Gamble even had the temerity to ask several of those former detainees for forgiveness and the cameras showed several of them giving him absolution.

'Of course all the past misdeeds and excesses were placed squarely on the late leader's shoulders. There was no mention of his sister. I suspect the new regime hasn't really figured out what to do with her.

'Probably the most important announcement was that a new government was being formed. The post of Prime Minister was being re-instated and – just wait for this – Tristram Pannell has accepted the assignment. I suspect he will be a toady and that his ministers will be mainly chosen for him. Sharon Burgess, the minister for social credit, will no longer be one of them. She has been detained, pending an investigation into her inhuman behaviour. Gamble announced that the social credit scheme was being wound up and that the targeting of the elderly would soon be phased out.

'Life will become less awful for a lot of people,' Lattimore said. 'There's no doubt about it. But I'm convinced that this is a Machiavellian move meant to entrench the Vanguard regime. The worst excesses will cease but, except for a few scapegoats, the people committed to, and benefiting from, the regime will remain where they are.

'I have serious concerns about the return of Pannell,' he went on. 'He has plenty of contacts in the deep American state and among the hi tech multi-billionaires. It would not surprise me to see him mounting a diplomatic offensive in the next few weeks. The aim will be to persuade US decision-makers to "give peace a chance." If he succeeds, the most significant outcome will be that England acquires a new dictator. Due to its broken and divided state, Sutton could be around for decades to come. It would not surprise me if he tries to deflect attention from the bloody transfer of power in southern England by stirring up trouble elsewhere. And the likeliest place is Scotland.

'As I say, I'm sorry to mess up what's left of your holiday. But I thought it advisable you heard about this as soon as possible.'

'Don't worry,' Crawford replied, 'we've had a great time. Thanks to the extended Scottish public holiday, we don't return to Edinburgh until the 3rd. But the PM and I will be weighing up the implications of what you told us.

'We also have an "informed" source of our own which is yielding up information about the last nine months of Vanguard rule just as Gamble was establishing his ascendancy.

'I can't say too much about it but you will understand what I mean hopefully very soon.

'So Ray, a new year, new challenges and a new bastard in charge in London. But I think Gamble will be contained and hopefully divested of power. But it will need fresh thinking and you are someone whom we can rely on to supply that.'

'I'm going to the USA in the next few days,' he said. 'I'm likely to acquire fresh perspectives and naturally, I'll be seeing my partner Lucy. If there was going to be any shabby peace deal with Gamble, naturally she'd walk out of the State Department rather than be part of it.'

Crawford ended the conversation by urging Lattimore to drop by his Edinburgh office before he left as he had something to show him. He and Gavin Ogilvy then left the others, to discuss Lattimore's news. When they rejoined them in the library, the PM told his guests what he had learnt.

'The main thing' he concluded, 'is that Vanguard seem set to pursue pro-active diplomacy. If the new front man Pannell succeeds, it will be at our expense. I am not prepared to discreetly cohabit with this regime even as it makes a show of washing away the copious amounts of blood on its hands.

'In the next few days, I will discuss where we go from here with Colin Ewart, my chief of staff and of course with the cabinet. But we have another day on Vatersay. We were talking about Philippa Sutton's diary before the phone rang. I am sure there is plenty more to say about it.'

Armstrong spoke up: 'if Vanguard are being given a fresh lick of paint, there is evidence aplenty from this diary which exposes the duplicity of the whole scheme.

'Philippa Sutton is adamant that both she and her brother only learned of Greer's kidnapping after the deed had been carried out. It was justified to them as an operation "designed to throw the Scottish government into crisis." A sudden opportunity had arisen to seize him and there was no time for authorisation. The Irish dimension, she claims was probably also a ploy to place the British Liberty-American coalition at loggerheads with the Macklin regime in Dublin.

'I fail to see how it will be possible for Gamble to claim that he had no role in the kidnapping' Armstrong continued. 'Even if he decides to get rid of the now disabled Philippa, her testimony points to him as someone at the centre of vile actions during the second half of Vanguard's rule.

'I suspect also that the truth is bound to come out about how Clive Sutton met his end. The ones who bundled him out of Hampton Palace and up to the stadium in Bradford where, probably drugged up, he was slain allegedly by a dupe like Hedley, are sure to talk. They won't owe Gamble any deep allegiance. If he fails to stabilise the regime and scatter his enemies, they will be thinking about their own exit strategies.

'It would be a clever move if British Liberty announced that it was launching an international enquiry into the deaths that occurred under Vanguard, including that of Clive Sutton.

'Tristram Pannell might even be asked to appear before it. He emerges with little credit from Philippa Sutton's testimony. Not once did he intercede on behalf of anyone who had been detained other than for Tessie his wife. She was held to ensure that he would not abscond when he was away in foreign capitals on Vanguard business.'

Ogilvy then spoke up, saying: 'it is clear to me that we should ensure both wings of the coalition, in Washington DC and Liverpool, are informed about the existence of the diary. The Americans need to be left with no illusions about Gamble or Pannell.'

'Ray Lattimore is flying to the USA later this week,' Crawford said 'You might consider if he could take a copy of the diary and deliver it personally to Secretary McKenna.'

'That idea makes sense to me,' Ogilvy responded. 'Otherwise there is bound to be a delay if the document is handed to a US diplomatic official here in Scotland.'

'Where does this leave us here in Scotland,' Anatoly asked?

'I'm not complacent,' Ogilvy responded. 'Parliamentary elections are due in the middle of the year. It will be very difficult for me to go into the campaign committed to some kind of limited co-existence with Vanguard. It leaves the refugees in an awkward situation. Many will wish to remain in Scotland or try and move elsewhere if a neo-Vanguard continues to rule. The media will ask why did we show so much hostility to Vanguard in the past if we are ready to cohabit with a new leader.

'Nobody should be complacent about his electoral prospects. But as long as the Nationalists are split then the chances of the Scottish Citizens Party losing office in June are slim.'

'But' Greer intervened, 'doesn't that leave open the danger that the militants might stage some kind of rebellion rather than accept the alternative of sliding into irrelevancy?'

Brian spoke up and said: 'Just now Ray Lattimore was worried that some kind of diversionary action might be attempted in Scotland to distract the attention of the world from the bloodshed in England.'

Gavin Ogilvy took up the point: 'Certainly if there was serious unrest here it would devalue Scotland's importance as a steadfast ally in the eyes of the Americans. When I was in New York at the UN General Assembly, it was only too clear that more than a few Americans had written off the whole of Europe. They were glad Scotland wasn't shooting any of their soldiers but their impatience with the old continent was running high.

'There are the arms and explosives caches which so far we have been unable to locate,' he went on. 'Sometimes I wonder if there isn't a pillar of the establishment who has concealed his fanatical views and has allowed these arms to be concealed on his land or premises. I know there are diehards who will stop at nothing to ensure that Scotland hurtles down the path of militant separation. I suspect it will be impossible to reason with them even if England quietens down.

'I don't think England will ever get back to anything like its former self unless Vanguard is toppled and its influence eradicated from all walks of life. Too much blood has been spilled for any kind of compromise peace to work. These past four weeks have been a lull. Of course, the release of Greer has been a welcome by-product of this strange time. But it is only an interlude. I am not hopeful about the immediate future,' Ogilvy said.

Before their spirits could be further darkened, it was time to drop in on a ceilidh being held in the island's community centre. There was dancing, singing and storytelling. Everyone got up on the dance-floor as the fiddles and accordions played spirited reels. The villagers were friendly but respectful towards their guests. Gavin and his guests returned to their fishing lodge with their spirits partly restored. There was one more day of the Scottish holiday left and then it was back to confronting the challenges of a land still menaced by war.

On the morning of 2 January Anatoly and Moira bade farewell to everyone. They were heading north to visit Luke and Chrissie Tanner, Anatoly's oldest English friends. While still a free man he had met Luke at a conference in Kiev. A decade later, shortly after his release from prison, Anatoly had been a guest at his home in Windcambe in Lincolnshire.

Luke was a fellow re-cyclist. He had surprised Anatoly when he had told him that his family would shortly be departing to start a new life on the island of Lewis. He had been the first person to confess his fears to the Russian about the dark valley which England seemed to be plunging into. That was in the autumn of 2020. Anatoly regarded Luke as a down-to-earth guy. But, at the time, he thought his fears were exaggerated. However, a year later, with Vanguard in power and fighting tearing apart English cities, he could see how right Luke had been.

This would be the first opportunity to see how he and Chrissie were faring in their retreat. He had picked up a hire car on Barra. Moira had offered to do most of the driving as Anatoly was still not entirely at ease with driving on the right. They were on their way by 8am and, an hour later, were on board a ferry that would take them across the sound of Barra to the much smaller island of Eriskay. It was where Charles Edward Stuart, the pretender to the British throne, had planted the flag of revolt in 1745. At Moira's request they paused on the Prince's cockle beach where this doomed but evocative phase in Scottish history had begun. Then they were off across the causeway to drive up the long narrow island of South Uist, past crofters villages, sandy beaches and the machair. By Noon they were on a second ferry that would make a short crossing from North Uist to Harris. A two hour drive lay ahead before they would reach Luke's place, perched on Lewis's northern tip. It was a blustery but clear day and they would like to have lingered on Harris. But there was no time to enjoy the scenery of picturesque bays and dramatic uplands, that is if they were to be at the Tanner's place by dusk. It would start to get dark by 3.30 pm and, for most of the time, the scenery now comprised monotonous peat bog. Only in the last stretch did it become absorbing again.

They were presented by the sight of a golden sun sinking into the western sea as they reached their destination. They were met by Chrissie. Not many cars passed by and she was standing at the gate in anticipation that it was them. Luke was elsewhere on the croft feeding some of the larger animals and he wouldn't be long.

By now their son Jack was 19. He was in his second year of studying electrical engineering at Stirling University and would be returning to college in a week's time. Moira was curious to know how the transition from a bustling English town to a sleepy Scottish island had been for him. He said it had taken a lot of getting used to but that, even without the troubles, he was glad dad had talked them into making the move. He had now got used to the slower pace of life and at university he found himself missing the atmosphere and sights of the island.

Luke had appeared at the doorway of the kitchen where they were sitting as Jack talked.

'It took our two visitors for Jack to fondly offer his thoughts about the place,' he said sardonically. He kissed Moira and gave Anatoly a bear hug.

'You've been through some hard times,' he said to the Russian as he looked him up and down. 'But I'm glad you managed to come and see us in this far-flung place.'

Looking around at the neat, simple kitchen Anatoly said: 'You seem to have settled in. Was it easy?'

'No, at first it was really hard even for me, trying to break free from urban living. Naturally, the transition was made easier by the awful fate that overtook the

England so many of us had taken for granted. But at least Windcambe was spared the worst.'

'I know' Anatoly said. 'I briefly returned last year. I even met our old friend the Romanian Pentecostalist Daçian Ursu. He's indestructible and did a lot to rescue vulnerable people in the town. He sends you his regards.'

'The civil war in England galvanised us into making a new life here,' Chrissie said. 'At first some of the locals were cool and distant. But once it became obvious that we intended to adapt to most of the ways of the community, the barriers soon fell away. I got a lot of help from neighbours about how to raise chickens and what feed to provide in order to get the tastiest eggs.'

'It was the same with me concerning the sheep farming,' Luke said. 'Archie, just up the road from here, offered me a young sheepdog when it was clear that I was struggling to gather in the sheep. The tradition of communal solidarity is still a real one here. Folk who struggle with the harvest due to ill-health or whatever can usually rely on neighbours rallying around.'

'Jack and Elaine are obliging youngsters and they won respect by doing errands, especially for elderly folk. We're very proud of both of them,' Chrissie said.

'Moira,' she went on, 'you might be interested to know that my daughter is training to be a nurse in Glasgow at the moment. I think she's suited for the role, especially the pastoral side of it.'

Moira smiled and said: 'I'd like to meet her one of these days. Turning to her partner, she said: 'Sure we could invite Elaine - and for that matter Jack also – to stay with us in Edinburgh when they have a free weekend.'

'Of course, a wonderful idea,' Anatoly said. 'And you two are welcome to stay for as long as you want that is if you can be coaxed off the island.'

At that point there was a knock at the door.

'Come in,' Jack called out.

A tall straight-backed man rather hesitantly stepped inside. He bore a resemblance to Luke but appeared slightly ill-at-ease.

Luke immediately sprang up and ushered him over to a spare place around the kitchen table.

'This is Freddie my cousin. He joined us here two years ago. He's a mechanic in a garage down in the village where he now has his own place.'

'Unlike Chrissie or me, Freddie has even managed to become conversant in Gaelic.'

'He's even read the Scripture lesson at the Free Presbyterian Church,' Chrissie interjected.

'What did you do Freddie before you came to the island,' Moira asked?

Anatoly wondered how Freddie would react because, by now, he had recalled who he was. Luke had told him about the cousin who had gone to pieces after military service in Afghanistan, hitting the bottle and eventually disappearing from Windcambe.

'I was in the army for ten years but ended up on the streets after leaving,' he said. 'I'd had recurrent nightmares and fits of anxiety after my time there. My marriage fell apart and I couldn't hold down a job because of the state of my nerves.'

Anatoly was relieved that Freddie could talk about his hard times but he noticed that a nervous tick affected his right eye.

'One of the hardest things about quitting the mainland for a new life up here was the thought that Freddie was being left on the streets,' Luke said.

'Anatoly, you may remember that in the autumn of 2020 I had mentioned that he had gone missing and that nobody could find him.'

'I just wanted to run away and hide from everyone at that time,' Freddie said.

'After we started to get established here,' Luke continued, 'I returned to Windcambe for a month, determined to try and find Freddie. The country was teetering on the brink of disaster then and I knew that if our cities became virtual war zones, then Freddie would be gone from us forever.

'Just as I was about to give up hope I found our lad here in a night shelter in Leicester. At first he just told me to bugger off. But I managed to talk sense into him. I told him he could join us in starting a new life which would hopefully have no upsetting memories.'

'I said I'd give it a try,' Freddie said, 'convinced it would be no good and that I'd return to the streets after a month or two. But I'm still here after thirty months. The place and most of the people have been good to me. The nightmares have gone. I've kept off the bottle even though it might not be the easiest part of the world to manage that.'

'Freddie's active in the local temperance movement' Chrissie said. 'He's dating Shona, a fellow stalwart.'

'Well that's everything about me,' he diffidently smiled. 'I'm sure you didn't come all this way to hear about my story from hell and back.'

'No we didn't,' Anatoly said 'but it's an uplifting story and there have been so few of those over the past few years.'

Chrissie had already prepared a succulent lamb stew garnished with local vegetables. Their guests marvelled at how tasty the ingredients were. Luke said nearly everything had been locally-sourced and was grown organically. Of course there is plenty that we miss and sometimes we sneak down to one of the supermarkets in Stornoway to buy treats, but not often.'

'No, he and Jack prefer me to wave my magic wand in the kitchen' Chrissie said as she hugged her husband.

Before going to bed Luke turned to Anatoly and said that there had been times when he had felt a coward for clearing out of England just as bad trouble erupted.'

'But you told me in 2020 that trouble was unavoidable,' Anatoly said.

'I presume you must have felt powerless to stop it.'

'Well I did,' Luke replied. 'But if England finds peace again I'll be prepared to go back for a while and help folk recover. I am sure there will be even more toxic material that will need to be cleaned up and recycled than there was at the end of the Soviet Union.'

The next day the visitors spent sightseeing either alone or with their hosts when they could put aside their chores. Jack took them to the Butt of Lewis, the most northerly point on the Outer Hebrides. There was a blustery wind and they spent a few hours observing the cormorants, kittiwakes and fulmars nesting on the sheer cliffs. Offshore gannets and skuas could be spotted scanning the choppy waters in search of food.

The visit heartened them and, as darkness began to encroach, it was time for goodbyes. Anatoly and Moira were flying to Edinburgh from Stornoway airport. Before they arrived they sensed something wasn't right. They were stopped and asked to show their papers a mile from the airport. There was a huge amount of activity for such a small place. Vehicles from the Scottish Army were entering and leaving the airport. Uniformed staff seemed preoccupied. When they looked up at the electronic timetable, all they saw was the word 'CANCELLED' after each scheduled departure and arrival.

A lot of other people were milling around. Moira asked what was going on of a friendly-looking woman who turned out to be a midwife returning, like them, to Edinburgh.

'Oh you haven't heard,' she replied. 'There's been an awful lot of trouble in both Edinburgh and Glasgow, buildings seized, politicians attacked, bombs set off, and even tourists kidnapped.

'No flights have come in or out of here since Midday, an hour after it all started to happen.'

Anatoly and Moira looked at each other. They realised just how cut off they had been up at Luke's croft. There was no television and nobody felt compelled to put the radio on for news. Only a few times a week did Luke bother to log on to the internet.

The news had grown so terrible that the Tanners preferred to learn about it in stages. Anatoly and Moira had assumed that Scotland would be uneventful until the country gradually stirred itself after the long holiday.

'It looks as if extremists have mounted some kind of rebellion,' the midwife continued. 'Nationalist nutters by the sound of things. A state of emergency was declared at 2pm.'

Anatoly wondered about Gavin Ogilvy and his party. They were due to be landing in Glasgow mid-morning. He presumed they had not been caught up in the drama and he hoped that the Prime Minister's steadiness under pressure was making a difference to the situation.

As these thoughts were racing through his mind there was a sudden announcement:

'Once again we apologise for the delay preventing flights from taking off. It is due to events beyond our control. Serious violence broke out in both Scotland's main cities this morning. Thankfully, the airports were not greatly affected. But the scale of the trouble meant that it was necessary to declare a state of emergency. For a while use of airspace was restricted. However, we have now been informed that once again it is possible to land at both Glasgow and Edinburgh airports. So our flights will be taking off ninety minutes from now.

'Anyone who has not checked in,' the announcer continued, 'must do so immediately. We wish everyone a pleasant flight and a safe onward destination.'

Moira remarked to Anatoly that security was very tight. Every person was being given a thorough search and she noticed a young man, wearing an SFF badge, being taken aside for questioning before being able to board his flight.

As an added precaution everyone had been asked not to use any electronic devices even before reaching the aircraft. The eighty minute flight proceeded normally until, just before the descent, the chief pilot, Captain McPherson made an announcement.

He said that the tram service to and from the airport was unable to go to the centre. This was due to the seizure of the Grand Nevis Hotel which lay at the west end of Princes Street. Transport going east was disrupted due to the occupation of St Mary's cathedral at the top of Leith Walk. Parts of the New Town, Charlotte Square and Albany street, close to both incidents, were currently inaccessible. So was Lothian Road as far as Tollcross.

There were also reports that the National Library of Scotland, on George IV Bridge, had been taken over. It meant the top of the Royal Mile was closed off. Thankfully, attacks on the Scottish Parliament and Glasgow City Chambers had been fought off.

Captain McPherson commiserated with people who would doubtless have difficult homeward journeys due to these shocking events. Like everyone else he hoped and prayed that 'the worst would soon be over.'

The resumption of a backlog of flights in and out meant that Edinburgh Airport was bursting at the seams. Anatoly was fearing that they would have a long wait before a taxi could take them (no doubt by a circuitous route) when he heard a familiar voice rise above the din.

It was Ray Lattimore.

'Anatoly! Moira! This way!,' he called out. The journalist even had a placard with 'Anatoly' scrawled on it.

'There was no need for you to come to the airport,' the Russian said. 'I'm sure we'd have made it home eventually.'

'I didn't,' Ray said. 'I'm heading out of here in three hours on the flight to Washington. If I wasn't I'd be covering the events unfolding here.

'We know very little,' Anatoly said. 'We were along with Gavin Ogilvy and others whom you know until yesterday. But I think you know that, otherwise how could you track us down here?"

'That's right,' Ray replied, 'the Prime Minister and his party flew in just before the rebellion started.'

'You're calling it a rebellion,' Moira interjected. 'Is it that serious'?

'Basically yes,' he replied.

'How much have you heard' Ray asked?

'Probably not much' Anatoly responded.

'We were with friends on a remote corner of Lewis until this morning and nobody felt like even turning on the radio.'

'The pilot mentioned various buildings seized,' Moira said.

'Yes, they were carefully chosen' Lattimore replied. 'It means that traffic in and out of Edinburgh is severely restricted. The main centre of resistance is the Grand Nevis Hotel. Clova Bruce was seen entering there at lunchtime flanked by bewildered-looking American tourists with armed young men hurrying them up. The latest I saw is that a special proclamation is due to be made tomorrow morning.'

'Has there been trouble elsewhere in the country'?

'Well the whole of the east right up to Aberdeen has been very quiet. But in Glasgow, Kelvingrove Museum is in the hands of the rebels. It's a very large sandstone building, one of the city's architectural jewels, and it is strategically placed on a thoroughfare going west from the city centre. Hospitals are nearby as is Glasgow University. The district contains not a few middle-class supporters of the radical separatists.

'Other groups tried to storm Glasgow City Chambers and the BBC offices on the banks of the river Clyde but they were overwhelmed and quite a number detained. It was the same story at the Scottish parliament where a small number of SFF MSPs tried to overpower security guards so as to enable armed militants to occupy the building. There were thirty minutes of scuffles and exchanges of gunfire. The last I heard is that the folk-singing MSP Ariadne McDowell was shot and seriously wounded after going for a moderate nationalist MSP with a claymore that she had grabbed from its place on her office wall.

Lattimore went on: 'Some of the diehards sought out fellow nationalists in the Independence Party who they believed were now traitors to the cause. Several appear to have been taken hostage in Glasgow. Tony Shand, the party leader, had an incredible escape. He had gone jogging on Edinburgh's Blackford Hill and when he reached the Royal Observatory, he looked down and saw there was a large fire a mile away on his street. He raced down to investigate and, just as he was about to turn into it, a paper-boy stopped him. He told the politician that it was his own house that was on fire and that armed men were out looking for him.'

'It seems to be a mad undertaking by desperate people,' Moira said.

Anatoly added: 'But I fear there are a lot of these extremists still around, otherwise they wouldn't have been able to cause this level of havoc.'

'I'm afraid Anatoly is right on that score,' Lattimore said. 'There may be no more than seven or eight hundred involved in the rebellion but several thousand will have helped them. Safe houses, alibis and money will have been provided. The silence of many has ensured that the conspiracy never reached the ears of the authorities. I expect a fraught time lies ahead before the whole thing is snuffed out.'

'So why are you not staying around to cover the story if the trouble is on such a scale,' Anatoly asked.

A frowning Lattimore sighed deeply and said: 'It seems there is even bigger trouble brewing across in Washington.

'It looks as if a so-called "peace party" has got going and has won the ear of the President. There was always a large trans-party group on Capitol Hill opposed to expending yet more American blood and treasure in a foreign war even if it was to rescue an old ally like Britain.

'The demise of Sutton has galvanised this faction. It has plenty of allies in the US media and I believe Tristram Pannell is crossing the Atlantic just now in order to blitz the news networks and speak at a few prestigious campus venues.

'These events in Scotland definitely play into his hands. Influential commentators in the East Coast media are saying that the British isles are now as complete a basket case as the Balkans once were. Ireland is a narco state. England is divided, now entering its third year of a civil-war that is shaping up to be much worse than the one seen in Spain ninety years ago.

'Only Scotland was a bright light in the darkness. A lot of Americans could relate to Gavin Ogilvy not only because he was a Hollywood star. He had also matured into a serious and wise leader, very few of whom are on the horizon either at home or abroad.'

'How is the Prime Minister? Any word?,' Moira asked.

'I am sure he is doing the best he can to stop the situation spiralling out of control and he has good people around him,' Lattimore replied.

'The government hasn't cracked under pressure, nor had I expected it to. That might have happened if the rebels had rubbed out Ogilvy. But he remains one step ahead of them. As long as he is the one in charge in Scotland, ultimately I refuse to despair about the future.'

'But nevertheless you seem pretty fed up Ray,' Anatoly observed.

Lattimore looked at both of them and said: 'Let's go outside and find a place where there's absolutely no chance of being overheard.'

With difficulty they made their way through the crush of people and found a spot near the terminus for the trams which were lying empty.

'The fact is,' he said glancing at his watch, 'Lucy may not be Secretary of State for much longer. I had great difficulty in talking her out of resigning once it became clear to her that Casper Wallace was beginning to come under the influence of the "peace party."

'What Pannell will be hoping for is a meeting with the President. Even if it takes place well away from the cameras, it is bound to be seen as a turning point. The President will be signalling that he is prepared to explore a way of living with Jason Gamble in charge of most of our island. Of course, the US won't cave in to Gamble. It will demand that the arsenal of repression be dismantled and wrongs done to innocent people corrected. Possibly his administration will be prepared to stump up a lot of money to encourage stability and reconciliation. But it will be a cold peace very much on the terms of Gamble, one of the most brutish warlords employed by Sutton. He doesn't acquire a clean identity just because he has ruthlessly disposed of his old boss. Does he?

'As daybreak arrived in the States Lucy and I had a long conversation. She made it clear that she was walking straight out the door if Wallace saw Pannell. I can see her point entirely. The US is just shredding whatever influence it has left in Western Europe if it consents to Gamble being a 21st century Marshall Tito, a ruthless but indispensable tyrant who can keep the lid on Britain's troubles.

'So I asked her to sit tight until I showed up. Since we got together, I've respected Lucy's instincts and judgement but she can be impulsive. So I'm hoping that she'll just sit this out for a few days at least.'

Looking again at his watch he said: 'I really must get a move on given the crush and the tighter security, otherwise I might miss my flight.'

Anatoly said: 'You mustn't go without this.'

He then reached down and removed a leather-bound journal from his holdall.

Lattimore said: 'I'm travelling light. It will be a struggle to add this to my hand luggage.'

'You must,' Moira said. 'Tell him quickly Anatoly what it is.'

'This is the journal of Philippa Sutton. She kept it right through the rise and fall of her brother. She gave it to Phelim Armstrong. Several copies are in existence. Brian Crawford said it was time I read it.

'I was planning to do so but it is far more important that you do. A six hour flight lies ahead. There is plenty of material that will make it hard for President Wallace to establish any kind of pragmatic link with a brigand like Gamble or a slimy toad like Pannell.'

'On Vatersay the diary was reviewed and discussed by those who had read it. They are convinced of its authenticity. I hope you will be too Ray.

'In your hands it could make a big difference and prevent the Americans making a truly colossal blunder.'

'Anatoly's right,' Moira said as she pecked a momentarily stunned Lattimore on the cheek.

'Off you go now' she said. 'Make sure you catch that flight. We wish you God speed.'

Chapter 13

Revolution at the Grand Nevis Hotel

A circuitous route, bypassing the city centre, eventually got Anatoly and Moira back to their flat in Cyprus Row. Going along Ferry Road they could see palls of smoke rising up in different parts of the city. The taxi-driver said that unrest had flared in housing schemes where the SFF had built support among disaffected youth. Tyres and old cars had been set on fire but he was sure less than one hundred hotheads were involved.

To their surprise they found that knots of people were standing around in their gardens or else on pavements in Stockbridge, talking quite animatedly. What a contrast to normal times when the face Stockbridge showed to the world was that of a demure, early-to-bed urban village. But Moira was able to recognise an architect, an estate agent and a university professor standing around the corner from the Admiral pub with glasses of wine discreetly on a ledge behind them.

Stolid people had been galvanised by the sinister turn of events in the city. Just above was the New Town, on the top-right-hand-side of which stood the Grand Nevis hotel, now in the hands of insurgents.

Murdo Toner, their nearest neighbour was up and about. After they waved to him, he came across. After first asking about their holiday, he said: 'Do you want to hear Gavin Ogilvy's statement? I've got it on my smart phone.'

'The PM gave a short address on television a few hours ago. He admitted that violent groups were seeking to usurp the authority of the government. But he was very composed, I suppose what we've come to expect by now. He said his response would be firm but measured. Unlike the SFF which appears to have taken lots of people hostage both here and in Glasgow, he promised not to place citizens in harm's way.'

They peered into Toner's device and saw the gaunt but determined-looking man they had been relaxing with days earlier:

'There are people in the public eye, including ones sitting in Parliament, who are backing this insurgency. It is an assault on civic order which has no justification. It is a desperately stupid gesture as I am sure will become clear in the hours ahead. Elections are due in the summer when all opponents of the Scottish Citizens party will have the chance to peacefully dislodge us from office via the ballot box. Instead, some have chosen to be insurgents. Public buildings have been seized, hostages have been taken ranging from foreign tourists to fellow politicians, in both our main cities. I am convinced that the support these insurgents have is minimal. It is a crazy and futile gesture by them. But my government and our security forces will be calm. We will resolve to ensure that these senseless events are brought to an early conclusion with minimum disruption and hopefully no loss of life.'

It was indeed the kind of measured response that Anatoly and Moira had expected though they wondered just how this emergency could be brought under control. Local residents were not panicking but instead were wondering how they could reach their offices and institutes in what was the first working day after the long break.

Moira would need to make a long and circuitous journey to the Royal Infirmary in the south-east of the city while Anatoly had to cross the city centre in order to reach his office near the Meadows. But they badly needed sleep. So did Gavin Ogilvy. He finally got it at 2am once it was clear that the police and army had ringed the three buildings which had been seized in the centre of the capital.

He was back on his feet by 6.30am. Greer McIver had already left to pay visits to refugee reception centres in south-east Scotland. Thankfully, the English refugees seemed to have been overlooked by the insurgents. Ogilvy expected most of his attention would have to be focussed on the Grand Nevis hotel where nearly two hundreds hostages had been seized.

The politician who, until a year ago, had been his chief rival, was holed up there with about fifty followers, some of whom were heavily armed. The assailants had confiscated the mobile phones of the guests but he was hoping that some might have managed to conceal theirs. He knew that most of them had been herded into the large Palm court which was the showpiece of the hotel.

The Grand Nevis was just two years old. With her castle business stagnating due to the sharp drop in tourism, Bella Munday had decided that a bold statement, expressing confidence in Scotland's future as a high-end tourist hub, was needed. A large 19th century classical stone building which had ended up as one of central Edinburgh's largest banks, was now lying empty. It stood at a major crossroad. Situated at the west end of Princes street, it faced the castle and Lothian Road. Trams passed it heading westwards to Haymarket Station and the airport.

Munday was a tough-minded entrepreneur blessed with occasional grand vision. After the destruction of Wilford University of which she was a co-founder, she needed a place to rest the insurance money. She was not keen for the proceeds to gather dust in a bank given how unstable conditions were. Instead, she decided to erect a hotel that would match the Langham or the Dorchester in London.

It would not be on their scale, with just two hundred rooms. But it would stand out from the garish and tacky buildings which had been thrown up from the early 2000s as philistine corporate and political elites sought to capitalise on Edinburgh's attraction as a low-risk destination for long-haul travellers.

The Grand Nevis stood out for its stylish art deco facade. There was an imposing entrance hall with marble floors, high ceilings and glittering chandeliers. Lush potted plants concealed elegant chairs meant for guests awaiting transport or merely observing the comings and goings.

Peggy Tyrell had been sitting on one of these seats at 10.45am on 4 January. She was thus able to see the Grand Nevis becoming famous for all the wrong reasons. She was a news analyst for an American cable network. She had just returned from a gruelling fact-finding trip to South India. Edinburgh had seemed an ideal spot to recharge her batteries. The hotel was now only half full. Most of the guests who had used it to see in the Scottish New Year had departed or would soon do so. She was waiting for a limousine to take her to Rosslyn Chapel seven miles away. She had heard about this late medieval building as a result of reading the *Da Vinci Code*. The place had an aura of mystery. Admittedly the associations with the Knights Templar and lost artefacts from Jerusalem sounded arch. But the journalist was ready to be taken out of herself for half-a-day. The building had a sumptuous facade and had recently been restored. But she hadn't bargained on receiving a box-office view of a mass kidnapping which would surpass in melodrama many an airport pulp thriller.

It started when a family group of four Americans were rudely pushed into the foyer by men in dark blue uniforms and white sashes.

'Hey fellas what's your hurry? Where's all that Scottish courtesy gone all of a sudden?' This was the response of the male adult Floyd Erlanger. He did not know whether to be bemused or indignant but he clammed up when his wife Megan said: 'Honey, I think they've got guns. We just better do as we are told.'

Suddenly anxious, Floyd asked: 'Where are Eben and Melanie?'

'The kids are right here,' Megan said.

As the gun-wielding youths moved away, Floyd said to nobody in particular: 'What the hell is going on here? Back in Minneapolis, the travel agent said Edinburgh was about as safe as you could get in Europe these days.'

Suddenly his reverie was interrupted by a yellow-haired rather gangling youth who seemed to be swallowed up in the commando outfit he was wearing.

'You are guests of the Free Scottish Army. As long as you just shut the fuck up, no harm will come to you. Now go over to the corner and don't say another word.'

The Erlangers shuffled over towards a large canna lily next to another even larger aspidistra. They didn't see Peggy Tyrell until she whispered: 'Hi folks. It looks as if our stay in the Grand Nevis is just about to become pretty eventful.'

'Is there a revolution going on here,' Eben asked?

'We'll soon find out,' the journalist replied.

'My name's Peggy by the way.'

They watched as the foyer filled with about fifty people. About half were wearing the blue shirt and pants and white sash that was the uniform of the SFF youth wing. Some were carrying baseball bats. Most had pistols and they also saw older brawnier men lugging heavy machine guns and even an artillery piece into the hotel.

Melanie said anxiously: 'It looks as if these folks are preparing for war and we are right in the middle of it.'

'Don't worry sweetheart,' her mother replied. 'Whatever they want, they won't need tourists like us standing in the way.

'I just hope they let us go back to our rooms so that we can pack and leave.'

Floyd raised an eyebrow as he looked at the journalist and said:

'We can only hope Megan is right. We'll soon find out.'

Clova Bruce and Teddy McCusker had just walked past, surrounded by a phalanx of bodyguards.

'They look like the leaders,' Eben said.

'A guy in his sixties in a flash suit and with a bit of a swagger and a dame who looks like a poor imitation of Madonna – you know it could be much worse,' Floyd said.

At that point a young man in civilian clothes and brandishing a pistol approached and said: 'You lot line up in front of me, I've orders to take you through to the main hall.'

As they headed towards the Palm Court adjacent to the restaurant, they could hear shouts. Some guests were being recalcitrant, perhaps not grasping that this 5-star hotel was turning into what could soon be a battlefield.

A German couple were objecting to being brusquely pushed towards one corner of the Palm Court. Losing patience, a fierce-looking captor whose chest hair protruded from his open-necked blue shirt, said:

'Another word out of you Herr Hitler and you'll be history just like the fuhrer.'

With the shocked guest still wagging his finger at the gunman, some of those nearby had a sickening feeling that something really bad was about to happen.

The tense situation was then lightened by a temperate voice that seemed to convey authority. Everyone looked over to a man in a sober but well-cut dress suit.

'My name is Matthew Forsyth. I am the hotel duty manager.

'There is no need for any trouble to occur,' he said turning to the belligerent man with the gun.

'I don't know why you are all here. I hope somebody will tell me soon. But I will try and prevent the guests getting in your way.

'Meanwhile I hope you can see that it doesn't advance your cause if people get injured or shot.'

By now Teddy McCusker had come over. He introduced himself and said:

'It looks as if you have the correct attitude. Your hotel is being requisitioned by the Scottish Freedom Front. Tomorrow we plan to issue a proclamation. It will be a historic one. It was necessary to select a place in the capital of our country where it would have the impact that it deserves.'

'I see,' Forsyth said in response. 'It means history will be made in the Grand Nevis hotel sooner than many people had expected. But would it not be better to let the hotel guests go free? Otherwise they will simply get in your way.'

McCusker scrutinised the duty manager and realised that he was nobody's pushover. He could be awkward but he might also be needed if things did not go entirely to plan.

But he also needed to be told what the new hotel rules were: 'Mr Forsyth, absolutely nobody is leaving until I say so. Perhaps it will be appropriate for some people to leave tomorrow. But the SFF needs to secure this place. That's our priority. If you know what is good for your guests, you and your staff will help us to do this.'

Forsyth worked long shifts and devoted what free time he had to fishing. The man in front of him, puffed up with revolutionary zeal, was not a stranger to him. He'd seen him on television and read a few of his articles until quickly concluding that his florid and bombastic style didn't match his own ordered approach to life.

He believed in the status quo. It wasn't perfect. But it enabled a civilized living to be had in this city for lots of people from all classes. These rude and volatile people had a different code for living than he had. He didn't want them to succeed. He didn't want a beautiful hotel that it was a pleasure to work in, to be trashed or even destroyed. He wanted all the guests and his staff to walk out of here unharmed. He needed to draw on all his people skills for that to happen. He would need to show quick wits and quiet determination. He hoped that others in a staff, carefully chosen by himself and Bella Munday, would, in turn, rise to the occasion.

'Sir,' he replied. 'it is clear we are in your hands. It is futile to offer defiance. Neither I nor my staff will do so. But can you allow me to get them together in one place so that I can explain the situation we are now in and suggest how they should behave in order to minimise difficulties.'

'Go ahead,' McCusker said. 'But this is no time for suggestions. Tell them that we are the acting managers and that any defiance will come with a heavy price.'

Forsyth gathered together the thirty or so staff at that moment in the hotel and told them that their priority was to prevent the situation getting any worse. As he said this the pair of SFF overseers in the room shuffled uneasily.

Forsyth quickly went on to say that they should not offer any resistance but try to cooperate with the SFF people, particularly when their demands were reasonable.

Forsyth had been due to go off duty at lunchtime after a twenty hour shift but he was glad to still be here. Before his phone was confiscated, he sent a discreet text message to Ralph Riach who had been due to relieve him, urging him to stay well away. He was relieved that it was him and not Ralph who had drawn the short straw since he doubted if he would have had the temperament to cope, at least as well.

Forsyth was also glad that his staff had been trained to be polite and composed in situations of difficulty. He watched, as supervised by SFF men, they went through each room in the six floor hotel. Guests were quietly ushered down to the ground floor and divested of their mobile phones.

Spotting what was happening Peggy Tyrell removed a nail file from her handbag. Pretending to be re-setting a loose plant in one of the large pots, she dug a hole and there she secreted her mobile phone. The plant, with fleshy green leaves, was near to a stout pillar and she made sure that the mattress she was given, was placed adjacent to it.

The duty manager's office allowed a view of the main dining room. Tyrell was not the only one who noticed Clova Bruce bent over the desk, busy writing and then often crossing out what she had written. Next to her was the lawyer James Hinde. Both of them were spotted first by several of the Scottish guests and their identity was soon common knowledge among the other captives.

One person who noted the identity of the leader of the assailants with special interest was Ross Bryden, the young hotel masseur. He was studying physiotherapy at Edinburgh University. He had known Davy Trainer. They had gone to school in the Battlefield area of Glasgow and had often played football together. He had finished escorting guests from the fourth floor to their area of confinement when he heard a woman shouting and cursing.

It was Bruce. She was complaining about the hotel flautist who was trying to soothe the spirits of the elderly guests in the Palm Court.

The young woman stopped after a mouthful of expletives from the politician prompted some of her heavies to snatch the flute from the hands of the musician.

She was concentrating on her address for the next day. The proclamation was still a work in progress and, along with Teddy, she had to figure out who exactly would do what in the provisional government that was to be announced. Bryden could see that she was clearly on edge.

At least she was alive and kicking unlike Davy, Ross thought. At school, he had been the most talented pupil in his year. He had the lot, brains, energy and looks. For him to end up dead at the feet of the creature who had now got several hundred people imprisoned riled him. He wondered how on earth he could halt the misery that she was causing. In a way he was glad that she was so close at hand. When Hinde got her off, he had wanted to kill her. Fat chance of accomplishing that here with her surrounded by armed heavies.

But he had an idea. The Trossachs Spa was in the basement of the hotel. It was rather dark down there. Most importantly the assailants had failed to detect that built into a recess and facing onto a back lane, was a shute in which laundry was taken out. It was also just about big enough to carry a human being.

If he could somehow entice Bruce down there – alone – there was a chance that he could overpower her and place her in that laundry shute. The only feasible way was to persuade her that a massage would relax her, un-knot those stiff muscles, and clear her head. She would then be fit and ready to give a bravura performance at 10am the next day.

Bryden told the duty manager not to be alarmed if he saw him in conversation with Bruce. Whatever he did was in the interest of preserving the hotel and keeping its captive guests alive. It wasn't the whole truth but he respected Mr Forsyth and didn't want to leave him absolutely in the dark that something might be afoot. He was one of the volunteers who answered Forsyth's request for staff to stay busy at least for part of the night. He noticed that Bruce remained closeted with McCusker and Hinde until after midnight. When she emerged, she looked wan. Taking a deep breath Bryden went over:

'Can I have a word Ms Bruce,' he asked. Her two young guards grimaced at him and she snapped: 'What do you want?'

'I'm Ross the hotel physio. As a believer in freedom for our land I applaud what you are doing and I want to help you.'

Her glare softened into a terse smile as she said: 'That's marvellous Ross. But how do you propose to do that'?

'Simple,' he said. 'I could give you a massage before your speech. You'll need to be at your best and a massage from me will relax your muscles and pressure points from forehead to ankles.

'If you have any doubts,' he went on, 'have a look at what many of the guests have written about my treatment on Trip advisor's Grand Nevis page. I know what I'm doing.'

In the looks department, the clean-cut Ross with his wispy moustache wasn't up there with his late pal Davy but he knew that he was handsome enough.

Bruce, despite her tiredness, had been persuaded by the sales pitch. She looked Ross up and down and said: 'How about giving me that massage right now'?

Ross knew that the chances of successfully spiriting her from the hotel at this hour were remote. It was nearly 2am and probably her guards would intercept him before the security folk outside the hotel could seize Bruce.

'I can be ready in ten minutes,' he said. 'But if you have a massage before retiring and only allow yourself 4-5 hours sleep, the benefits will be wasted. It's really so much better if you have it in the morning before a light breakfast. It will then have you firing on all cylinders.

'And' he threw in for good measure, 'Scotland deserves you to be in the peak of your condition.'

'What do you say Teddy,' she asked, turning to McCusker?

'If the boy can do what he promises, then I'm for it,' he replied. 'We need you to be fresh and vital and I doubt if you will be if you are relying on a short sleep.'

'Well that's agreed. Show Calum my minder where I should go.'

The tough with surly good looks looked disgusted with the whole idea as Ross showed him where the Trossachs Spa was located.

Peggy Tyrell had woken up during the conversation. It had occurred out of earshot but her journalistic antennae sensed that something might be cooking. She looked over at Ross: he had the professional bearing that she had come to associate with the staff at the Grand Nevis. He was a fine-looking young man in an unassuming way. She had heard of Bruce's penchant for men of his age-group.

Thirty minutes later, as she drifted between sleep and wakefulness, the young man re-appeared.

She thought that she had nothing to lose by engaging him in conversation. As he passed near her, she discreetly waved and said: 'Have you a minute'?

When Ross came over, she said: 'I just wanted to say that in the circumstances you and the staff are doing a first-rate job. Without your display of grace under pressure, a lot of people here would simply have gone to pieces.'

'Thank you madam, it is the way we were trained but I never thought we would have to show our fortitude in such circumstances.'

Extending her hand, Tyrell introduced herself and said: 'By the way, I'm a journalist. I don't cover Scottish matters and have just returned from India. I was sitting near the front entrance when the whole drama erupted.'

Ross stared at her: 'You're a journalist. Are you going to write about this?'

'If and when we get out of here I probably will,' she replied. 'It looks as if I'm the only member of my profession who is here in an involuntary capacity.'

Ross then spoke: 'I hate Clova Bruce and her sordid exploitation of people's emotions. She fooled a lot of people into thinking she was a national redeemer, Scotland's Joan of Arc. After she killed Davy Trainer her star waned. This is her last throw of the dice in my view. She is dangerous because she's really a socio-path as so many of these radical nationalists are. She simply doesn't care what happens to anyone around her. People are there to be used and discarded.

'The SFF claim to be on a mission of liberation. But that lot haven't the first idea of how to take Scotland forward, They are a bunch of misfits, opportunists and outright nutters. They only know how to destroy. It's their own appetites and interests they are seeking to indulge. And in that poisonous, immoral bitch Clova Bruce, they have the perfect vehicle!'

Tyrell could see that Bryden's suave deportment had deserted him and that this bright young Scot was genuinely angry.

She replied: 'you speak with feeling and what you say chimes with me. I checked in here with no strong views on Scottish matters. But twelve hours spent observing how these rebels behave, makes me see your point – absolutely' she said with emphasis.

She continued: 'But I saw you talking in a very friendly manner to Bruce a short time ago'?

He looked closely at her and said: 'there are times when it is definitely better to conceal what you really think from someone like that.'

He then excused himself and said: 'I'm sorry for unloading my feelings on you when you should be trying to rest. Let me wish you goodnight and perhaps we'll have the chance to talk when this is over.'

'I'd like that a lot' she said. Then her next words caused Ross to spin back on his heels just as he was moving away.

'By the way, I still have a mobile phone.'

Ross stood rooted to the spot and said:

'Really. I thought they had all been confiscated.'

'Where is it'?

She pointed to the large pot her mattress was rested against.

'Can I use it'?

'Yes provided you have a very good reason for doing so.'

'Believe me I have' and by the way my name is Ross, Ross Bryden.'

'It is one thing to retrieve it from the pot but another thing to use it,' Tyrell said.

'If you try it here, you'll soon be detected.'

Looking over she said 'At least three of the guards are still wide awake.'

'I won't use it here but I think I know a place where I'll be undetected.'

'Okay then. Just give me a minute until I scoop it out,' she replied.

'On doing so she discreetly slipped the phone to Ross who then went over to Calum, the chief guard.

He was playing the card game of solitaire on his smart phone and snapped at Ross: 'what do you want now'?

'Before I get some sleep, I'd like to make sure the fitness room is ready for Ms Bruce when she has her massage,' he said.

'Can't it wait,' the guard replied?

'I think it might be better if it was cleaned up now. I may have other duties at breakfast time.'

'Oh alright then.'

He signalled for another guard to accompany Ross to the basement. The air in the fitness room was stale and there was a slightly acrid smell.'

Peering in the guard said to Ross, 'I'd better leave you to it then. Don't be long mind. I'm expected back up there in fifteen minutes.'

'Don't worry I'll try to be quick,' Ross replied. In reality it would only take him five minutes to make the place presentable and he flew at the task.

At the spot furthest from the door he took out the smart phone and rang a number. It was that of Bella Munday, the owner. He had only obtained it thanks to being hired to offer work-outs and massage sessions to guests who were staying at Traquane Castle in East Lothian.

It was 2.30am. She would not be pleased to be wakened at that hour and her phone might not even be switched on.

But it was. After one minute, there was an answer: 'Just who is calling at this hour'?

'Ms Munday. It's Ross Bryden from the Spa at the Nevis. I'm there now. For a few minutes I've got access to a mobile phone. Can I speak'?

'Gosh,' Munday said. 'Right, go ahead Ross. I was fast asleep but now I'm all ears.'

Bryden outlined his plan and said the chance for success would be boosted if security men were positioned outside once he had bundled Bruce through the laundry shute.

'Just one thing,' Munday said. 'Do you recall when you were last down at Traquane'?

Ross paused and then said. It was a rainy Monday in early October, the Edinburgh autumn holiday. You'd had to cancel excursions for the visitors because of the bad weather.'

'Just checking Ross,' she said.

'You're a brave lad. I'll do all I can to ensure you pull this off. If you do, then Scotland will have been saved from a lot of misery and strife.'

'Good night Ms Munday, sorry to have wakened you at this hour,' Ross said.

'No worries, I'll be waking others up now so as to ensure help awaits you tomorrow morning.'

Back upstairs, on the pretext of fetching her a glass of water, Ross slipped the phone back to Peggy Tyrell. He was so exhausted that he then slumped in a corner of the Palm Court and managed to get a few hours sleep despite the hair-raising assignment that lay ahead.

At 8.30am as instructed, Ross was waiting at the entrance to the lift that went down to the Trossachs Spa. Bruce was accompanied by Benny one of her older guards. She preened herself in the mirror during the few seconds in the lift. The guard followed them into the massage room. Bruce had already been given the standard cotton robe provided by the hotel which she was wearing under her silk dressing gown.

Ross was obliging. He asked her was she rested and she confessed that she had probably got less sleep than him due to further amendments to the speech to be given an hour from now. He said he would do his best to banish the fatigue and activate her reserves of energy.

Benny could not repress a disdainful smirk as he spoke. Out of the corner of her eye Bruce observed his manner and said: 'Okay Benny. You're not needed here. Just go and wait outside.'

Looking peeved, he reluctantly did as he was told.

Ross was dressed in light cotton trousers and a sleeveless vest. He had buffed his hair with gel and liberally applied the male fragrance which his girlfriend Chloe claimed exuded a subtle and calming effect.

Smiling, he asked his client to disrobe and rest on the treatment board face up. He could see that she was wearing skimpy panties and a bikini top.

'I hope this will be good,' she said as he asked her to close her eyes.

'Oh it will be,' Ross replied. 'You can be sure that I know what I'm doing.

'I'm going to release chemical charges in your body that will enable its internal balance to be restored.'

'Well I can't wait, let's get on with it,' she said.

He used both his index fingers to massage the centre of her forehead twenty times. He kneaded the temple area for a similar number. After ten minutes, he had reached her upper abdomen which he rubbed with the palms of his hands for some time.

When he asked her to turn over, he planned to repeat the procedure from the top of her buttocks to the base of her skull. But as he pinched the muscles near her lower spine, he felt her hand wandering up his right thigh and resting on his groin. He wasn't surprised that Bruce was groping him. She was, after all, known for her erotic drive and for making younger Scots in particular the object of her lust.

He was a good actor. He could pretend to go along with it. But he suspected that if she had an orgasm, she would hastily leave, her passions sated and leap into the shower.

At all costs he must get her to stick to his routine. So, in what he hoped was a seductive and compliant voice, he whispered:

'Clova that feels brilliant. Let's just wait a few more minutes until the treatment is over and, believe me, it will be even better.'

'Let's,' she rasped and he got to work on her back and shoulders, relaxing her neck and applying the kneading technique to the back of her head. By now he knew she should be drowsy. His procedures had been designed to induce sleep rather than release energy.

He then said: 'Please turn over. I'm ready for you now.'

She was groggy now but still awake. As she leered expectantly, he produced a cotton swab and pressed it down on her mouth. Her arms and legs started flailing but soon her body went limp. She had absorbed a lot of chloroform which Ross had applied to the swab and, within seconds, she fell into unconsciousness.

The masseur wasted no time and, within seconds, hoisted the politician onto his shoulders. She was big boned but he could just about bear the weight. But, as he passed a side table, her left foot brushed against it and a metal pan clattered to the floor.

Benny heard the noise and called out: 'Is everything all right in there'?

Ross called back with as much composure as he could muster: 'We just tipped over a small dish. We'll be back out in two minutes.'

His heart raced as he expected the door to open. But Benny despised the massage game and was impatient for it to be over, so he didn't stir.

There were only a few seconds to go before he would be at the laundry shute. Normally, there would be a laundry basket at the other end to receive the waste linen. He wondered if instead, there would be help from the authorities. Otherwise his goose might well be cooked.

But as he shoved the unconscious kidnapped politician into the shute he felt good. She was an unprincipled wrecker totally bound up with her ego and her unbridled lust. He was a young Christian, a segment of the population which, in Scotland, was now as rare as it probably had been in the ancient Rome of Emperor Nero. For Ross, Bruce was one of the worst things that had happened to Scotland. She had legitimised a selfish 'me first' attitude and along with media agitators like McCusker had dressed it up in patriotic garb.

These were the thoughts running through his mind as he bundled the comatose politician into the shute. Instead of a loud thud which meant that she would have made contact with the concrete pavement, he hardly heard anything. As he climbed up after her, he heard the door open and Benny cry out: 'What the fuck'!

He landed on a pile of duvets and looked up into the eyes of a masked man in the uniform of the Scottish Army.

Clova Bruce was being carried away. The soldier said: 'Great work son. You had better get out of the way as we are just about to make a controlled explosion so as to blow in the outer wall of the spa.

He clambered to his feet and moved away. Two small explosions followed, exposing a hole in the wall through which soldiers rushed.

Upstairs in the Palm Court all was nearly ready for the declaration. Genuine Scottish independence and the installation of a provisional government were to be the main centre-pieces of Bruce's address. The frequent re-writes had been caused by uncertainty over who would fill which posts. Several sympathisers from the world of business and public relations who had been assigned economic portfolios, had got cold feet. In the end, the cabinet was dominated by 'B' list people some of whom had in the past made claims about Scotland's economic viability which had turned them into laughing-stocks.

The area set aside for the media was filling up with journalists and several television crews. Teddy McCusker would be the master of ceremonies. This was a moment where he felt he would be on the cusp of history. To his surprise and delight, the government had allowed the conventional media to come into the besieged hotel to film this momentous event.

It just shows, McCusker thought, the naivety of Ogilvy and his gang. They have no idea how to run a country.

Not far off were the captives forced to sit through this bid for liberation. The hotel guests were tired and bewildered but also curious.

'I thought Scotland was already independent,' Eben said to his dad Floyd Erlanger.

'Well it looks as if these nutty folk are so in love with the idea that they have to do it over and over again,' he said.

'This is something amazing that you can tell your kids about,' Megan Erlanger said to her children.

'It means we won't need to go to another movie,' Floyd said. 'No plot can beat this one for sheer goofiness.'

Ed Cargill of BBC Lowland TV had been sent to cover Bruce's declaration. It had too many of the hallmarks of a comic opera, with the sinister overlay of a lot of jumpy guys totting guns, in order to be credible. Maybe that was why the Scottish government had allowed the media to go into the hotel, he mused. He and the other hacks would be able to see just how desperately contrived this whole affair was.

As 10am drew near, he and the other journalists started to receive messages from their studios and newspaper offices. A major news story was breaking in Glasgow. It seemed Jerome Roxburgh had surfaced there. In fact he had stormed the Kelvingrove Museum and was warning that he was poised to make a declaration that was sure to strike fear in the hearts of the 'criminals' running Scotland.

The press pack were wandering what to make of it when the sound of explosions in the basement were heard. Twenty or so armed men jumped up and ran towards the scene of the noise. Then pandemonium broke out. Noticing that most of their captors had suddenly left, almost in unison the captive guests concluded that now was their chance to get away. There was a great rush of people from the Palm Court towards the foyer and through the exit and on to Princes street.

Eagle-eyed journalists spotted members of the provisional government, as well as the lawyer James Hinde, slipping into the dense fleeing throng. They included zealots like Miranda Pittock, Finlay Jardine and Murray Cairns who, just a short time earlier, had been jostling for a good position in the government line-up.

They had concluded that this was not, after all, going to be the moment when Scotland gave birth to its progressive republic so it was time to slip back into the shadows.

After the hotel emptied of its hostages, Teddy McCusker was left alone on the platform where he would have hosted the historic event. To his chagrin he saw that the journalists were now also making a swift exit.

'Guys why are you all leaving,' he shouted to a few who used to be drinking mates in Glasgow's Merchant City. 'Our proclamation's only been delayed. Clova is sure to appear soon. You still have a dynamite story here.'

'There was a story here' Cargill said. 'The story is in Glasgow now and from what we are hearing it's a big one. If you had the sense to steer clear of fringe politics, you'd be covering it. Instead, you've messed up. I hope they find you a cosy cell in Barlinnie.'

For once McCusker was left speechless as his former press chums headed out of the hotel. But by his side there was suddenly the duty manager. Forsyth looked weary but was clean-shaven and his white shirt was clean and well-pressed. His manner betrayed his relief that the hotel was returning to normal.

'Mr McCusker both I and my staff are always here to serve even rule-breakers like you and your men.'

'I'd like to think that your last memory of this place is that you were treated with some consideration. So I'm inviting you and those of your people who are still at liberty to come into the restaurant for breakfast.

'We want you to leave here on a full stomach.' The journalist-cum-revolutionary looked at the duty manager. He showed no trace of sarcasm on his face.

Shrugging his shoulders, he followed him into the restaurant, wondering where on earth Clova had got to.

Chapter 14

The Bomb in the Museum

Bella Munday managed to get through to Major Malcolm Leckie after the surprise phone call from inside her occupied hotel. They had known each other since 2022 when he had commanded the unit of the Scottish army which had rescued thousands of people in Wilford from likely death at the hands of foreign fighters.

Thereafter they had cooperated on charity matters. When out-of-uniform Leckie worked to ensure that Scottish soldiers wearing British uniforms who had lost limbs in action were not forgotten in an independent Scotland.

Leckie had been stationed outside St Mary's Cathedral which had been occupied by religious activists who hoped that the declaration of independence would enable Scotland to be dedicated to the cause of Latin American-style liberation theology.

He contacted the government's crisis centre. It was Colin Ewart, Ogilvy's civilian chief of staff, who was the main person on duty. He gave the immediate go-ahead for the army to facilitate Ross Bryden's abduction of Clova Bruce.

By 11 am of 6 January it was clear that the emergency in Edinburgh was all but over. The dozens of armed men in the Grand Nevis hotel either surrendered or attempted to flee. Nobody was killed or even wounded. Bruce had suffered a few bruises and was closely-guarded in a hospital bed. The rebels holding out in the National Library and the Catholic cathedral gave up once many realised that Scotland's freedom day had instead descended into the most ludicrous of farces. The city returned to its wintry normality as high pressure over Scandinavia enabled the east wind to gust along Princes Street, bringing snow and a collapse in the temperature.

Gavin Ogilvy briefly stopped off at the Grand Nevis hotel. He issued no statement but was photographed with Ross Bryden and Peggy Tyrell whose retention of her phone had enabled the young masseur to set in train the events ending the siege. Mr Forsyth, the duty manager, had been invited to join the group but he preferred to stay in the background. However, the Erlanger family were introduced to Ogilvy and secured his autograph. The Minneapolis family's account of the siege would dominate the news schedules back home for the next couple of evenings.

Ogilvy carried on to the crisis headquarters which were at the Gallery of Contemporary Scottish Art. This large neo-classical building had been requisitioned since the collection had been receiving few visitors due to the precipitous decline in the appeal of abstract art work.

E mails and text messages sent by leading players in the Edinburgh rebellion revealed something of their motivation. They had been planning a kind of grand gesture to distract attention from the fact that the radical nationalists were heading for electoral defeat in the summer. But they had brought forward their plan in light of the upheavals in England which had produced a new leadership in London. Direct action was agreed upon as soon as it appeared that the Americans might be wavering in their resolve to drive Vanguard from power.

Ogilvy had been right to surmise that Scottish extremists might try to use the uncertain diplomatic picture to try and stage some kind of disturbance. Perhaps several of its perpetrators even knew, in their hearts, that it would have little chance of success. Stories of prominent radicals running away from the hotel showed that they felt it was time to leap off the revolution escalator. But the SFF had partly achieved its objective even with its leaders under arrest or in hiding. Scotland was no longer the place of stability it had previously been seen as. The dramatic scenes in Edinburgh would no doubt embolden the Washington faction which cynically argued that no strong moderate side was left in Britain and it was time for a compromise peace with Jason Gamble.

But the post-mortem into the 5-6 January unrest lasted only minutes. The main issue was the seizure of the Kelvingrove Museum and Art Gallery. The media pack had raced from central Edinburgh to west end of Glasgow after it was confirmed that Jerome Roxburgh was in the building. He had made a broadcast with his camera phone in the aftermath of the Edinburgh trouble in which he was surrounded by armed men. Few were wearing the uniform of the SFF. Several were wearing Celtic football tops. It was an indication that some of them had been recruited from Irish-minded factions around Glasgow. Their links to Scottish nationalism were probably tenuous or only very recent. Anti-British sentiment prevailed among them. Others, it was thought, possessed links to Emmett Macklin's narco-state in Dublin.

There was no point in mulling over whether the seizure of the museum had been a separate operation or a late-starting part of the SFF's rebellion. The belligerent language used by Roxburgh, in the brief address that he had posted online, suggested that he meant business. He had seized the few museum staff in the building as well as politicians who had been kidnapped and assaulted before being taken there.

But there was a menacing new twist to the polemics of this longstanding thorn in the side of the Unionists. Roxburgh was claiming that a dirty bomb had been brought into the building. It was the term that he had used as he gesticulated in the main gallery of the culture palace, his voice echoing along its corridors. He warned that if it went off, then the combination of explosives and radio-active material meant that a wide area of Glasgow would be contaminated. The dispersal area would take in the university quarter, Hyndland and Kelvingrove, desirable middle-class areas also containing some of the city's top medical facilities.

In his address Roxburgh made sure that the camera panned in on the ten hostages chained to radiators in the gallery containing the works of the painters known as the Scottish Colourists. He insisted that he meant business. He had faced death frequently after an abortive love affair had propelled him into the French Foreign Legion. He was ready to do so again. He would set out his terms at 7pm that evening. He also promised to display pictures of the bomb which he vowed was ready to be detonated.

Before the crisis committee could fashion any kind of response, an aide handed a piece of paper to Ogilvy. Rising from his seat he said: 'the President of the United States is on the line. It's just 5am in Washington. I better see what he wants.'

Casper Wallace had been notified immediately about the situation in Glasgow. He got right to the point in his conversation with Ogilvy:

'Gavin, this is a scary situation. This Roxburgh claims to have a dirty bomb. If he's right and it goes off, it will be the first time that it has happened anywhere in the Western hemisphere.'

'I appreciate your concern Mr President,' Ogilvy replied. 'The government is already evacuating the area likely to be affected if the bomb is detonated. Perhaps 100,000 people may have to be moved. But this is a war that we are in which I'm sure you understand.'

To Ogilvy's consternation, Wallace appeared far more concerned with the wider political situation.

'I appreciate that,' he said. 'But if the bomb goes off it could jeopardise the prospects for peace that have opened up since the Sutton regime was brought to an end.

'I implore you to keep this fact in mind as you grapple with the awful situation.'

This was the first time Wallace had talked to him about peace being such a priority. A war of attrition was being waged against Vanguard and there were plans for what was hoped would be a decisive spring offensive. The President seemed to think that Gamble replacing Sutton had initiated a new situation. He knew that it had not – and not only from reading the diaries of the dead leader's sister. Wallace's remarks just confirmed that his administration seemed poised to adopt a very different approach to the British conflict.

He knew that it would be futile to have it out with Wallace, especially at 5am, when he was likely to be half-asleep. If only the President could obtain a concise summary of what was in Sutton's diaries. But events were moving so fast that perhaps it was simply too late for that.

Ogilvy decided to wind up the conversation in a cordial manner: 'Mr President, I appreciate the concern you have shown by phoning at such an hour. It is our express wish to prevent the worst happening. The siege in Edinburgh, involving over a hundred hostages, many of them American, was peacefully ended. I assure you that our approach to the Glasgow crisis will be no different.'

Since military figures were present at the crisis meeting, Ogilvy kept back details of the conversation. In his absence new information had emerged about the siege. Ogilvy had learned to be no longer surprised by anything but even he was taken aback when the facts were laid before him.

A previously disused tunnel, dating from the Second World War, linking the museum to the university, had been discovered. It seems to have been the route which Roxburgh and his followers had taken in order to enter a museum closed over the holiday. Ogilvy ruefully assumed that the university had also been used as a depot for the many small bombs which had gone off across Scotland in the previous two years. He observed to himself that given the lurch to extremism across the island, he should not have been that surprised.

There were red faces at the university. Suspicions were directed at Professor Mungo Kemp. He was one of the deputy Principals. His particular remit concerned the maintenance of the built environment and health and safety matters. It was a demanding and unglamorous task. Many people had been surprised when, four years earlier, Kemp had put his name forward for the position. Beforehand, and for at least a decade, he had been one of Scotland's academic firebrands.

He was a criminologist who argued that criminals were mainly morally upright people. Their misdeeds usually involved a redistribution of property from the rich to the poorer in society. He brushed aside evidence that in fact it was poorer-income citizens who suffered the most from crime. It was the criminal justice system which was criminal and criminals who were unsung heroes, promoting social justice!

Rather than being a joyless and intense academic, Kemp was cheerful in manner, relaxed in debate and very middle-class in his mannerisms. He was the son of a charity executive and had grown up in rural Stirlingshire far away from areas where crime was prevalent. He was able to utter extreme comments without provoking reprisals because of his outwardly sympathetic demeanour. His jokey style meant that trainee police staff attended his classes even though he had baldly stated that too many tears were shed for dead policemen or women: 'they were servants of a rotten social order,' he insisted. The police was simply a poor career choice, he informed students in his quieter moments.

Kemp would probably have remained a picturesque and fringe figure in Scottish academia but for the fact that around 2013, he had been given £5 million with which to set up a criminology department encompassing the most radical thinking in this field. The heir to a multi-million pet food business who had come under the influence of student radicals while studying in America, had been swayed by Kemp's ideas. Woodrow Tucker was committed to the closure of prisons and the release of imprisoned men to the community where they could support families or at least exercise their democratic rights. Of course violent offenders would need supervision but, in time, even that would not be necessary.

Kemp convinced the impressionable young Tucker that an institute, naturally named after him and shaped by his emancipatory ideas, would shake up criminology. A year after Tucker managed to part with £5 million in a contract drawn up by Kemp which ensured it could not be claimed back, he had been divested of control of the company through a shareholders revolt. But by now the institute was already a reality. It had a gleaming building on its own free-standing site, one looking down on the Kelvingrove Museum.

Kemp had generated non-stop controversy but the University of Glasgow managed to shelve its reservations about having him among the senior staff because he had dangled such a rich bequest in front of the management.

When Ogilvy became Prime Minister, some of his MSPs urged him to keep a watch on the most outspoken academics who had flirted with Vanguard or what became the SFF. He had instructed the intelligence services to keep an unobtrusive watch on some of them. But by now Kemp was deputy Principal at Glasgow and it was felt unnecessary to do so in his case. He had taken leave of absence from his department. He seemed to be engrossed with responsibilities like managing fire risks and keeping hazardous substances in secure areas.

The accepted view was that the smiling and once sinister hell-raiser had settled down and become an adornment of the university. But in reality he had not changed at all. He had been appalled that the weak-willed nationalists had allowed Gavin Ogilvy to assume office in 2020. A year earlier he had risked blowing his cover by writing to Janey Snodgrass and urging her to do anything possible to prevent this - from gerrymandering the electoral system to declaring a state emergency - if it appeared that Ogilvy's Unionists were on course for victory. He had no fears that the SNAP leader would report him to the police despite harsh laws against sedition and 'hate speech' which she had introduced. But he was disappointed when all he got back was a bland acknowledgement that his concerns were always appreciated.

He reckoned that the time was over for his high profile stunts and statements. But he needed to avoid exposure. The new times required a more Machiavellian way of undermining a rotten order. Thus he busied himself not with shocking bourgeois sensibilities but – outwardly – at least maintaining the university fabric as one of Glasgow's most dutiful senior academics.

Convinced, correctly, that nobody was looking over his shoulder he had control of storage space in one of the city's most important civic institutions.

As bombings and kidnappings periodically shook Scotland, the government stepped up its vigilance on public buildings and private individuals. But it never really focused its gaze on Scotland's diminishing number of universities. Ogilvy was sensitive to accusations of being a dictator who trampled on human rights. Besides ever since a past Principal of Glasgow University had backed the independence bid of the nationalists a decade earlier, he had been wary of getting entangled with this particular university. To discover that one of the senior staff had been using the criminology department to store weapons and explosives had come as a sickening blow. In retrospect, it was an ideal place. He expected that the planning of the bombings that had occurred in the past few years in all likelihood would be traced back to Kemp. In time his supposition would prove to be correct.

The police soon discovered that university porters had noticed unusual out-of-hours movements during the recent holiday. Kemp and men known to him who were clearly not university staff, had used a fork-lift truck to transport heavy boxes from his department to the basement of the main university building. As he was un-conventional by nature, nobody bothered to challenge him. But one porter recalled an incident he could not get out of his head. A large box had fallen off the forklift after being carelessly placed there by a helper. Kemp had gone berserk and, for a few seconds, gripped the man by the throat ready, it seemed, to throttle him.

As the crisis committee was absorbed with this information, a slip of paper was placed before Grant Stevenson. The security minister read it and then informed the others that Kemp's Jaguar car, by now burnt-out, had been found in a gulley at a small fishing port in Galloway. This suggested that he wasn't holed up in the museum and had made a getaway most likely by sea.

Ogilvy and his advisors faced a dilemma. Whereas the hostages in Edinburgh had been used as a shield for a planned freedom declaration, it looked as if Roxburgh would demand concessions in return for leaving them unharmed. What these concessions were became clear when he delivered his broadcast at 7pm.

He enjoyed his media performances and this one was no exception. His thickset features and spiky reddish hair were contrasted by a wide range of facial techniques, body movements and voice registers that made him a compelling propagandist, at least for some. His showmanship drew in listeners often against their better judgement only to be disgusted with themselves for listening to what ended up as crude and abusive tirades. This time Roxburgh dealt in specifics. He said that Glasgow's precious palace of culture had been seized in order to speed up the resumption of peaceful relations between Scotland and England, by which he meant the shrinking area under Vanguard rule.

He said the world was tired of the British war and this included the United States. But Scotland's insistence on allying with so-called British Liberty in Liverpool, amounted to a huge roadblock on the road to peace. He demanded that Ogilvy sever ties with British Liberty and agree to meet Jason Gamble around an agenda of peace and reconciliation. If he did not have the stomach to be a statesman then he should quit office and allow someone more capable to take over.

He promised that he meant business. The cameras zoomed in on a hapless group of Unionist and moderate Nationalist politicians chained to railings surrounded by bucolic pictures drawn by artists known as the Glasgow Boys. He also showed pictures of a bulky package in thick black plastic wrapping with wires protruding from it. He said that the package contained the bomb that he had earlier warned about. It was placed on the first floor in a section devoted to the Glasgow artist and designer Charles Rennie Mackintosh. He warned that the bomb contained a mixture of radio-active material and high explosives. It would cause destruction over a wide area if the continued unreasonable stance of the Ogilvy government left him with no option but to detonate it.

He placed himself in the footsteps of World War II commanders. They had sometimes found it necessary to carry out acts of terrible destruction to hasten the arrival of peace and he had no hesitation in emulating them unless the government saw sense.

No sooner had his crisis committee convened than Ogilvy was called to the phone to take another transatlantic call. This time it was President Wallace's national security advisor Harvey Brinton. He had never been an enthusiast for the administration's existing British policy. He was phoning to convey the President's feeling that the crisis should be brought to a conclusion as swiftly as possible. When Ogilvy said that this was exactly his intention, Brinton came back to suggest that talking to Gamble might indeed now be the way forward. Ogilvy felt the anger rising within him. Here was confirmation that Washington was indeed walking away from its commitment to topple a regime which had so much blood on its hands. But nevertheless he kept his cool.

He said that he did not rule out any option so grave was the threat posed to life by Roxburgh. But he thought it worth reminding his caller that Scotland and America were on the verge of signing a defence pact at the centre of which was an undertaking to remove Vanguard and work together to help reconstruct England.

Brinton cleared his throat and said that treaties like that one were laudable but they often had to be adapted in the face of changing circumstances. 'That might be the situation we are in now Gavin,' he observed.

Stung by his insouciance, Ogilvy ignored his familiarity, concluding that the sooner this conversation finished the better. He thanked Brinton for keeping in contact and said that he expected any change of policy on the part of the United States towards Britain would not occur unilaterally but would be made in consultation with its allies.

No military officials were present at the crisis committee. They were busy supervising the evacuation of scores of thousands of people from west Glasgow and the city centre. So Ogilvy felt able to broach the political dimension of the Kelvingrove crisis with his advisers. He feared that however it ended the government would be left isolated. The trend in the White House was clearly towards reaching a compromise peace with Vanguard. Tristram Pannell had been pushing that line all day on US cable news networks. There were also rumours that Lucy McKenna was only hours away from resigning as Secretary of State.

'I hope she reads Philippa Sutton's diaries before she does anything,' Brian Crawford said.

'Did you manage to pass on a copy to Ray Lattimore before he flew out,' he was asked?

'No I gave my copy to Anatoly Yashin. I didn't expect Ray to be leaving for the States as early as this. But don't worry. I heard last night that he now has a copy.

He and Anatoly met up at the airport and he insisted that he take his copy and read as much as he could of it on the flight to DC.

'Let's hope what's contained in the diary helps policy-makers across there to see reason once again,' he concluded.

The spirits of Ogilvy and his team might not have been so low if they had been aware of conditions inside the Kelvingrove Museum.

Except for his provocative broadcasts from England, Roxburgh was an enigma for a lot of his accomplices. Most had been recruited by Pearse Mellick. He had built up a flourishing business that traded in artefacts relating to Celtic football club. Everything from beer mats and key rings to old match programmes and books and videos relating to Celtic were traded by McCelt Inc, the name of his company.

The Glaswegian had operated out of Dublin until the political violence there made him decide that it was prudent to transfer his base to the Isle of Man in 2021. He was not only concerned to earn a living from his passion, one shared by tens of thousands of people, but he wanted to make it a springboard for political influence.

He was adept at public relations. His twin bugbears were Rangers football club and Britain's unbroken record of meddling in Irish affairs. He fostered a sense of indignation online, magnifying and sometimes inventing scandals and incidents. The political dimension of the whole Celtic phenomenon had only usually appealed to a minority of fans. But this minority had grown in size due to the collapse of European-level football and the depressed state of the game generally arising from the political crisis. Mellick cultivated links with those fans who saw Celtic more as a political religion than as a magical football side. He touched base with the angry evangelicals in speaking tours through Scotland and at conventions further afield in the Canary islands, Florida and the Costa del Sol.

It was Mellick who took the initiative and sought out Roxburgh. This occurred not long after he began his propaganda onslaught on the Scottish government. Mellick slipped in and out of the Isle of Man, Dublin and London. He had stopped coming to Scotland because he knew that the intelligence services were on his trail, especially after Grant Stevenson had become minister of public security.

For his part Roxburgh regarded Mellick as a temporary ally whom he could use and then discard if he no longer suited his designs. He never divulged it to Mellick but before entering the Foreign Legion, he had followed Rangers. It had been a tradition in his family. His father, who was a foreman in an engineering firm, had possessed anti-Catholic and anti-Irish views and some of them had rubbed off on his son. When just a child Jerome had gravitated to Scottish Nationalism after his father was thrown out of work with the closure of the firm in the 1980s. He had campaigned for the SNP as it then was and found that Catholics in and around Glasgow were the most resistant voters. He found it hard to regard Irish-minded Scots on Clydeside as true Scots. They were too bound up with Ireland and its complex grievances. By the time they went over in large numbers to the nationalist cause during and after the 2014 referendum he was far away in French Guiana. He had joined the Foreign Legion in almost suicidal despair after a love affair cut short by his fiancé dying of cancer.

She had died in an English hospital where a suspicious Roxburgh had become convinced that she had been neglected due to her Scottishness.

His anguish found an outlet in an all-consuming hatred for Britain. It was this that created the conditions for an alliance with Mellick. Both of them increasingly focused on mounting a special operation in Glasgow. The hope was that it would throw the authorities off balance and might even have international repercussions.

Mellick had purchased weapons in Dublin which were then landed clandestinely in Scotland. Instead of being stored in remote locations, they were housed just a few hundred yards from the building which they hoped to capture.

Kemp and Roxburgh had known each other for several years. They were kindred spirits, mischief-makers intent on toppling the existing social order, not knowing or really caring what followed. By now Roxburgh's attachment to Scotland was primarily sentimental. It had grown during his service in the Foreign Legion in remaining French imperial outposts. But he had lost touch with Scotland and it had become a platform for what grew into insensate hatred for Britain. Kemp for his part claimed to be an internationalist but he was committed to the destruction of bourgeois capitalism before peace and virtue could finally have their chance to shape the world.

It had been decided that Kemp would slip away on the eve of the seizure of Kelvingrove Museum. In Ireland, he would then act as a spokesman for Roxburgh's 'Scotland First' movement. He himself had headed for Dublin after his propaganda broadcasts abruptly ceased immediately after the killing of Clive Sutton. Far from being silenced by Jason Gamble, he had been asked to take a break and, if necessary, find new and better ways of harrying the Scottish government.

Vanguard had no advance knowledge of what he was cooking up but Roxburgh continued to be supplied with political intelligence. He was among the first to learn that the Atlantic front against Vanguard was starting to crack, leaving Ogilvy's government suddenly exposed.

Roxburgh retained a similar arms length relationship with the SFF. Scotland First was his own preferred flag of convenience. He had never possessed much confidence in the conspiratorial talents of Bruce or McCusker. He had retained contact primarily because they were also dedicated to toppling the Scottish government by openly defying it.

Roxburgh was a natural conspirator who, to press ahead with his venture, kept his collaborators in the dark about vital details. Thus Mellick was unaware of the existence of a dirty bomb until it had been mentioned in Roxburgh's first museum broadcast.

When he broached the matter with Roxburgh, he was told that the bomb was an elaborate ruse. There were indeed explosives. After all he had bought them for the cause and smuggled them to Scotland. But there was no radio-active component.

This was a lie. Roxburgh had acquired the knowledge to manufacture such a bomb and Kemp had helped him construct it. The authorities were soon convinced that there was indeed a bomb inside the museum since strong radio-active signals were emanating from the Mackintosh room where it was being kept. Ogilvy had discussed with his advisers whether a swoop on this part of the museum was feasible but they decided that if Roxburgh had already linked the bomb to detonators, it was far too great a risk.

Roxburgh had issued instructions through Mellick that the fifty or so accomplices were to keep a close watch on the prisoners during his broadcast. He wished his underlings to have as little knowledge as possible about the operation. They were there to obey orders and lay down their lives for the cause.

The men with Roxburgh could be split into two groups. There were a smaller group of hardened criminals mainly recruited by Kemp who were drawn to an implacable leader like Roxburgh. They were likely to obey his orders especially if mayhem and destruction were promised. The larger group recruited by Mellick were more varied. Most lacked a vicious streak. They had been swept up in what some saw merely as an escapade out of boredom or from a sense of bravado. The thought of storming Glasgow's palace of culture and making a stand there as Scotland's premier online propagandist ranted and raged, was a diverting one. The trouble was that nobody had thought through what followed. The thoughts of the brighter youngsters swung in this direction after it became clear that Roxburgh had no intention of mixing with them. He remained cooped up on his first floor headquarters located in the gallery exploring 'Scotland's First People.'

Only Mellick was permitted to occasionally enter. Roxburgh declined to even go down to the restaurant in the main hall. Instead, one of Kemp's criminal pals left a tray of food outside his HQ.

Roxburgh expected Mellick to act as a pliant subaltern. But the head of McCelt Inc was finding it difficult to keep his young recruits in line. Word was spreading about the dirty bomb. Mellick tried, but never quite succeeded, to convince his men that it was a clever hoax. Grumbling spilled over into dissatisfaction on the second full day of the siege when news arrived that the match between Celtic and the Spirit of Freedom was still on. Celtic Park was outside the zone likely to be contaminated if the dirty bomb went off. Ogilvy authorised it to go ahead because he thought Glasgow's inhabitants badly needed their morale boosting.

Most followers of football had forgotten that the Spirits were an English team. They were welcomed because of the quality of the football that they so often played. This applied also to most of the thirty or so Celtic fans in the museum even though few stated this outright.

Roxburgh ordered the televisions in the museum to be turned off. He was angry that the match was going ahead. It seemed to suggest that the threat he posed was not that severe after all. Many of the youngsters were livid for a different reason. People evacuated from their houses would be able to watch the game but it would be a pleasure denied to them. Some were muttering that if things spun out of control, they might never see their beloved Celtic playing ever again.

Mellick tried to persuade Roxburgh to change his mind and allow the broadcast to be shown but he was unbending and bawled him out. Danny Roarty and Ricky McGrain, two of the most assertive youngsters decided that the only option was to confront Roxburgh. But when they walked into his den, he sprang to his feet from the couch he had been resting on and fired a volley of shots over their heads.

Later Mellick tried to explain that he had mistakenly thought they were assailants who had crept in from outside. But his authority was fast diminishing among the lads he had recruited. A lot of them had lapped up Roxburgh's stormy broadcasts echoing their own hardly profound anti-British feelings. But the horrible thought was dawning on some of them that they were just as much prisoners of Roxburgh as the politicians chained to the railings.

Mellick was now having second thoughts of his own about his involvement. He had started out believing that taking part in what admittedly was a gamble meant he stood a chance of becoming a figure of real importance in the new Scotland. He had assumed the chances of being personally harmed were low. But as soon as it became obvious that the dirty bomb existed and Roxburgh was prepared to blow himself and everyone up if necessary, he realised that he had very badly miscalculated. By the third day of the museum's occupation, he knew he had made a terrible mistake and that his life and the lives of those whom he had recruited like some kind of Pied Piper, were in jeopardy.

However, it was no easy matter to escape from Roxburgh. Kemp's mean-spirited guards were increasingly in control. Roxburgh had dropped his stern and unapproachable manner and had decided to cultivate them. They became his praetorian guard and there were always several with him in his first floor operations room.

One of these grim lieutenants caught Mellick as he tried to get clear of the museum by climbing down a drainpipe from a window that he had prised open.

He was hauled before Roxburgh who, there and then, placed him before an impromptu court-martial. He was accused and quickly found guilty of betraying Scotland First. Roxburgh's frustration at being holed up in the cavernous museum for half-a-week got the better of him. After twenty minutes he pronounced the sentence of death on Mellick for desertion.

He begged for mercy and when Roxburgh jeered at him he said that without his money and planning, this enterprise would never have got off the ground. Standing over him clad in his dressing-gown and vaping, Roxburgh laughed contemptuously. He ordered a minion to hold Mellick's head down on a pillow while another put a bullet through the back of it.

The intermittent sound of shots had been heard outside. It convinced Stevenson that the situation might soon boil over. The next morning Roxburgh made another broadcast. He warned that unless there were tangible signs that the government was prepared to extend an olive branch to Vanguard, he would detonate the bomb. He said that he had no fear of death (which was true) and that the others with him were prepared to lay down their lives for a glorious cause (which wasn't).

He assumed that the blocking system preventing mobile phones being used was on but several of the by now disaffected youngsters had found a spot in the museum where it didn't work. When news spread that Roxburgh was planning to blow everyone up, there was mounting anger. All but the ex-criminals had been divested of their weapons and the misguided Celtic fans were hauled off into detention.

Roxburgh issued a deadline of 1pm and, when it passed without a response from the government, he left his den and headed to the Mackintosh room where the bomb was located. As he did so he was being watched from the outside. Soldiers had managed to clamber on to the roof undetected. Long-range cameras from the Kelvin Hall on the south side of the museum and the University at the back, were able to follow much of what was happening inside.

By the time Roxburgh had got close to the bomb it was intended that a sniper, positioned in Glasgow University's staff club, would take aim with the intention of killing him instantaneously.

But the sniper's view was blocked by large marble pillars and he feared that he would have no time to get his quarry properly in his sights before he could carry out his deed. Seconds passed and then he was able to spot him as he passed a large window. The sniper wasted no time and pressed the trigger.

It missed, the bullet ricocheting off a pillar. A cry of pain was audible, first to those inside the building and then to the troops and special police outside.

The bullet had hit Roxburgh's bodyguard, entering his neck. He dropped to the floor, rolling in agony.

The bomb-master only briefly averted his fixed gaze as he strode towards the device. But as he picked up the detonator, as a preliminary to blowing himself and much of the museum sky high, the legs suddenly went from under him. He was floored in a rugby tackle by Danny Roarty.

He was the Celtic youth who had been the first to see just what a terrible fate was about to befall them and much of their city. It had given him the determination to loosen the cords with which he was bound when he and others had been pushed into a cloakroom. He overpowered a guard who had been watching over them

Pinning Roxburgh to the ground, he lost no time in knocking him out cold with a metal torch which he had grabbed as he made his way to the Mackintosh room.

Realising what was happening, Roxburgh's remaining guards bore down on him. But before they could reach him, the chambers of the museum filled with smoke and sirens wailed furiously.

Once Roarty's desperate attempt to halt Roxburgh had been spotted by the armed units outside and on the roof of the building, they had entered from at least four directions. Masked men in commando gear crashed through the windows of the Mackintosh room to prevent anyone else reaching the explosive device. A fire-fight ensued between the armed police and some of the ex-prisoners. Only after twenty minutes was it apparent that the danger had been averted.

Thankfully none of the captive politicians or staff were seriously hurt and the youngsters recruited by Mellick were relieved that their terrifying escapade was over. As they filed out of the building, they passed the body of their mentor Mellick slumped in a corner under a sheet. A few openly cursed him, furious at themselves for getting swept up in his deadly stunt. After questioning it was decided to release the Celtic youth. They had been caught up in what they saw as an escapade. Once it had gone badly wrong, they had shown their horror at what they had got mixed up in.

Without Roarty's courageous act, it was impossible to see how total disaster could have been averted. When he and the others were released from police custody, Rory Savidge was there to greet him. They were cousins. They had disagreed in the past about the right future for Scotland. But the terrifying drama and its outcome had finally banished the misunderstanding.

Glasgow returned to some semblance of normality in the hours ahead as people were gradually allowed to return to their homes. Ogilvy and his key advisers grabbed a few hours of sleep. His office had been notified by the Scottish embassy in Washington that a debate between Ray Littlemore and Tristram Pannell would be taking place around midnight British time. All the main American news networks would be broadcasting it live.

The question for the evening was should peace be given a chance now in Britain? It would be a 45-minute encounter and Lattimore began first. He argued that the poison of Vanguard needed to be uprooted completely or peace would never return to England. He branded the government in London as no different from the former one. Jason Gamble had come to power by arranging the murder of his predecessor, the architect of the regime. He would not hesitate to use violence in order to stay in power and any hopes that he would mend his ways were simply delusional.

Pannell was more relaxed than he had been in years according to those who had closely watched his long period in the wilderness. He said that he pitied Ray Lattimore for being anchored in the past. England now had a new leadership which spurned violence. It wished to stretch out the hand of reconciliation as widely as possible. The government that he had just been asked to form would be a natural and, in time, trusted, ally of the United States. Lattimore was expressing the viewpoint of those in US politics who would soon be viewed as political dinosaurs with no appreciation of the new political spring that England was poised to experience.

Pannell's line about dinosaurs had been aimed at Lucy McKenna. By now it was common knowledge that the US Secretary was in a relationship with Lattimore. He had learned of a warning that she had been given by Wallace just prior to the debate. A source in the White House informed him that she had been told to vacate her office if her British partner sought to undermine what would shortly be the altered US policy line.

Viewers waited to see what Lattimore's last throw of the dice would be. The strain was clearly etched across his saturnine features. He began with an unusual gesture. He put a briefcase on the table and extracted a bulky leather-bound journal which he unbuckled.

Turning to the cameras, he said:

'What I have before me is a diary. It was kept for thirty-seven months by Philippa Sutton. She is currently being held in detention by Mr Pannell's government. But for the last three years she was a loyal acolyte of her brother when he controlled most of England.

'Mr Pannell will no doubt insist that the diary is a clever forgery. Or else he may say that it is indeed Sutton's words but that what she wrote for three years was a pack of lies. She is clearly mad is the current view of the regime which no doubt he concurs with.

'It is true that this diary is the record of a misguided woman who hopefully one day will answer for certain misdeeds in a court of law. But she is most certainly not mad as Phelim Armstrong, the lawyer who defended Greer McIver in London's Old Bailey, knows. He met her when she fled to the South African embassy in London, carrying this diary.

'He and others in Britain as well as several US officials, have read it. Their unanimous view is that it provides an important account of how power was exercised at the heart of the Vanguard regime.

'Mr Pannell appears frequently. Thus, on 28 December 2021 an entry reads:

"Tristram Pannell came to Hampton Palace at 10am. I sat in as he and Clive discussed the trip that he would make to the Middle East in early January. He would be meeting with Nureddin Shaheedi and Adnan Mistret. He would be carrying with him £12 million pounds as a down-payment for the recruitment of foreign fighters who it was expected would be put into battle by the summer of 2022."

"Pannell agreed to the assignment. I hoped he might ask for something in return. The obvious request would be to seek an improvement in the condition of the VIPs languishing in the basement of football stadiums. Many were known to him and several had served in his government. I had already suggested to Clive that no useful purpose was being served through having such a harsh regime. But he didn't raise the subject. Instead, he asked that his wife be released from house arrest upon his return to London."'

Pannell's relaxed demeanour had vanished and he was suddenly flushed and agitated. He turned to the moderator Peyton Duncan and said :

'This is outrageous. The debating rules are being thrown out the window here.'

Duncan briefly conferred with the studio through an earpiece before saying: 'So far Mr Lattimore appears to have broken no rules. He is citing from a document which he believes is relevant to his case. Naturally, if the document contains extreme language, then I would stop him from reading further extracts.'

Turning to Lattimore he said: 'Please continue.'

He turned a few pages of the diary and said:

'15 January 2022, Clive has informed me that Pannell is satisfied with the terms agreed with the Middle East warlords Shaheedi and Mistret. They are supplying eight thousand foreign fighters for a six month contract in England. They will mainly be recruited from Syria, Eritrea, Tunisia, and Iraq and from among the Chechyan diaspora.'

Closing the journal he turned to Pannell and said: 'I expect you will deny the authenticity of these extracts. But can I ask you this? Where exactly were you on 15 January 2022. Did you happen to be in Beirut?'

Pannell avoided his gaze and stared into the distance.

Lattimore continued: 'you may deny it but the intelligence services of several countries will have a record of you being there.'

'If you concede you were, it is reasonable to ask about the purpose of your visit.

'Middle Eastern factions had not played any role in the British conflict until mid-2022. But from that point on, they became key players with devastating consequences for Britain.'

Lattimore paused and looked over to the moderator who said: 'It's now over to you Mr Pannell. Feel free to respond…'

Pannell continued to blankly look ahead and then he said: 'I travelled extensively in that period. Yes I recall being in the Middle East around then. All my trips were meant to further peace and I'm absolutely sure that this one was no exception.'

He abruptly stopped, his mouth now set in a tight grimace.

Lattimore resumed:

'I think not. The foreign fighters who were recruited, and paid for, by you managed to carry out devastating acts in the summer of 2022. Several million people were forced from their homes out of fear of being slaughtered. Many of these people are now living as refugees in Scotland. You even spent time there a year later seeking to prevent its government taking in people whom your actions had displaced.

'And now you are back as Prime Minister. The country you are supposedly in charge of used to be a decent place to live but now large parts of it are one huge morgue.

'Once your record during this time of torment becomes better known, only you will still believe that you have what it takes to bring peace to England. You are too intimately bound up with the suffering that it may take a generation or more to recover from. Anybody in the United States who, no doubt for the best of motives, believes that creatures like you can restore peace, will only be cruelly deceived.

'Now in the minutes remaining,' Lattimore said, 'let me turn to several of the entries concerning Jason Gamble.'

But before he could start Pannell noisily got up from the table and said: 'I repeat this is outrageous. This debate is being turned into a monstrous witch-hunt. It is one I have no intention of enduring a moment longer.'

Open-mouthed at the dramatic turn which the encounter had taken, the moderator struggled to find the right words with which to wrap up proceedings. Instead frantic hand signals from the producer indicated that he must bring them to an end now. It had been riveting television but if Lattimore made claims about Gamble as sensational as the ones he had thrown at Pannell, it could cause a huge diplomatic scandal.

So the programme credits started to roll and an extended run of ads followed.

Martha Kirchbaum had been one of several million Americans who had watched the debate. She had more than the usual interest. Her son Jeff had been the pilot of a US airforce plane in 2022 which had been trying to prevent foreign fighters landing in West Yorkshire. His plane had been downed by artillery fire from Vanguard batteries and the airforce had eventually written to say that her son was missing, presumed killed in action.

While the ads were running, Mrs Kirchbaum picked up the phone and rang the District Attorney's office in west Long Island. Doug Schell III had been elected promising accessibility to the voters in his district. It was 7.30pm and Mrs Kirchbaum knew that someone would still be at the office who would hopefully act on her complaint.

As requested she filled in an online form reporting a crime carried out by Mr Tristram Pannell, a British citizen currently in the United States. In the box headed 'Type of Crime' she wrote: 'MANSLAUGHTER, Pannell handed over a large sum of money to two Middle Eastern nationals which resulted in mercenaries arriving in Britain in June 2022. My son Jeff was killed carrying out his duties as an American airman in opposing their landing on British soil.'

Two hours later she received a call. It was the District Attorney. He had persuaded a judge to issue a warrant for Pannell's arrest. The FBI in Washington had been notified. He was not at his hotel suite in the affluent north-west of the city but they would keep looking.

Watching late night news, one of the officers saw that Pannell was due to meet informally with several Senators from the foreign relations committee at Capitol Hill the next morning. The agents closed in on Pannell just as he was sitting down with the senior law-makers. He was informed that he was under arrest. A warrant had been issued by a district attorney in Long Island arising from the shooting down of a US airforce pilot over the British city of Leeds in June 2022.

Pannell had struggled to regain his poise after the disastrous television debate. He had received instructions from London to head to Dulles airport and get on a flight to Paris as soon as his meeting was over.

He knew that he was cornered at least for now. He could not claim diplomatic immunity. Only British Liberty had representation in Washington. Vanguard's affairs were being handled by the Turkish embassy.

The politicians whom Pannell had been due to meet were sympathetic to the idea of a compromise peace. There were awkward disbelieving glances as Pannell was led away. But there had already been a few rumours from inside the White House that the President was swinging back to the previous policy of all-out-confrontation with Vanguard.

An aide rushed in to the room to say that Lucy McKenna would be on television in a few moments. Only a short time before, those present had assumed that by now she would be out of a job .

They filed into a dining room to gather around a television in a far corner. McKenna appeared tired but there was a gleam in her eyes and her voice was firm. She said that graphologists had compared the writing in the diaries with that of Philippa Sutton and had offered the opinion that they belonged to one and the same person.

That being so, she urged the Vanguard authorities to ensure that no harm befell Ms Sutton while in their custody. Otherwise it would be yet another stain in the dark record of political violence that had occurred in England.

She concluded by announcing that she would soon be travelling to Scotland in the hope that it would be possible to conclude the negotiations for a mutual defence pact.

This return to the limelight of the Secretary of State signalled to many observers that her job was safe and the policy she embodied was not about to be junked. In the next few days extracts from the Sutton diaries were published in the *New York Times*. These entries dwelt on Philippa Sutton's state of mind and her relations with her brother. They indicated her growing sense of dismay and even remorse over what had happened since Vanguard had swept to power. There were further revelations indicating that Tristram Pannell had been party to other decisions which had compounded the misery of the British people. By 11 January he had been transferred to a top security area of a New York detention centre. Another judge had concluded that he had a case to answer and there was no basis for offering him bail.

The published diary entries made no mention of Jason Gamble. There were in-criminating entries which the US authorities decided to withhold. It was thought better not to force him into a corner and to wait and see how he would react to the reversal in his fortunes. His ace card Pannell was now stewing in a US jail. The chief US diplomat was heading to Scotland in all likelihood to sign a treaty with Vanguard's northern rival. British Liberty in Liverpool would also continue to receive US backing.

The diaries did, however, contain shocking revelations about the Macklin regime in Dublin. Excerpts from early 2023 were published showing that the Irish government was involved in the human organ trade. It was selling the body parts of individuals who had died in accidents or in the violence that was scarring a Dublin now awash with hard drugs. The remains of the dead were only handed over to the next-of-kin after various organs such as heart, liver, kidneys and lungs had been removed. There had been rumours of such an illicit trade but the Irish media had been dissuaded from following them up.

Now there was concrete proof. Philippa Sutton had found out because Vanguard officials were involved in arranging the shipment of the human organs to East Asia. They received a part of the massive profit which senior Irish officials (in reality Macklin himself) made. Sutton named the individuals. Several were high in Gamble's entourage. She had pressed her brother to end Vanguard's involvement in the trade, sparking resentment among regime officials who had made enormous gains and expected more in the future.

As Secretary McKenna prepared to cross the Atlantic news came from Dublin of serious disturbances in several of its working-class areas. A family whose 14-year-old son had been killed in a hit-and-run accident had organized a march on a local police station. They were driven off with tear gas and rubber bullets. This only caused the unrest to spread. By 8pm an estimated 10,000 people had massed in the city centre. In an overnight operation many were herded into the Aviva stadium south of the river Liffey by the Sunrise party, Macklin's political arm.

The Scottish Army's special operations unit took advantage of the turmoil to mount a daring operation and seize Mungo Kemp. The fugitive professor had been holed up in a cottage in a secluded valley south-west of the capital. He was taken in an unmarked vehicle on the two hour journey to Northern Ireland. Within 24 hours he was languishing in a Scottish jail, facing interrogation over a terror plot which could have devastated much of Glasgow.

The sudden eruption of conflict in Ireland prompted Secretary McKenna to turn back from Dulles airport. The pace of Irish events did indeed merit high-level attention. A ruthless crackdown in Dublin bought the narco-regime some time. But there were protests in each of the devolved regions where Macklin's reach was fast diminishing. Within days each of his puppet leaders was swept aside. Democratic juntas were set up with members of the late Paschal Rogan's movement playing a prominent role.

People right across the island had been affronted and horrified when the revelations about the government's active role in the organ trade spilled out into the open. A moral outlook which had seemed to be expunged by the 'anything goes' attitude of Ireland during the previous twenty years, re-asserted itself. A march on the capital was launched from four points, Cork, Galway, Limerick and Sligo and by the third day, it was estimated that one-fifth of the adult population was taking part. Leading the march from Cork was Phelim Armstrong. It was his home town and he had returned to Ireland within hours of the unrest starting.

Each of the foreign embassies in which Macklin and his chief accomplice Louis Carmody sought refuge, slammed the door in their faces. Finally with their lynching seeming imminent, the US government authorised its Dublin embassy to take them in. This occurred just after Gavin Ogilvy had made an announcement about the desirability of a special international court to try people in the British Isles guilty of high crimes since 2021. While at the UN General Assembly in October he had discussed the mechanisms for setting it up. He had obtained guarded support from the upper echelons of the UN and finally the US authorities seemed to be offering backing.

The toppled Irish leaders, as well as the imprisoned academic Mungo Kemp and a Jerome Roxburgh recovering from his wounds, seemed prime candidates. Of course there were hundreds of people in England who had acquired notoriety over the past few years for their crimes. Sharon Burgess, the former minister of social credit who had sent thousands of elderly citizens to an early death by withholding credits from them, was just the most notorious example. Ogilvy feared that only a small portion of the horrors that had occurred in England when Vanguard was in charge, had surfaced and that awful discoveries remained to be made.

The winds of change were, however, blowing vigorously through the tormented isles. As well as working to bring the guilty to book, Ogilvy was increasingly thinking of what fresh arrangements could lead to permanent forms of cooperation between them. Britain still had resources, material and human. He believed that close inter-island cooperation provided the best chance of recovery. But he was well aware that peace was still only a distant prospect. Gargantuan efforts would be needed before reconstruction could get underway.

Chapter 15

Conclusion

In some quarters there was surprise when Gavin Ogilvy accepted an invitation to deliver a short address at a thanksgiving service in Glasgow's St Andrew's Cathedral for the city's deliverance from disaster. At times senior Catholic clergy had acted as cheer-leaders for political nationalism. They had forgotten their role as spiritual pastors as many young Catholics were swallowed up in a tide of hedonism. But, as far as was known, no clergy had got involved with militant extremists. Now the church appeared to be re-evaluating its stance and stepping back from political engagement.

In his address Ogilvy expressed relief that the city had emerged unscathed from the dirty bomb episode and that no innocent people had lost their lives. But he struck a sombre note:

'Too many people on our islands had become obsessed with the present and with satisfying their egos. Self-absorption had enabled grievances to be manufactured by unscrupulous individuals. They had promised paradise on earth, a state of being which was supposed to be the pinnacle of existence. Political alchemists had exploited the human craving for material comfort and emotional release in order to carve out a path to power. Once power was in their grasp, they used it to unleash a wave of cruelty and wanton destruction.

'One of the few benefits to have arisen from the foulness of recent times has been the growing realisation that evil exists in men and that vigilance is needed if it is not to rise up, again and again, and destroy what has been patiently constructed.

'The present has to be a time of recovery and reconstruction rather than a time devoted to hedonistic fancies and the pursuit of sterile disputes. Future generations have to be left tangible legacies in order to provide a basis for civil behaviour. But it will all be pointless unless we find means to check the periodic urge for self-destruction. A sense of the spiritual, going beyond merely enjoying happiness in the here-and-now, is essential to save us from falling so low in another generation or two.'

Anatoly Yashin found echoes in Ogilvy's speech in what his fellow Russian Aleksandr Solzhenitsyn had warned about the West's capacity for self-destruction forty years earlier. When he quizzed the Prime Minister he said that he had indeed dipped into Solzhenitsyn's writings as he could find few contemporary Scottish thinkers who could adequately explain the grim point the island had now reached. But he had also drawn on English thinkers like Roger Scruton as well as Scottish writers of the past such as John Buchan.

As he emerged from the Cathedral, the Prime Minister was cheered. It was one small indication that the mood in Glasgow was shifting. There was a swing away from cultivating ethnic identities and challenging authority. It was confirmed four months later when the governing Scottish Citizens Party won a majority of seats in the city, ensuring another four years in office.

One of his acts was to announce an amnesty for those who had been involved in the January rebellion without having been responsible for any serious assaults. Ogilvy felt it was important to dispel any sense of martyrdom which could be the basis for fresh grievances to fester. Clova Bruce was released from custody. She and Torquil Niven were re-united and headed back to the Moray Firth. They settled down to running a small hotel which specialised in New Age meditation courses as a profitable sideline. Bruce candidly informed any guests who asked that she had been on a journey and the political phase of her life was now finally over.

But on the eve of her departure, and in an uncharacteristic gesture, she had sought out Tony Shand. She apologised to the moderate nationalist for the burning of his house and for seeking to do him personal harm during the rebellion. She confessed to him that she was finally learning that she was not really made for politics.

'Tony, what is it about our generation', she ruminated? 'We've done precious little for Scotland through our behaviour'.

'Some like me, have dragged the country into strife. Scotland has been little more than a stage upon which a lot of overwrought people unloaded their personal frustrations and resentments. This has been all too true in my case'.

'Hopefully, I'm getting over this phase. At least I can see that politics has reduced me to an inconsequential figure. It became an outlet enabling my personal defects to be magnified. In the Grand Nevis hotel, I finally realised that we were going nowhere and was relieved that Ross Bryden spirited me out of there before I could make an even bigger fool of myself.'

'Far too many of our activists see nationalism as a hobby. It became a magnet for obsessives and egotists who wanted to strut their stuff. In a quieter age, they might have been trainspotters or stamp collectors. The new noisy era of self-dramatisation turned them into folk who imagined they could somehow create a new country.

'I now think it might be for the best if we step aside and see if Gavin Ogilvy can really take the place forward with his reforms. I'm certainly thankful that he has allowed me to be a free women despite all that has happened.'

Shand wished her well but said little, inwardly relieved that a belatedly more philosophical Clova Bruce had replaced the hell-raiser.

Immediately after the January crisis Ogilvy had received an offer to return to Hollywood for the shooting of a British Western which Chuck Redwood promised would be a blockbuster. His four years governing Scotland, avoiding it being dragged into war but helping many of the English victims, had been taxing. Soon he would be forty. There would not be much more time for him to play the lead in action man roles. But he decided to soldier on. At least he had a life partner to share his existence with. There was too much unfinished business. He would devote his energies to public service until others came forward to take the burden from him. Then he could step aside.

He and Greer wanted to keep their own lives private. Neither of them were keen to opt for marriage. They had enough fulfilment in their lives. The redefinition of marriage was just part of a wider movement to redefine humanity and banish norms which had stood the test of time, a bulwark against chaos they both felt. The institution of marriage between a man and a woman was the natural order of things. More gays believed this than was often assumed. Of course, the militant utopians keen to endlessly experiment in human relations saw the pair of them as sell-outs. But by now his own back was strong enough to endure such brickbats.

As he had anticipated, Vanguard was not proving easy to crush. In London, Gamble was still in charge. In the spring, his regime had been rocked by another crisis. Realising that he was the only one of those who had eliminated Clive Sutton who had not simply disappeared or been involved in a mysterious accident, a senior Vanguard official defected. He talked, filling in the blanks about how Sutton had met his end.

He had been murdered in a basement of Hampton palace and a double had been sent to Bradford where the assassination reported to the world had occurred. But Gamble shrugged off the affair. He dug in, confirming Ogilvy's prediction that it would be an arduous task for the British-American coalition to capture cities like London and Birmingham. They were now full of ethnic and religious enclaves which it would be difficult for any outside army to subdue and police.

In Scotland Ogilvy resolved to build up the country by emphasising modernisation, improvements and respect for each individual. A slimmed down state was a necessity due to severe financial restraints but he was confident that a state with an ethos of accessibility could better serve citizens than had been the case hitherto.

He launched a programme of improvements at the first sitting of the Scottish Parliament after his victory. The initial emphasis was to be on education and its overhaul from primary school to university level. The turmoil across much of the world meant the comparative league tables in which Scotland had steadily slipped back, were no longer in existence. But it was still obvious that the level of functional illiteracy was alarmingly high. Meanwhile at university level students were too often encouraged by their teachers to cultivate a rebellious spirit well into adulthood rather than equip themselves with knowledge to make a positive mark on life.

Mungo Kemp, the vice-principal of Glasgow University and the brains behind the bombing campaign which had culminated in the seizure of Kelvingrove museum, had revealed the rot in higher eduction. His exposure gave Ogilvy the opportunity to press ahead with a daring series of university reforms. Two-year degree courses were introduced in the arts and humanities. Shorter degrees would provide financial savings both to students and to the public purse. Ogilvy had long felt that too many students were opting for liberal arts courses. Many had emerged after three or four years with closed minds and a sense of grievance. They had been easy fodder for extremists and opportunists like Clova Bruce. He wanted it to be harder for the latest rising nationalist star James Hinde to capture the minds of some of the best Scottish youth. Moreover, the professional jobs to absorb them were simply not there and many ended up unemployed or else working in supermarkets or call centres - jobs they could have had without bothering with university. His goal was to restore the reputation of Scottish universities to what they had been in the mid-18th century – the age of the Scottish Enlightenment.

Ogilvy was mindful of the example set by Wilford University. Its priority had been to cultivate an independent and enquiring spirit that was not a slave to any dogma. Absolutely none of the dogmas that had arisen in modern times had all or even most of the answers for problems arising from human existence. These were perennial ones arising from mankind's imperfection.

In the hands of malign individuals like Clive Sutton, dogmas promising salvation and redemption had brought terrible consequences in their wake. Scotland had avoided the worst. But the fact had to be faced that, except briefly in the 18th century, a spirit of free enquiry had never really flourished there. It needed to spring up if the country was to avoid being swept away by demagogues like Fergus Peacock or Clova Bruce. People not just of intellect but with strong character would be needed to guide the country through stormy times. Judgement and insight were more likely to be found in the next generation of leaders if the country was equipped with institution that gave them the scope to govern effectively but limited their ability to carry out harm. Finding the balance would be his challenge.

He had been able to gather people of merit around him to steer Scotland through its time of troubles. They came from unlikely backgrounds. Brian Crawford had helped Vanguard prepare its assault on power. Grant Stevenson had started out in politics as a convinced nationalist. It was wrong to judge people by their backgrounds or to assume that they could never evolve or improve.

It had been consoling that the trust placed in the foreigners who had come to Scotland to find the means to ease the torment of millions of casualties of violence, had been amply rewarded. Anatoly Yashin had, along with his own partner Greer, enabled several million refugees to come to Scotland to recover from their ordeals. Zach Mbarra had helped build up the Spirit of Freedom football team which had done so much to dispel antagonism towards these newcomers.

Friendships and new relationships had been forged. Hopefully, most of the refugees would be able to return to the homes from which they had been driven. But enough would be left to forge a new synthesis in the human make-up of Scotland. It would ensure that appeals to chauvinism and small mindedness could not succeed with such ease in the future.

Now here he was, on 15 August 2024, witnessing the final blossoming of one such encounter. Anatoly Yashin and Moira Torrance were getting married. They had asked him to be their best-man and he had happily agreed.

At Moira's suggestion they had chosen a church associated with St Margaret. She had been a Saxon princess from Wessex who had fled to Scotland after the battle of Hastings in 1066. She had married King Malcolm Canmore and was known for her good works. In time, she also became a symbol of reconciliation between the two parts of the island of Britain. It would be one of his priorities, in whatever time was left to him, to make a difference in the search for a balanced set of relationships across the British isles.

On hearing of the couple's affection for Queen Margaret, Ogilvy had offered to try and secure Queen Margaret's Chapel in Edinburgh Castle for them. It was the oldest building in Edinburgh and a favourite place for high society weddings. But they preferred a more modest location. St Margaret's Presbyterian Church in Dunfermline was chosen. The place had been Scotland's capital in the past and it lay across the Firth of Forth in the county of Fife.

He could see that they were right to aim for a modest venue to celebrate the most meaningful day in both their lives. The wedding day was overcast but the rain kept away. On this typical Scottish summer's day two people in love with one another, but devoted to human service, were formally united. There would be a reception in the evening but beforehand Anatoly's friend Zach Mbarra had arranged a surprise.

Five of the Spirit of Freedom's players turned up and, for an hour in a nearby park, played a five-a-side match with youngsters from Fife selected for their prowess on the pitch. A Souvenir programme had been prepared. Not only the team stars but Zach, Anatoly and the others from BEAST who had helped put it on its feet, were mentioned. For thirty minutes Gavin was mobbed by people requesting that he sign theirs.

Afterwards he was approached by Arthur Gorman. In his hand he had a book for him. It was another Margo Forbes mystery. He had shaken off his writing block. The police widow, burnt out of her Manchester home, had arrived in Scotland with thousands of other refugees. In the inner city Edinburgh district where she was located, she soon found herself duelling with people traffickers who preyed on vulnerable refugees.

Soon Arthur would be returning to Wilford for the opening of the rebuilt university. The pioneering work of Professor Euan Garland in the field of arthritis would go on. Zach Mbarra vowed to continue in his mentor's footsteps. A centre for palliative care was being established by Prof Edgar Hale. Livia Morariu would be his chief assistant. Ogilvy hoped that soon there would be Scottish emulators of Wilford as it rose from the ashes as a centre of learning committed to the freedom of the human spirit.

So life went on for these friends who had come through the fire somehow unscathed after years of conflict. There would be other battles. Britain hopefully would be re-founded on a newer and more enduring basis. It was hard to see London remaining as its capital given the damage Vanguard rule had caused. A new union, perhaps encompassing an Ireland where Phelim Armstrong had just been elected President, might just work. But it would need to be founded on a very different footing from the last one.

So challenges in abundance remained. Dark shadows pressed in but there was a light and energy which for the first time was causing some to think positively about the future that might await them.